SOUTH WIND

SOUTH WIND

DON COLDSMITH

BANTAM BOOKS

NEW YORK   TORONTO
LONDON   SYDNEY   AUCKLAND

SOUTH WIND

A Bantam Book / June 1998

Library of Congress Cataloging-in-Publication Data
Coldsmith, Don, 1926–
    South wind / Don Coldsmith.
      p.   cm.
   ISBN 0-553-10641-4
   I. title.
   PS3553.O445S66   1998
   814'.54—dc21   97-46704
                                 CIP

Published simultaneously in the United States and Canada

Bantam Books are published by Bantam Books, a
division of Bantam Doubleday Dell Publishing Group,
Inc. Its trademark, consisting of the words "Bantam
Books" and the portrayal of a rooster, is Registered in
U.S. Patent and Trademark Office and in other
countries. Marca Registrada. Bantam Books, 1540
Broadway, New York, New York 10036.

To all the people who have lived these stories . . .

To all who have helped me with the telling of them . . .

To all whose stories could not be included because there simply wasn't space for such a massive body of material . . .

But especially to my wife, whose patience is only exceeded by her sense of humor. She has needed vast quantities of both during the creation of *South Wind*.

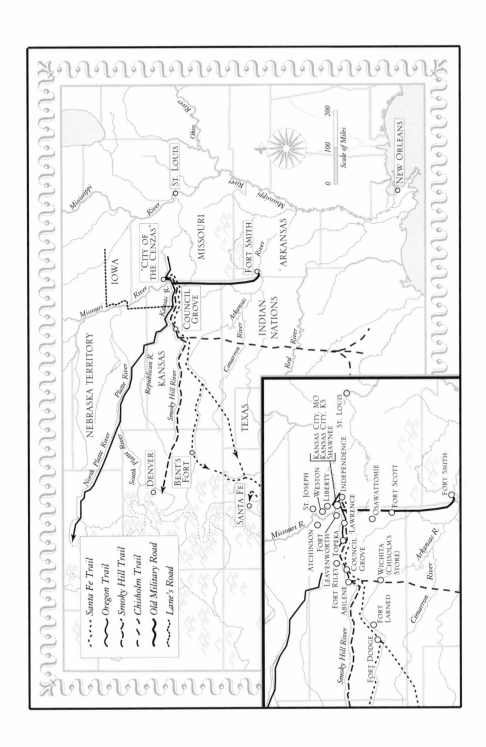

Scale of Miles

200

100

0

NEW ORLEANS

ST. LOUIS

Ohio River

Mississippi River

MISSOURI

"CITY OF THE CENZAS"

FORT SMITH

ARKANSAS

Mississippi River

IOWA

Missouri River

COUNCIL GROVE

Kansas R.

Arkansas River

INDIAN NATIONS

NEBRASKA TERRITORY

KANSAS

Republican R.

Smoky Hill River

Cimarron River

Red River

TEXAS

North Platte River

South Platte River

Platte River

DENVER

BENT'S FORT

SANTA FE

·········· Santa Fe Trail
⎯⎯⎯ Oregon Trail
⌣⌣⌣ Smoky Hill Trail
– – – Chisholm Trail
▬▬▬ Old Military Road
- - - Lane's Road

ST. JOSEPH

WESTON

KANSAS CITY, MO
KANSAS CITY, KS

SHAWNEE

LIBERTY

INDEPENDENCE

ST. LOUIS

OSAWATTOMIE

FORT SCOTT

FORT SMITH

ATCHINSON

Missouri R.

FORT LEAVENWORTH

FORT RILEY

TOPEKA

LAWRENCE

COUNCIL GROVE

ABILENE

WICHITA (CHISOLM'S STORE)

Arkansas R.

Smoky Hill River

FORT DODGE

FORT LARNED

Cimarron River

BOOK I

✠

THE GROVE
1846

1

Suzannah finished sweeping the rammed-earth floor of the little cabin, and stood in the doorway, enjoying the warmth of the spring morning. It was good. Her husband should be back soon, and that would be even better. She longed to see him. She would never have thought her life could be like this, missing him every moment of his absence, yet happy with the expectation of his return.

A smile came to her face as she thought of how they had met. Three years they had been together now, but it had only been a year since Jed had decided to settle here at the Grove. He had built the cabin, promising her a better house as soon as they could. She could wait. This was so much better than anything she had expected when he bought her. It seemed impossible now that it had happened at all.

But she could shut her eyes and still see the horror of that morning in New Orleans. Her master, always kind to her, had been killed in a poker game on a riverboat. She had found herself half naked on the auction block, while men joked and laughed and made ribald remarks about her anatomy. She dreaded the touch of the highest bidder, who seemed so sure of himself. He had been pointed out earlier as a buyer of female flesh for the brothels. In a panic, she thought of killing herself as soon as she could.

Then, out of the crowd strode a tall, middle-aged man, well dressed, who made a single bid, and she was his. She had resented him, too, of course, and had reason to suspect his intentions. At least, he had not made her skin crawl at the thought of his hands on her body.

It was a complete surprise, then, to find that he had no such motives.

He had only been passing by and on a whim had tried to help her. Only much later did she learn that he had practically impoverished himself to do so. He had been reminded by her looks, he said, of his dead wife, who had been a Pawnee. She had been killed a few years earlier. To his credit, he had never made a comparison.

Jed's background was as unlikely as her own. He, too, was well educated, but had been living as a trapper, trader, guide, and hunter. She did not know that until they reached St. Louis. He had schemed to get her out of the area where slave law would be a threat. She still had no idea what his original plan might have been, or if he had one. To free her, possibly. But in Memphis, where they changed boats, he had bought her some genteel clothing, and she had been mistaken for his wife.

It was easy to let it pass, and she had shared his first-class cabin instead of being relegated to the slave holding area on deck. It was there, on the packet steamer upriver, that they had realized their need for each other. They "jumped the broom," figuratively speaking, and became man and wife.

In St. Louis, he had changed to buckskins, which made the whole thing much easier. Many of the frontiersmen had Indian wives. The attitude of the public was not always approving, but it was acceptable. . . . Another mountain man with a younger, dusky wife . . . A "squaw man."

They had considered several places to settle. Jed did not want to rejoin his wife's people. They visited the Cherokees in the "Nations," and were welcomed, but felt like outsiders in the unfamiliar culture. Similarly, among Creeks. They talked of the buffalo tribes that he knew, Kiowa or Cheyenne, but he was not happy with any of these possibilities.

Eventually they found themselves at the Council Grove, which seemed a logical place to settle. It was Indian Territory, but her husband seemed to get along with them quite well. In fact, he was sometimes in demand for his ability to use the hand signs and some of the Indian tongues. She was proud of him.

They had hardly moved into the cabin, however, when the Kaws were relocated from farther east and assigned the area around the Grove. Jed assured her that it would make no difference. A few more whites, maybe. This had been Osage country when he came west, but they too had now been relocated, to a more southern part of the Indian Territory. In fact, their boundaries were adjacent to those of the Cherokee Nation. There had been border incidents while she and Jed were there, one of the deciding factors in choosing the Grove instead.

It was familiar country to Jed, a traditional meeting place for centuries for the natives. It lay on the old Southwest Trail, now called the Santa Fe Trail by the whites. This grove, Jed had told her, was the last point where there were any hardwood trees on the road west. Many had been cut now to use as material for replacement wagon tongues and axles for the freight wagons. Still, there were many magnificent oaks and walnuts and sycamores. Beyond that, to the west, mostly treeless prairie. A few trees along the rivers to the south, maybe, Jed told her. But not on the Trail. Just willows and cottonwoods, not usable for wagon repair.

Commerce on the old Santa Fe Trail had been slowed for a time because of impending war with Mexico, but would surely recover. Even now there was talk that the United States would win the contested lands from Mexico when the war was over. The Texas Republic had just become a state. Wagon trains were beginning to organize to start on down the trail with trade goods for the new territory, replacing the trade with Mexico.

From where the cabin stood on the west bank of the river, she could see the big freight wagons easing their way down the hill and onto the trail toward the ford. They'd pause at the Post Office Oak sometimes to pick up messages left by previous travelers. Then on across the river into the main part of the Grove.

Beyond, the grass . . . She was fascinated by the grassland, a panorama she had never seen before. Wide, open skies with far horizons. Tall stalks in autumn, bearing seed heads that nodded above her. Jed had told her, that first season together, that this would come, but she hardly believed him. *As tall as a man on a horse,* he said, and she thought he was teasing. Maybe he was talking about a canebrake.

But no, during their first September together she saw the slender seed stalks shoot up almost overnight and open into the three-awned seed head that gave that variety its Indian name. Turkey-foot . . . Jed had ridden his horse into a growth of this tall grass to show her its height. She could hardly see him. As a joke, he took a stalk from each side of the horse and tied them in a knot over the saddle without breaking or uprooting them. This grass was also called "big bluestem," she learned, because of its color in the earlier season. There were several other grasses, too. She especially liked another tall variety called Indian grass, with a feathery golden plume.

Farther west, Jed told her, was "shortgrass country." He showed her patches of a short, curly blue-green variety, never more than a few inches tall. Buffalo grass, he called it, a favorite graze of the great herds. Suzannah had seen a few buffalo but none of the great migrations yet.

She sighed, impatient for his return. He had expected to be home this week, but it was never a sure thing. He might be hindered by any one of a number of unavoidable delays. The military was like that, and this was his present mission. . . . Helping with the relocation of some of the Indian Nations, in his role as interpreter. She knew that he was trusted by both the natives and the military in this role.

But I need him, too! she thought. Well, maybe this afternoon . . . She must be patient. . . .

·   ·   ·

"Mr. Sterling? Jedediah Sterling?"

"Yes . . . What is it, sir?"

"I would speak with you. . . . I am told you might be able to guide a party for a tour of the Rocky Mountains?"

The man in buckskins did not take long to answer. "Not likely. But I'll listen."

"Of course . . . Allow me to introduce myself, sir. Parkman . . . Francis Parkman . . . I am here in Westport to organize an expedition."

"For what purpose, may I ask?" Jed inquired.

The man shrugged, a confident smile playing over his features.

"Curiosity . . . Amusement . . . I propose to follow the Oregon Trail past Leavenworth. We've been told that there are many travelers from Missouri and Illinois, heading for the West from there."

"That's true, I guess. You'd travel with them?"

"Partway. But we hear there are Mormons starting from St. Joseph. We would hate to encounter them."

Jed nodded. "Your Illinois folks aren't on good terms with 'em. Well, Missourians, either. But I've been to St. Joe recently. I heard nothing about such a party."

"But that was not my main concern, sir," Parkman went on. "I intend a pleasant summer in the mountains, and then return via the same Oregon Road."

Jed looked the man over more carefully. A "gentleman," to all appearances. He was wearing a trendy outfit such as an affluent dandy might choose to explore the woods. . . . Well, for "curiosity and amusement . . ." His boots were of expensive make, not interchangeable right and left like most. These were expensively custom made, not on a single last, but on *two*, one right, one left. . . .

"I'm afraid you're looking for trouble, Mr. Parkman," he said. "The Oregon Trail's probably safe enough if you join a wagon train. But there's disease. . . . Cholera, dysentery . . ."

"But we won't stay with them," protested Parkman. "That's why I need someone like you. A man who knows the mountains. We'll leave the Trail when we approach the eastern slopes, and explore on our own."

Jed sighed inwardly. It was bad enough to have the hundreds of inexperienced travelers setting out for the promised land, without such men as this, looking for "amusement" in the country of the Cheyenne and Arapaho. *I'm getting too old for this,* he thought.

"I'm sorry," he said. "I'm on my way home. My wife is expecting me."

"Pity," mused Parkman. "I'm certain we could get on well. But perhaps you can tell me . . . Mr. Parks, the owner of the trading post here . . . He is an Indian? A savage?"

It rankled Jed, just a trifle, the way the man said it. A slight curl of the lip, a touch of contempt . . . *Even if I were able and needed the work,* he thought, *I doubt that I could work with this man.*

"That's true," he said aloud. "Joseph Parks is a chief of the Shawnees. He has the store, a large farm operation, and a considerable number of slaves."

"I see. . . . That accounts for the nigras I've seen. But tell me . . . which is the best route to the fort?"

"Leavenworth?"

"Yes, that's the route I had planned."

Without much information with which to plan, Jed thought. But there was little point in arguing.

"Follow this road," he pointed. "You'll pass the Shawnee Mission, and then you'll see some of Mr. Parks's fields. . . . Corn, tobacco, although most of his crops aren't up yet. You'll hit a north-south road, which is the military road from Fort Leavenworth to Fort Scott, to Fort Gibson. Turn north on that trail. You strike the river. . . . The Kansas, at what they call the Lower Delaware Crossing. You'll need rafts for your wagons. You can probably make one or buy one that others have used. That's a good crossing."

"I thank you for the information, sir. Are you certain you won't change your mind and join my expedition?"

"Quite sure . . . My wife . . ."

"Yes, yes . . ."

Jed turned away. Suzannah would be expecting him. If he hurried, and there were no storms, he could still reach home in a few days. He hated to be longer.

It worried him to leave her alone. Odd, when he had been married to Raven he had always felt that she was safe with her people. Now, with Suzannah living among whites, he was more concerned. There were so many coming into the area, with so many different purposes. Suzannah might be safer among some of his Indian friends. Yet, Raven had been killed in a raid by Delawares on *her* people. Raven and their two children, along with others. That was a lifetime ago.

There was, too, the ever-present fact that Suzannah had been a slave. One of light complexion, she could pass for an Indian or even a dark-skinned European. But it bothered him. A few years ago, he would hardly have noticed the slaves of Joseph Parks farming the plantation near the Shawnee Mission. Now, he observed them more closely. Some were quite dark skinned, others little different in complexion from Suzannah. They had her papers. . . . A bill of sale documenting his purchase of her. His written page giving her freedom, signed and sealed by a judge. Still he was uneasy. If something should happen to him . . . Papers can be lost, sometimes intentionally. Besides, there were no laws yet, except those of the natives, in this new territory.

And, there was so much more feeling about the whole matter of slavery now. People moving into the area, sometimes for the express purpose of forcing their views on others. He might not have noticed, a few years ago, the rising resentments on both sides. Now, it was closer to home.

There would be a nearly full moon tonight. . . . Maybe he could travel, at least partway, and save a day on the road home to Suzannah. He turned toward the hitch rail, untied and mounted his horse.

2

The area was not yet even a territory as such. Legally, Indian Territory. Yet in every Indian village, representing more than thirty tribes and nations, there were a few white men living. Some were trappers and mountain men, who had never quite been able to give up the old ways when the fur trade collapsed. Others, adventurers, who had seen excitement in the vast skies of the West. Some were renegades, with vague backgrounds and even more uncertain futures. Among these were a few who preyed on unsuspecting travelers on the trails across the prairie.

This was a part of Jed's concern. When he had come to the grassland as a young man, it was different. The Indians were as they had been for generations. Some were friendly, some dangerous and unpredictable. Yet when he had begun to understand their ways, there was usually a reason for their customs. Sometimes it was obscure, based on a fragment of a legend or creation story. Yet he had learned to respect even that which he did not understand. At first it had been merely a matter of politeness and a wish not to offend. *When in Rome, do as the Romans do,* he had once heard a preacher say. Gradually, he had learned that no matter how bizarre a custom might seem, there had probably once been a reason.

This helped him in his dealings with each of the various nations with whom he had come in contact. He was respected by both natives and whites, and had acted as guide, scout, and interpreter in many tense situations.

But now, he saw new people coming in. A new breed, whites with no understanding and no wish to understand the ways of those already here. Strictly speaking, there was no legality in this new influx. The area had been set aside for the use of the native Indians and those relocated here. But there had always been traders, trappers. Now, "Indian Agents," representatives of the government to regulate dealings with the nations . . . Some of these were honest though misguided. Others, self-serving opportunists.

Then there were the missionaries. Jed had respect for some of these. For others, only contempt. Some were broadly accepting in their interpretations, others so extremely narrow that Jed was amused. *You must think exactly as I do about God,* some seemed to say, *or you are doomed to hellfire and damnation.* He doubted that everybody could ever think exactly the same way about anything. Maybe they *shouldn't.* Otherwise, how could there ever be any new ideas at all?

Yet, on the Shawnee reservation alone, at least three religious denominations were represented. The Methodist Episcopals, whose goal was education, had established a mission school a few miles west of Chouteau's store. Southern Baptists also opened a mission, and the Quakers a manual training school nearby.

In other parts of the Indian Territory there were Catholic missions, as well as others of several denominations. The Mormons, almost universally feared, hated, and misunderstood, were moving through on the Oregon Trail, bound for their own promised land.

There were also whites who formed the support and supply system for both the Santa Fe and Oregon Trails. Blacksmiths, farriers, outfitters . . . At first these had been on the Missouri side, but were spreading into the area now being called the "Platte Country" . . . The areas drained by the Nebraska, or Platte River, and that drained by the Kansas River. These traders and artisans also supplied the Indians in their area.

But more and more, each newcomer on the frontier seemed to have an ax to grind, a need to force ideas on others. And, the newcomers had a wide variety of goals.

There were a few whose goals were quite personal. Free Negroes and runaway slaves . . . It made no difference here. Many of these felt far more comfortable among the Indian nations. There was no slave law of any sort here, and these people were not so impressed by color of skin. Soon, many Indian nations had adopted a few "black white men."

These presented no special problem for Jed, although he had become much more aware of their problems since Suzannah had come into his life. How had he ever lived *without* her? She was much like Raven in many ways. . . . The way she moved, the way she smiled . . . But she was not Raven. She was Suzannah, a woman of her own, and to be with her, sharing the immensity of their love, was a thing of wonder.

Once, early in their relationship, he had inadvertently called her "Raven." If she noticed, she pretended not to, and quickly it was no problem.

Now, as he traveled, Jed was eager to see her, to hold her close. There was the gnawing of concern each time he left her. . . . He must really consider how to avoid leaving home for more than a short while. He was not sure he was cut out for farming. A store or trading post, maybe . . .

The sun was setting beyond the giant trees of the Grove as he rode in and stepped down from the tired horse. Suzannah came running from the cabin and flew into his arms.

How wonderful, the firm feel of her body against his, the warmth of her lips, and the sparkle of delight in her eyes at his return . . .

"Wait, now," he said with a grin. "Let me take care of the horse!"

"All right . . . I'll come with you. How are you? Is there any news?"

"One at a time . . . Yes, I've been well. No real news. We're at war with Mexico, of course, but it won't last long, it's said. But what of *you*? Lord, I've missed you, Suzannah!"

"I'm well. . . . The black hen hatched her chicks. A lot of wagons on the trail. I thought maybe the war would have stopped that."

"Not really, I guess."

They reached the shed and he loosened the cinch and pulled the saddle from the animal's back to hang it on a rail inside the shed. He returned with a curry comb and began to groom the sweaty back where the saddle had rested.

"Texas claims a lot of the trail to Santa Fe," he went on. "So does Mexico, but they don't have troops to support the claim. And, if things get too sticky, the traders can trade in the pueblo towns south of Bent's Fort."

He slipped the bridle from the horse's head and turned him into the little pole corral. Suzannah was already forking hay into the manger.

"Now," she said, a teasing sparkle in her eyes. "We gwine in de house. You gwine pleasure me, Massah?"

"Suzannah, don't do that!" he scolded. It had always bothered him when she reverted to such talk.

Originally it had been a defense. She had been well educated in the household of her owner, who was probably also her father. She was a companion to Miss Annabel, about the same age. From her earliest memories, though, Suzannah had realized that Miss Jennie, Annabel's mother, resented her. The favoritism Mr. Frank lavished on the little girl was considered unseemly.

After Annabel's death from a fever as both girls reached young womanhood, the resentment had ripened into hate. When her husband was killed, Miss Jennie took the opportunity to sell some of the slaves, and one of the first to go was Suzannah, his favorite. Miss Jennie had always acted strangely toward both Suzannah and her mother, who worked in the kitchen. Only after she was a young woman had Suzannah realized that there was jealousy involved. Miss Jennie considered her a *rival.*

It had been in that situation that she had unconsciously adopted the maneuver used by many slaves to defuse a dangerous confrontation with whites. Particularly in the case of an intelligent or educated Negro, there was always a risk. The sidelong glance of disapproval, a remark about "uppity niggers" . . . The best defense was to revert to the subservient, fawning darkie talk expected of a slave who "knew his place." The implied ignorance allowed Massah to reinforce his own position of superiority. It was something learned early, because it provided some degree of safety.

Suzannah had used it on Jed when they began to become acquainted. She had assumed that his motives for buying her were not the most noble. In reality he had not been sure of those motives himself. When he had seemed to become confused or irritated at her cultured language, she would retreat into dialect. . . . "Yas, Massah . . ."

It had become a source of amusement between them as their relationship ripened into love. Jed had hated to see her demean herself in that way, and would scold her gently. In turn, she would tease him with it. Now, it was a private joke, a reminder of the unlikely start of their romance.

She took his hand and led him into their home.

Sometime later, they lay in the darkness, content in each other's arms. They had eaten, and after dark had taken a swim in the river and made love with the hunger of long separation. Their appetites, physical and spiritual, were satisfied, and there was complete contentment. The full moon, rising over the bluff across the river, made a pool of silver on the foot of the bed and across the floor.

"Jed . . . ," she whispered softly.

"Yes . . . What . . . ?"

He sounded half asleep. He was often like that for a little while after a romantic interlude.

"I wasn't sure you were awake."

"I'm not, really. . . . Lord, Suzannah, it's good to be home. . . ."

"Yes . . . I know. For me too, to have you home."

She kissed his lips softly, and he drew her closer.

"Jed," she whispered, "wait a moment. There's something I must tell you."

Instantly, he was wide-awake.

"What . . . ? Is there something wrong?"

There was alarm in his voice.

"No, no," she soothed. "Maybe it is good."

"For God's sake, Suzannah, what is it?"

"Well . . . I think I am with child."

"You are not sure?"

"No . . . I . . . I have never been, before. How would I know?"

"I don't know. I supposed a woman can tell."

"About some things, yes. But I have no older woman to talk to about this. I never have had. My own mother died, you know, before . . ."

"Yes, you told me. But I never realized, Suzannah. You missed much of the woman talk, growing up as you did."

"I guess so. I never thought of it much."

"We can find a woman. Not many white women here, though."

"That doesn't matter." She paused for a moment. "Do you remember how it was for your wife?"

He smiled and tickled her gently.

"How could I know that? I know how it was for *me,* to have her with child."

"You know what I meant," she chided. "But you have not said, yet. . . . Are you happy for this, my husband?"

"Forgive me!" he blurted. "Of course I am. Suzannah, nothing could make our life together more complete."

A tear rolled down her cheek in the moonlight.

"What is the matter?" he asked.

"I . . . Nothing . . . I don't know why I am crying."

"Ah! That is one of the things! I remember, now."

"What things?"

"The things a woman feels when she is with child."

"But I am *not* sad. I am happy, if you are happy for this."

"Of course. You feel happy and sad, all at once. You laugh and cry, all at the same time."

"This is expected, then?"

"I am made to think so. Look, Suzannah, we must find a woman for you to talk to."

"That would be good."

And, he thought to himself, *I must find a way not to be gone as much as I have been.*

3

He had, in the intervening years, forgotten how it was to live with a pregnant woman. Of course, his previous experience, with Raven as his partner, had been in a Pawnee earth lodge. Some forty other people of the extended family had shared the close confines of the lodge.

That had bothered him at first, but when he realized that romantic coupling was an accepted norm, his embarrassed anxiety decreased. Never, though, had he ever experienced the carefree abandon that he now did with Suzannah in the privacy of their own lodge.

During Raven's pregnancies, Jed had traveled quite a bit. But he had been around her enough to see a change in her attitude. She had been unpredictable, crying unexpectedly for no apparent reason. Then he would try to comfort her, a futile gesture.

"What's the matter, Raven?"

"Nothing!"

"But, you . . ."

"If you do not know already, I am not going to tell you!"

And she would stalk away, furious. It was very confusing to the young man.

In bed, too, he had noticed a remarkable transformation. Always before, he and Raven had reveled in the feel of each other's bodies as they snuggled for warmth in the thick buffalo robes. When she became pregnant, all of that changed. Where he once had welcomed the soft warmth and sensual curves, he had encountered only knees and elbows. It was very hurtful and confusing.

Finally, Swimmer, brother of Raven, had shared with him the wisdom of experience. Swimmer had two children already.

"It is a woman's way when she is with child," Swimmer advised him. "It will pass."

"When?"

"Well . . . I am made to think this way: It has to do with her moon periods, no? When a woman needs to have one, her power is at its greatest. She becomes dangerous to be near."

"That is true."

Swimmer spread his palms in confirmation.

"So . . . At this time she will need, but cannot find the release of the moon period for a whole season, almost. *Aiee!"*

"It will be the whole time?" asked Jed in alarm.

"No, no. Not so long. Another moon, maybe. Then her body becomes happy with this *new* power, and things become much better for us."

"That is good."

And it had been good. It was as Swimmer had said, when the time came. Raven had seemed to regret the way she had behaved and to want to make it up to him. Sometimes he wondered if he could keep up with her romantic desires.

Now, all this was recalled as he saw Suzannah go through the moodiness, the alternating joy and tears, for no apparent reason. And she had no woman to turn to. Had never had, he now realized, since the loss of her own mother many years ago.

He tried to explain to her what he knew of her moodiness, but this was completely unproductive. Not only was he unable to comprehend the moods of a woman, but there was another factor. Talking to Suzannah of this required mention of his previous experience with Raven. By implication, a comparison, and there could be no worse time. He abandoned all attempts at discussion of this subject.

I must find a woman for her to talk to, he thought.

But whom? There were plenty of Kansa women moving into the area, with the relocation, but he was hesitant. One does not simply approach another man's wife with a discussion of such subjects. At least, not among most cultures, and he was not well versed in the ways of the Kaw Nation. A Cheyenne woman might be good at this. Their marriage customs were similar to those known by Suzannah. . . .

The best friend Suzannah had had since they had been together was a Cheyenne woman, wife of a traveling trader who had wintered there at the Grove. But Owl Woman and her Scottish husband had moved on, about the time Jed had been called on by the army on this last absence. That had been one of his concerns, that they had no close friends for her to call on while he was away. But it would be only a short time, and Suzannah insisted that he go. No matter, now. He was back, and to himself he vowed he would not leave her again. There were too many strangers coming in.

But still, especially at this time, she needed the sympathetic counsel of a woman. Best would be a white woman. Maybe there would be wives of the Indian Agents or preachers for the expected mission school. Yet he was not sure that would be a *good* thing. Some of them had very strange ideas.

He wandered through the Grove, idly observing the preparations by the teamsters for the long haul to the southwest. A blacksmith had set up a portable forge in the shade of a sycamore tree and was shaping a muleshoe. The man's thick red hair and beard caught his eye. . . .

"Kesterson?" he asked.

"Jah . . . Ach! Sterling, wasn't it? Jed . . . You was Long Valker to der Pawnees!"

"That's right, Sven. Long Walker. What are you doing here?"

The big smith pointed to the anvil with his heavy hammer.

"Poundin' der shoe. Vat else?" he laughed.

"But you had a smithy in Independence."

"Jah. But too many people. Anyway, I'm think 'Sven, better go see some country. Dem folks needs mules shod, too.' So ve come!"

"We?"

"Jah . . . Mine wife, Ilsa, dere!"

He pointed to a nearby tent. A young woman with hair the color of ripe wheat poked her head out to look around.

"You called me, Sven?"

"Nein, not really. But come! Meet mine friend Jed."

The woman came forward, wiping her hands on her apron and extending her right one in greeting.

"Pleased to meet you, ma'am," Jed said genuinely.

It had never occurred to him to wonder whether the smith had a wife until now. He saw two small children peeking shyly from behind their mother's skirts.

"Dot's how long ve ist married," laughed the big man. "Vun, two, t'ree. The baby's inside der tent."

Jed nodded, an idea forming in his head.

"Will you be here for a while, Sven?"

"You mean today?"

"No . . . For the summer, or just a few days?"

"Oh. All summer, maybe so." He swept the surroundings with a glance and a wave of the hammer. "A plenty to do!"

"Well, I . . . I have a new wife, too," Jed began.

"Ach! Goot! I heard you lost your family, and I had sorrow. Dis is anodder Pawnee woman?"

"No . . . I . . . We met in New Orleans."

"A Sothern lady!" grinned Sven.

"I was wondering. . . . Could I bring her to meet Mrs. Kesterson?"

"Of course," Ilsa smiled. "I am hungry for a woman to talk to!"

So, thought Jed, *maybe this will solve more than one problem.*

Despite their widely varied backgrounds, the two women seemed to form an instant bond of sisterhood. Jed and Suzannah talked in advance about the dangers of too much information about her background. The less, the better.

As Jed had revealed initially, they had met in New Orleans, where he had met members of her family. All of this was true. It should not be necessary to go into more detail than that. The fact was that he had met and played poker with Mr. Frank Sullivan on the riverboat. He had first seen Suzannah there among the other slaves. No one had even questioned her status since Memphis.

But there remained the gnawing fear, the doubt. . . . Would someone, sometime, accost them with the accusation that Suzannah was a runaway slave? It was better that absolutely no one know anything at all about her. Attitudes toward the slave question in the new territories were a nebulous thing. One could never quite tell who might turn up unexpectedly on which side of an argument. It would be far better to avoid such things if they could.

In the case of the friendship between these two women, it was no problem at all. Their common thread of interest and understanding was Suzannah's pregnancy. They talked easily and enthusiastically. Ilsa's English was somewhat better than Sven's, and she was as delighted as Suzannah to find another woman with whom to visit. Her mothering instincts came quickly to the surface as she learned of her new friend's pregnancy.

"Jah! When I had my first pregnancy, with little Olaf, there, I cried all the time. Poor Sven . . . He did not understand! It is the way. . . . Happy and sad all at once. But that part is soon over. You will see."

"And the feeling sick in the morning?"

"Oh, yes! You feel like you never want to eat again, no? In another month or two, you'll be past that. Then, you'll want to eat for two. . . . You, and the one inside."

It did Jed's heart good to hear the chatter of the women as they discussed the problems of pregnancy as well as housekeeping on the frontier. "Girl talk," Ilsa called it. He felt a great deal of confidence that Suzannah now had someone who could help her with her questions.

He had determined that he would not leave her again for more than a day.

There were things he could do. He would help the Kestersons build their house, and he could supply both families with meat for the season. The women had estimated that Suzannah's time of delivery would be in late autumn.

He tried to ignore a small whisper of doubt in the back of his mind. . . . Would this child, his and Suzannah's, show the dark coloring of its slave background? It did not matter to him, but this could be quite important to the child and to Suzannah's own safety. More and more, he overheard talk among the travelers from farther east. North, South, free, slave . . . He had thought that he had removed Suzannah from the threat of such things, but was it to follow them here?

He recalled, a few years before, a conversation with his father and his sister's husband. It had been at the time of his one journey back to Baltimore, after his retreat from the unacceptable situation at home. He wished to keep contact with his family, but a stepmother only slightly older than himself made it impractical if not impossible. He had left law school and fled to the west.

On that visit, however, he had been interested in the conversation with the two men. Both were watching the developing political situation and the balance of power between North and South. There was also the shifting position of federal power as opposed to that of the individual states. Was that, too, to follow him here?

4

During the pregnancy of Suzannah, Jed remained near the Grove. He had determined not to leave her. Even so, he picked up a great quantity of news about political developments in the country. All sorts of people were passing through, and many were willing and eager to talk.

He soon realized, however, that he had to be selective. As his friend Kesterson put it, "Ef a man knows vat he talks of, he says it. Ef he don't, he says it anyway."

The big migration just now was on the trail along the Nebraska River, traditionally called the Platte by the French. These were people heading for Oregon and California. That was now called the Oregon Trail, and branched off to the north, crossing the Kansas River at a settlement a few miles west of Topeka.

The Santa Fe Trail, the trail of commerce, bent southwestward from the Grove and continued to serve its function. Jed and Suzannah had followed it west the previous year, as far as Bent's Fort. It was there that he had realized that he wanted to be a little nearer to civilization for her sake. Oddly Suzannah, even as a slave, had been exposed to more education and culture than most women on the frontier.

It was at Bent's Fort that August that they had encountered an expedition headed by John Fremont. Joe Walker, who knew the geography of the West like no one else, was one of the guides. A dozen Delaware Indians were included in the large, well-armed party, which made Jed quite uneasy. He recognized Swanok, a Delaware with a militant reputation. It was rumored that Swanok had led the Delaware raids against the Pawnees in which Raven had been killed. It was hard to turn away, and until a short while ago he might have openly challenged the man. Instead, he had renewed old acquaintances. He *had* killed a Delaware once, and was not proud of it. The unfortunate Delaware had probably been entirely innocent.

He found several of the men he had known on Fremont's first expedition to South Pass a few years ago. He had been astonished to find that their mapmaker was none other than Charles Pruess. The German had seemed so disgusted with Fremont on that first expedition, Jed had been sure that he would never sign on again. Yet this was his third trip with the "Great Pathfinder."

"Sterling!" called a short, freckled man.

"Kit! Good to see you."

"And you," replied Carson. "Are you going with us?"

"No . . . You're guiding Fremont again?"

"Yes. Joe Walker and I. I just joined them here. What are you doing?"

"Just lookin' around . . . Kit, this is my wife, Suzannah."

Carson looked puzzled, touched his hat, and nodded to Suzannah.

"My pleasure, ma'am. But I thought . . ."

"Yes, my wife, Raven, was killed some years back. You met her, I think. . . . When I was with the Pawnees?"

"Yes, so I was thinking." He smiled politely at Suzannah. "But you are very fortunate, Long Walker, to find another such as this."

She blushed and smiled. "Thank you, sir," she said with a little curtsy.

Carson still appeared confused. Suzannah was wearing a buckskin dress, and Jed realized that the scout believed her to be another Pawnee, perhaps Raven's sister. That would have been appropriate to Pawnee custom. He did not attempt to clarify the situation. It had been gratifying to find that Suzannah could be mistaken for Indian as well as white. Jed was still uneasy about her former status. The runaway slave laws were very strict, and often abused. She was not and had never been a runaway, but it would be hard to prove if he was unable to vouch for her.

"Do you know Senator Benton?" Carson asked him, returning his thoughts to reality.

"Fremont's father-in-law? Just know who he is. Never met him. Why?"

"Well, I talked to him a while back. He's interested in how the West will open up."

"What do you mean?" asked Jed.

"Jed, you know Texas was just admitted as a state?"

"Yes, I'd heard that."

"That's botherin' some of the Northern folks some, I reckon. On account of the slavery thing . . . Some think they'd ought to admit one Free State for every slave state, to keep it even in the Congress."

"But Missouri came in as a Free State."

"True, but they're still arguin' about that. There's a lot of slave owners in Missouri. And they've got that law about no freed niggers comin' in."

"What are you getting at, Kit?"

"Well, the Republic of Texas was given statehood with strings attached. They can split up into as many as four states if they want. So, more votes in the Congress."

Jed began to see the situation. . . . A power struggle within the government. Still, it seemed to have no meaning here.

"Jed, I sort of liked the senator. He understands a lot more about the West than some."

"How so?"

"Well, I guess when Missouri came in as a state, he was purty much for havin' it be slave. He's sort of mellowed out now. He said he figgered slavery's already dead in the North, and will be in the South pretty quick. Its cost don't pay out in goods produced, or somethin'."

"Then what's the problem?" Jed was somewhat surprised to find Carson so well versed in politics.

"Well, I guess there's some that are bound to pass laws to try to keep it goin'. If they bring in enough states to swing the vote . . ."

"Yes, I see. . . ."

"Seems there's a tendency to think of everything north of the Ohio River as free, and everything south of it slave."

"But what . . . ?"

"I'm comin' to that. There's a move to make the whole Platte Country a territory. From Missouri and Iowa, west to the Divide, the Rockies."

"That's a lot of territory, Kit."

"Yes . . . Bigger'n Texas, you see. . . ."

"And enough to swing the vote in the Congress, if they come in Northern."

"Right!"

"How far south would it reach? Clear to Texas?"

"Depends on where you call Texas. They're still talkin' about that. Texas still claims *this* area. . . . The whole front range. That would be part of that 'Nebraska Territory.' Then there's the Indian Nations to the south. It's a matter of where they'll decide to draw the lines. Of course, that territory has several Indian reservations in it, even as far north as the Platte."

There would have been a time when Jed had very little concern with all of this. He could move on west, away from it. He had done it. Now, with the responsibility of a wife who was quite vulnerable to the changing politics of the day, he had become much more aware.

"I guess you and I won't get it worked out today," Jed told him. "But tell me about this trip of Fremont's. It's pretty late to be crossing the mountains, isn't it?"

"No, we'll take the south route. West from Santa Fe and on to California. The captain wants to prove it can be done, I reckon. And then, California's part of this, too. She's tryin' to break away from Mexico. Mebbe we'll have a state out there."

"Oh, surely not!" Jed laughed.

"I'm serious, Jed. Senator Benton's talking states plumb to the Pacific. Look at all the folks headin' to Oregon! Some of 'em figger it's God's will. The Promised Land out there, just askin' to be settled. There's others that think so, too. Just a question, I guess, whether those would be free or slave states."

"You said something about the Ohio River. . . ."

"Oh! Yes. It appears if you draw a line east and west across the Indian Territories, from the mouth of the Ohio where it joins the Mississippi, it would come out a ways south of here. The thirty-six-thirty parallel, I think they said."

"But that would cut through Missouri!"

"Sure. But Missouri's already in. This would just only affect new states. North of that, free. South of it, slave. Anyhow, that's what the senator said."

Jed had thought much about that brief conversation in the ensuing months. Before a year had passed, the war with Mexico had started over some of those territorial claims in California and the Southwest. Word filtered back that Fremont's party had become involved in a revolution in California. Word was scarce and unreliable. But there was little doubt that major changes were in the making.

Joe Walker came through, heading back toward St. Louis, and spent a short while visiting with Jed.

"That damn fool Fremont," he sputtered. "Led us into all sorts of trouble, tryin' to make a name for hisself. Damn near got us killed. And he's a coward, Jed! I'd say he's got no more bravery than a woman, except I'd hate to give a bad name to the fairer sex. And an explorer? Shit! I knew more about the West fifteen years ago than he'll ever know."

"Is Kit still with him?" Jed asked.

"I reckon so. Kit's so impressed with his reputation, he cain't see that the man's a hazard to be around. Fremont better hope Kit stays with him, keep him from getting hisself killed!"

Old Joe went on his way, still mumbling to himself in indignation. He had never been very tolerant of greenhorns and tenderfeet.

.   .   .

Suzannah was growing larger now as autumn approached. She still did not show much but was very self-conscious of the fullness in her belly. She tired more easily. There were times when she was sure she would never be attractive again.

To Jed, she was more lovely than ever. There is something, maybe, in the latter months of a pregnancy, that makes a woman even more attractive to the man who loves her. Perhaps a primal urge to protect, to preserve the race . . . Many men feel this attraction to any pregnant female. It is not a sexual attraction but an outgoing of sympathy and understanding and of male helplessness to *really* understand. When the object of this emotion is a cherished partner, it becomes ever so much stronger. He wants to hold and comfort and protect her as never before.

In this way, as the tall seed heads of the prairie grasses ripened into the fullness of the season, the love of Jed and Suzannah ripened in all its fullness. He loved to hold her, to feel her firm body against his. As they shared the warmth of the buffalo robes, the slight protrusion of her lower abdomen against him was a sensual thing. Not a thing of sexual excitement and desire (though there was still that), but a sense of the life that they had created and which was theirs alone. He could feel, sometimes, the gentle, placid movement of the child inside her. Or, on occasion, even see the motion of the kick, transmitted to the outside as he watched.

He tried to remember how it had been with Raven's pregnancies, but then was touched by guilt as he did so. That had been different, and he should not compare. He had been blessed, he felt, with two wonderful women, yet so completely different that there was no comparison.

The two were much alike in appearance: tall, long-legged and long-waisted, graceful in their way of moving. But so different . . . Raven strong, as a Pawnee woman is strong, bold, fervent in her love, proud in her heritage. Suzannah, equally strong, but able to swing from strength to submission to meet the needs of the moment. Flexible . . . Yes, that was it. . . . Her survival as a slave with varying fortunes had depended on her ability to adjust.

That's it, Jed thought. *Ability to bend and to spring back . . .*

Like two trees he had once seen after one of the violent storms that lash the prairie. One was a medium-sized oak, twisted and broken off a few feet above the ground. But nearby, a willow . . . Tattered yet standing upright, it had been able to bend with the force of the howling wind, and yet recover to continue survival. That was Suzannah.

5

I lsa swung through the doorway, happily talking as she did so.
"Good morning, mein friend! I have brought you a little something."

She drew aside the cloth that covered a small crock and held it out proudly.

"Look! A starter! Smell it, Suzannah."

Suzannah sniffed the yeasty smell, like that of rising bread. "Mmm . . . Where did you get it?"

"From a teamster's wife who was passing through . . . We can make bread again!"

"But you have no oven, Ilsa!"

"I know. . . . Neither do you. But we can make spider bread in a skillet, and pancakes. . . . Biscuits, in a covered pot. You have not done those things?"

"Well . . . Yes, and corn dodgers and johnnycake. My mother had an oven."

"Really?"

"Yes . . ." Suzannah paused, uneasy. She could not go into much detail here. Absolutely no one must know that her mother had worked in the kitchen of the big house as a slave. Suzannah's education had been as a companion to the daughter of the plantation. Jed had cautioned many times since they came north that there must be no hint of her background.

"Do you know about hush puppies?" she asked brightly.

"Hush puppies?" Ilsa laughed.

"Yes . . . When you're cooking fish, the cornmeal you're using to roll it in . . . To save it . . . You can't put it back in the sack, of course. Add a little milk to hold it together . . . Or water, if you don't have milk. Then roll it in little balls and fry them with the fish."

"Like corn dodgers!"

"Well, yes . . ."

"Why are they 'hush puppies'?"

Suzannah laughed. "I don't know. I suppose you could use them to appease puppies while you finish cooking. But they're fine for children, too."

"How many brothers and sisters you had, Suzannah?"

There it came again. . . . *Be careful, now.* . . . *Talk about something else.*

"Just one sister. She died when I was about fifteen."

"I'm sorry, Suzannah."

"It was very hard."

There was silence for a few moments, and Suzannah noticed the sensation she had felt from time to time lately. It was a firming of her abdomen, and really uncomfortable, but . . . She placed a hand on the rounded surface, hard as a board. In a few moments the firmness passed, and the texture was as before. This had been happening a few times every day, but more often now the past week.

"What is it?" asked Ilsa.

"Nothing, I guess . . ."

"You touched your belly. You hurt there?"

"Not hurt, really. My belly gets firmer, and then soft again. But it has done that for weeks, Ilsa."

The other girl nodded. "Your belly muscles practice, to get ready. When it happens again, tell me."

"All right. Well, here it comes now!"

Ilsa leaned over to feel the hardening belly. "Yes. That is it."

"But how is it different from labor?"

"That gets more regular. You know when to expect the next one. You'll know."

"But this doesn't hurt, Ilsa."

"I know. There's a bit more later. But a lot of women have done it. I have, a few times, myself. A lot of it is how you feel about it. I help you. . . . You do fine. My mother was a midwife."

"So you have helped before?"

"Sure, sure . . . Are you wantin' a boy or a girl?"

"I don't know. . . . My husband had one of each, before. They were killed in an Indian fight, along with his wife."

"Yes, you told me that. Too bad. But now, you give him one! Shall we see which?"

"What do you mean? Can you tell?"

"Sometimes."

"But how?" Suzannah's voice was anxious.

"Different ways," Ilsa said with a little smile. "No, we can't look inside, but . . . Here, stand up. . . . Smooth your apron out tight over your belly, while I look from the side. . . . Mmm . . . Yes . . . See, some babies stick out pointed in front. Some are rounded and flatter."

"What does that mean?"

"Well, boys stick out more in front, don't they? And girls are wider in the hips?"

Suzannah had her doubts. "So which is this?"

"Hard to tell. You don't show much, girl. You sure you're in the family way?"

"I'm sure!"

Both women laughed.

"There's another way," Ilsa said brightly. "Do you have some silk thread?"

"Yes . . ."

"And let me use your wedding ring."

Suzannah slipped the gold ring from her finger, a simple slender band. Jed had bought it for her in St. Louis as they came through from New Orleans, to symbolize their strange relationship that had ripened into love. She doubted that anyone could have a love any greater than theirs, even though he was considerably older. He was kind and gentle, and . . . Well, he was Jed.

Ilsa stripped a foot or so of silk thread from the wooden spool, bit it off, and tucked the loose end back into the tiny slit in the spool's rim. Then she tied one end of her short thread through the ring.

"Lie down on the bed," she pointed.

Suzannah did so, and Ilsa suspended the ring over her belly like a pendulum, swinging it in a gentle circle. Then she stopped, holding her fingers still. The gold ring twirled and swung, slowly assuming an alignment with Suzannah's body.

"Mmm—a boy!" said Ilsa. "That's odd. I'd have said a girl from your shape."

"So, we still don't know?"

"Well, there's one sure way!"

"How, Ilsa?"

"Get it out and look between the legs!"

Both laughed and Suzannah rose.

"One thing's sure, though. It has a lot of hair. Your heartburn early on proves that!"

Suzannah nodded. She had heard that as a child from the grannies in the slave cabins, but preferred to change the subject.

"Nights are getting chilly," she observed.

"Yes. You ready for winter?"

Suzannah shrugged. She had experienced only two winters here. . . . A far cry from Louisiana, but Jed had provided well for them.

"I guess so. Somebody said you're never ready, it just comes."

"That's right," Ilsa laughed. "At least we both have houses. But I like the autumn, don't you?"

Suzannah nodded. "Except for what comes next!"

"You'll be busy, though, with the babe! Well, I'd best get along, Sue. . . . Oh . . . Here comes your husband!"

Jed stepped inside and nodded to Ilsa.

"What are you two up to now?" he smiled.

Suzannah leaned against him, and Jed circled her with an arm.

"Just girl talk," Suzannah told him.

He nodded, pleased. Ilsa had been good for Suzannah. He felt easier when he was gone for a day now and then. He knew that with the Kestersons only a stone's throw away, he could be more confident about Suzannah's safety.

Besides, there would be someone to help her when her time came. He knew nothing about that. He only remembered dimly when, as a youngster in Baltimore, his mother had given birth to Jed's sister. The boy had been sent to spend the night with relatives while the doctor came to Judge Sterling's house to attend the birth.

"You have a baby sister," his father had told him the next morning.

When Jed's wife, Raven, had given birth, they had been living among her people, the Pawnees. Mere men had been banished completely from the lodge until it was over. At the time of Raven's second birthing, Jed had been away on a scout.

He resolved this time that he would be on hand. Probably he would be excluded from the process again, but he was determined that he would be near. Somehow, Suzannah seemed more vulnerable to him. She would need the support that only he could provide with the closeness of their spirits.

Maybe I'm getting more sentimental, he thought. Maybe, though, he was just admitting it. . . .

Suzannah reached into her apron pocket and drew out a shiny gold coin.

"Look, Jed!"

Her time was drawing ever nearer, and she now "wore her apron high," the string drawn up over the bulge of her belly in front. This had made the motion into the pocket and out quite obvious.

"Where did you get that?" He had only been away from the cabin for a short while.

"One of the teamsters."

"Suzannah, you shouldn't be talking to teamsters. . . . But . . . He gave it to you?"

There was anger and a little jealousy in his face.

"I sold him some eggs, Jed. It was all right. Ilsa was here, and we saw him looking at the chickens. Ilsa was about to tell him to move on, when he came over. He was polite, and took off his hat when he talked to us. I think he was homesick, Jed."

"But . . . Eggs?"

"Yes! He said our chicken coop reminded him of his mother's, and how long it had been since he's had a fresh, fried egg. He offered a dollar for one."

"A whole dollar? But this is a five-dollar gold piece!"

"Yes, I know. I found three eggs, and he said that was all right, take the five, and he'd collect his other two eggs on his next trip."

Jed nodded, amused. "They don't like to carry many silver dollars. . . . Too heavy and bulky for the trail. But *eggs*!"

"Yes, Jed! I was thinking. If we had a few more hens . . . There must be other teamsters who feel like this one. Ilsa and I could sell them eggs, make them feel at home."

"I don't know, Suzannah. I don't really want teamsters hanging around. Besides, you know how hard it is to keep the coons from killing chickens."

"I know. But if we sell only a few eggs . . ."

She held the gold coin toward him on her palm, and it glittered in the sunlight.

"Well," he said, "we can think about it."

She smiled happily. "Ilsa and I were talking about it. She says she thinks people would buy fresh milk and butter, too, Jed. Cheese, maybe. She knows how to make cheese!"

"A *cow*? You want a *cow*?"

"Well, maybe we could think about that. . . . Later, maybe?"

He laughed and hugged her expanding waist gently. "We'll see. One thing at a time."

In his heart, he knew two things. One was that he could never deny Suzannah anything that was in his power to give for very long. The other, that he was being recivilized after many years on the frontier.

He was a little surprised that he did not really care. Eggs . . . He had enjoyed the luxury himself, and could see how travelers would crave fresh eggs after trail fare, dust, and jerky. *A dollar apiece* . . . A few hens could make more money than he'd be paid scouting for the army. But he'd really have to think of something to do about the raccoons.

6

Suzannah woke him in the early morning, before first light of dawn.
"Jed," she whispered, "it is my time!"

Instantly, he was wide-awake, his mind full of questions as he sat up.

"What . . . ? When . . . ? How . . . ?"

Suzannah giggled. "No hurry, I think. But, I'll build the fire while you go for Ilsa."

"No, stay in bed. I'll start the fire."

He knew how hard it had become for her to bend over the cooking fire in the fireplace. Quickly, he uncovered a few hot embers, placed tinder on the glowing lumps, and blew gently until a cheery flame flickered to life. A few small sticks, then three larger ones . . . The flame began to grow and he rose, looking toward the bed.

Suzannah's face was tight and drawn in the new light. Then she began to relax and smiled at him as the contraction faded.

"Thank you. Now go for Ilsa."

"You have been awake awhile?" he asked, and then felt stupid for asking.

"Yes. They're getting stronger. . . . A little closer, too . . . Here comes another."

He was already buttoning his coat as he reached the door and lifted the latch.

"I'll be right back!"

There was a pale glow in the east, the first hint of predawn change. He hurried to the log cabin upstream and knocked on the plank doorway.

"Sven! Ilsa! It's me, Jed. Suzannah says her time has come."

There were sounds of motion inside, and in a moment the door opened.

"Yust a minute," said Sven. "She be coming. Suzannah does well?"

"Yes, I think so. She just woke me."

"You come inside?" invited Sven.

"No, I'll go back." He turned to go.

"Wait! I'm ready," called Ilsa. She picked up a bundle that appeared to be prewrapped and ready. Sven had turned to build up the fire.

The two hurried back through the crisp November dawn. Jed was shivering, not only from the cold but from his excitement and concern. He had not felt this before. Maybe he had not been mature enough when he and Raven had had their babies, he thought. Of course, for the one he had not even been there, and a pang of much delayed guilt washed over him for an instant.

He opened the door and stood aside, holding it for Ilsa. She stepped in, followed closely by Jed. Suzannah's face was tense with her next contraction.

"They comin' quicker, now?" Ilsa asked as Suzannah's face relaxed again.

"Yes . . ." She took a deep breath. "Much shorter between."

"That's good! Now don't push yet. Loosen up all you can. Breathe deep, get a lot of air for baby."

Suzannah smiled. "How long will it be, Ilsa?"

The other girl held her hands out a foot and a half apart. "Oh, 'bout like that."

"No, I mean . . ."

"Sure, honey, I know. . . . I can't tell you yet. Did your water break yet?"

"I don't know. . . . I'm pretty wet. . . ."

"But no splash, huh?"

"No . . . Ah! Here comes another one!"

Jed was standing, helpless, watching the tense expression tighten on Suzannah's face. He wished he could help her. . . . Do it for her, even. Then, as the tension faded again, Ilsa seemed to notice him.

"Here, Jed, you can't help here. Out!"

He looked questioningly to his wife, who nodded assent. He hated to leave. He would have liked to hold her, to be with her in her pain. Instead, he took her hand for a moment, kissed her cheek, and stepped back.

"I'll be outside," he said gently.

"Might as well go over to our place," called Ilsa after him. "Have some coffee."

Jed waved his thanks, stepped outside, and closed the door. He did not want to be at Kesterson's, with a houseful of children. What he really wanted was a swig of good bourbon whiskey, but he quickly rejected that idea. He had tasted very little liquor for the past three or four years. It had become a big problem at one time after he lost Raven. There were still many blank spots, in which he had no idea where he had been or what he had done. How he had survived, actually. He had seen men frozen to death in their sleep, too drunk to realize the danger of merely lying down on the board sidewalk to catch a few winks. The cold was unforgiving of such mistakes. He thought that he must have had a close call or two.

So, the temptation passed. But, if he could not be with Suzannah, he did not want to be with anyone else. He'd rather be alone, and near her. He leaned against the outside of the logs of the cabin wall and slid down to a sitting position, and something close to panic gripped him for a moment. *What if something goes wrong?* He did not know whether he could handle the prospect of another loss. Suzannah had completely become a part of his life . . . a part of *him.* He wanted to rush inside, to be with her in this, her time of trouble.

It seemed like a very long time, the little while before the sun showed its rim of molten gold over the horizon to the east. It was fully daylight, because the hills on the east side of the river prevented the sun's rays from striking the Grove until well after dawn. In actual time elapsed, it was not long, but it seemed an eternity to Jed. He slumped against the cabin wall, suffering with his concern for the woman who had so quickly become a central part of his life. Sometimes it seemed as though he had never been without her. At others, their life together seemed always new and exciting and rewarding. . . .

He could hear the women talking inside the cabin, and from time to time a low moan when the spasm of another contraction swept over Suzannah's body. Maybe he *should* go to the Kestersons' . . . No, he could not leave. . . . There was a pang of guilt that it was he who had caused this to happen. Suzannah was suffering because of *him.*

Finally the voices rose, and he could hear Ilsa's firm command.

"Now! Now, it's the time. *Push,* Suzannah. . . . Yes, I can see the head! Once more . . . A big breath, and . . . No, it's gone now. Wait for the next one. . . ."

Suzannah said something, but he could not understand her soft tones. There was a space of a minute or two, and then Ilsa spoke again.

"Yes, it's firmin' up for the next one. This is the last push, honey. Take two big deep breaths. . . . That's it. . . . Now, fill your lungs and *push.* . . . Long and hard as you can . . . Yes! Yes! Here it comes! Push. . . . *Now!* There!"

There was a frightened little squeal from Suzannah, and in a moment, the startled squall of an infant, arriving in a cold and unfamiliar world. To Jed, it was the most welcome sound he had ever heard. Her labor was over. But was she all right?

Impatiently, he knocked on the door.

"Hold your horses, Jed!" Ilsa called. "We're not quite through here, but she's fine. . . . Got to get the afterbirth . . . Yes, here it comes. . . . Ah . . . Good!"

Another eternity passed before the door opened and Ilsa motioned him inside.

"Come see your daughter, Jed."

Suzannah lay there in the firelight, looking tired but happy. In her arms was the tiny blanket-wrapped bundle that represented the culmination of their love. The infant had stopped crying now and was staring at the world in wide-eyed wonder.

Jed knelt beside her, and she smiled at him. He had never felt such love as he now felt for her. He took her hand.

"Isn't she beautiful, Jed?"

He nodded and finally found his voice. "Are you all right?"

"Of course. What shall we call her?"

"I hadn't thought about it. What do you think, Suzannah?"

"Well . . ." She hesitated, and finally continued. "We've moved around a lot, Jed, but I am thinking . . . Well, this is the home you built for us, here on the river. . . . Maybe we should name her after this place."

Jed was puzzled. How could a child be named for a place called Council Grove?

"The . . . the Grove?" he stammered.

Suzannah laughed, and the sound of her laughter made his heart glad.

"No, silly! Not for the Grove. For the river. 'Neosho.' "

So the child was named Neosho. Jed went outside into the crisp autumn air and sought an outlet for his feelings of joy and relief. For some odd reason, the influence of his years with Raven's people rose up within him, and he had need to mark this occasion with a ceremony.

He built a small fire a short distance from the cabin and prayed a prayer of thanksgiving and joy, improvising a song as he went. As an effort to please the spirits, he offered a pinch of tobacco on the little fire.

As he danced around his fire, still singing, Ilsa emerged from the house, carrying her bundle. She paused to watch him for a moment, considering whether to speak to him or not. Finally she decided against it and moved on toward her own home. She could come back later. She shook her head and clucked her tongue at the strange ways of the frontiersman. Or maybe the ceremony was that of Suzannah's people. *Odd*, reflected Ilsa. *She has never said which tribe is hers. Well, no matter . . .*

.   .   .

Later that day, they examined the baby in better light.

"Her skin's pretty light," Jed observed.

"Were you worried about that?" Suzannah asked.

"No," he lied, "not really."

"I was."

"Well, I was, too," he admitted.

He had been greatly concerned. Although he reasoned that the child probably carried no more than one-eighth African blood, what if it were very dark? In the South, he had seen slaves whose Negroid features could hardly be noticed. *Any* amount of African blood in the pedigree made an individual legally a "person of colour" . . . a Negro. Jed did not wish a child of his and Suzannah's to be faced with this, as she had been. He had decided that if this baby proved to be dark, they would leave civilization and make a home among the Indians, who were more tolerant of such things. Cheyennes, probably . . . Their marriage customs were more like those of white civilization than most.

But now Suzannah spoke again.

"Jed," she began gently, "we both knew that it could be a big problem for this child. But, my mother's people have learned many things. What to expect, how it will affect their lives."

"How so?" he asked.

"Well, first, lighter is better for a slave. The darker men end up as field hands. A lighter-skinned boy, especially if he's handsome, might be lucky enough to rise to status as a servant. . . . A 'house nigger.' Same way with a girl. She might even get to be the mistress of the massah. You know what 'high yellow' means?"

"Yes, I've heard the term, but . . ."

"I'd be a high yellow. Almost light enough to pass . . ."

"You did . . ."

"Yes. So far. But let me finish about this, Jed. There are some things we've learned. . . . Folktales, some of it. But some fact, I think. First, as a rule, a baby will never be darker than the darker parent. Still, every woman wonders . . . *will my baby be the exception? The throwback?*"

"I wondered that too," he admitted.

"Of course. I knew. . . . Then there are things to look for. All babies are lighter at birth, you know."

"I never thought about it."

"You've had no need to. But my people *have*. So they've learned the signs."

She gently took one of the infant's tiny hands and pointed to the skin of the fingers, next to the cuticle of the nails.

"If that area of skin is very much darker, the complexion will become more dark," she said. "On a boy-child, same with his private parts."

"But there is no difference here," he observed.

"Exactly. This child will be no darker than I am."

"I would love her anyway, Suzannah."

"I know. But we were both concerned about what life would bring for her, no?"

"Yes . . . Maybe so."

"So . . . We know more than yesterday!" she smiled. "We did not even know she was a girl then." She paused. "Are you disappointed in that? That it was a girl?"

Jed thought for a moment. At one time he would have been. A man needs a son. . . . But he had had a son, and had lost him, along with a daughter and a much beloved wife. That had served to put things in perspective for him after his plunge into the depths of alcohol and depression, and his recovery.

But today, after his concern for Suzannah, it was a great relief to have it over, and to see the beautiful girl-child in her mother's arms.

"Suzannah," he told her, "I could not be happier."

7

The child grew quickly, and from the first moment seemed wise beyond all reason. An old spirit, Raven's people would have said. Her hair was dark and shiny, not curly but with a slight wave. Her smile, which came early and often, was that of her mother. Likewise, long curling lashes over deep dark pools of wisdom. Jed knew in his heart that this girl-child would some day be a striking beauty, drawing the attention of all men.

He worried some about this. An odd situation . . . In his previous marriage among the Pawnees, there had been little concern. Even in the community lodge with some fifty people, there was a feeling of safety. Maybe because of the closeness of the extended family. The moral and the ethical codes, though quite different from that of the civilized whites, were strictly enforced by the community.

A similar enforcement existed in the small settlements and villages, in any part of the country, among the whites. This community morality only started to break down, he had noticed, in two situations. One was in the larger cities. Sheer numbers of people made each one a faceless, nameless entity. Responsibility and accountability for one's actions began to disappear with this facelessness.

The other situation was that in which he and Suzannah now attempted to make their home. In the restless, ever-changing population of the border there was a danger. . . . A lawlessness that, after all, was because of the complete absence of laws and lawmen. Most of the people to be encountered were travelers, here today, somewhere else tomorrow. Most of these, though rough and hardy, were honest and forthright. Yet, because of sheer numbers and the strange lure of the unknown, there were an increasing number of questionable individuals on the trails. They might never be seen again, and there was little or no accountability. There were the adventurers, the curious, the greedy, the shiftless. . . . Sorting out the scoundrels from the legitimate, hardworking teamsters, frontiersmen, suppliers, and hunters was an impossible task. There must be some trust, but a healthy amount of suspicion and self-defense, too. And Jed Sterling was still alive because he had learned to keep his senses sharply honed, alert for danger.

Times were changing rapidly. Sometimes he longed for what he now perceived as simpler times, when he had first crossed the Missouri and learned to trap and hunt. It was a shock to think that that was now nearly thirty years ago. Well over half of his years had been spent on the prairie. Sometimes he felt that the other world, that of his family in Baltimore and of his own years as a student at Princeton, had never happened at all.

In a rush of family feeling over the birth of Neosho, he wrote to his father. There was no way of knowing, even, whether Judge Sterling would still be alive, but Jed felt that he must try. He had always felt some guilt about the manner in which he left home. He had never written before, and had made only the one brief visit a decade ago.

He told of the loss of his wife and children and of his remarriage to Suzannah. He did not mention her background, only that they had met in New Orleans, and they had now been blessed with a daughter, named Neosho for the place of her birth.

He sent the letter with a friend who was traveling east, to be posted in St. Louis. It would be months before he could expect a reply, if at all. But there was a sense of relief and accomplishment at having tried.

1848

More people were coming into the area. . . . Kansa Indians, from their former towns along the Missouri and Kansas Rivers . . . Whites, to operate the Kansa Indian Agency . . . Missionaries and teachers and the necessary people for their support and operation . . . And traffic was again increasing along the Santa Fe Trail. The war with Mexico was over, although there were still negotiations going on about where the international boundaries were to be drawn. Some areas were claimed by three entities: Mexico, the United States, and the former Republic of Texas, recently admitted to the Union.

Jedediah Sterling and his family were well aware of all this. They could not fail to be. The traffic on the Trail, hardly a stone's throw from their cabin, was obvious in its increase.

This also provided more of a market for Suzannah's produce. They had enlarged the henhouse and sold all the eggs they could manage to gather. A cow, too, produced enough milk and butter not only for their own use but to sell to travelers and other settlers. Ilsa was experienced in the making of cheese, which allowed the salvage of any excess milk and cream.

In the other end of the shed that Jed had erected for the cow, he made a box stall for his saddle horse. With the growing population of the Grove, Jed was able to participate again as a scout and hunter for the army from time to time. He was becoming more confident about his family's safety, with the Kestersons' home only a few steps away.

Neosho was coming two, a bright, alert, and happy child. It seemed amazing to Jed that here was a small person, who walked and talked, laughed and cried. Only a short while ago there had been none. He had forgotten the joys of fatherhood in the intervening years. True, it had been much different among the Pawnees. Swimmer, the maternal uncle of his children, had played an important role as teacher and adult confidant. This time, such a role was his, and he treasured it. Maybe his previous loss had made him more aware of this treasure, that of a small child. Even more importantly, a child born of his union with Suzannah.

In that respect, he had never been happier. With more maturity, he was more appreciative. Then too, Suzannah represented a contact with his own culture that he had not had with his former marriage.

There were two events that following spring that would have a major effect on their future. One seemed insignificant at the time. Kit Carson, passing through, brought news. He had been on yet another expedition with Fremont in 1848. He had also talked again with Senator Benton. The news was that the Wyandot Nation, an Indian tribe from farther east, had petitioned the Congress to become a Territory. They were now settled in lands formerly held by the Kansa, Osage, and Missouri.

"But why?" asked Jed.

"Don't know. But figger this, Jed. The Wyandots are pretty civilized, compared to those we know. A lot of mixed bloods. Lots of 'em storekeepers and such. They know somethin' about politics, and that all this *will* be a territory. That gives 'em a chance to form a government, right?"

"Well, yes. But . . ."

"Well, it comes back again to the slave question. Would such a territory be free or slave?"

"I . . . I wouldn't know, Kit."

"Neither does anybody. And what they're asking is a strip four hundred miles wide north and south, from Missouri . . . the state and the river, clear to the crest of the Rockies."

"You mentioned that before, Kit. But you didn't say it was Wyandots."

"It wasn't. And it was just talk, anyway, then. At Bent's, wasn't it? Two . . . no, three seasons ago?"

"I think so. But what will the Congress do?"

"Well, the senator says he thinks there's no way they'll pass it. Too many unknowns. Oh, it'll be a Territory, and soon, maybe. But not for Wyandots. That would confuse the North-South thing too much."

"I see. . . . Wouldn't all that land be north of your imaginary line . . . thirty-six-thirty, wasn't it?"

"Exactly. Too many folks in the Congress are bothered by that. Suppose the Wyandots had a Southern tendency. There's a lot of territory lost to the Free State folks there."

Jed nodded. "Kit, what do *you* think about it?"

"The Wyandots?"

"No . . . The whole slave thing."

"I dunno, Jed. In a way, it seems like it's more of a power thing. Who'll have the say-so. But I'm no politician. Seems like trouble ahead, though. You can't have so many big and powerful men arguin' about it without some trouble."

Again, Jed was amazed at Carson's grasp of politics. But then the frontiersman had been in close contact with Fremont and Senator Benton, and was greatly impressed by these public figures. But it was a far cry from the early days, when Carson was a young man on the frontier, and named "Rope Thrower" by the Indians for his skill with a lariat. A feeling of nostalgia washed over him for a moment, along with a feeling of uneasiness for the future.

"Well, I'd best be goin'," Carson said. "Much obliged for the dinner, Miz Sterling. My, the fresh eggs are nice."

Suzannah smiled. "Y'all come back!"

The other event, far more important from a personal viewpoint, was a letter. It was handed to Jed by a teamster who had received it in the same way in St. Louis. An answer, of sorts, to the letter he had written to his father a year earlier. He recognized the bold flowing strokes of Judge Sterling's hand. It was largely uninformative. . . . *We are well, hope this finds you the same, etc.* . . . The wish that Jed would return to look after family affairs, or at least for a visit . . .

The startling thing, though, was on another scrap of paper. A narrow slip had fluttered to the ground as he slit the envelope. He glanced at it for a moment and then turned to his father's letter. Now, he looked again at the extra note and its delicate feminine handwriting. It had apparently been slipped into the envelope, probably without his father's knowledge.

Dearest Jed,
Please come home if you can. Your father is not well.
Phoebe

Phoebe . . . His stepmother, only a little older than himself. His father had remarried shortly after the death of Jed's mother. Jed had been away at college, and resented Phoebe anyway. The trollop had tried to seduce him when they first met, though she was already married to the Judge. He had left Princeton and fled to the frontier.

Then, on his only visit home, she had made another attempt. He also suspected that Phoebe was cheating on her husband with the husband of her own stepdaughter.

But he pushed such thoughts aside. This note seemed sincere. His father *was* getting on in years. He had never thought much about it, but who *would* administer the estate on the death of his father?

Much as he might dislike Phoebe and suspect her motives, it was probable that in this she was sincere. At least, partly so. She had contrived to smuggle that note into his father's letter. How? He wondered. . . . Maybe she had offered to affix the wax seal to the envelope. It would be a nuisance thing to his father. She would melt the crimson blob of wax. In the process of handling the envelope, slip her own note inside before imprinting the hot wax with the metal stamp. He fingered the broken seal with its fancy Old English letter *S,* and looked again at the letter and the note.

Phoebe must have felt strongly about wanting him to return. But why? At one time she had stated her intentions to eventually bed with him, but that was years ago. Surely she would have matured to the extent that this . . . No, that would not be her motive. The woman was an opportunist, but he doubted that she would set up such an intricate plot just to create the opportunity for an illicit tryst.

The other possibility kept coming back to mind. . . . She must be genuinely concerned about his father. She had married him to better herself socially and financially. There was little doubt of that. Yet, she must have developed a sense of responsibility. In her own way, she *was* concerned.

There flitted through Jed's mind the thought that her concern might be mostly financial. He did not know who might be expected to handle such affairs for Judge Sterling. Peter Van Landingham, the young lawyer who had married Jed's sister, Sarah? Jed did not entirely trust him. In fact, he had suspected strongly that Peter and Phoebe were involved in an illicit romance. Had *they* had a falling-out?

His guilt was rising. He felt that he had not carried out his responsibility to his father, his sister, and yes . . . to his mother's memory. He could see no way out of this situation but one. He must honor the pitiful request of his stepmother. He must make the long trip to Baltimore.

8

Jed was reluctant to approach his wife with his need to travel back to Baltimore. He was not certain why, except that they had never been separated for more than a few days at a time.

At first it had been essential that they be together for Suzannah's protection as he tried to get her out of New Orleans. Then, as they traveled back to the prairie country that had become his life. After they settled at the Grove, he had taken only short-term jobs due to concern for her. With the arrival of their baby, even more so. Yet, gradually, with the security of the Kestersons' nearness, he had begun to scout for the army a little more.

Still, a journey such as this would involve several months. There were moments when he considered it out of the question. In other moments, he told himself that he *must* go. Finally, he decided that the matter must be decided by the two of them together. He had not yet told Suzannah about the letter that had been handed to him.

He watched while she read it clear through to the end, including the extra note. Her eyes were wide when she finished and looked at him again.

"You must go, of course."

"But . . ."

"Phoebe is your stepmother, no?"

"Yes . . . But I . . ."

"A woman knows of these things, Jed. She sees a need for you to come. There is such a wish in your father's letter, too."

"What? I did not see that."

"No? Maybe it is hidden in his lawyer talk. But, yes, Jed. Look, let us read it again."

They reread the letter together, Suzannah reading aloud. She emphasized the points that Jed had skipped over rather quickly, the Judge's expressed wish to see his son, to meet his wife and see their baby. Yes, it was there. . . . There was also something that both had overlooked, a mention of Judge Sterling's interest in the frontier country.

"Does it say *interest* or *interests,* there?" asked Jed.

"I . . . I don't know. That would make a great difference, Jed. Look . . . Is that little curl after the *t* meant to be an *s* or is it just where his pen skipped?"

"I can't tell. But it *is* important."

They discussed it further, but could not decide. The word was used in a paragraph about wishing to see his son.

> . . . *to renew family ties and to answer my questions regarding my interest in your frontier country.*

Or was it *interests?* In the one case, it would express only the fascination of all Americans with the expanding West. But if the word were plural, it might imply financial interests. Had the Judge invested in some business or stock companies operating on the frontier? Was this a veiled request for Jed to look into such investments? It might be. . . . To add to that possibility was another factor. It had taken the Judge well over a year to reply to Jed's letter. There must have been a reason for Judge Sterling to write at this particular time. The date on the letter was now three months old, easily accounted for by unreliable and often nonexistent mail service. But that was to be expected. Maybe he had been distracted by Phoebe's note.

As if in answer to that thought, Suzannah spoke.

"Is this not odd, Jed, the slip of paper from your stepmother? Tell me more of her."

He had never told Suzannah much about his family. Especially, about Phoebe. They had been preoccupied with other matters. But surely, this was the time.

"That is a long story, dear one. I was away at college when my mother died. Then very soon . . . too soon, I thought . . . my father remarried. I met Phoebe when I came home for Christmas that following year. I knew of the marriage, but had not realized that Phoebe was very young. I . . . She tried to seduce me, Suzannah."

Suzannah looked startled, and then laughed, her clear musical chuckle of pure amusement. Soon she sobered.

"You're serious! She really—"

"Yes, really," Jed said irritably. "She came to my bed."

"I'm sorry, Jed. But I can understand her motives, you know, if not her ethics."

He could see a twinkle of amusement in Suzannah's dark eyes, but decided not to make an issue of it.

"She was unsuccessful," he mumbled.

"It would not matter, Jed."

"I know. Not now. But then she tried again, years later, when I went home."

"*Again?* Jed, is this why you have not been close to your family?"

"Well . . . Yes, partly, I guess. It's not that I'm afraid of her. Not exactly . . ."

"You are afraid of the complications for the family, then?" she said helpfully.

"Yes. That's it, I suppose."

"But they've been together for many years now. . . . *Still* together."

"Yes, I know. Thirty years."

"Your father must be nearing seventy?"

"I guess so. That seems impossible."

"Do you know the nature of his poor health?"

"No. When I was there, he suffered from gout. It could be anything, now, I suppose. But, you see why I have to go."

"Of course," Suzannah agreed. "But you see why, after what you have told me, why I have to go, too?"

"*You?* But what . . . How . . ."

"I don't know yet, but we'll work it out."

In a way, Jed was greatly relieved. Suzannah teased him occasionally about going along to protect him from predatory females. He was well aware that it was only half teasing, and in fact was partially quite serious.

They began to plan. It would be a very expensive undertaking, and their money was scarce. But Suzannah had saved from her butter and egg money.

"It's still not enough," Jed worried. "Coach fare is expensive, and riverboats even more so. We can't walk, with a small child. Maybe I'd better go alone."

"No!" said Suzannah firmly. "Look, Jed. You have your horse. We can buy another for me, and a pack horse to carry supplies. Neosho can ride the pack horse."

Jed nodded thoughtfully. He had been surprised to find that Suzannah was an excellent horsewoman. She had received instruction back on the plantation, as companion to the planter's daughter. They had been taught sidesaddle, but the girls would sneak out to the stables and ride bare-back. . . . Yes, maybe it would work. . . .

"You would ride sidesaddle?" he teased.

"No. I'll wear buckskins, and appear to be your Indian wife. We'll carry a supply of jerky for food, and there will be fresh fruits and vegetables as we travel."

"And occasional game for fresh meat," he agreed. "Yes, I think it will work. I'll start to look for the horses. Sven will help with that. And we have to discuss it with the Kestersons anyway. Will Ilsa look after the chickens and cow?"

"I'm sure she will. If not, we can sell them. There are more when we return."

Ilsa Kesterson was not only willing but eager to take over the dairy and egg business. Its income was not to be overlooked. She had often helped with the churning and cheese making anyway. She had her own cow, too, but the older Kesterson children were old enough to help with the milking and churning.

Jed was able to find a suitable pack horse almost immediately. A discouraged traveler, daunted by the prospects of the Trail's hardships, was ready to sell out and return to civilization. He had offered the little mare to Kesterson at the smithy.

A small, sturdy blue roan about ten years old, Jed estimated by her teeth as he "mouthed" her. Good feet and legs . . . Quiet disposition. The owner, down on his luck, offered to throw in the well-worn sawbuck pack saddle. It could be padded and modified for Neosho to ride. Maybe he'd even add a pair of stirrup straps. . . .

"I'll take her," he decided.

A mount for Suzannah was a harder problem. Most of the animals passing through the Grove were draft animals. About half were oxen, most of the rest, mules. Saddle animals were already in use, and needed by their owners. An occasional trader still drove a herd of half-wild Mexican horses back from Santa Fe on the return trip. But these were unsuitable for the purpose, and scarce at best because of the war.

Another thought occurred to him. The Kansa Indians were now pretty well settled on their allotted reserve, with the Agency at Council Grove. They had always been proud of their horses and owned many of good quality.

Jed rode out to the nearest of the three Kansa towns and asked directions to the home of the chief. His experience would now stand him in good stead. It was always good manners, when entering an Indian camp or town, to pay a formal visit to the leader. He had found that to ignore this bit of protocol was unwise. He had seen the reaction of Raven's people to trappers and traders who neglected the niceties of the customs of their hosts. He had been present when one missionary, in his zeal to save souls, had been virtually invited to leave.

"You are very rude," the band's holy man had finally told him. "It is not done so among the People."

From that point on, everyone simply ignored the presence of the visitor.

With this in mind, Jed sought out the house of Wah-Shun-Gah and called out at the doorway, using the Kansa tongue.

"May I speak with you, Uncle?"

A woman looked out of the doorway of the half-buried lodge, studied him for a moment, and called back inside. There was an exchange of words, and she turned again to Jed.

"Who comes? How are you called?"

"I am Long Walker," he answered. "Called Jed Sterling by the whites."

There was more conversation, and a tall well-formed man stepped out to study the visitor.

"You *are* a white man," observed the chief. "Do I know you?" He spoke in English.

"Probably not," Jed admitted. "I come to pay my respects."

"For what purpose?"

"Because it is right to do so, Uncle. But I would also trade for a horse."

"You are not like the others. You are called . . . how?"

"Long Walker, by my wife's people."

"I have heard of you," the chief said glumly. "You are *Pawnee*!" His tone was accusing.

This was unfortunate. Pawnee and Kansa were traditional enemies.

"My *wife* was, Uncle. She was killed by Delawares, maybe ten, twelve summers ago."

He did not mention that the raid had been carried out by Delawares *and* Kansas. The chief would know that.

"I have another wife now," he added.

"And what is *her* tribe?" Wah-Shun-Gah demanded.

"I am not certain. She is mixed blood, brought up by whites. Cherokee, maybe."

He was trying to be scrupulously honest.

"So . . . Go on."

"Yes, Uncle. I am looking for a horse for my wife. Kansa horses are well thought of. . . . May we smoke and talk?"

Wah-Shun-Gah nodded and motioned to a small, dying fire outside the lodge. The two men sat, and Jed took a pinch of tobacco from his pouch and tossed it on the embers. His host called out, and a young man emerged from the lodge with an ornate ceremonial pipe of red stone. Jed handed the chief his tobacco pouch and watched as the man filled and packed it, and lighted it with a brand from the fire. . . . A puff of smoke to the four directions, then to sky and to earth. He then handed the pipe to Jed, who repeated the ritual and returned it.

"Now," said Wah-Shun-Gah, "let us talk about horses. What have you to offer?"

Jed smiled. "First, Uncle, let us *look* at horses, no?"

A trace of a twinkle creased the crow's-feet at the corners of the chief's eyes.

"You are really not like the others." He rose. "It is good. Let us look at horses."

9

Suzannah did prove an excellent horsewoman, and Jed had chosen her mount well. A coppery sorrel mare, easy in her gaits, docile but with a look of eagles in her eye. Suzannah, as she had suggested, wore buckskins, with the short but full skirt of the buffalo-hunting tribes of the prairie. It lent itself well to riding astride. With knee-length moccasins and her hair in braids to the sides, she looked every bit the Indian wife of a trapper or frontiersman.

They could find no suitable saddle, but decided to make do with a blanket pad until they could obtain one. One of the outfitters in Independence would surely have an assortment of used saddles.

For Neosho, now coming three, it was a time of excitement. Almost from the time she could sit, Jed had allowed her to sit on his big gelding while he fed and groomed the animal. This was a common custom among Raven's people. In fact, among the hunting tribes Jed had often seen the women use this to good advantage. The hard and urgent work of preparing meat and skins after a hunt often required a mother's full attention. She would tie her infant to the back of a dependable old mare and turn it out to graze. The gentle rocking motion as the animal walked was a soothing comfort, and the child would sleep or wake, according to need.

There was an unrecognized side benefit to this custom. A child was confident and secure on a horse. Comanche, Cheyenne, or Kiowa children could ride well, almost before they could walk, and being on a horse was second nature to them.

For Neosho, to have her own horse to ride on their journey was beyond her wildest dreams. She spent hours in grooming and talking to the roan pack horse. Jed modified the pack saddle to accommodate a small passenger as well as their light baggage of blankets and supplies.

After the horse trade, the Kansas were helpful in providing not only the buckskin garment for Suzannah but dried meat and pemmican for their journey. They had quickly realized that here was a white man who treated them fairly. . . . One who understood and respected their ways.

Jed estimated that they could cover an average of twenty miles a day. It would take at least two months to reach Baltimore. There was, of course, no way to inform his family that they were coming. It would take that long, or nearly so, for a letter to reach Maryland. There was an understanding with Sven and Ilsa Kesterson. . . . If they did not return in a year, the chickens and cow would belong to the Kestersons. There was little else of value. The house would be maintained and probably used. There was no deed or title. These were nonexistent, since the region was not even a territory, merely *owned* by the United States. It had no other legal status except as an Indian Territory. Any claim to ownership of real property depended largely on possession.

It was a bright spring morning when they crossed the ford, waved to their neighbors, and turned the horses up the hill to reach the high ground and the trail to the east. They traveled well, and in a day or two had overcome the stiffness that always bothered the unaccustomed traveler.

There was a great deal of change in the area around the junction of the Kansas and Missouri Rivers. Several small towns and communities were springing up. The Shawnee Mission, the Wyandot Agency, Westport . . . Jed could not even locate Chouteau's trading post. There was an active ferry, but their route lay south of the river, crossed into Missouri, and on to Independence. It, too, had continued to grow. A pang of nostalgic regret struck him. This had been the wild and free frontier of his younger days.

They paused to shop for a saddle for Suzannah's mare. Jed found an outfitter with whom he had traded, and with his help acquired a good used saddle. Now Suzannah would be much more comfortable as they traveled.

They moved on quickly. Jed found that the larger towns made him uneasy, and he longed for more open country. Even so, he realized that this feeling would probably grow worse, not better.

Blue Springs . . . Oak Grove . . . On toward Booneville. Jed pointed out where the town had originally stood on the other, the north bank of the Missouri River. It had been called Franklin, and was one of the main staging and supply areas for travelers to the West. The entire town site had slid off into the river some twenty years before.

Columbia . . . On to St. Louis. It had been nearly a month now since they had left the Council Grove. They crossed the Mississippi on a ferry to start across Illinois. Here, they received more curious stares, and sometimes a sidelong glance of disapproval. This made Suzannah quite uneasy. Jed, with his somewhat broader experience, realized the nature of this reaction.

"They're not used to seein' a frontiersman with an Indian wife," he told her. "I've been called a squaw man lots of times."

"They'd disapprove of *that*?"

"Sure. Some would. Some would disapprove of 'most anything."

"But this is Northern country. . . . 'Free State,' don't they call it?"

"Yes . . . Antislave," he answered.

"But these people . . . Some, anyway . . . They want Negroes freed, but no intermarriage, even with Indians?"

"That's about it for some, I guess."

"This Maryland, where we're going, Jed. Is it a slave state?"

"Hard to say, Suzannah. A lot of people have slaves. Virginia, next door, is slave."

A thought occurred to her. "*Your* family has slaves?" There was panic in her tone.

"Well . . . I'm not sure . . . When I was a child, we had an old servant. He lived above the coach house. I never wondered . . ."

"You don't even *know*?" she blurted angrily. "They may have slaves *now,* and you would take me there?"

This possibility had not even crossed his mind. He tried to remember his previous visit home. . . . Slavery had not been of much concern to him a decade ago. There had been a Negro girl, a house servant. . . . But was she a hired servant, or a slave? He had not even wondered and was embarrassed at the realization.

"I don't know, Suzannah. I'm sorry. Such things have much more meaning for me now than they did then. But remember, you are my wife, and nothing will change that."

They rode in silence for a long time. It was a clumsy silence, and he longed for talk, but feared it, too. There were so many things involved. Religion, for one. His mother had been a staunch Episcopalian. He did not know whether Phoebe had any beliefs, other than her own agenda. He was certain that she and his father attended church because it was the thing to do. The Judge had a social responsibility that went hand-in-hand with his office.

Jed considered himself a devout man, but had been away from any organized church setting for more than half his life. His concept of a creator was along the lines of the Indians with whom he had been in contact. He had not been wholeheartedly able to accept the Pawnee religion of his wife's people. There was a dark side to the story of Morning Star. But, there was no coercion about it. He was welcome while he lived with them to have his own beliefs. The same was true among any others with whom he had been in contact. There was tolerance of the beliefs of others and of their ways of worship.

The thing that now began to trouble him was along this line. He had never thought about it before. *How does a devout Christian accept slavery?* he asked himself.

"Suzannah, was your plantation owner, Mr. Sullivan, a churchgoer?" he asked suddenly.

"What?"

"Did they go to church?"

"Why, yes. Why do you ask?"

"I was just thinking. . . . *You* went to church with them? You were companion to Miss Annabel, no?"

Suzannah laughed. "Of course. But I couldn't sit with them, naturally. I sat in the balcony with a few nigras. A mammy or two, a couple of house servants."

"I see. . . . What about the plantation Negroes?"

"They had their own services. Mostly singing. Annabel and I used to sneak down to listen. That and watch them baptize at the river."

"Who did the baptizing?"

"Gideon . . . He was an old coachman who was a preacher. No field work on Sundays, so they'd hold services. Some plantations didn't allow Sunday rest. They'd have services at night, in secret."

"So, most Negroes were Christians?"

"Of course. What else?"

Jed was embarrassed never to have wondered before. "I don't know. No African religion?"

"A little, maybe. Most of them lost or left it behind, I think. Some were Christian in Africa, of course. Then in some places there's a mix of Indian tribal religions, too. Cherokee, Seminole . . . My mother used to tell Annabel and me stories from that side of *her* background. You know the Rabbit stories I tell to Neosho?"

"Yes. I thought they were Negro stories."

"They probably are, now. But I got the idea they came from the Cherokees' creation stories."

Jed shook his head. It was all far too complicated, and the more he thought about it, the more confusing it seemed. Even more so, when he thought about the Christian teachings of brotherly love, knowing that there were Christians who *owned* other Christians like livestock. Of course, he realized that few Christians agreed with each other on everything anyway. And oddly, he could not recall a single instance of argument or even disagreement between Indians of different tribal religions. It was simply inappropriate to argue such a thing as the meaning of God to someone else. But then he would come back to the meaning of *slavery* to someone else.

At any rate, he was much more comfortable with the fact that Suzannah was being accepted as his Indian wife rather than his slave mistress. On their first journey together, on a Mississippi riverboat, that had distressed him greatly. He had traveled first class, while she had been confined to a roped-off slave area as a deck passenger. It troubled him, though, that there was any question in her mind about his family and their attitude. He had decided, however, that they need not know the entire story. As far as anyone they knew was concerned, they had met in New Orleans and married soon after on a riverboat. Most people assumed that her high cheekbones implied Indian blood, and questioned no further.

As he thought about the impending homecoming, an idea began to form in his mind. He wanted to make the best possible presentation to his family. One that would make Suzannah as comfortable as possible. He did not want to arrive at his father's doorstep dusty and trail-worn, in frontier clothing. He would discuss his idea with Suzannah, and they could plan together. It would take a little money, but they had been spending very little.

With this in mind, he shot a deer as they traveled across Indiana, dressed it out, and packed it into a nearby town where he sold it to a butcher for a few dollars. Yes, it might make his idea work. He could do this another time or two. . . .

10

They crossed on into Ohio. Nearly two months had passed, and it was early summer. At one point their travel was held up by three days of summer rain. They took refuge in a roadside inn near Zanesville, and Jed paced and fretted at the delay and the cost.

It was there, however, that he fell into conversation with a talkative and curious individual. The man was interested in the politics of the day, and wanted to talk about the Western Frontier. He was full of questions about the trails to the West, trade, and travel. Jed became uneasy when the conversation turned to the question of the status of the new territories. . . . Slave or Free? A bill was being introduced into Congress, said the man, providing Territorial status to the Platte Country.

"I heard that," Jed said cautiously. "The Wyandot Indians' petition?"

"No, this is another. Similar, I understand. Proposed by Congressman Douglas of Illinois."

"May I ask what is your interest, sir?" inquired Jed.

Instantly the other became defensive and a bit hostile.

"The cause of righteousness and humanity!" He gestured dramatically, a forefinger pointed toward heaven. "The new territories must come into the Union as free soil!"

The man must be a preacher of some sort.

"But that's still Indian Territory," Jed protested mildly.

"And the heathen must be brought to the Lord!" insisted the other, his voice rising.

Jed found himself in a strange position. He agreed with the man's basic premise on slavery, yet objected to his entire approach. This was no way to try to reconcile a problem, *any* problem. To dogmatically insist that everyone think alike was to invite trouble.

"Mark my words," the preacher went on, lowering his voice somewhat. "Your Territory will be filled with the righteous. We will send settlers!" He paused, and a look of suspicion flitted across his face. "I assume, sir, that you are on the side of the right?"

Jed was caught completely off guard by this demand for a commitment. How could he have formed such an instant dislike for a man he had just met and with whom he basically *agreed*? At least, on the question of slavery. He wondered what the preacher would say if he knew that Jed had bought a slave at auction only a few years before. He had seen the man's slightly disapproving glance at Suzannah, who appeared to be an *Indian* wife.

"Well," said Jed mildly, "I'll want to know more about the wording of the bill granting Territorial status. Meanwhile, we're just going to visit family in Baltimore."

"Baltimore? Maryland's almost as Southern as Virginia!"

The tone was accusing.

"I haven't been home for more than ten years," Jed said apologetically. Then he was angry at himself. Why should he feel that he had to justify himself to this zealot? "I haven't been able to follow her politics," he added, "so I really couldn't comment on that."

And my opinion is really no concern of yours, anyway, he wanted to add. He refrained, knowing that either to agree or to disagree with such a man would only fan the flames of his chosen crusade. It was discouraging to realize that there were hundreds, maybe thousands, of such men and women out there. And on *both* sides of a knotty problem. This approach could lead to no good.

"Well," said the preacher, "the situation can lead to no good."

It was disconcerting to hear his own thought echoed by this extremist.

They were glad when the sun came out and they were again able to travel. At Wheeling they crossed into Virginia, and on across the narrow isthmus into Pennsylvania. . . . Over the Cumberland and into Maryland.

As they approached Baltimore, Jed began to look for a livery stable that would meet the needs of their plan. He remembered well the different reception that Suzannah had received in St. Louis when she had been dressed as a lady. It was time to shed their buckskins, so practical and comfortable for travel, and to prepare to meet his family.

A cooperative livery owner agreed to stable their horses for a few days and to rent them a team and a buggy.

"I've a good team of bays. . . . A pair of dapple grays if you'd want something with a bit more class . . . You want a good buggy, or a light carriage?"

"Don't know yet," Jed explained. "We just got here. Let us shop for some clothes, and pick our team and rig when we come back."

They had spent the night just outside the edge of town, to give them most of the day to ready themselves for the meeting with Jed's family. Now, they walked toward an area of town where shops and dry-goods stores gave access to merchandise that would fill their needs.

Suzannah had brought clothing for Neosho and a plain gingham for herself. During the years of their marriage there had been no opportunity or need for more civilized finery. She had, however, grown up with the niceties of aristocracy. Within an hour, she was decked out in tasteful but not elegant finery, from hat to shoes, and had also found a shiny pair of new shoes for Neosho.

Jed, meanwhile, bought a white linen shirt, trousers, and a topcoat, top hat, and cravat. He looked at boots, and even tried on a pair, but decided that he could not go that far. His years in the comfortable hard-sole moccasins of the plains had conditioned him. Anyway, he was wearing a fairly new pair. They would look better and be more appropriate than the rough straight-last boots that would be in his affordable price range.

The trio walked back to the livery.

"Yes, sir, can I help . . . ?"

The liveryman's jaw dropped in amazement. "Sterling?" he finally blurted. "I . . . I'm sorry, sir. I didn't recognize you."

Jed was amused yet a bit troubled at the deferential treatment they now received. Before, the man had been easygoing and friendly. Now, he was almost fawning in his desire to please.

"Be you kin to Judge Sterling, sir?"

Jed had given his name when they arranged for the hire of the team and buggy. At the time, there had been no reaction. But now, dressed in more civilized clothing, it was a different matter. He tried to brush it off lightly.

"Distant relation, I guess," he joked. "You know the Judge?"

"No, sir. Just by reputation. A good man, I've heard. Retired, now, I guess."

"He's still alive, then?"

"I suppose so. Yes, surely we'd have heard."

"Good. Maybe we'll stop by and see him. Now, let's look at the buggies."

The shiny pair of bays drove well, and the light carriage, not too pretentious, still lent a touch of class. They turned into the circle drive and drew up before the steps at the doorway. He noted that the place was well kept, the hedges trimmed and flower beds immaculate. A well-dressed Negro stepped quickly from somewhere behind the house and came to take the horses' heads. The man quickly sized up the situation.

"You be drivin' youself, suh? I'll take 'em."

Jed stepped down. "Thank you."

He would not have wondered, at the time of his last visit, but now . . . *A hired free Negro, or a slave?*

He turned and gave his hand to Suzannah, who stepped daintily to the flagstone pavement and waited while he lifted the little girl from the carriage.

"Will you be long, suh? I can feed the horses," offered the Negro.

"I don't know. Just wait a bit for now." He pointed to the hitching weights on the floor of the driver's seat in the carriage. "You can move the rig out of the drive if you need to."

The man nodded. "Yes, suh. I'll take care of it."

Jed rang the bell, and a middle-aged Negro woman opened the door. She looked puzzled for a moment, glancing from his hat to his moccasins, and then at Suzannah, who smiled at her.

"Jed Sterling," he told her. "Is my father in?"

"Yes, sir. I . . . You were here before!"

"Yes, a long time ago."

As before, a woman came up behind her. . . . A sort of déjà vu . . .

"Jed!"

Phoebe swept past the servant . . . or slave . . . into his arms.

"Phoebe . . . I . . . This is my wife, Suzannah. My daughter, Neosho," he said hurriedly.

His stepmother had aged, but rather gracefully. Still a handsome woman, though there were hard lines around her mouth and eyes. She backed off a step and extended a hand to Suzannah.

"A pleasure, I'm sure," she gushed.

Suzannah nodded, with a trace of a curtsy. "Mrs. Sterling," she acknowledged.

"My father?" Jed inquired. "Your letter said he was not well?"

"He's better, now. His gout . . . He was bad at the time. He'll be glad to see you, Jed."

She took his arm and almost pulled him into the house, leaving Suzannah and Neosho to trail along behind. The maid smiled sympathetically and ushered them in.

"What is it?" called a deep voice from the library.

"Jed's here!" called Phoebe.

"Our Jed?"

"Yes! Come and see!"

Judge Sterling stepped into the room, dressed immaculately in a white shirt, embroidered vest, and expensive-looking trousers and boots. In his hand he held a meerschaum pipe, from which a wisp of bluish smoke rose.

"Jed!" he exclaimed. "Good to see you! It's been so long, we thought you were dead."

His hair was white, but as Jed recalled, it had been nearly so on his last visit. In general, his father appeared healthy, although the years showed in his face. A thought struck Jed that maybe Phoebe had exaggerated his father's condition to draw him home. Maybe not. When the gout was active, he knew it could cause great disability. It must now be in a period of remission.

"Father, my wife Suzannah, and our daughter Neosho."

Suzannah curtsied, and the Judge was obviously charmed. He bowed like a gentleman.

"Delighted, madam! Welcome to our family!"

It was a gallant gesture, but he spoke a trifle too loudly, and in a slightly patronizing manner. Jed realized that he was sincere, and was truly trying. But why, he wondered, does anyone do that? He had seen it many times. When talking to a person of another culture or language, one has a tendency to raise his voice, sometimes almost to a shout. . . . As if somehow, louder could eliminate the language barrier. It was amusing to see this in his father.

"Suzannah understands English quite well, Father," he laughed. "A fair amount of French, too, and she reads Latin."

"Oh, yes. Forgive me, Suzannah. I was being a boor."

"Not at all, sir. It is a pleasure to meet the father of my husband."

The look on Phoebe's face was her glassy, fixed smile for social situations. It was apparent that her feelings for Suzannah were less than charitable.

11

It was a strange sort of déjà vu, the conversation in the library after dinner. Jed, his father, and Sarah's husband Peter sat over brandy and cigars, discussing politics and business.

Fourteen years, it had been, since this scene had played out before. Since then, the death of Raven, his own battle with grief and alcohol, and his recovery. He still did not trust himself with strong drink, and his crystal glass sat untended after the first pretense at a ritual sip.

He was glad, this time, to be accompanied by Suzannah and little Neosho. It would simplify his refusal of any misguided attentions of his predatory stepmother, Phoebe. Suzannah had charmed everyone at dinner with her culture and her intelligent conversation.

"You have married well, Jed," the Judge remarked as he lighted a long black cigar. "Tell us more of her family."

"I don't know much, sir," Jed said truthfully. "Louisiana plantation . . . Suzannah's father was dead before we met, and her mother much earlier. I met a man whom she referred to as Uncle Charles. Sullivan, I believe the name was. Pure vintage Southern gentleman."

"As I would assume," agreed his father. "A charming lady, my boy. Dark Irish, I suppose."

Jed wondered what these two would say if they knew the full truth of Suzannah's background. He smiled to himself.

"I suppose so."

"Well, things move swiftly in your West," observed Van Landingham. "A lot of water down the river since last we spoke."

"That's true," agreed Jed. "We're glad to have the Mexican War behind us. I understand they're still negotiating on the exact boundaries."

"So it seems," the Judge agreed. "My guess is that the United States will simply buy out both Texan and Mexican claims to disputed territory."

Jed took a moment to marvel that these men, so far removed in location, had better information than those in the area affected. They were, of course, in close proximity to the seat of government, and hence to the political figures involved.

"It would be good to do so," Jed admitted. "No use to spill blood over a line in the sand."

"True, but it's happened many times over the years," said the Judge. "But is the traffic on the Santa Fe Trail increasing again?"

"Oh, yes. On the Oregon Trail, too. The war didn't bother that, of course. Lots of settlers moving to the west coast."

"Have you heard anything about gold, Jed?" asked his brother-in-law.

"Gold? No, why?"

"Rumors. Northern California, I believe."

"Yes," grunted the Judge. "So it's said. But Jed, all these things are part of the pattern."

"I beg your pardon, sir. 'Pattern'?"

"Yes. The whole country, shifting westward. 'Sea to shining sea' . . . Manifest Destiny!"

Jed now recalled that his father had mentioned something like this before. He waited.

"We're interested in being a part of this, Jed," his father went on. "You can help us."

"You want to *move* west?"

"No, no," the Judge laughed. "Not *move*. *Invest*. Look at the possibilities. A supply line for a continent! Peter and I are considering investments. *Transportation*. Maybe even the new steam trains."

"*Steam* trains?"

"Yes, my boy. Locomotives, the engines are called. Think of it. . . . One engine can pull several cars or wagons with freight or passengers. Already in use in Britain, we hear. They'll roll on rails."

"But in the *West*?"

Judge Sterling laughed. "In time, maybe. We'll see. Meanwhile, Peter and I are looking at steamboat investments. Several companies operating on the Mississippi, you know."

"Yes . . . I've traveled on them, Father. On the Missouri, too."

"Excellent! You can answer some of our doubts, maybe. Peter, let's show him the map!"

Van Landingham nodded, and the two unrolled a paper that spread across most of the top of the big desk. As they weighted the corners with books and paperweights, Jed began to see that it was a rather detailed map. It included all of the eastern portion of the continent. The United States, her territories and lands from the Gulf to the Canadian border. The western edge, however, lay only a little way beyond the Continental Divide, the summits of the Rocky Mountain range.

"You know this country, Jed?" asked his father, gesturing at the area between the Mississippi and the mountains.

"Of course. Not the Lakota lands, or Texas, but the central part. That's where we live."

"Ah! Good . . . Now, we're looking at the rivers. How many are navigable?"

Jed had never thought seriously about it. There were steamers on some of them.

"Well, there's regular service now on the Missouri, at least to Leavenworth. It should be possible to go on upstream. A few boats on the Kaw River, now. I'd guess the lower Arkansas is navigable, maybe this far upstream." He pointed to an area at about the eastern border of the state lettered "Arkansas."

"Yes. Now this Kansas River . . . 'Kaw,' you say?"

"Yes. Both terms are used."

"Very well . . . Now, how far upstream could one take a packet steamer?"

"Well . . . I don't know," Jed pondered. "I'm no sailor. But, I'd guess maybe this far." He pointed to the map. "Probably to this junction, where the Republican joins the Kansas. It's pretty shallow in some places. Sandbars, shoals . . ."

"Yes, yes." The Judge hurried on. "We know about that. They're working on new designs for the prairie steamers. Think of it, Jed. . . . A boat that will carry more than two hundred tons of freight, and draw only eighteen inches of water!"

"Can this be done?" Jed asked.

"Yes, it has. We have them coming. But what about this upper Kansas River?" He pointed to that portion west of the junction with the Republican.

"What about it? Well, it flows from pretty much straight west. The trappers and traders sometimes call it the Smoky Hill River."

The Judge seemed to ignore that bit of information. "Now," he said, "I want you to look at this."

He unrolled a second map, not quite so large as the first. Jed leaned forward to study it in the light of the whale-oil lamp. In the lower left corner, the title legend, in flowery script, read "The Great Central American Waterway." The upper Kansas River, or Smoky Hill, appeared considerably larger and straighter, and seemed to extend much farther westward than Jed remembered.

"I don't understand. . . ."

"A *canal system, Jed!*" The Judge's eyes glittered with excitement, almost equally matched by those of Van Landingham. "What do you think?"

"A *canal?*"

"Yes! A series of locks, raising the boats as the land rises. We'll be able to ship freight into the mountains."

Jed wanted to laugh but felt that it was too serious a situation. His father and brother-in-law might already . . .

"We?" Jed asked. "You have invested in this canal system?"

His father saw the alarm in Jed's face.

"Yes . . . Some. Anything wrong?"

"Well, yes, I would think. There's not enough water in the Smoky Hill to operate canal locks, Father."

The Judge chuckled. "The engineers know that, Jed. They'll use snowmelt, from the front range, here."

Jed sighed. "Father," he said seriously, "I don't know whether the promoters of this scheme are swindlers or not. Maybe they honestly think it can be done. But I seriously doubt it. The Smoky Hill isn't a snowmelt river. It rises from springs, more than a hundred miles east of the mountains. The Nebraska River, or Platte, gets some snowmelt. So does the Arkansas, which rises in the mountains. But not this one."

It was apparent from the expression on Van Landingham's face that he, at least, had invested substantially in the canal scheme.

"Can't it be channeled there?" Peter asked hoarsely.

"I doubt it, Peter. The soil is sandy. The Indians say the rivers run upside down in that country. There's moisture underground, and it may come to the surface somewhere downstream. But often, the stream bed is dry and dusty for weeks in the summer months. People die of thirst if they don't know how to dig for water."

"Dig for it?" asked the Judge.

"Yes . . . A seep hole. 'Indian wells,' people call them."

The silence became uncomfortable.

"It's possible I'm wrong," Jed admitted, "but I don't think so. And there is a rise in elevation. It would take a lot of canal locks."

"How much rise?" asked the Judge.

"I couldn't say. Hundreds of feet. Fremont took some survey figures. Are those available?"

"Surely, somewhere. But you think it not feasible, Jedediah?"

"That's my feeling, sir."

"Good enough. We may have to take our lumps. But about the river steamers?"

"Oh, yes. A very good future, I'd think, where possible. Some problems with sandbars. They're never where they were, after the next rain upstream. But practical, for people or goods, if that's where you want to go."

"But where else would one want to go?"

"Well, Santa Fe . . . Oregon . . . Anywhere across the mountains would be by land, of course. Even so, the upper Missouri is navigable. I don't know how far."

The other two men looked at each other.

"You say you've traveled on these river packet steamers?" asked Peter.

"Oh, yes. That's how I happened to be in New Orleans to meet Suzannah. On the Missouri, too. There are regular runs from St. Louis to Fort Leavenworth."

"Ah, good!" sighed the Judge with apparent relief. "We have an interest, Peter and I, in a company based in St. Louis. They want to expand into the Platte region if it becomes a Territory. What about the rivers there?"

"Well, the Platte, or Nebraska River isn't too good a possibility. Too shallow and sandy most of the way, I think. The Kansas, for a ways, anyway, as I said. But that's still Indian Territory. I think there's a move to change that, no?"

"So we hear. There's a push to move the tribes south."

Jed shook his head. "I can't see the Comanches and Kiowas being as docile as the eastern tribes have been."

"You expect trouble, then?"

"If they try to put them on reserves, yes," Jed assured him.

"They have a strange concept of land, apparently," mused Van Landingham.

"Strange? Maybe. Their whole concept of ownership is different, Peter. Land cannot be 'owned,' in the sense that private property can. It isn't bought or sold or even traded, only used, by the group."

"But they fight over it?"

"Only over the right of other groups to *use* it. Some of the treaties have been misunderstood. The natives believed that they were selling the *right to use,* not the land itself."

The Judge nodded. "Never thought of it that way. That puts a new light on the whole thing. Mmm . . . A completely different system of real estate law . . ." He shifted in his chair. "But, back to the expansion . . . We hear that there are several moves in Congress to establish Territories in your area, but some reluctance."

"I don't understand, Father."

"Politics, Jed. Democrats versus Whigs. I've always been a Whig, you know."

Jed had never been really interested in politics, and had not gone to any effort in trying to understand the forces involved. Now, it seemed, these were the forces that would shape the frontier.

"Politics, sir? How do you mean?" he asked.

The Judge pondered for a moment. "Well," he said finally, "how much power should the federal government have? Under the Constitution, the federation is bound to protect the sovereign rights of the individual republics. But I'm afraid there's too much power centered there. We . . . the Whig party . . . want to limit the president to one term, for instance. We've tried to elect Henry Clay, who understands the concept of states' rights, but can't get him elected. He'd push for a federal system of canals and roads, financed by selling federal lands in the West. But he's a Southerner, you see. Not electable. We were lucky to get Zach Taylor in this time."

The North-South thing again, Jed thought.

"Is this about slavery?" he asked.

"Not really, Jed. There are those who'd make it so. It's about whether the federation or the separate states should have the greatest power. Slavery's just something to argue over. It's dead anyway. Economically unfeasible. Another generation . . . Well, you know. Missouri . . . Infants born to slaves there *now* are free."

"But what does this have to do with the Kansas area becoming a Territory?"

"Power. Power in Congress, in the Senate. It could shift the balance, toward the Democratic-Republican federalism, or to the Whig, states'-rights view. Both sides are uneasy. And then there's this third-party talk. National Republicans, they call themselves. A pity. It will split the vote. Steal mostly from the Whigs, I think. A lot of them are Whigs who are nervous that the Whigs won't take a stand on slavery. I'm hoping we can reunify the party in the next election by running General Winfield Scott. Good, solid military man. Popular public figure."

"Taylor won't run again?"

"I think not. The party wants to limit terms in office. Well, we'll see. But I fear, if we don't keep the slavery issue out of the Whig platform, it will split the party. There's a very vocal minority who want to hang our campaign on that, and not on *states' rights,* which is our heritage. It could destroy both the Whigs and states' rights. Even the Union itself."

He sighed deeply. "Well, enough doom and gloom. We'll see. . . . Anyway, Jed, your West is to be important, and to invest in it, in transportation, is to our interest. Peter's and mine. Let us talk about how you could help us as a representative in that area. Would you be interested in a partnership, of sorts?"

There was one short conversation that evening, overheard by no one but the servant girl. Sarah, Jed's sister, was busy with the children, and for a few moments Phoebe and Suzannah found themselves alone in the dining room, at opposite ends of the table.

"So good to have you here," gushed Phoebe. "I've always simply adored Jed, you know."

Suzannah was equal to almost any social situation. She smiled sweetly.

"Yes, I know," she purred, pausing just enough to let that thought sink home. "Be assured that he's well cared for, though."

The subject did not come up again, and the two women understood each other.

12

Jed had never thought of such a thing. A representative of an eastern
firm looking after their interests on the frontier? He had protested, but
his father and Van Landingham had an answer for every argument.
They had apparently given this much thought. Jed wondered, even, if the
note from Phoebe had been part of the scheme to get him back home.
Probably not. That was likely her own agenda.

Actually, as he thought about it, this was a logical move on their part.
The partners could trust him, he had wide experience, education, he knew
the region, the people, and the need for expansion of transportation. The one
major drawback, as he saw it, was that he and Suzannah must move to a
more populated area, nearer the mainstream of commerce. The partners
favored St. Louis, but he flatly refused. There were too many people. More
importantly, too much Southern influence along the Mississippi. There was a
point beyond which he was unwilling to go, out of consideration for Suzannah's feelings. By contrast, the Council Grove was too far into the frontier,
and with too few resident whites for their purpose.

They discussed other possible sites where he might settle. Independence? Possibly, but it might be good to be nearer the rivers. Leavenworth?
Another good possibility, but farther from the land trails than he'd wish. He
kept thinking of the area of the old Kaw town where the Kansas and Missouri Rivers join. The westward roads all passed through there. In addition,
the north-south military road between the frontier forts led *across* the others.
Of most importance to their interest in the riverboat industry, here was

access to the upper Missouri River, the Kansas River, the St. Louis portion of the Missouri, and on into the Mississippi. He could find the right spot. . . .

Suzannah was agreeable, but with some reservations. She would hate to leave the home they had built and the anonymity of the frontier. Yet she had thoroughly enjoyed this return to civilization for a little while, and had gained much confidence. The possibility of a school for Neosho was a great inducement, too. They began to plan the changes that such a new life would bring. There were arrangements for Jed to draw a salary at St. Louis until a line of banking could be established in the rapidly growing Kansas City area.

Jed also decided to drive a team and wagon back to Kansas, instead of riding.

"Let's shop for some clothes here," he told Suzannah. "The farther west we go, the more expensive they'll be. The same with the team. We can find a light wagon, take along some supplies, anything else we might want where we'll live."

Suzannah readily agreed. She also had some further suggestions.

"Why don't we take some yard goods and some other things that people need back on the frontier? They'll increase in value with every day's travel west."

Jed laughed. "You'd have made a good trader's wife! Yes, it's a good idea. You choose what we'll take, and buy it, while I see about the team and wagon. I'm sure one of the servants can go with you to shop."

"All right . . . But Jed, we'll take the saddle horses, won't we? I love my chestnut mare."

"Of course, if you like. I'd planned to keep mine. We won't need the pack horse, though."

He was becoming excited at the prospects, now.

The next few days were a whirlwind of preparation. It was a long trip as autumn drew near. Jed was still undecided as to whether they could find or build suitable housing for the coming winter. Maybe it would be more practical to winter in the cabin at the Grove and move the following spring.

Finally the wagon was loaded, the good-byes said. Suzannah and Phoebe embraced briefly, and exchanged a peck on the cheek. Jed assisted Suzannah into the wagon, lifted Neosho to the seat, and shook his father's hand.

"Thank you, sir. Let us hope for a useful business venture. I'll write."

"And I," agreed the Judge. "May your mail arrive in more timely fashion!"

"It will, Father, after we move. Where we are now, they leave it in a hollow tree."

The Judge laughed. "Let us know as soon as you have an address!"

Jed clucked to the team and flapped the lines, and the wagon rolled forward.

"He thought you were joking about the Post Office Oak," Suzannah giggled.

"I know. No use trying to explain."

There was silence for a little while, and Jed spoke again.

"I was a little surprised to see you and Phoebe getting along so well."

Suzannah smiled. "We understand each other quite well."

They paused for two days in Kentucky while Jed had the wagon fitted with bows and a canvas top. He had not thought to do so in Baltimore, but a rainstorm in the Cumberland had caught their attention. The merchandise in the wagon was sheltered under canvas tarpaulins, but needed more protection.

"Now we'll look like settlers headed for Oregon," Jed remarked with a wry smile.

They were, of course, better equipped than most. Some of the ramshackle outfits they passed looked as though they couldn't make it to the next town.

Beyond St. Louis, the road was clogged, not only with emigrants but with a different sort of traveler. At first, Jed did not understand. Mostly men, traveling light, sometimes on horseback and leading a pack horse, or walking and leading a donkey or small mule. They had encountered a few such travelers, but here were many more. It did not take long to learn their goal.

"Gold! Layin' on top o' the ground in Californy," a grizzled old man assured them, without missing a step as he passed.

There were others, from all walks of life. Gentlemen, laborers, a few with families, but mostly single men with a single purpose: to get rich, quickly. The air fairly crackled with excitement.

Jed wondered how many would actually become rich. In fact, how many would even survive to reach California? Most of these appeared to have no idea at all of the distances involved, or the necessary supplies and equipment.

They spent a few days in the rapidly growing area near the junction of the Kansas and Missouri Rivers. They established a temporary camp while Jed looked for a place to build or buy. The whole situation was complicated by the many Indian claims and assignments in the area. Boundaries were indefinite and often conflicting because of faulty surveys and treaties that were even worse.

He finally decided on a general area along the military road from Fort Leavenworth to Fort Scott, on high ground south of the crossing of the Kaw known as the Lower Delaware Crossing. He exchanged most of the trade goods for credit with one of the trading posts in the area.

That decision made, they moved on toward the Grove, another week's journey. Mornings were crisp and cool, and days sunny, and traveling was good, but it was even better to be nearing home.

"Mama! Mama! They're back!" shouted a young Kesterson as they pulled up before the cabin.

It looked smaller than Jed remembered, but was in good shape. Ilsa came from the doorway of her own cabin, wiping her hands on her apron.

"Velcome home!" she called. She hurried on over. "Ve missed you! But mein Gott! You're goin' to Oregon?" She stared at the wagon. "Or you have become traders?"

"Not Oregon, Ilsa!" Suzannah laughed. "Traders, maybe, in a way. Jed's going into business with his father. A shipping company."

"Ach! You go back east, den?"

"No, no. But we'll move, in the spring. He needs to be near the river. I'll tell you all about it."

"All right. I vill miss you, Suzannah."

"And I'll miss you too, Ilsa. But tell me . . . how is everyone?"

"Jus' fine. Sven's busy. Your cow freshened. . . . A nice heifer, so we kept her for you to decide about. Plenty milk anyway, till you get back. Chickens fine. Trouble mit 'coons in der chicken house at nights, but Sven got a dog, and dat helps some."

"Well, we'll catch up on visiting. Right now, let me start to unload our things. Most of the goods can stay in the wagon for now." She paused and looked around the shady Grove and up the river past the houses. "It's good to be home, Ilsa."

It was equally hard to plan and accomplish the move when spring came. Jed had made several trips on horseback to put things in motion to build a house in the selected area. It would be a frame house because logs were becoming scarce. But there was also more prestige in a house made of sawn lumber. He chafed a little at the need for such recognition, but if he was to represent the shipping firm, it would be necessary.

He found and rented a small cubbyhole of an office near the docks, and arranged for a sign to be lettered on the inside of the single window that faced the traffic. It was rather startling to him as he rode down the street the next day.

The company name was in large and fancy gilt lettering, in an arching design like a rainbow. The business of the firm was indicated just below in a neat black block style.

Sterling and Van Landingham, Inc.
Transport and Shipping

BOOK II

❈

THE
RIVERBOATS
1853

1

Jed pulled his horse to a stop at the overlook and dismounted to let the animal rest for a few minutes. *Life is good,* he reflected.

He had had his doubts when they returned from their visit to Baltimore, nearly four years ago now. He had never considered himself much of a businessman. Yet he found that he rather enjoyed it. Maybe it was a matter of having been in the right place at the right time. That had certainly helped. The country was rapidly opening up to settlement. The area west of Missouri was not yet even designated as Territorial, beyond that of Indian Territory along the Kansas River. But, there being no formal law, there was nothing to prevent settlement. The area around the old Kansa town, the Shawnee Mission, and the Wyandot and Delaware reservations now held more white settlers than Indians.

Jed did regret the "civilizing" of an area that he had known in its unspoiled state, but had learned to live with it. It helped that he had been busy with the expansion of the riverboat company. There were those from the old days who had not taken well to the onrushing tide of civilization.

William Bent, for instance . . . Who could have foreseen that the trader would have become so disillusioned. Maybe it was the mad rush to the California goldfields, the trespass of greenhorns across the prairie that had supported the traders and trappers of an earlier day. Bent had simply removed most articles of value and then blown up the fort, the landmark where the Santa Fe Trail turned south. Bent's Fort would be missed by the teamsters.

But *then* . . . Bent was said to be building, even now, a *new* "fort," a trading post some thirty miles nearer civilization, at a place called Big Timbers. It made little sense to Jed. In a way, he longed to go and see Bent's New Fort, to talk to the trader and discover his motives. But he had more pressing things to do.

The transport business was thriving. Communities were springing up along the Missouri River, in Iowa, and also in the territory west of the river. All of these needed merchandise to stock the shelves of storekeepers supplying the settlers who were pouring into the area. Sterling and Van Landingham had owned only two riverboats in 1849. The fleet had now grown to six packet steamers, not including one that had been lost. She had struck a snag in the lower Missouri near Rocheport, the old French landing above Columbia. Snags and shoals were always a problem in the shifting channels of the prairie rivers. Jed figured that the life of a river steamer averaged only about five years. Sterling and Van Landingham had been lucky.

They now had several regular runs from Leavenworth to St. Louis. There was a schedule from Leavenworth to Kansas City to Fort Riley, the new army post on the Kaw River. About halfway along that run was the port of Silver Lake, with good berths for several packet steamers, a few miles above the ferry at Topeka.

The gold rush to California had caused an increase in overland traffic, too. California had joined the Union as a state, and there was talk that Oregon, too, was seeking statehood. With Jed's experience as a scout and guide, he had seen a great deal of overland travel. Why not take advantage of that knowledge? He had proposed such expansion to his partners by letter. . . . Mail service was improving now, slow but more reliable. His suggestion was met with enthusiasm, and Sterling and Van Landingham now had three freight wagons as well as a passenger coach. The coach was new, and even Jed admitted that it was an experiment. But it seemed logical to him that there would be interest in such a conveyance, faster than the lumbering freight wagons.

There was no regular passenger run as yet, but there was talk of mail contracts on the Oregon Trail. Jed had envisioned a regular loop from the Kansas City area on the old Santa Fe road, then north from Bent's along the front range of the mountains to meet the Oregon Trail. Eastward, back along that road on the Platte River to the starting point. Now, with Bent having destroyed the old fort, the plan was at a virtual halt. Still, shorter irregular runs had proved practical among the towns and military posts along the border. There were always those who felt the need to be somewhere else. Jed saw this as an opportunity to demonstrate the company's ability to accommodate.

Today, he was in Missouri to have a look at the road to St. Joseph. They already had riverboat service from Kansas City to Leavenworth to St.

Joseph. But with the coach, it should be possible to cut at least a day off the time required. A two-day passenger run, if the road was good.

There should be a town about halfway there, he thought. Weston . . . An overnight stop for the passenger coach, perhaps. Today he could evaluate the road and the town, possibly stay there overnight, and on to St. Joseph. He remounted and moved on at an easy trot.

It had been a big help to have his nephew, Ben, join him in the operation of the business. That had occurred two years ago. Ben was the son of Jed's sister, Sarah, and Peter Van Landingham. In his mid-twenties, Ben had decided not to follow his father into law. He had done well in college, was quick and witty, yet quite businesslike when occasion required. Jed had liked the boy immediately on the few occasions when they had met.

Ben had been working for a newspaper in Arlington, Virginia. When his grandfather the Judge suggested that Ben join the family shipping company on the frontier, Jed was willing. He was always somewhat bored and restless with the paperwork, and hated to be tied to an indoor desk. To have a bright young man, trustworthy and a member of the family, to take on a major portion of this work was little short of emancipation. Ben had brought his young wife, Lorena, and their three children, and settled them in a house near that of Jed and Suzannah. The two families had a comfortable relationship, and Ben's help had been good for the company.

Jed noticed a crowd gathered in the street as he entered the town of Weston. He pulled the horse from a trot to a walk, and out of sheer curiosity reined in that direction. On a soapbox in front of a store stood a long-faced, heavy-set man who was haranguing the crowd. A traveling drummer, maybe? No . . . A politician . . . Jed reined to a stop and stepped down.

"Who's that?" he asked a youngster who trotted past.

"Senator Atchison!" grinned the boy. "He's talkin' about the territories!"

I'd better listen, thought Jed. Jed turned to the boy.

"Could you take my horse to the livery yonder?" he asked.

"Sure!"

"Have them give him some oats, and tell them I'll be over directly."

He tossed the boy a coin and made his way toward the speaker. He had never met Senator David Atchison, but had heard rumors of the man's enmity toward Senator Thomas Benton, also of Missouri. Atchison was now stumping the frontier to promote his ideas about the status of the proposed territories.

At this point the senator, his face flushed and sweating, was warming to his subject. He would oppose the admission of Nebraska, the all-inclusive name for the area, as "Free" territory with the last drop of his blood, he said.

"American citizens should be privileged to go where they please," he shouted, "and carry with them their property. . . . Furniture, mules, or niggers!"

Jed felt his hackles rise and his palms began to sweat.

"On that question," the senator continued, "I pledge myself to be faithful. The Missouri Compromise must be repealed! Will you sit down here at home and permit the nigger thieves, the cattle, the vermin of the North to come in and take up those fertile prairies, run off your Negroes, and depreciate the value of your slaves here?"

He paused a moment and seemed to soften, but the change was deceptive.

"I know you well," he said, smiling. "I know what you will do. You know how to protect your interests. Your own rifles will free you from such neighbors and secure your property."

Unbelievable, thought Jed. *Is the man calling for murder?*

"You will go in there if necessary with bayonets and with *blood!*" Atchison shouted. "We will repeal the Compromise. I would sooner see the whole of Nebraska in the bottom of hell than to see it a Free State!"

To Jed this inflammatory rhetoric was chilling, but the next occurrence even more so. The crowd was cheering wildly, yelling support. A few turned away in disgust, or perhaps in fear. But, the senator stepped down from his rude platform, flushed and sweating, to the howls of approval.

" 'At's right, Senator!"

"We're with you!"

"We'll show them Yankees what for!"

Jed turned away, sick at heart. It was one thing to have political views, quite another to encourage border ruffians to wreak death and destruction. He knew of several Missouri families from this area who had crossed the river to settle in Kansas, between St. Joseph and Leavenworth. They anticipated Territorial status, and assumed Northern orientation on the basis of location. They had no particular political ax to grind.

But how vulnerable this border incitement would make them! No legal protection for these squatters . . . And here was a senator of the United States, urging the killing of such families fully two hundred miles north of the accepted North-South dividing boundary.

It made him angry. In a younger day, he might have voiced a protest. Now, he was more cautious. Today, it would have been foolhardy to challenge any of the statements of such a powerful speaker.

The crowd began to disperse, and Jed watched small groups in heated conversation. They seemed eager to go somewhere, to do something. Anything, almost, to relieve the excitement and tension generated by the tirade of the senator.

No good can come of this day, Jed told himself.

He picked up his horse at the livery and rode out of town. He would spend the night elsewhere, even on the trail, if needed. With regret, he abandoned his tentative plans for a passenger line here. It would simply be too dangerous, not only for drivers but for passengers. The riverboats would be safer.

On the ride home, Jed's thoughts were troubled. He had not realized how deeply the troubles of the frontier were affecting people. Most of the people he knew were not really concerned with politics, but with making a living. But now, political opinion was threatening to make a great deal of difference in the lives of his family and in the business. He must discuss these developments with Ben.

And, of course, with Suzannah.

2

"**B**en, you have no idea!" Jed told his nephew. "The man was actually urging these ruffians to pillage and kill."

The younger man shook his head sadly. "And they seemed to be in sympathy with this idea?"

"It was hard to tell. There were maybe thirty or forty men there. Some, I suppose, would have left already, when they saw where his talk was going. I saw others turn and walk away. But he had a hard core of listeners who were *cheering*."

"Well, no one who disagreed would have spoken up at that point, would he?" asked Ben.

"That's true. I suppose we knew that this sort of feeling existed. It was simply a shock to see it out there in the open. . . . A public figure . . . A United States *senator*, Ben!"

Ben pushed aside the shock of sandy hair that always seemed to go awry and leaned back in his chair.

"You know, I guess, that he was president of the United States for a day?"

"*Atchison?*" Jed blurted. "No! I . . ."

"Yes! 1849 . . . President Taylor was to be inaugurated on March fourth, but that was a Sunday. Taylor's a Quaker, and deferred till the next day. Atchison, as president of the Senate, would have been next in line in an emergency."

"My God! I had no idea. But his position, Ben. That's frightening!"

"This is more complicated than it looks, Uncle Jed. I saw these feelings in Virginia. Not this incitement to violence, but arguments about the rights of the new states as they're settled."

Jed studied the thoughtful young man.

"Ben," he said finally, "we've never talked much politics. Maybe we need to."

The young man nodded. "I guess so. You know something of the ideas of my father and of the Judge?"

"Somewhat. My father, the Judge, has always been active in the Whig party. When I was there four years ago, he was fearful of a party split."

"Over states' rights?"

"Not exactly, Ben. His preference for the Whigs has always been that they opposed the growing federal power. He favored Henry Clay's ideas: *help* the individual states but let them run their own affairs."

"I know. But Clay's not electable. He's a Southerner."

Jed agreed. "To me, it makes sense that a big, powerful government in Washington can't solve all the problems of farmers in Iowa, mining in California, growing cotton in Georgia, manufacturing in New England. . . . And shouldn't try, probably. But it's become a North-South conflict, somehow. That's what concerns your grandfather."

Ben nodded. "I'd understood that. But I can't go along with the Whigs' proslavery stand."

"Neither can he. And that's what he's afraid will destroy his party. The proslave faction have let *that* become the issue instead of the rights of the states. The more thoughtful Free-Staters will back off from that argument, and probably join the new National Republicans, who favor states' rights but *oppose* slavery."

Ben nodded again. "And the more argument there is about slavery, the more it plays into the hands of the federalist, big-government Northerners."

"Exactly. We see things pretty much alike, then?"

"It would seem so, Jed. I think my father's ideas are much the same. What about the Judge?"

"When I last saw them, his main concern was that the conflict would destroy his Whig party."

"That seems likely. But there's a likelihood, it seems, of the new territories going slave or free by vote of the new settlers. Did you hear any of that over in Missouri?"

"I wasn't really thinking about it, after hearing that speech. But, I think that's the only logical way to do it, don't you?"

Ben nodded. "It has to be. But that doesn't solve the basic problem, does it? Who deserves the right to govern? The federation or its member nations?"

The two had reached a better understanding, but there remained a dread in the thoughts of both. Judge Sterling, the family patriarch, could worry about a rift in his political party. In the nation, even. More to the point for the families of these two men was the plain fact that Jed had observed in a frontier town. If this spark ever fanned into flame, it could start a wildfire that could destroy the nation. And it would start not in Washington but here, on the frontier. Their hearts were heavy.

Meanwhile, discussion and argument continued regarding Territorial status for the Great Plains. Each proposed plan met with objections from one faction or another of the complicated North-South, free-slave, states' rights–federalist arguments. The traditional dividing line between North and South at the thirty-six-thirty parallel was all but forgotten. All factions were eager to claim any territory possible, to gain representation and political power in the Congress.

A few decades earlier, there had existed a gentlemen's agreement to admit one Northern state and one Southern at the same time. This distinction was breaking down. Little territory was available to those of Southern persuasion. Texas had the right to divide into four states but had refused to do so, despite urging by the proslavery minority. This would have provided eight Southern seats in the Senate instead of two, and could have swung a vote.

California, although Southern geographically, was being settled largely by Northerners due to the massive rush for gold. It had been admitted to the Union in 1850, as a Free State, further upsetting the balance of power.

Ben returned from a business trip with newspapers from Baltimore and Washington, as well as St. Louis.

"Senator Atchison and others have introduced a new bill into Congress," Ben pointed out.

The plan would divide the territory in two along the fortieth parallel. The area south of that line would become Kansas Territory, and that to the north, Nebraska Territory, after the major river of each. Both would extend westward to the summit of the Rocky Mountains. This plan was introduced as a compromise, with the further provision that each of the new territories would decide at the first election whether it would permit slavery. With this concession, it seemed probable that the southern, or Kansas Territory, would elect to Southern loyalties, and leave Nebraska Territory to the North.

"Don't you think this will stir up more trouble?" asked Ben.

"It surely could," Jed agreed. "The abolitionists are going to resent concessions to Southern interests."

"Yes," agreed Ben, "but there are a lot of Southerners who'll oppose it too. Even slave owners. I think a lot of them would like to avoid a public confrontation. And as we've agreed, that's not what it's about. It's about power."

Jed nodded. "Ben, I think this can only lead to more trouble. Now both sides . . . *all* sides, really, will see a need to rush settlers in here, just to swing the votes in disputed territory."

The Kansas-Nebraska Bill made its way to the President's desk and was signed into law in May 1854.

A few weeks earlier, a meeting had been held in the city hall in Worcester, Massachusetts. Eli Thayer, serving his second term as a representative in the state legislature, chaired the meeting.

Thayer was an entrepreneur, a dreamer and visionary who had already been involved in a number of schemes to acquire money. He had a business interest in a factory in Kentucky designed to extract oil from bituminous coal. This "coal oil" would be used in place of whale oil for fuel and for lighting purposes.

Mr. Thayer's meeting was a proposal to encourage investment in a project that would capitalize on the growing antislavery sentiment in the country. If he could somehow connect this sentiment with a speculative enterprise . . .

"I pondered upon it day and night," he wrote. "By what plan could this great problem be solved . . . ? Suddenly it came upon me in a revelation. It was *organized and assisted emigration.*"

At the organizational meeting he spoke eloquently. He proposed to fill up Kansas with new settlers . . . "with men who hate slavery and would drive the hideous thing from the broad and beautiful plains where they are going to raise free homes." Thayer scarcely mentioned that it was primarily an investment scheme, soliciting stockholders with attractive promises like "large returns at no distant day" and "very handsome profit to stockholders upon their investment."

He immediately drew up a lengthy and complicated charter for the "Massachusetts Emigrant Aid Company." The proposal was to colonize the new Territory with foreigners from Europe, at an estimated forty thousand annually, and, in addition, twenty thousand citizens of Massachusetts who were opposed to slavery. The company would send mills and machinery and printing presses, and purchase land to be resold for ever-increasing prices to incoming settlers.

The charter was submitted to the Massachusetts legislature as a plan to "organize emigration to the West and bring it into a system." Linked to the emotional antislavery issue, the charter proceeded rapidly through the legislature and was signed by the governor.

A report of Mr. Thayer's plan was published in the *New York Tribune* in May 1854, attracting much favorable attention in the Northeast and in

New England. Editorially, such celebrities as Horace Greeley himself gave enthusiastic support. In a short while, other emigrant aid societies sprang up. The "Emigrant Aid Company of New York and Connecticut," chartered in Connecticut, listed as its president Eli Thayer. The "Union Emigration Society" was formed in Washington City within a month. Many other smaller societies followed, and the rush of settlers began.

Naturally, this rush alarmed the South. Whether or not they were proslave, this massive infusion of Northern ideas and voters presented a threat. The new Territory's policies were to be determined by ballot, and this was a challenge not to be ignored by those believing in the rights of the individual states. Nothing so far had so influenced the South. Especially, this became true along the border. Missourians, pro- and antislave alike, rallied to the cause. If they could fill the border counties with squatters, there would be no room for emigrants.

Quickly, a "Squatters' Claim Association" sprang up in the Salt Creek Valley near Leavenworth and similar groups in other areas along the Missouri side of the border.

In Liberty, Missouri, a large meeting passed a Declaration and Resolution:

> Therefore, we the citizens of Clay County, believing self-preservation to be the first law of nature, and learning that organizations have been effected in Northern States for the purpose of colonizing the Territory of Kansas with such fanatical persons as composed the recent disgraceful mob in the city of Boston, where a United States officer, for simply attempting to obtain justice for a Southern citizen, was shot down in the streets; and learning, too, that these organizations have for their object the colonization of said Territory with "eastern and foreign paupers," with a view of excluding citizens of slave-holding States, and especially citizens of Missouri, from settling there with their property; and further, to establish a trunk of the underground railroad, connecting with the same line, where thousands of our slaves shall be stolen from us in thwarting their attempts upon our rights, we do
>
> *Resolved,* That Kansas ought of right to be a slave State, and we pledge ourselves to cooperate with the citizens of Jackson County (Missouri) and the South generally, in any MEASURE to accomplish such ENDS.

A similar meeting in Weston, a few miles north in Platte County, Missouri, produced a resolution that was much shorter and to the point:

Resolved, that this association will, whenever called upon by any of the citizens of Kansas Territory, hold itself in readiness together to assist and remove any and all emigrants who go there under the auspices of The Emigrant Aid Societies.

In June 1854, a correspondent of the *Baltimore Sun* ended his dispatch to the paper with this statement:

It is estimated that some two thousand claims have already been made within fifteen miles of the military reserve (Fort Leavenworth), and in another week's time, double that number will be made.

The lines of battle were being drawn, and storm clouds of trouble began to gather over the new territory.

3

J ed and Ben found little occasion to discuss the rapid changes around them in the ensuing months. The rush of settlers brought such an increase in the business of Sterling and Van Landingham that time for anything else became quite scarce. Jed reflected many times that being in the right place at the right time is the major factor in success . . . or in survival. Sometimes the misfortune of the *wrong* place and time is equally disastrous.

Maybe, even, they were experiencing a combination of both. There was a growing uneasiness in the entire area. To meet a stranger on the road, always a matter of cautious assessment, now became a major concern. A traveler must try to guess the stranger's motives, his politics, the potential danger he presented. This was not always easy. Jed had some advantage. He was well known in the area, was a respected early settler and businessman. He was also known to "keep his own counsel." One may be friendly, honest, and helpful without delving deeply into either his own opinions or those of others. He had always been a private person, and even more so in the past decade. He was certain that no one suspected that his wife, olive-skinned and beautiful, was once a slave in Louisiana. Everyone they knew was aware of his background as a scout and hunter, and seemed to assume that he had married an Indian wife in some of his travels. No one even appeared to wonder. At one time he had experienced some sidelong remarks about being a "squaw man," but even that did not occur anymore. No doubt there were some who disapproved, but such marriages were usually accepted. Especially, since the "Civilized Tribes" had arrived and settled in the Indian

Nations to the south of Kansas Territory. Cherokees, especially, were thrifty and hardworking, and were earning the respect of their border neighbors.

In the decade since his marriage to Suzannah, they had confided the actual circumstances to no one. At this time, Jed was glad. Even his nephew and partner in business had been allowed to assume that Suzannah was Indian or half-blood. With the present developments and settlement in the new territory being manipulated by both sides in the political arena, this was very fortunate.

The worst of the new influx of settlers was that with the touchy politics of the times, one could not be sure of trusting even old friends. There were those whom he had known and liked for years, who were now unsure of each other. As a businessman, he had need to retain the friendship of everyone, if possible. The same was true of any of the established businesses. "A trader needs the good will of all," an Arapaho friend had once told him. This explained why the Arapaho, "Trader People" in hand signs, had traditionally had few enemies.

It was the same with Sven Kesterson at his smithy in Council Grove, and with Moses Grinter, who operated the ferry at the Delaware Crossing on the military road. Jed did not have much of an idea of the political position of these men. It had not mattered. Now, it was becoming important. He found himself listening for any trace of an accent in a stranger's speech. It might be quite important, the slow drawl of a Southerner, or the clipped speech of a New Englander, who might add an *R* at the end of any word ending with an *A*. This had once been a source of mild amusement. Now, it might easily indicate to which faction one belonged, and how dangerous a given situation might be.

Sometimes Jed longed for the early days on the prairie. It had been dangerous. There were those who might want to kill a lone trapper or hunter, but they would do so honestly and openly, and within the understood framework of their respective cultures. Now, there was distrust, dishonesty, and chicanery. Whom could a man trust? And all of this was made worse by Jed's own confusion. He could see both sides. States' rights, yet slave or free . . . Why did people have to link the two together? These were separate problems, as far as he could see. He firmly believed in the sovereignty of the individual republics, but was just as strongly opposed to slavery. There must be many Southerners who felt as he did, but the extremists on both sides would not let it be. He could see no simple solution.

Well, meanwhile the transport and shipping business was thriving. He'd continue to tend to that.

By autumn of 1854, several town sites were laid out and settlements sprang up. The town of Leavenworth, just south of the fort, was growing rapidly, populated mostly by settlers from Missouri, just across the river. Some of these seemed to Jed to have Free State sympathies, but were totally eclipsed by the more vocal and aggressive proslavers.

It was apparent that this was an ideal location for a town, with access to river ports, and also to well-used roads for commerce. The first newspaper in the new Territory, the *Kansas Weekly Herald,* was printed there in September, under an old elm tree on the levee, near the corner of a new street designated Cherokee Street. It was strongly proslavery.

A few miles to the north, Senator Atchison and his Missouri followers staked out a town site that he dedicated to the same cause. In a speech on the morning when the sale of lots began, Atchison stated that if he had his way, he would "hang every abolitionist who dares to show his face here." Then, as if to soften this stand, he admitted that there might be Northern settlers who were "sensible, honest, right-feeling men" and would be as far from stealing a Negro as a Southern man.

Atchison did not establish residence in the town that bore his name, but the name was well known throughout the South. The town became a rallying point for the more extreme proslavers from all over the Southern states.

By contrast, Free State settlers had a tendency to enter the Territory at Kansas City, having come by riverboat. From there, they followed the Kansas River westward, or the land trails to the west and south. Communities sprang up along the Santa Fe and Oregon Trails, and along the military road to the south.

The first party of the Massachusetts Emigrant Aid Company settlers arrived from Boston in July 1854, and traveled westward to a site selected by the company's advance agents, arriving there August 1. The town was called Lawrence, after a Massachusetts town of the same name. A second party, including women and children, arrived at Lawrence in September, and a third in October. This third group felt that they had been deceived by Thayer and his agents, and most of them returned to Massachusetts, completely disillusioned. Yet there would be two more parties to arrive before the year was out.

Jed saw that the lines were being drawn. The Atchison-Leavenworth area was becoming the headquarters of the proslavery faction. Lawrence, on the Kansas River, and ironically, to the *south* of the proslavers, was becoming the bastion of Free State sympathy.

More newspapers entered the confrontation. *The Herald of Freedom,* organ of the Emigrant Aid Company, issued a paper dated October 22, 1854, at Wakarusa, Kansas Territory, but it had been printed in Pennsylvania.

In June 1854, President Pierce appointed a governor for the Kansas Territory, a Pennsylvanian named Andrew H. Reeder. The *Kansas Weekly Herald* announced his arrival at Leavenworth on the steamer *Polar Star* on October 7.

The new governor attended a reception in his honor at the fort.

There were the traditional welcoming speeches and Governor Reeder's response. He lost no time in announcing that he would make a brief circuit of the Territory, as far west as the Council Grove and Fort Riley. Then he would announce the date for the territory's first election, that of a delegate to the United States Congress.

He did so, and on November 10, issued the proclamation: The election would be held on November 29, 1854.

4

G overnor Reeder arbitrarily divided the Territory into sixteen voting districts for the election.

> *First District*—Commencing at the Missouri State line, on the south bank of the Kansas River; thence along the south bank of said river to the first tributary or watered ravine running into the Kansas above the Town of Lawrence . . . to the west side of Rolf's house; thence by a due south line to the middle of the Santa Fe Road . . . etc.

The place of election was also stated for each district, usually a private home. Election judges were appointed.

The governor also published the suffrage requirements for voting in the election.

> Every free white male inhabitant above the age of twenty-one years, who shall be an actual resident of said Territory . . .

The proclamation excluded federal officers and those in the armed forces serving in the Territory. There was provision for newcomers to declare their intention to become citizens by taking an oath administered by a panel of the three election judges of the district involved.

·   ·   ·

"What will happen?" asked Suzannah.

"I don't know," Jed admitted. "I've never seen anything like this before. Ben has been involved with politics, but not frontier politics. He says the governor is pretty heavy-handed, but somebody has to start somewhere, I guess. Did you know that Reeder brought with him a man he expects to elect to Congress?"

"No. How can an outsider stand for office, Jed?"

"Take the oath that he intends to settle, I suppose. Fellow name of Flenneken, from Pennsylvania. It seems he was an ambassador to Denmark under President Polk."

Suzannah smiled. "That's not likely to make an impression on the people here, is it?"

"Not those we know. But, Suzannah, there are so many coming in. No way of telling where they stand, or how the election will go. It's a little frightening."

She gave the little chuckle that he loved. "Jed, you're just not accustomed to so many people. What does it matter who they send to Washington?"

"It *could* matter a lot. This is turning into a power struggle. And, though I don't quite see how, into a free or slave question."

Now there was alarm in her eyes. "Do you think we should leave? Go north?"

"No . . . Not yet, anyway. Let's see how the election goes. I'd hate to leave what we've built here. Besides, we have the family business to think of."

Shortly before the election, the outspoken Senator Atchison was quoted in the newspaper *Platte Argus,* from a speech in Weston, Missouri, a favorite pulpit for his ideas.

. . . Colonies are to be planted in all places where slavery and slave institutions can best be assailed; Kansas is now a favorite position, from whence they can now assail Missouri, Arkansas, and Texas. Men are being sent from Massachusetts and elsewhere for the avowed purpose of excluding slaveholders from Kansas, and as a matter of course to seduce, steal, and protect fugitive slaves. The first thing, however, they have to do is to throw into Kansas a majority of votes to control the ballot boxes. This is the policy of the abolitionists.

The senator went on to suggest that if each border county in Missouri were to do only its duty, to send five hundred young men to vote in the Territorial elections of Kansas, "The question will be decided quietly and peaceably at the ballot box."

He admitted that there might be honest persons who held abstract views in conflict with his own. They should not be punished for those views. However, if they "stirred up insubordination and insurrection among our slaves," no punishment was too severe. Notwithstanding his pacifist views, he would "hang these Negro-stealers."

Three candidates declared themselves for the office of delegate to Congress from the Kansas Territory.

Robert P. Flenneken of Pennsylvania, who had arrived on the *Polar Star* steamer with the governor, obviously expected to carry the vote for nomination by the Democrats, due to the influence of the governor. However, he obviously did not understand frontier politics. The Missouri Democrats had declared themselves proslavery and backed another candidate, General J. W. Whitfield, of Jackson County, Missouri. He was a known quantity, the Indian Agent of the Potawatomi reservation, and well respected in the area. He presented his platform, of moderate and tolerant tone, and convincingly stated that he was his own man, unswayed by any indebtedness to any supporters, and willing to abide by the decision of the ballot box.

Notwithstanding, he became the candidate of the proslavery faction. Disappointed, Flenneken immediately filed as an Independent.

A third candidate, John A. Wakefield, chief justice of the "Mutual Settlers' Association of Kansas Territory," became the Free State candidate. It was to be assumed that the settlers recently arrived under the auspices of the Emigrant Aid Company would support him as a Free State candidate.

"What do you think, Uncle Jed?" asked Ben. "Will there be enough votes to override those who intend to come across from Missouri and vote proslave?"

"I don't know, Ben. I've talked to some of the settlers. Looks to me as if there are a lot who are really here to settle, not because of the free or slave thing. A lot from Missouri, the same way. The Missourians have to keep quiet if they're Free State, of course. Their neighbors might turn on them. It's a dangerous time."

Ben nodded. "Jed, I rather like this General Whitfield. I know he's backed by the proslavers, but he seems moderate. And I'd bet he *is* his own man."

"But Ben, look who's backing him. *Atchison!*"

"I know. Of course, I guess it doesn't matter much anyway. The Territorial delegate doesn't have much say in the Congress."

"That's true."

The young man could not realize how critical this election might be to Jed and Suzannah, and Jed could not tell him. Meanwhile, they had business to transact. Despite the many questions revolving in a cloud of confusion about the election, the world must go on. The expansion of trade was bringing an ever-increasing burden on the transportation system.

"How are Lorena and the children?" Jed asked. "I haven't seen them for some time."

"Fine. The girls get together occasionally, you know. They sew and let the children play. Say! You're wearing new boots!"

"Yes!" Jed laughed. "You know I prefer moccasins. Too many years on the prairie, I guess. But these"—he lifted a foot—"these are different. Right and left . . . See?"

"I'd heard of those. Made on two separate lasts, no? Where did you get them?"

"St. Louis. Saw a pair in a store window and thought I'd try them. You know, they're actually comfortable, Ben."

Ben laughed. "But not to rival moccasins, of course?"

"No, but pretty close. Ben, the world is changing, and very rapidly. Not always for the good, I fear."

"Even with comfortable boots?"

Jed smiled ruefully. "Even so. I worry about this border conflict, Ben. It's much like two traditional enemies among the Indian Nations. They kill each other just *because* they're Pawnee, or Comanche or Osage. No room for compromise. I fear the border is being taken over by the extremists from both sides. There's no room for plain, friendly neighbors. No room for *any* neighbors, actually. Too many people!"

As he spoke, he thought of Daniel Boone, long ago. Jed had met Boone in Missouri when he first came west, and knew that the old frontiersman had left Kentucky because it was "gettin' too crowded. . . . Folks movin' in just twenty miles away."

On the day before the election, Jed and Ben boarded one of the Sterling and Van Landingham steamers to travel to their assigned voting place near Leavenworth City. It would be a full day's round-trip. They would board another boat on the downstream run after voting. Ben was somewhat irritated at the fact that they must travel so far to vote. There was no polling place within twenty miles of the populated area around the mouth of the Kansas River.

"You have to figure," Jed observed, "that the governor's new to the area. He doesn't rightly understand the patterns of travel. And look at it this way, Ben: If we lived just across the river, there, we'd be in another district, and would have to vote in Lawrence. That's even farther from home."

"I suppose so. And, I am able to experience travel on one of our company packets." Ben smiled ruefully.

"Right. Fresh air will do you good."

It was a crisp, sunny day, and travel was pleasant. They watched the bluffs on the right bank of the river slide past, and felt the throb of the steamer's engines as she breasted the current. As they neared Leavenworth along toward noon, they began to see groups of people camped in tents on the Kansas side of the river. Some waved at the steamer.

"Settlers?" asked Ben.

"I think not," Jed mused. "Look . . . These are mostly men. . . . Light camping outfits, camping in groups . . . Ben, I'm afraid we're looking at men who crossed the river yesterday just to vote."

"But they can't do that, can they?"

"Who knows? They'd have to take the oath that they intend to stay, but it would be hard to enforce, at best."

At the dock they disembarked and inquired the way to the polling place.

"Be careful!" advised the citizen who gave directions.

The reason for such advice became quickly evident. The dooryard at the designated house was full of armed men, many of whom appeared to be ruffians. They encountered an acquaintance from the fort, who also advised caution.

"The Missourians have rather taken over the polling place," he confided. "Be careful!"

Their right to vote was not challenged, but they felt concern for the election judges, who sat behind the table in obvious fear. One ruffian elbowed his way to the front of the line, refused to take the oath, and demanded to vote. The trembling judge decided that the safest course was to comply. Jed wondered how many times this had happened today.

They voted, returned to the docks, and boarded their packet steamer for the trip downriver. It seemed a great relief to reach the relative safety of the riverboat, and the feeling for the day was not good.

It was several days before they learned the results of the election. The total number of votes cast in the Kansas Territory's first election was 2,833. The official record showed the following results:

Whitfield, Proslavery candidate	—	2,258
Flenneken, Independent	—	305
Wakefield, Free State	—	248

There was a smattering of write-in votes, amounting to twenty-two more.

"There aren't that many voters in the whole Territory!" sputtered Ben indignantly. "This election is not valid!"

"It doesn't matter much, Ben," Jed noted. "The delegate to Congress has no power anyway. We'll have the election to form the Territorial legislature in the spring. Maybe that will be better."

He was not as optimistic as he tried to sound. He knew full well that there were probably not half that number of qualified voters in all. The discouraging part was that the proslave Missourians would not even have had to cross the river. The proslave candidate, General Whitfield, would have been elected anyway.

5

J ed and Suzannah discussed the election results in privacy. Women were assumed not to be interested in politics, and of course had no vote. Still, she had a vested interest in this situation. Jed often talked with her. Probably his attitude toward women was influenced by having lived among the Indians, where women had greater status than among whites. Suzannah's mind was quick and insightful, partly from years of self-preservation, he thought. She had a way of cutting through the confusion to the heart of a matter, and saying so in a few words.

"So . . . There are more proslavers in the Kansas Territory than Free-Staters?"

"It would seem so from the vote," Jed agreed. "But I would not have thought so. Something's not right."

Suzannah nodded. "But look at the candidates, Jed. General Whitfield, known in the area, a states'-rights Southerner, but not really heavy-handed on the slavery question . . . The other two . . . Outsiders. One wants to vote out everybody *but* people who think as he does. And he's a Northerner, against states' rights. The other, just off the boat, an unknown, but again, a Northerner. How did *you* vote?"

Jed hesitated, and finally sighed. "I had a hard decision, Suzannah. I wanted to vote against the whole slavery system, but both the antislave candidates are against states' rights. It wasn't a single issue."

"*You* voted for General Whitfield!" she accused softly. A flash of mixed emotions fluttered across her face, and a tear glistened for a moment.

"Suzannah . . . I . . ."

"Ssh . . . It's all right, Jed. There's no way you could agree totally with any of them."

She was quiet for a moment, then spoke again. "Ben, too, I suppose?"

"I don't know. We didn't talk about it."

"I understand. What will happen now?"

"Who knows? There will be another election in the spring, to form the Territorial Legislature. Probably more voters rushing in, sponsored by both sides, trying to swing the election. And both will force it to be about slavery."

"And you think it's *not?*" she demanded.

"It *shouldn't* be, Suzannah. It *should* be about whether the states individually or the federation should have the most power. The South joined the Union with the understanding that each separate state is its own republic, as the Constitution says. The slavery issue should not even come into federal politics."

"So . . . You agree with the Missourians on states' rights, but disagree on slavery?"

"Exactly, Suzannah. That's it. . . . And the South must keep the attention on states' rights. If they let the issue become slavery they're asking for trouble."

"But Atchison and his Missourians are trying to *make* that the issue."

"Yes . . . And I'm afraid that plays into the hands of the Emigrant Aid Societies. *They* want it about slavery, too. They'll keep bringing in settlers, and there's sure to be trouble. Suzannah, do you want to leave?"

"And go where? We've made a home here, Jed. Let's see what the spring election brings."

"All right. I'll talk to Ben, too. We need to understand how he and Lorena feel about it."

It was a very uncomfortable situation, one that could become dangerous at any moment.

The explosive situation did not go unnoticed in other parts of the country. The *Journal and Courier* of Lowell, Massachusetts, published an article on March 26, 1855:

> Some thousands of emigrants are now at St. Louis waiting for the opening of Kansas navigation; 500 arrived at Alton on their way on Friday, and as many more were expected on Saturday. 600 are ready to start from Cincinnati; while from that city last week 130 Germans with their families, household goods, stools, fruit-trees, etc., marched in true German style with their fine band of music on board the steamer and started. In Kentucky,

an association of some hundreds of *temperance* and *anti-slavery* men are to set forth soon to found a city on the Kansas River. . . . A similar company of 500 families is expected to start by detachments from Wayne County, Indiana. The waves of emigration are rolling mightily.

The first party of these emigrants, led by Dr. Charles Robinson, consisted of some two hundred people. His intention was to reach the territory before the coming election. They reached Kansas City on March 24, 1855. This alarmed the border Missourians, and the newspaper *Squatter Sovereign* fired off an inflammatory rebuttal:

> We are credibly informed that quite a large number, probably several hundred, of these purchased voters are now on their way up the Missouri River, consigned to Messrs. Park & Patterson, Parkville, and other consignees at different points for distribution in lots to suit, subject to the order of A. H. Reeder, Esq., President of the Underground Railroad, in Kansas Territory. . . . We hope the quarantine officers along the borders will forbid the unloading of that kind of cargo.

Governor Reeder had announced the election date for the Territorial Legislature to be March 30, 1855. He also rearranged the voting districts, adding two and apportioning them according to numbers of registered voters in an area.

The Council, or upper house, would be composed of thirteen members. The House of Representatives would have twenty-six members. At the time of the election, there were 2,905 legally registered voters in the territory.

Literally thousands of people of both factions poured into the Territory in the last few days of March.

Jed encountered a friend from the Missouri side of the river the day before the election. It was prudent not to question the motives of others, but he was caught by surprise and blurted out a greeting that would have been appropriate under most circumstances.

"Sam! What are you doing here?"

Instantly, his friend became defensive and suspicious.

"I have a right to be here!"

"I . . . Of course, Sam . . . I only . . ."

"Jed, I intend to vote. Don't *you?*"

"Certainly . . . Will the election judges allow a man from Missouri . . . Oh! You've moved to Kansas?"

"No! But by God, sir, a man from Missouri has as much right to vote here as a man from Massachusetts!"

Jed found that argument hard to deny, but feared the problems that this attitude would bring. As his friend hurried on, he saw a twist of white ribbon in the buttonhole of the man's lapel. It was a thing easily overlooked, but now that he had noticed it, he began to look at the lapel of each man he passed. A surprising number wore such a ribbon. Most of these appeared to be the border Missourians. There were dozens, perhaps hundreds. . . . Some kind of identification? This seemed to be an organized effort, with means to identify in case of trouble.

This is borne out by a letter written some years later by one of the participants:

> . . . We knew that Eli Thayer and Horace Greeley had organized the New England Emigrant Society to send Free-Soil voters to Kansas. . . . They were passing up the Missouri River on steamboats continually and was well armed. Our opinion was that if the North had the right to hire men to go to Kansas to vote to make it a free state, the Missourians had the right to go there without being hired to vote to make it a Slave State. 800 men went to Peoria's on Bull Creek, forty miles south of Lawrence; and as more voters were there than was needed to carry that precinct, many of us was sent to Lawrence. . . . Where we were welcomed by many other Missourians. . . .
>
> . . . The Kansas judges insisted that every voter should swear that he was a bona fide citizen of Kansas. . . . A few took the oath at the start, which was soon dispensed with. Then it was free for all. . . . The second time I voted (I only voted twice), I went up over the roof (of the cabin, to approach again from the other side).
>
> Some voted many times. One old planter near this place said he voted 144 times. . . .
>
> The Missourians went to that election well armed. . . .

After much soul-searching, Jed elected to stay at home on election day.

"This election will accomplish nothing except trouble," he told Suzannah. "My first duty is to you and Neosho. There may be very dangerous trouble."

"Will Ben vote?" she asked.

"I don't know. I think he'll try it, but I rather hope not. A man could be killed by either side, intentionally or by accident."

Young Ben did vote, and also took it upon himself to challenge the votes of a couple of Missourians. But they were well armed, and he backed down, in fear of his life.

On the way home, Ben stopped at a country store to speak to the proprietor, a friend of long standing. There was a discussion in progress, and congratulations for a young farmer who lived nearby. He had successfully prevented the voting of a group of Missourians who had ridden over to take part in the election. Several men had offered to buy the hero a drink, and they were seated at a table across the room from the sales counter, still discussing the day.

"I don't know, Caleb," Ben said. "I tried to do that, and I backed down when they threatened me. I'm not very proud of it, but I . . ."

The conversation was interrupted by a booming report from outside the open window. The young farmer lurched forward, unseeing eyes still wide open and glazing with the absent stare of death. Outside, the hoofbeats of a rapidly retreating horse faded into the night. There was the smell of gunpowder, heavy in the room.

"Damn!" said Caleb. "I was afraid of this."

They rushed to the young man's side, trying to support the body as it slid from the chair. A brown paper bag protruded from one of the farmer's pockets, and as he fell, several pieces of hard horehound candy rolled out onto the plank floor.

"Damn!" said Caleb again. "He just stopped by here on the way home. Said he promised to bring his kids some candy . . ."

The election of the Territorial Legislature was a complete debacle. Many of the legitimate, eligible voters, like Jed Sterling, avoided the polls entirely. Less than half the eligible voters participated. Even so, 6,307 votes were cast, of which more than five thousand were proslavery. Only 1,410 could be identified as legal votes.

Meanwhile, more trouble was quietly brewing elsewhere. Dr. Robinson, of the Emigrant Aid Society, dispatched a secret emissary to Boston. Within hours after his arrival in Boston, the messenger was supplied with an order for a hundred Sharp's rifles. The rifles were packed the next day, a Sunday, in wooden boxes marked "Books," and on Monday he started back to Kansas.

The rifles arrived at Lawrence on the steamer *Emma Harmon,* but their arrival was kept secret.

Another shipment arrived in August 1855, a hundred more rifles and a short-barreled brass cannon, of the mountain howitzer type. Large quantities of ammunition were also smuggled into the territory by the New Englanders.

In a letter to Eli Thayer, carried by his second emissary, Dr. Robinson penned words that were to become prophetic:

We are in the midst of a revolution, as you will see by the papers. How we shall come out of the furnace, God only knows. That we have got to enter it, some of us, there is no doubt, but we are ready to be offered.

There were many Free-Staters who objected to the importation of arms and asked that they be returned. But their voices were drowned in the roar of approval.

The fact was that the real point of contention, that of the rights of the states versus the power of the federation, was all but forgotten. The emotional issue of slavery had captured the imagination and emotions of both sides, obscuring the reasons for disagreement. What had been the muddy water of confusion was becoming quicksand.

6

In the aftermath of the election, Jed and Ben held a serious conversation about the results.

"I'm afraid it will be worse before it's better, Ben," Jed admitted. "There are madmen on both sides. Do you want to take your family back to Virginia?"

"I've thought of it, Uncle Jed. But . . . Well, we have a stake in it here, now. To leave is to admit that the extremists have won. I don't want to abandon our home, the place I've come to think of as ours, to your 'madmen.'"

"*Which* madmen?" Jed asked, with a wry chuckle that really held no humor.

"*Either* side, Jed. I'll give up if I have to, but . . . Lord, I never expected to meet a stranger on the road and try to guess from his accent whether he's likely to attack me. We must be careful!"

"True. And stay out of it as much as we can. Sterling and Van Landingham have to deal with both sides."

Ben nodded. "So far, so good. I guess it helps that we're already established."

"I'm sure it does."

"And of course we don't talk like Yankees or own any slaves."

"True," Jed chuckled. He wondered what young Ben would think if he knew the full story of Suzannah's background.

"You heard," he went on, changing the subject, "that the legislature's meeting at Pawnee?"

"Yes . . . Where in the world is Pawnee?"

"Near Fort Riley, I guess. New town site."

"But Jed, that's a hundred miles west of the populated area."

"That's true. I'd guess somebody's got an interest in land develop-ment. I'd also guess that there will be a shake-up. You know the governor has challenged the election?"

"Yes. Will they have another?"

"Who knows? We'll see."

Some time later, Jed was returning home from a trip to Silver Lake to check on the berths for steamers there. He had decided to travel by horse on this trip, admitting that he enjoyed the feel of freedom that it provided. He was nearly home when he met a man driving a farm wagon drawn by mules. The fellow was a stranger, which was not unusual.

Each was sizing up the other as they approached a meeting on the road with no one else in sight. The stranger drew his mules to a complete halt and waited for the horseman to pass. Jed was uneasy, for reasons he could not have explained. Maybe the old plainsman's instinct for survival was revived in these troubled times. Possibly, though, it was the burning intensity in the dark eyes. The stare of the stranger was quite disconcerting. Especially when coupled with a facial expression that was almost hostile.

Jed had formulated a ritual that he had found useful when meeting strangers. He did not speak but smiled pleasantly and nodded a greeting, touching the brim of his hat in a polite salute. Then the other could speak if he wished, revealing any trace of regional accent or not.

In this case, the man did not react at all. He merely sat, his hands on the lines, staring. . . . He did not even blink or in any way return Jed's greeting. He was bareheaded, and his gray hair seemed wild and unmanage-able, in keeping with his lanky frame and disheveled clothing.

Jed's impression was that the stranger had traveled a great distance. He also noticed that the wheels of the wagon had sunk deeply into the hard clay of the road. A heavy load . . . *Weapons?*

He felt the icy stare on his back and glanced over his shoulder for another look. The stranger had not moved, and was still staring, with the wild-eyed look of a madman. Jed was very uncomfortable.

It was somewhat later that events would identify the man and make his name a household word: *John Brown.*

"Ben, you have no idea. . . . The fellow looked crazy!"

Ben shook his head sadly. "I know. These are crazy times. Uncle Jed, one of our teamsters told me a frightening story. He was on a haul up near Atchison and stopped at an inn there."

"Drinking? They're not supposed—"

"Yes, yes, that's not the point. He was there, and a group of men were talking politics. They were laughing about a friend with whom they had a bet. This fellow had bet them that he could bring back the scalp of an abolitionist before sundown!"

"*What?* They were serious?"

"Not only that, Jed. The man *came back,* while our driver was still there, and he *had* a scalp."

"My God . . . What was their reaction?"

"That's the worst. They were laughing, threatening not to pay off the bet, because he had no proof of the victim's politics!"

Jed shook his head sadly. "That makes my experience seem pretty tame, I guess. What's next? Has the whole world gone mad?"

The Territorial Legislature met in July at Pawnee. Because of the unsuitability of the facilities, one of their first decisions was to transfer the Territorial capital to the Shawnee Mission, at least temporarily. The permanent capital was later designated as Lecompton, west of Lawrence.

Governor Reeder, denouncing the legislature as an "illegal body," vetoed the bill. It was promptly passed over his veto.

On a more grassroots level, the newspaper *Parkville Luminary* published editorial comments that were radically pro-Northern. This proved unwise in an area where Missourians were proudly accepting the name "Border Ruffians." The newspaper office was destroyed, and the *Luminary*'s press and type cases were thrown into the Missouri River. The owners and publisher were warned to leave town, lest they be tarred and feathered.

Such treatment *was* accorded to another Northern sympathizer, William Phillips, a citizen of Leavenworth. He was warned to leave but showed no inclination to do so. He was kidnapped by the Southerners, taken across the river into Missouri, near Weston. Stripped, tarred, and feathered, he was warned again to leave the territory. Since he made no move to do so, he was murdered at his home in Leavenworth a few months later.

These happenings were viewed with alarm by the Northern sympathizers in the new territory. Meetings were held at Big Springs and at Lawrence, a few miles to the east, chaired by men of the New England Emigrant Aid Societies.

The Big Springs Convention created a Free State political party and issued a resolution with a strong antislavery platform. It declared the Territorial Legislature to have been created by *"force* and *fraud,"* and stated "we do not feel bound to obey any law of their enacting."

They nominated the ousted Governor Reeder as a candidate for Congress, and he made an eloquent but quite inflammatory speech.

A movement also developed at Topeka, which resulted in the drafting of a constitution and a move toward statehood. The growing Free State party held an election of state officers, with Charles Robinson as governor. Wilson Shannon, of course, was still the legitimate governor by appointment.

This election, proclaimed by the "Executive Committee of Kansas Territory," was virtually unopposed except at Leavenworth, where a mob destroyed the polling places.

The constitution and application for statehood were forwarded to Washington, where President Pierce reacted quickly. He had already endorsed the Kansas Territorial Legislature, elected in the earlier flawed election. He now reacted with a proclamation, sent to the military commanders at Fort Leavenworth and Fort Riley, by his secretary of war, Jefferson Davis, as an order.

> The President has warned all persons combined for insurrection
> or invasive aggression against the organized government of the
> Territory of Kansas . . . to abstain from such revolutionary
> and lawless proceedings, and has commanded them to *disperse
> and retire peaceably* to their respective abodes . . .

The constitution issue never reached Congress.

There were other incidents. The Territorial government learned of the stockpiling of weapons in Lawrence, and warrants were issued for the arrests of several Free State men. As word spread, several hundred of the proslavery Missourians assembled and camped around the town. The cooler heads on both sides requested intervention by the cavalry stationed at Leavenworth, but Colonel Sumner, in command, had no authority to do so. This, in spite of the fact that at the time a congressional committee was in session at the fort, investigating the worsening situation.

On May 21, 1856, a posse of Ruffians, armed with warrants and under the authority of Sheriff Jones, entered the town of Lawrence. They were followed by a mob of several hundred militiamen, volunteer units of cavalry and artillery, mostly Missourians. It had been decided by the Free State faction to avoid bloodshed, so they met with no resistance. The warrants called for surrender of the several hundred Sharp's rifles. This was impossible, since most had been issued to individuals. S. C. Pomeroy met the posse in front of the Free State Hotel and explained this, offering compliance otherwise. The brass howitzer, concealed under the foundation of Blood's Hardware store, was brought forth and turned over to the posse.

In accordance with the sheriff's warrants, the Free State Hotel was then subjected to at least fifty rounds of cannon fire, and burned. Under further legal authorization, the presses of both Lawrence newspapers, the *Herald of Freedom* and the *Kansas Free State,* were broken up and the pieces thrown into the river. Even the stocks of paper were destroyed.

There were only two fatalities, both accidental, and both to members of the mob, not the townspeople. A brick or stone, falling from the chimney of the doomed hotel, struck a young man on the head and killed him. In the other accident, a young Ruffian accidentally shot himself with his own gun.

The compliance did not sit well with extremists on either side. A Free State boy, carrying a sack of meal and unarmed, had been wantonly murdered near Lawrence a few days before. Two friends who ventured out to retrieve the body were also harassed, and one of them shot and killed.

This and the burning of the hotel greatly incensed a New Yorker named John Brown. Brown had come to Kansas at the request of four of his sons who had settled there. He brought a wagon load of assorted weapons, including a number of antique broadswords.

Now, he set out to avenge the incidents at Lawrence. Under protection of darkness, the Browns and other Free-Staters descended on the homes of those on Brown's list with Southern sympathies. They would use only swords rather than guns, "that the neighbors might not be alarmed." The moon was a little past full, so they waited for it to rise. By means of its light, they approached the house of James and Mahala Doyle and their five children at about 10 P.M. The Doyles' dog ran out to sound the alarm, and was struck down with a sword by one of the party.

They entered the house, rousing the Doyles from their beds, and dragged out James and his two oldest sons, aged twenty and sixteen. A short distance from the house, the three were hacked to death with the swords.

The procedure was repeated at the home of Allen Wilkinson, though only Mr. Wilkinson was killed there. One of their intended victims, "Dutch Henry" Sherman, was not at home, so his brother William was killed instead, though his political views were not known to the raiders.

John T. Hughes, in a communication to the newspaper *Missouri Republican* in June 1856, closed his letter with this paragraph:

> *. . . But I have not time to give you further details of the horrid war which has been raging in Kansas for some weeks and which if not speedily checked, may eventually widen its circle, and involve all the States of the Union in a devastating civil war, and if it*

*shall ever come, which may God avert, it will be one of the bloodi-
est upon the records of time . . .*

A force of Missouri Ruffians under Captain H. C. Pate captured a
Free State man who was a native of Missouri near the town of Palmyra,
several miles south of Lawrence. He was "tried for treason against Missouri," taken to a ravine, and executed.

7

Despite all the political activity and the growing tendency to bloodshed, life must go on. Nebraska Territory, organizing more slowly, still had the major advantage of less political friction. It was assumed by both sides that Nebraska would become a Free State. With less controversy, towns were springing up along the Missouri River above St. Joseph . . . Savannah, Iowa Point, Council Bluffs, Omaha, Linden . . .

"Ben," suggested Jed, "what would you think of extending our line on up the Missouri a ways?"

Ben frowned. "I don't know, Uncle Jed. You know the Ruffians have boarded and searched some steamers. They confiscated cargo from the *Sultan* at Leavenworth. And the *Star of the West* . . . She was stopped at Lexington, Missouri, and again at Kansas City. At Leavenworth they robbed the passengers."

"That's true, Ben. But the *Sultan* was carrying weapons for emigrants. The *Star*'s passengers were abolitionists from Chicago. We don't carry weapons or emigrants."

"But it's not right for them to do that."

"I agree completely, Ben. But right now we have to stay neutral, for the safety of our families. The Territorial Legislature at Lecompton *is* the legal body. They're using the Border Ruffians, yes. But it's legal."

"But what about the Free State legislators in Topeka?" Ben asked.

"Yes. I know. I also know they were ordered to disperse by federal troops. For now, we have to stay neutral. And upstream, Nebraska and Iowa, should be safe. We'd carry no munitions or questionable cargo."

"Have you been up the Missouri, Jed?"

"Not by boat. Horseback, as far as where Nebraska City is now, I'd guess. I was thinking of booking as a passenger on one of the other lines, to see how it goes."

"Good idea! You want me to go?"

Jed smiled. "No, you're better with the bookkeeping. I thought I might book on the *Arabia*."

"You just can't stand to stay inside, Uncle Jed! But go ahead. The *Arabia*'s certainly a handsome boat. How far does she go?"

"I don't know. I'd get off at Nebraska City, probably. By that time, I'd probably have an idea whether such a run would be practical for our packets."

"Sounds good . . . When will you go?"

The "Great White *Arabia*," a Missouri River packet, had been built in Brownsville, Pennsylvania, only three years ago, Jed learned. One hundred and eighty feet in length, she could carry two hundred tons of freight as well as a hundred or so deck passengers. There were several first-class cabins, and a dining room for those not carrying their own food.

The *Arabia* incorporated the latest developments in the field of water transportation. Jed looked her over with admiration. Sterling and Van Landingham owned two of the earlier packets built in Brownsville, and knew of their reliability. This one, new and exciting, appeared to be quite special. Jed was looking forward to the voyage. He had kissed Suzannah and Neosho, and Ben had taken him to the dock in his buggy.

He always hated to be away overnight, but the immediate area of their house and Ben's was relatively safe. Still, the way things were going . . .

"Be careful!" Suzannah had told him as they parted.

"And you . . . Call on Ben if you need to."

"Bring me something, Daddy?" Neosho pleaded, her most appealing smile turned up to full power.

"If I can, honey. But I'm not going to St. Louis this time. We'll see."

In his heart he knew that he'd have to find something. . . .

The *Arabia* was an hour out of Westport, approaching Quindaro Bend. Jed had walked her decks and admired her way of going. He rather enjoyed the throb of the big engines, the life in the vibration of the deck under his feet. He could see how this could get in the blood of a river boatman. He circled the main deck, noting the carpenter's mule tied to the rail aft.

He decided to step into the dining room for a bit of supper before dark. Days were beginning to grow shorter now. Not long until autumn, and the river packets would have ice to contend with. Last winter had been hard, with much snow and ice. . . .

He was halfway through the doorway. . . . Hatch, the crews called it. . . . He'd never understood why. . . . Then it happened. A loud jarring crash. The *Arabia* shuddered and the deck tilted sharply to the left. Jed was thrown against the bulkhead and almost fell. A woman screamed, and people were running in all directions.

"She's sinkin'!" a man yelled.

Jed evaluated the situation quickly. People were trying to scramble up and down the ladder. His carpetbag with a clean shirt, socks, and a razor was in his stateroom, on the upper deck, but there was little chance to reach it. It could be replaced.

He looked toward the banks. The *Arabia* was in mid-channel, slightly closer to the west bank. The crew, a handful of men, were frantically launching the lifeboat. There seemed to be only one.

"Women and children first!" a man called.

Then, to Jed's amazement, the crewmen jumped into the boat themselves and shoved off toward the west bank. The air was filled with angry cries and curses. Most of the *Arabia*'s passengers were women and children, and the boat could have held perhaps twenty had the crew tried to help them.

"Come back here!" yelled an angry man in buckskins. "Ye can't leave these young'uns!"

Jed joined a group of furious passengers at the rail, and caught the frontiersman's arm.

"Do you have a weapon?" he asked as he drew the derringer from his own waistband.

"Not one of them," said the man. "My rifle, here." He displayed a short, heavy Hawken.

"Good. Show it!"

Jed pointed his pistol well above the heads of the boatmen and fired. The report echoed along the river bluff and resounded again.

"Back here with the boat or we shoot you!" Jed yelled. He had only the one shot, but it had certainly drawn their attention. A few other men drew weapons, and the frightened crew quickly returned to evacuate the passengers.

Several trips were required, and most of the men and a few women swam to shore. In only a few minutes the *Arabia* had struck the bottom, nose down, and settled on her ruptured underbelly, the crew's quarters, tacks, and pilot house protruding above the surface. Jed had seen the frantic mule struggling to free itself as the waters closed.

"Where's your mule?" someone asked the carpenter as the survivors gathered on the bank.

"Stupid bastard," sputtered the carpenter, "I cut him loose but he wouldn't leave the boat."

Jed said nothing.

People were rushing toward the scene from the nearby town of Parkville and from the surrounding area. Some to help, some to try to steal any unguarded item of passengers' luggage. Human nature is strange in emergencies.

People built fires, and many of the survivors huddled around them in the lengthening shadows of evening. Some started on foot to the nearer towns in the vicinity. Some merely stood or sat, and cried or talked softly, still in awe of the tragedy.

Jed's clothes were wet. He had swum to shore after helping the first few loads of passengers into the lifeboat. Now he felt the uncomfortable squish of water in his boots. His topcoat hung heavy with its sodden weight. He removed it, squeezed from it what water he could, and held it before the fire. Water dripped from his other clothing. The evening was fairly warm, but he knew that at this time of year nights could be uncomfortably cool. Pneumonia was a strong possibility for the very young or the old or infirm, unless they kept moving.

He removed his boots, poured water from them, and set them near the fire. He must put them back on before they dried completely, or they would stiffen. Later, he'd have to oil them. Jed began to make plans. He could probably catch a ride to somewhere, but saw no need. He'd spend the night here, dry his clothes, and walk or find a ride after the sun rose and began to warm the day. To Leavenworth, maybe. No, too far . . . But maybe he could board a packet somewhere, and go there, back downstream to Kansas City.

He knew that Suzannah would be worried when she heard of the wreck, and was concerned for her worry. But, with such news, which would travel swiftly, would surely be the news that there was no loss of life. And, he'd be home as soon as possible.

Meanwhile, he began to enjoy the warmth of the fire, turning to let its welcome heat soak into other areas of his wet body. It was not an unpleasant sensation. In his years on the frontier there had been many evenings far more uncomfortable than this.

Jed watched the sunset and the purpling of the shadows along the river as the sky darkened. One by one, stars began to dot the sky. The crowd of people along the bank began to thin as they found rides or started to walk toward civilization. There was a certain peace about the evening. It had been a long time, he realized, since he had spent a night on the open prairie. It was a good feeling. A hunting owl sounded his hollow cry from the timber along the river. Jed smiled.

"Good hunting, *Kookooskoos,*" he murmured.

He had not realized how much he missed life on the frontier since he had settled in as a respectable businessman. A coyote called from a distant ridge, sounding like at least a dozen as his cry echoed along the bluffs across the river.

The buckskin-clad hunter from the *Arabia* came over and squatted by Jed's fire. The man took out a short pipe, filled it from a pouch at his waist, and tossed a pinch of tobacco into the fire. He lighted the pipe with a brand and blew a puff to each of the four directions, to sky and earth, and then offered it to Jed.

Jed nodded, and repeated the ceremony, handing back the pipe. He had recognized, when the man offered the pinch of tobacco to the fire. . . . Here was one who knew. . . . An offering to the spirits of the place, a thing of respect, a ceremony to be performed at each new camp. *I am here, I intend to camp, and ask your hospitality.*

Jed squatted, trapper fashion, stretching leg muscles not used for a long time.

"How are you called?" the man asked in hand signs.

An interesting approach . . . The hunter had recognized a fellow frontiersman, but was unsure, even after the ceremony with the shared pipe. This was a test. A real buckskinner would understand the hand signs. A tenderfoot would not, in case the judgment was wrong.

Jed chuckled. "I am Long Walker . . . Pawnee . . . Or was, a long time ago."

The man nodded. "I have heard of you. . . . Sterling?"

"Yes. We may have friends in common. Chris Carson?"

"Kit? The 'Rope Thrower'? Of course!"

"And how are you called?"

"Oh . . . Sorry. 'Star Looker' . . . I've no special tribe. Kiowas gave me the name."

Jed nodded. He knew much about the man already. A newcomer to the wide sky of the prairie country might easily be known for his habit of watching the stars. . . . He felt at home with this stranger, in contrast to the usual distrust in meeting new people, which had come with the current political situation. It was good, this chance to escape from the cares of the complicated world. It was easy to long for simpler times, if in fact those simpler times had actually existed. He was not sure, but looking back, it *seemed* so. . . .

All in all, there had been no loss of life as the *Arabia* went down, except for the mule. In the next few days, her two hundred tons of freight settled into the silt of the muddy bottom, and not even her stacks could be seen.

8

Jed found one major drawback to his return to old ways for a night. He was stiff and sore after such unaccustomed exertion, followed by the damp chill of the night. Somehow, he reflected, the cold of many winters had invaded his bones. It took a little longer now to limber up than it had taken twenty years ago. He had heard men talk of this all his life, but was just beginning to understand.

He caught a ride on the back of a farm wagon heading toward his own area. He could have walked, and it probably would have been better to loosen his tight muscles. Had he not once walked all the way from Maryland? That had earned him the name "Long Walker," bestowed by Daniel Boone himself. But that was long ago. He'd been "wearing a younger man's clothes," as Boone would have said.

A great many memories came floating back as the wagon rattled over the rutted road. They'd been stirred by the long visit with the hunter at last night's fire. It had been good, to talk of simpler times and old friends with one who understood. That world was fast disappearing, and both men knew it. Yet for a little while they had shared a pipe and a memory across a fire under the stars. Jed wondered when or whether their trails might cross again.

The accident and the sinking of the *Arabia* had touched him deeply. It was long ago that he had realized the frailty of human life. He well remembered when. A young person often considers himself immortal until circumstances call attention to one's vulnerability. An illness or injury . . .

The death of a friend . . . Life is fragile, and one forgets, until a close encounter such as this.

The wagon jolted to a stop, and the driver called back to his sleepy passenger.

"This here's where I turn off. Good luck to ye!"

Jed swung down stiffly. "Much obliged for the ride!"

The walking did warm him, and he began to feel better as the sun rose. His clothes were rumpled, but dry. His boots were still damp, but drying. He'd oil them tonight.

It was past noon when he stepped into the offices of Sterling and Van Landingham. Ben rose to his feet.

"Thank God! We heard about the wreck, and figured you'd turn up!"

"Is Suzannah worried? I need to get on home."

"No, no. The word was that there were no casualties. She said you'd take care of yourself. She'll be expecting you. Tell me about it."

Jed briefly outlined the events of the sinking, omitting the details about the mule. He also failed to go into detail about the emotional impact of the chance reunion with the old life.

". . . So, I spent the night keeping warm by a fire, with another man who'd been on the boat," he finished.

"You think the *Arabia* hit a snag, then?"

"I'd suppose so. You know how treacherous the Big Muddy is. 'Too thick to drink, too thin to plow,' the settlers are sayin'."

"Yes, I've heard that. I guess this ends our thoughts of an upriver line, Uncle Jed?"

"Not necessarily . . . Ben, people are coming in so fast. . . . New towns, all along the rivers. No end to the freight they'll need. Plows . . . Every kind of tool and implement, actually. Shoes, clothing, dry goods. The cargo of the *Arabia* . . . Ben, she carried two hundred *tons* of goods, besides people. No, I'm thinking *expand,* rather than turn back. Look, our pilots are the best. Sterling and Van Landingham loses fewer steamers than most. We're big enough to take the risks."

"But insurance comes high, Jed. There are companies who won't insure prairie steamers."

"I'm not talking insurance. Cover it ourselves. Our safety record speaks for itself. Go ahead and figure it, both ways, based on the last two years. Insure or not. You're the accountant. See which way's best. We'll talk again, but right now I've got to get on home. Suzannah will be worried."

"Of course. She's put up a brave front, but I know she'll be relieved to have you home."

·   ·   ·

Suzannah flew into his arms.

"I'm so glad you're home! I knew you'd be all right, but oh, Jed . . . The first word we had . . . No one knew if there were any lost. . . ."

Now, with the pressure relieved, she began to cry, laughing at her reaction at the same time. He held her, rocking gently as they stood. Finally he released her and stooped to hug Neosho.

"I couldn't bring you anything, honey."

"I know, Daddy." She clung to him, understanding that it had been a dangerous situation. "It's all right."

"Let's see your clothes," Suzannah said, practical as always. "You do smell like a wet sheep."

He shucked out of his coat and handed it to her.

"I'll oil my boots. They're nearly dry, I think. I lost the carpetbag, my razor and all."

"Do you have another?"

"I think so. Or, I can buy one."

"Take off your trousers, Jed. I'll rinse them and the jacket in cold water, and spread and shape them as they dry. They may not shrink too much. Your shirt's muddy, but that will wash. Here, step in the bedroom. . . . I'll get you some clean things."

"Daddy, tell me about it. The shipwreck," Neosho pleaded. "Were you scared?"

"Well, maybe a little. Let me get changed, and I'll tell you all about it. Oh, I have to clean my little pistol, too."

"You fired it?" asked Suzannah in alarm. "Jed, was there trouble? Something I don't know?"

"No, no. I fired it in the air to attract attention. . . . Some men in a boat. We needed their help."

"This had nothing to do with the political situation?" she asked anxiously. "Promise?"

"I promise, Suzannah. This was one thing, among all the recent killing, that had nothing to do with it."

"Thank God," she murmured, busy with laying out a fresh shirt and trousers. "Jed, you haven't said . . . Were you able to learn anything about the upriver freighting?"

"Not much. But I did decide that it's a good area for our packets. Suzannah, that boat was crammed with freight. New cities upriver need *everything*. New settlers are starting from scratch. They need tools, household goods, supplies of all kinds, and we can carry it to them."

"But the *Arabia* was lost, Jed."

"True. We've lost steamers, too. But it's rare. And as a rule, the loss of the freight isn't ours. That comes under an 'act of God' situation. Our loss would be only the boat. The freight might be owned by a dozen or more consignors."

"I see. But Jed, I can't help but be concerned about all the killing. What's going to happen?"

He took a deep breath and thought for a moment before answering. Suzannah's inquiry had served to drive home to him something he had not fully understood. It was far easier to think about something else. . . . About the freight line, the river steamers of Sterling and Van Landingham, than about the political murders that seemed to be occurring everywhere. Easier to retreat into the past, as he had done the night before at the makeshift camp on the river. Things had been simpler, then. Or had they, really? Or was it simply that now he had immensely more responsibility to others?

"I don't know, Suzannah. . . ."

How could he tell her that he, too, was concerned? Sometimes he hated to think about it, even. Maybe his trip upriver on the *Arabia* was only an escape from the reality of hate and murder and civil warfare. If so, it had failed.

"I don't know, but we'll face it together. We can handle it."

He took her in his arms, and she smiled as she snuggled close. Her body was warm against his, and he knew that he had spoken the truth.

Meanwhile, discouraged by the interference with emigration by river steamer transportation, James Lane began to devise other means. By following the centuries-old Indian trails, a road was mapped for emigrants to follow. It became known as the Lane Road. From Illinois, it crossed into Iowa, through Iowa City and westward across that state to the Missouri River. Crossing was by rafts or ferries into Nebraska Territory at Nebraska City. Towns along the route were supplied with agents to expedite the movement of travelers and supplies. The Western Stage Company was formed to transport passengers across Iowa for the sum of twenty-five dollars.

From that point, the trail turned southward, crossing into Kansas Territory and leading into Topeka from the north. Topeka was becoming the Free State stronghold, as Lawrence was now under heavy pressure from the proslavery Territorial Legislature. This new route to Kansas would avoid entirely the crossing of Southern land.

9

The national election in 1856 had a great influence on life in the Kansas and Nebraska Territories. More to the point, though, the border wars had a tremendous effect on the election.

The Whig party was shattered over the question of slavery. Their leadership had taken a firm proslavery stand, destroying their effectiveness as a voice for states' rights. More moderate elements clustered together in several different reform parties with various views on the problems of the day. Some joined the ranks of the Democrats, whose platform was a somewhat vague and indecisive "let the people decide" statement on the nation's pressing problems.

The Democratic party of Missouri refused to endorse the national party's platform. Instead, they wrote their own planks, one of which subscribed to a strict proslavery stance.

In the summer of 1856, a convention was held in Philadelphia to form a new party from the disenchanted fragments of the collapsing two-party system.

"Have you seen the papers, Jed?" asked Ben as his uncle entered the office. "A new party. 'National Republicans.' Here, read it!"

Jed scanned the sheet.

"I knew there was a convention to be held. . . . Good Lord! They nominated *John Fremont?*"

"Yes. Didn't you know him, Jed?"

"Yes, I scouted for him on one of his expeditions."

"Will he make a candidate?" asked Ben eagerly.

"I don't know. I never thought . . . I just can't envision him as president, Ben."

The younger man laughed. "He's surely popular with the public, I gather. The 'Great Pathfinder' of the West."

"Yes, I know. Very forceful leader. Ben, he's hard to explain. He can ask you to do something, and somehow you feel honored that he asked. Still, you think about it later and . . . Well, what he asked you to do seems a little crazy in the first place."

"He's crazy?"

"Not exactly . . . Crazy like a fox, sometimes. There are those who can't stand him, of course. Joe Walker, for one."

"The mountain man? You knew *him*?"

"Of course. In the old days . . ." Jed was feeling old, suddenly. "But, to go on . . . There are some who'd follow Fremont into the jaws of hell. Kit Carson, for one. Ben, Fremont is a man you have to understand for yourself."

Ben nodded. "Did you see his party's platform, there?" he asked, pointing at the newspaper.

"Let's see . . . Eight or ten planks . . ." He paused, surprised. "Ben, most of these deal with Kansas!"

"Yes, so I noticed. Jed, they're actually aware of us, out here on the prairie!"

"Hmm . . . Strong antislavery, antipolygamy . . . Review of the Declaration of Independence . . . Railroads, rivers and harbors, encourage trade . . . 'Freemen of all parties . . .' Ben, it's a powerful statement. I don't know whether they can do it."

"Nor do I. But isn't it a valiant effort? And they favor the Free State Constitution and statehood for Kansas."

"You sound excited, Ben."

"I guess I am. Maybe this will end some of our problems."

"We'll see." Jed was afraid to appear too hopeful. He had been fooled before.

A few weeks before the election, the country was flooded with handbills attempting to discredit John Fremont. ILLEGITIMATE! one bill screamed. There was a short paragraph about Fremont's parents, who had lived together for many years without benefit of clergy. His father was a French refugee named Fremonte, and his mother the runaway wife of a wealthy planter. The handbill concluded with advice for the coming election: "Don't vote for the Frenchman's bastard!"

Buchanan, the Democrats' candidate, was elected by only a handful of votes. Politics in the United States would never be quite the same again.

Toward 1860, the border became somewhat more quiet for a time. There had been a succession of six governors in the Kansas Territory. Each served for only a few months, sometimes a few weeks. In the intervals between, the Territorial secretary acted as governor until each new presidential appointee could reach the frontier. Some of the appointees were forced to resign by political pressure. Others fled for their lives under the threat of assassination.

During these years, four different constitutions were composed to be offered in application for statehood. The legally authorized version, written at Lecompton by members of the Territorial Legislature, was a proslavery document. It held such provisions as the death penalty for anyone so much as *aiding* a fugitive slave.

"Never mind, Ben," Jed advised. "When it's presented to the voters, it will be rejected. There are enough Free State voters now to prevent its adoption."

This was a likely guess, and one that was noted by the proslave legislature. Their leaders had no intention of allowing such a vote. They did cautiously allow a vote on the preference of the public for the constitution "with" or "without" the proslavery paragraphs. There was a decided shift to Free State thinking, but such a vote was not binding. The constitution was submitted to the Congress, but never reached the point of discussion in the federal legislature.

A Free State constitution was drafted at Topeka, but that political body had been declared an illegal, revolutionary group. It was ordered by federal authority to disband under threat of the charge of treason.

Another, semiofficial attempt at a constitution was formulated at Leavenworth, but lacked authority. It, too, failed to reach consideration by the Congress.

Meanwhile, each election shifted slightly more power to Free State legislators. In spite of differences on the slavery question, the Territorial Legislature was able to accomplish some quality lawmaking.

In 1857, Moses Grinter, the ferryman, began to build a handsome brick house. It stood on a hill overlooking the river and the Lower Delaware Crossing on the military road south toward Fort Scott. Such a structure seemed to Jed and Suzannah to suggest a stability and progress toward peace and civility.

This idea was somewhat offset by a visit from Sven Kesterson, the blacksmith from Council Grove. Sven had come to inquire about obtaining a supply of bar iron for horse and mule shoes. At the office of Sterling and Van Landingham, he drew Jed aside and talked very seriously.

"You know dat John Brown, Jed?"

"Know of him. We once met, a passing encounter. He's dangerous, Sven. Has he been out your way?"

"No. But a man was. . . . I'm t'ink maybe one of his sons. He vanted to ask about dis spear point."

"A *spear?*"

"Jah . . . He vanted some made. . . . Lots of 'em. Had a picture, like dis . . ."

Sven took a stick and drew in the dust of the street a strange design. It was a pointed spear or pike head, but on one side there was a projection, another blade, shaped like a large pruning hook.

"Dis inside curve, he vanted sharp," Sven explained.

"But what's it for? It would be on a pole?"

"Jah. Dis man said someding about cutting a horse's reins or hamstrings."

A cold chill crept up Jed's spine. Brown's killings had been deterred to an extent by the presence of the dragoons from Fort Leavenworth. Could this be suggestive of a move to arm foot troops with primitive weapons and send them against cavalry? Could the man be contemplating such a thing? It could wreak havoc on the mounted troops. . . . Cut a bridle rein, a cavalryman's horse could not be controlled . . . Or, cripple the animal by slashing a hamstring . . . A suicidal gesture, of course. The spearman would be vulnerable to the slashing sabers of the dragoons. Who would be willing to enter such an ill-balanced contest? Some of Brown's followers were as crazy as he, but Jed doubted that any were . . . He stopped short at his next thought. It would have to be desperate men in a hopeless situation. . . . *Slaves?* Could Brown be plotting a revolution, an uprising by slaves?

If so, where? There were not enough slaves on the border to carry out such a plan. Wait . . . Had it not been said that Old John Brown was no longer at Osawatomie? He had gone back east somewhere, under pressure by the federal troops.

"What did you tell them, Sven? Did you make their spear points?"

"No, no. Jed, I vant no part of dat. I tell him no, I got too much work on mules an' oxen shoes."

"I am made to think that was a wise choice, Sven. Brown's gone back east, they say. But I reckon we haven't heard the last of him."

All of this was noted by Jed and Suzannah, but life must go on. Sometimes, after rumors of trouble or news of atrocities by the lunatic fringe of either side, they talked of it with concern.

"Should we move farther north?" Jed suggested. "Sterling and Van Landingham could operate out of one of the ports on the Missouri."

"I don't know, Jed. I feel pretty safe here. We have good neighbors, and the shipping company has remained neutral."

"We've tried to, God knows. Our packets have been boarded a few times, but that's quieting down some now, it seems. The Border Ruffians aren't nearly so bold with the army in evidence."

Suzannah nodded. "Yes . . . Don't you think it helps, Jed, to have them see that someone will stand up to them?"

"Of course. But that doesn't help the ones who are killed for standing up. And, doesn't help their families either, you know."

"I know, Jed. But it is more quiet along the border, isn't it?"

"I think so. Hard to tell. There are always a few stories of robbery, abuse, sometimes killings. Yes, probably fewer now."

"Then let's stay a bit longer. Maybe . . . Didn't you tell me the governor has called for a new constitution?"

"Yes. But I don't have much confidence that he'll last any longer than the others. We'll see."

But now a new ingredient was added into the mix of confusion.

Gold had been discovered on Cherry Creek, on the eastern slope of the Rockies.

As if Kansas did not have enough lawlessness and strife, now the character of the incoming hordes changed again. Greedy, unscrupulous individuals from everywhere flooded across the prairie toward the Rocky Mountains and the lure of Kansas's gold.

The trail, westward along the upper Kansas River, now called the Smoky Hill, was dangerous at best. It was poorly mapped and unreliable, and under the traffic of inexperienced fortune hunters, it now earned a reputation as the Trail of Death. Robbery, murder, starvation, even cannibalism for survival occurred in these dark days on the trail to the goldfields.

Once they arrived there, the situation became even worse. There were more would-be miners than there was space for claims. Supplies were short.

Sterling and Van Landingham were able to take advantage of the need to move freight. Ben had ordered more freight wagons when he heard the news of gold. They now had six Studebakers on regular runs to the new settlement on the front range. Just a year ago it had been only a couple of trappers' huts. Now, it was becoming a booming town, though many of the dwellings and stores were still tents. People were calling the town "Denver," after the current governor of the Kansas Territory, James W. Denver.

By 1859, newly appointed Governor Medary, with considerable diplomatic experience, was able to convene a constitutional convention at Wyandotte. Once more, a Kansas constitution was created, to be submitted to the voters, then to Congress, with application for statehood. This proposal would create a new western border for Kansas at the twenty-fifth meridian. The gold country and the front range of the Rocky Mountains would be eliminated, along with all the necessary legislation for regulation of mining, and problems with gold-seeking riffraff pouring into the territory. It would help to establish a stable agricultural economy in the proposed state. This constitution, too, failed to make it through committee in the Congress.

In the autumn of 1859, word reached Kansas that John Brown had indeed tried to foment a revolution among the slaves in Virginia. Failing to convince them to use the hooked pikes against cavalry, he had attacked the federal arsenal at Harpers Ferry in western Virginia with a small force. He actually captured the arsenal, but had no escape. Federal troops under Colonel Robert E. Lee took Brown prisoner. He was tried for treason and hanged in December of that year.

Of passing interest in the capture of John Brown is the participation in Colonel Lee's detachment of a young lieutenant named George Armstrong Custer.

BOOK III

�֍

WAR
1861

1

Nancy looked up from her sewing and leaned forward to see what was troubling the dogs. Horsemen again, four of them, carrying long guns and with pistols and knives at their belts. They were passing down the road, only a stone's throw away. She could plainly hear the creak of saddle leather and the jingle of bridle chains.

No telling who they were, but it was always a nervous time when armed riders passed. She always hoped it would be soldiers, but that was seldom the case. Most of the patrols traveled the military road north and south from Fort Scott. That was only four or five miles away, but for her family it might as well be on the other side of the moon. It *was* on the other side of the border, which was almost as bad. In a scrape, the army would be little help. Settlers were on their own. She wished sometimes they'd gone ahead and settled on the Kansas side. They'd considered it, but John had the idea that since Missouri had already been admitted to the Union as a state, it would be safer. They'd move across into Kansas as things settled down, he figured. Nancy agreed. It had seemed like a good plan at the time.

Sometimes for a while things did seem to settle down. But about the time it seemed so, something would happen. . . . It didn't seem to matter much which side they were on. The riders from both sides robbed the settlers, and threatened them. Killed them, sometimes, if they tried to resist the theft of their poultry or hogs. Horses and mules, even, though their losses had so far been restricted to a few chickens. Well, that one pig, maybe. John had tried to make her believe that the shoat had just wandered off looking for acorns, and joined up with wild hogs. Maybe, but she didn't really think so. There had been armed men in the area. They'd not likely see that shoat again.

One of her greatest worries was that John didn't hesitate to talk politics when he was in town. Everybody knew they'd come from Indiana, and were probably abolitionists. But she wished he wouldn't advertise it. Over on the Kansas side, families had been killed just for their beliefs. Families on both sides of the slavery question. They'd heard that Old John Brown had gone back east and had met his end trying to stir up trouble. He'd done a lot of killing of proslavers first, over in Kansas. No worse, she reckoned, than what the Border Ruffians were doing. Some abolitionist had called them that in a speech . . . "Ruffians," and they'd taken the name proudly. They'd taken one of their own, a Missourian who spoke out against slavery, tried him for treason, and shot him, leaving his body in a ravine.

John had agreed to stop talking politics for a while, but things seemed to quiet down some. She feared it was temporary, and now there was more activity again. Small bands of armed men traveled the roads and camped in the woods. Mostly Southerners, it seemed, and mostly Missourians. A few from Georgia and the Carolinas. They'd be proslavers, of course. She was concerned for the safety of her boys. Brown had killed youngsters the age of twelve or so, and the Ruffians had done the same to Northern sympathizers. Her own boys were in their teens, three of them, out working with their father now. Her youngest, Ezra, was five. He'd been born in Illinois as they traveled west. He was playing by the window, and looked up to watch the men pass.

One of them raised his rifle toward the dogs, but another rider stopped him.

"Let it go, Hiram. We're pretty close to the fort."

The man contented himself with a threatening yell and a curse, and the dogs drew away. The riders moved on without pausing.

Jayhawkers . . . She'd first heard the term applied to the militant Kansans, abolitionists looking for a fight, like John Brown. Now, it didn't matter anymore. Settlers of either persuasion, or even those who tried to stay neutral, were at the mercy of these armed bands. An isolated family was in danger of being jayhawked by either faction.

Maybe it would be better now that the election was over. It remained to be seen whether Mr. Lincoln, the new President, could lead the country. His party had many of the same ideas that she and John did, but the party was new. Well, time would tell.

She was also fascinated that Kansas had finally achieved statehood. That was exciting. The thirty-fourth state of the Union! She looked down at the flag she was sewing. . . . Before long she'd have to decide on how to arrange the stars. It would have thirty-four, of course. But try as she would, she couldn't see how to put them on the blue field in a pretty arrangement.

The Constitution didn't specify, so she'd have to plan it out, like she'd do with a quilt.

She'd found some bright red material for the stripes, to be alternated with the white. She wasn't really happy with that. Her white cloth was linen, and the red was wool. She didn't like to mix them, but yard goods were scarce and expensive, like everything else. She'd managed a pretty good blue square by dyeing some of the white linen. But the stars . . . Maybe she'd start with a circle of thirteen, for the thirteen colonies. She'd need sixty-eight, of course, to appliqué on both sides of the blue field. She folded and cut a paper pattern, and began to cut out each individual star from the white cloth. Then she could lay out and arrange the pattern before starting to sew them on.

Wait . . . A smile crept over her face. Surely, the star for Kansas should have something to distinguish it. Put it right in the center . . . Somehow, the waiting and the anticipation had caused the push for statehood to grow in her mind. The new state would be *hers*. They'd move there, and begin a new life with the new republic. Her boys would grow with Kansas. It was frustrating that it could not be right now, but she understood. Not quite yet . . . It would be safer to make the move in a few months or a few years. Better for the boys. For now, she'd sew her flag, and the star, that thirty-fourth star that represented Kansas, would be the one in the center of the circle. . . . A trifle bigger and brighter, maybe. Smiling again, she found a scrap of paper and folded it. . . . With a single stroke of her scissors she cut a new pattern, to be used for only one star. The one in the center of the blue field . . .

John and the boys came back to the house along toward noon. Nancy had put the makings of the flag away. It was her special, private thing. John wouldn't have minded. Might even have approved and enjoyed the making of her flag for Kansas . . . *Their* state . . . She'd show it to him soon, but not quite yet. Until the flag began to really look like a flag, it would be her secret. Ezra knew about it, of course, and that it was special. But he also knew that it was some sort of a special secret, to be saved for a surprise.

"Ezra, you can set the table for me," she told the boy. "Your father and the boys will be back soon. I'm going to the well to get the butter."

The weather had been warm for late April, and she'd started keeping the butter and milk in the well. It was nice to have a good well, fed by a cool underground stream. She'd witched it herself, and was pleased when it came in clear and cold at the point she'd selected. Not many people knew about her gift with the wand, and she'd as soon keep it quiet. There were always some who didn't understand, or thought it the work of the devil. No matter . . . She took the cloth-wrapped mold of butter from its can on the string and dropped the empty can back into the well, hurrying back to the house. It was about time to take the bread out of the oven. . . .

She heard the boys come up on the porch, and John, washing hands and face at the basin on the bench. He dried with the towel and hung it back on the nail in the post to enter the house.

John came up behind her and touched her hair. He wasn't very demonstrative in his affection. Sometimes she wished he'd be a little more romantic. But he was shy about it. She had the feeling that he thought it wasn't proper, somehow, to carry on in front of the boys. But that little touch was a reminder. . . . He had no trouble in the privacy of darkness, or when they were alone. She turned to smile at him.

"Get out of the way!" she teased playfully.

He grinned and stepped back.

"Wash up! It's about ready," she called.

The boys were washing, taking turns splashing water with cupped hands from the basin to sweaty faces. Samuel took the bucket and walked to the well to refill it, lowering the dip bucket on its rope. Three dips to fill the big bucket . . .

"Fill the pan and bring the bucket in for drinking," Nancy called. "Don't get soap in it, William!"

The good-natured splashing and horseplay quieted somewhat at the warning, and the boys straggled in. Nancy set the big crock of chicken and dumplings on the table, and one loaf of hot bread. She'd save the other one if she could. Her menfolk were always hungry.

They folded hands and bowed heads, and John murmured a prayer of thanks for their many blessings. They did have a lot to be thankful for, Nancy thought. John mostly mentioned the food and its "intended use," and they all joined in the "Amen."

By custom, all waited until Nancy took the first bite, and then all fell to.

"Some riders passed today," she said conversationally.

"Yes, we saw them. Looked like they were moving on through. Could you tell who they were?"

"No," Nancy answered, "but probably Southerners. Sounded like it when they yelled at the dogs. Does it really matter, though? One bunch can jayhawk as bad as the other."

"Yes, I know, Nancy. I hate to have you in this troubled place. Maybe we—"

"No!" she said quickly. "We're here, this is our home, and when we move, it will be into Kansas, to grow with it. I'm not frightened, John. If it's meant to be . . ."

"All right," he chuckled. "I didn't mean to rile you. I know."

There was only the sound of eating for a little while, and John spoke again.

"I believe I'll ride over to Fort Scott tomorrow."

"Trouble?" she asked quickly.

"No, no! I just want to talk to their farrier. Ol' Fanny has that hoof that splits. Old injury, probably. But their farrier is good with special shoeing. I wanted to ask him what he'd suggest."

"You'll ride Fanny?"

"No, no. I'll ride Blue. But one day I do want a real saddle horse. It'll come."

"You'll be careful?"

"Of course. How could I be safer than with the army?"

"Well . . . Yes, I know, but things are so unsettled, John."

"I know. But maybe, now that there's statehood . . . We'll see."

It was quiet for a few moments, except for the sounds of eating. Hungry young men, filling their apparently bottomless stomachs . . .

Nancy knew that her husband probably had no real need to talk to the army farrier. Sometimes he'd just need to talk to another man, like she'd talk to a woman if she had the chance. That chance was pretty slim. Their closest neighbors were just a mile away, but were proslavers. The women were decent to each other, but it was an uncomfortable thing. Both Nancy and Abigail were quite conscious of the differences between them, and as a result they hadn't visited much. Of course, they'd help one another in an emergency, Nancy knew. The thing that made that an uncomfortable situation was that the likeliest trouble they might have would be from their political differences.

So, Nancy understood John's need to talk to other men. Likely, he'd hear some news, too. News was slow, here on the border. In the towns, of course, there were newspapers. They got news by wire, some of them. It was hard to see how that could work, but she guessed it did.

John could have ridden into Nevada, Missouri, the small town a few miles east of them. He could get the news and man-talk there, but she was glad he chose the other way. She was more comfortable with the thought that he'd be at the fort, or near it. In the town of Nevada, he'd more likely encounter some of the Ruffians, looking for trouble. At Fort Scott, they'd be officially neutral, but leaning toward Free State ideas. He'd be safer. She'd be interested in what news he'd pick up, too. Fanny's hoof was just an excuse. He worked the mares without shoes, and he could trim that hoof perfectly well *without* advice.

Still, she understood his need. There was a lot happening these last few months. Just a few weeks before Kansas had been admitted as a state, South Carolina had dropped out of the Union. "Secession," they called it. She'd had a bad feeling about it, especially since word had filtered in that other states were dropping out, too. Mississippi, Florida, Alabama, Georgia, Louisiana, Texas . . . It was over their right to drop out, it was said. This struck Nancy as odd, to secede just to prove they could. Of course, Texas could, under special agreement, but they chose to do so to support the other states.

Nancy could understand the wish of any state to retain the right to its own destiny and not become subject to the federation. But somewhere along the line, the reasons had gotten confused. Now, folks talked about "slave" or "free," as if that was the point of argument. It might as well be, because it seemed now that the free or slave sentiment was the thing over which folks were killing one another.

It was a worrisome thing. . . .

Life *was* moving on, bringing civilization to the frontier and across the West. Riders of the Pony Express (". . . wiry young fellows, preferably orphans . . .") brought the mail with news of Lincoln's election from St. Joseph, Missouri, to Sacramento, California, in only ten days. That was nearly two weeks faster than the conventional mail service via Butterfield Overland on the southern route to the west coast.

But now the telegraph had bridged the continent. The marvelous achievement of the Pony Express would be doomed to financial failure after only sixteen months of operation.

2

Nancy did not expect him back until late in the day. It was early afternoon when he rode the old work mare into the yard, slid to the ground, and tossed the lead rope he'd used for reins up over her withers. Blue ambled toward the barn, and John headed purposefully toward the house.

The boys had gone fishing down at the creek, and she'd let little Ezra go with them, so she was alone. Faced with this opportunity, she had spread her flag over the top of the dinner table, and was trying different arrangements for the stars on the blue field. She considered attempting to put it away, but John was hurrying across the yard. No matter. She'd show it to him soon anyway. Let him see what she'd been working on. He knew of her patriotism, as she knew of his, though they didn't talk of it much. But just now, there was a grim, determined look on his face. Normally he'd follow the mare to the stall and give her grain, or turn her out into the pasture. Today, he just let her go. Something must be wrong. . . .

Nancy flew to the door to meet him on the porch. Her first thought was that something had happened to the boys. But they were at the creek, in the other direction. John had come down the road from the fort. He couldn't have seen the boys yet. These were the fragmented thoughts that flitted through her head as she met him in the doorway.

"John . . . What is it?"

She had never seen such a look of sadness in his face. Hopelessness, almost. He seemed lost, confused, and angry, all at the same time.

He gave a deep sigh and put his arms around her. It was an uncharacteristic gesture for him.

"Nancy," he said seriously, "I reckon we're at war."

"At *war*?"

"Yes. They've fired on a fort in the harbor at Charleston."

"Who has? What are you talking about, John? Tell me!"

He withdrew his arms from her waist and took a step back. . . . Another sigh . . . Then he shuffled aimlessly to a chair and slumped down, staring into space. Finally, his eyes turned toward her.

"Well . . . You know several states have pulled out of the Union."

"Yes, but . . ."

He waved her down. "They've formed a union of their own, the Confederate States of America. We'd heard something about that. But now . . . I guess Mr. Lincoln declared that all property in the South that was owned by the United States still *is*."

"What property, John?"

"Not sure . . . All military bases, forts and such. Harbors, I don't know. . . ."

"But you said somebody fired . . ."

"Yes. Fort Sumter, in the harbor at Charleston, in South Carolina. They were the first state to secede, you know."

"The President was trying to force them out of the fort?"

"No, no, Nancy. Federal troops were *in* the fort. The *Confederates* fired on the fort with cannon. . . . The federal troops surrendered next day. April thirteenth. The President has called for the states to furnish troops, and has declared war."

"But *which* president, John? I suppose the Confederate States have one, too?"

"Yes. But I was speaking of Mr. Lincoln."

"How did you learn all this, John?"

"Met a fellow at the fort. A Mr. Sterling. He'd been traveling, and his horse threw a shoe. I was talking to him while the farrier reshod the animal. You remember the packet steamers on the Missouri? He's a partner in one of the companies operating those riverboats. They have freighters and passenger stages on the roads, too."

It was a long speech for John. He must have been quite impressed with this Sterling.

"How did he learn all this, John?" she asked.

"The transport company . . . Sterling and Van Landingham . . . They have somebody back east . . . Baltimore, I think he said. . . . Sends a telegram, when something of note happens. He lives at Shawnee, near the Delaware Crossing."

"Which side is he on?"

"That's just it, Nancy. He'd like to stay neutral, like us. We were talking, startin' out careful-like, and pretty soon realized we think pretty much alike. That's how he happened to tell me about the war news."

"What will *he* do? About the war, I mean?"

"Try to stay out. People still need freight hauled, I reckon. Oh, yes . . . Several more states are out of the Union."

"Which ones, John?"

"Let's see . . . Virginia, North Carolina, Tennessee . . . Arkansas, of course."

"Missouri? There's a lot of proslavers here."

"No, Missouri's declared for the Union. Kansas will too, of course. Sterling expects Maryland to go Southern, I think. Oh, yes . . . He said the western part of Virginia wants to stay Northern. They may try to secede from *Virginia*."

"What do you think *we* should do, John? Our family, I mean?"

"I don't know, Nan. We could move on into Kansas. They've become pretty solidly Union now, it seems. Maybe be better than here. Not much, though. There's still jayhawkin' across the border, both ways. Might even be better now, with Missouri declarin' for the Union. Let's just set here a spell if it's all right with you."

"Fine."

"Where are the boys?"

"Fishing. They took Ezra. I've been sewing."

She pointed to the table.

"What . . . A *flag*?" he asked.

"Yes. For Kansas. Thirty-four stars."

John smiled. "Don't recall that one star in the flag was bigger than the rest, Nancy."

She turned up her nose at him and tossed her head mischievously. "Wasn't any need till now," she told him. "There wasn't Kansas yet. That one goes in the middle of the circle."

He rose and circled her with an arm as he studied the scattered stars on the table.

"What is it with you and Kansas, Nancy?" he teased.

She could not have answered in words, but she knew that he felt it, too. Maybe as much as she. It was new country, out there, to be made whatever they'd want it to be.

"Maybe," John said sympathetically, "it won't be too long till we can homestead there. Let's see what this war situation does in a few months."

She smiled, contented. Then a sudden thought gripped her. "John! You're not thinking of going to *fight*?"

"Well . . . I hadn't thought so. I have a lot of family to care for. Besides, I reckon they can negotiate who owns what government bases. They'll let the South go their own way. Not everybody has to think alike, do they? It'll be over pretty soon."

•   •   •

Instead of quieting down, there seemed to be even more threatening activity along the border. Missouri raised troops for the Union in response to President Lincoln's request. But there were still bands of Border Ruffians with proslave loyalties. These loosely organized guerrilla raiders saw an opportunity to assume an air of legitimacy as riders for the Confederate cause. Some pledged allegiance and became units of the Armies of the Confederacy.

Others, however, already experienced in the art of guerrilla warfare, operated quite independently, continuing to raid at will, sometimes with the sanction of the Confederacy, sometimes virtually as privateers.

There came to be individual raiders who were known by name along the border, hated and feared by the vulnerable settlers, or admired and praised by those with Southern sympathies. Foremost of these was William Quantrill. With the sanction of the Confederacy, if not wholehearted approval, he raided along the border in a series of quick strike-and-run attacks. His successes drew more followers to his ranks. Among these were a wide variety of riders, some true Confederate patriots, some whose pleasure was to raid and plunder for personal gain. Worst of all were a few sadists who simply enjoyed the killing. Possibly the most loathsome of these was also a man with leadership ability, a lieutenant of Quantrill, William Anderson.

Unlike most of the irregular Confederate raiders, Anderson was a Kansan. His family had homesteaded quite early, a short distance south of the Santa Fe Trail, and only a day's travel from the Council Grove. This was nearly a hundred miles west of the area of most of the raiding and killing along the border. He would participate in a raid or two and then travel to his home in Breckenridge County, Kansas, safe from pursuit or even suspicion, to rest from his efforts. Most of the raiders, when they dispersed after a skirmish, would seek the safety of pro-Southern communities in Missouri, but Anderson seemed to virtually disappear between raids. Possibly his neighbors knew of his Southern sympathies, but few connected young William with the infamous Bloody Bill Anderson who rode into a fight wearing a bandolier of the scalps of his victims.

On at least one occasion after an encounter with Northern volunteers, he ordered the dead "Yankees" scalped, stripped, and sexually mutilated. Mutilation of the dead was a favorite pastime, which became a trademark of Anderson's raids. It may have been inspired originally for Anderson by the stories that Old John Brown, murdering Southern sympathizers, had sometimes hacked off the hands of a victim with his antique broadsword.

Further irony is reflected in a popular song of the times, which evolved as a tribute to Brown.

John Brown's body lies a-mouldering in the grave,
John Brown's body lies a-mouldering in the grave,
John Brown's body lies a-mouldering in the grave,
But his soul goes marching on. . . .

In 1861 Julia Ward Howe, visiting army camps, heard this song, and intrigued by its melody, wrote new words to it. This was published in the *Atlantic Monthly* as "The Battle Hymn of the Republic."

Ralph Waldo Emerson wrote that by Brown's execution, the gallows would become "as glorious as the cross."

And "Bloody Kansas," even with statehood, continued to bleed. . . .

3

More riders . . . They hadn't seen any for a few days, but there was tension in the air. News of the war trickled in from time to time, and it was becoming more uncomfortable to go to town. Black looks followed Nancy and her family wherever they went. Former friends smiled uncomfortably, passed the time of day as quickly as possible, and hurried on. Even Abigail, maybe her only friend, avoided her now. Even the storekeeper sold them flour, sugar, or coffee grudgingly.

John had never made any pretense when they came to the area. He had openly stated that the family was sympathetic to the Northern cause. Not abolitionists, of course. He'd always considered those to be troublemakers. He even leaned some toward the idea of states' rights. He just thought that some things were better accomplished by the federation.

But now, the war had been going on for a year, and feelings were running high. The South had done well on the field of battle. Names of unfamiliar places became common conversation. Fort Henry and Fort Donelson in Tennessee had been Northern victories. But Shiloh, with the skill of Confederate Generals Johnston and Beauregard, had become a great victory for the South. Beauregard had moved into Virginia and stung the Northern forces at Manassas, called "Bull Run" by the Yankees. He'd had to withdraw, but after Manassas, the Unionists had known they were in for a fight.

A Union sympathizer like John Willett was under increasing pressure. In the area of their farm, between Fort Scott on the Kansas side of the border and Nevada, in Missouri, Southerners were increasingly vocal.

"Nancy, they don't seem to understand. I'm not an abolitionist. I just want the Union to hold together."

"I know. But I'm afraid it doesn't matter anymore. Anybody who favored one side or the other is suspect. We're all tarred with the same brush."

John winced. "Don't say that!"

A few years earlier a mob had kidnapped and tarred and feathered a citizen in the Leavenworth area.

He smiled ruefully. "I really think, Nancy, that the war's makin' it pretty dangerous here. But we *can't* leave, right now. We have to get crops gathered. It's August, and we need to be hayin' right now. Corn, pretty soon. Let's get that done, and then we'd ought to talk about it. Sellin' out, that is."

Nancy glanced at the sewing box where her flag lay, nearly finished. A few more stars to appliqué on the back side, when she had time. "When the work's all done . . ." But the work was never all done. Never had been, anyway. That was just the way of things. She'd take pride in what they'd done together, and in the boys they were raising.

"Your flag will be just as good when we come back," John said softly. He teased her about it, but she knew that down deep, he understood.

"When we do come back," he went on, "it will be on the Kansas side."

"Promise?" she smiled.

"Promise!"

They were haying today, John and the older boys. Ezra, now six, could help with some things, but haying wasn't one of them. So, he'd stay at the house and keep her company.

It was hot, and all the doors and windows were open to let what breeze there was come through. She saw the riders through the open door from about a hundred yards away, and paused to watch them. They were a bit different, somehow, from some of the ragtag bunches that passed. They seemed to have a sense of purpose, a determination. Nearly a dozen of them . . . She watched them without moving, as they came along the road toward the house. They paused, directly in front, and there was a brief conversation among the three at the front of the column. Ezra crept close to her and took hold of a fold of her long skirt, silently watching. The dogs barked, a bit halfheartedly in the heat, and then drew back toward the barn.

Then, to her horror, the three leaders reined toward the house and rode directly up to the door. Nancy's heart fluttered and raced, and her palms were sweaty. Illogical thoughts tumbled through her mind. She should have put her sewing away. . . . The flag was almost in plain sight and would mark them as Northern sympathizers. Mixed with this realization was the wish that the riders would keep their horses out of her petunias by the path.

The men were grim-faced, and fairly bristled with weapons. She didn't know what to do. She wasn't even sure yet which side they stood for. One thing sure, she'd stand her ground. She thought of John's rifle, across two pegs above the door, where it could be quickly grabbed. Too late now . . . She stepped into the doorway so that they'd have to move her forcibly to enter the house. The big rifle was directly over her head now, but she had given up any idea of using it. She'd have only the one shot, and then Lord knows what. . . . She pushed Ezra behind her skirts, but he continued to peer around at the riders.

"Ezra," she whispered, "don't you say a word!"

The one who appeared to be the leader was a lean, bearded man. He wore a slouch hat and had a frightening stare that seemed to burn through her with the intensity of a snake's eye just before the strike. He brushed the brim of his hat with his right forefinger in a pretense of a salute, and spoke.

"This the Willett place, ma'am?"

A chill gripped her heart, despite the August heat. Although the question was polite, and a logical one, the implications were fearful. The soft drawl identified this man as a Southerner. A few Southerners were Free-Staters, but not likely in this case.

"It is," said Nancy firmly. "I am Mrs. Willett." Her heart beat even faster. They had asked *by name.* This meant . . . what? The bushwhackers were known to carry lists, and to seek out and harass those of differing political beliefs. Sometimes they'd kill a man, in his own yard, with his family watching.

"Where is your husband?" the bearded leader asked. "We need to talk to him."

Her worst fears were being realized. *Why* hadn't they moved last year? Now it was too late. What could she do or say?

She managed a sort of smile. "I don't know," she said dreamily, trying to appear as empty-headed as she could. These men had come from the east, so she'd have to send them west, or they'd know she was lying. She pointed vaguely in the direction of the fort. "He was going to help somebody with a horse, I think."

It bothered her just a little to lie about it. She'd been raised not to lie. A lot of people didn't pay much attention to truth, and that had always irritated her. But she figured that in a case like this, maybe the Almighty would give her some benefit of the doubt because her goal was good. Trying to save her husband had to carry some weight.

The rider was not impressed.

"How far?" he demanded.

"Oh, I don't know. . . ." She waved a hand in that direction. "He don't tell me much. . . ." She hoped she hadn't overdone the stupid role.

The bearded man bored through her with his beady eyes for a moment, and then hauled his horse's head around with a cruel jerk and a curse. Narrowly missing the petunias, he kicked the animal into a lope. The others followed.

Nancy took a deep breath and knelt beside Ezra.

"Ezra," she said quickly, "listen to me carefully. You know where they're stackin' hay?"

"Yes . . ."

"All right. You run there, as fast as you can. Tell your daddy the bushwhackers are lookin' for him. Do you understand?"

Ezra nodded.

"Good! Now *go*! Fast!"

She watched the child for a moment, his little feet and legs fairly flying, past the barn and across the creek at the ford. Then she took down the rifle and drew the hammer back to check the cap, returning it to half-cock. She set the gun against the wall by the door and turned to put away her sewing basket. She'd done all she could, for now. . . .

"What's the matter, Ezra? Is Mama all right?"

"Yes," panted the boy. "She says tell you the bushwhackers are comin'!"

"Where? When?"

"Now. At the house!"

The boys gathered round, and John thought quickly.

"What shall we do?" asked William.

"All right," said John. "They'll be here soon, I expect. Ezra and I will crawl into this haystack, here. You toss some more hay over us, and just keep on hayin'. Sam, you're the oldest. You do the talkin' when they come. Don't try to fight 'em. Tell 'em this . . ."

The last forkful of hay had hardly settled over the hiding place of John and the child when he heard the hoofbeats of the riders. Maybe a dozen, sounded like. He worried for the boys, now working on another stack a stone's throw away.

The hoofbeats stopped, except for the nervous shuffling and stamping of tired horses, fighting flies. A man's voice spoke, with a Southern accent. As he'd figured, Nancy had sent them on a wild-goose chase to give him a few minutes' time. They'd figured it out and had come back.

"Howdy, boys," said the Southerner. "Where's your daddy? We need to talk to him."

"He ain't here," said Samuel.

"I can see that," snapped the man. *"Where is he?"*

"Oh," said Sam. "He's workin' at the fort, I reckon."

"The fort? How come?"

"I dunno. He hires out as a carpenter sometimes."

That, at least, was true, and they might know it. . . .

There was a pause, and then another voice spoke.

"Hold on. The army has its own carpenters!"

Sam rose to the occasion.

"Sure!" he said. "But there's a lot of buildin' around the town site there, I reckon."

"Who's he workin' for, then?"

"I don't know. He don't tell me everything. I got to stay here and put up hay."

Good, thought John. *Just don't push it too far.*

There was a long pause, and then one of the men spoke.

"Well, looks like we came up dry today. But, it's gettin' late. Boy, is your daddy comin' home tonight?"

"How do I know?" grunted Sam. "Sometimes he stays over."

Careful, Sam . . .

"Well, no use to wait for him I guess," said the leader. He paused a moment, and spoke again. "Wait . . . We can camp here, wait for him. If he don't come home, we'll go on in the morning."

There was a mutter of assent from the tired riders.

"You boys go on home," the man's voice spoke again. "No monkey-shines, now. We'll be watching you-all."

"You got some chickens, boy?" another voice asked. "We could use some vittles."

"No!" said the leader firmly. "Stay away from the house. We don't want to scare him off. Now, you boys *git*!"

Nancy waited anxiously, watching toward the hay meadow. The riders had come back, far sooner than she'd hoped. They hadn't even paused at the house, but loped past the barn and across the ford. *Had they seen Ezra?* she wondered.

She considered taking the rifle and going up to the meadow, but that might cause John one more worry. She didn't know what might be happening, but if she heard any shooting, she'd be up there in a hurry, and she'd make her one shot count. That beady-eyed one with the beard, if she could. But that would be a last resort.

She stiffened. . . . Someone was crossing the creek. Sam . . . William . . . Ernest . . . *Where are John and Ezra?* she thought. She rushed outside with the rifle, even as Samuel began to motion her back. They straggled on up toward the house.

"Where's your father?" she called.

"We don't know, Mama," Sam called back, shaking his head and motioning with a hand to his lips.

She waited as they hurried on into the yard. Then, everybody tried to talk at once.

"Quiet! Sam, you talk!"

Quickly, Samuel spilled out the story.

"They're still in the haystack?" she asked.

"Yes. What will we do, Mama?"

She thought a moment. "So, they think he's at the fort?"

"I hope so," said Sam.

"Then we act like he is," Nancy decided. "William, you grain the horses and feed the pigs. Sam, milk the cow. Ernest, you gather the eggs. Take your time, all of you, do it just like we always do. I'll get some supper on. Your father will look after himself and Ezra."

At least, she hoped so. She wished she felt as confident as she tried to sound. But they had to act as if nothing out of the ordinary was going on. Otherwise those bushwhackers might get suspicious and poke around. But what if they came to the house? They might remember that there'd been a smaller boy. She shivered, though the air was hot. She wondered how her "baby" was holding up. . . .

Maybe later, John and Ezra could escape from the hay and come on home. Her mind refused to consider one question that kept cropping up: *What if they decide to burn the hay?*

4

John heard the boys leave, and the sounds of the raiders as they unsaddled and made camp. He tried to visualize where they'd make their fires and tie or hobble their horses. Nearer the creek, likely.

If they were specifically after him, John Wesley Willett, by name, they'd probably wait to see if he returned home. If he didn't come tonight, they'd move on. Such a raiding party would not stay in one place longer than overnight.

Well, one thing at a time. He shifted his position a little, trying to settle in. He'd need to be as comfortable as he could get, so as not to stiffen up during the long night's chill. There would be no sleep for him. Maybe they could slip out of the hay after dark, but even that would be risky.

The sounds of moving men and horses drifted away toward the creek, and he put his lips close to his son's ear. The boy had not made a sound.

"Ezra," he whispered, "don't say a word. . . . We're goin' to spend the night here, till those men leave. You just lay here in my arms, and don't make any noise. All right?"

The boy nodded, eyes wide. The dim light, filtering through the lacy pattern of loosely tossed hay, showed concern yet confidence in the boy's freckled face. John wondered if the child could comprehend the gravity of their situation. He gave him a gentle hug.

"That's my boy!"

The light began to fade as evening drew near. Locusts in the trees along the creek tuned up in their raspy singsong mating concert. They'd been singing since mid-July. Ninety days till frost, when the first locusts sing, some of the old-timers in the area said. He wondered where he'd be by then. Their noise was good, though. It would cover any chance sounds he and Ezra might make by accident. Maybe after dark they could slip away. . . .

There was one scary moment during the brief twilight just after sunset. A hobbled horse, browsing in the meadow, approached their hiding place and began to nibble loose hay from the stack. John kept still at first, but quickly realized that this could not continue. In a short while their cover could be eaten away.

"Shoo!" he hissed softly, making a slight motion.

The horse, hearing, seeing, and probably smelling an unsuspected living creature all at once, gave a startled snort. It lurched aside, almost falling because of the hobbles on its front legs. Another lurch, in the strange hopping gait of a horse with hobbles.

"Lookit yer horse, 'Lige," someone called. "Somethin' spooked him."

"Aw, he's just kinda spooky," a voice answered. "See, he's all right now."

"No, there's somethin' in that stack," the other answered. "We better have a look."

There was a sound of footsteps trotting toward them, and another puzzled snort from the horse.

"Mebbe it's somethin' to eat," suggested the one voice. "A 'coon would be purty good. Even woodchuck or 'possum would go right well."

"Let's burn the stack, an' get him when he comes out."

"No, you fool! You want the army chasin' us?"

The thought that they might fire the haystacks had occurred to John, along with a chill of fear. He quickly realized, though, that they wouldn't do such a thing until morning. The blaze of burning haystacks could be seen for miles, and the marauders would not expose their position when preparing to camp. There might be Northern jayhawkers prowling the border, too. Even army patrols from the fort . . .

"Well, mebbe we could *grab* it. I got gloves, here. . . ."

"Fergit it, Jack. You'll be grabbin' a snake er a badger. Even a 'coon would chaw you up purty good."

"Well, seems we'd ought to try somethin' . . . Say, did them boys leave one o' their pitchforks? We could poke in there. . . ."

John's heart sank. If they started jabbing in the hay . . . He knew the boys *wouldn't* leave a fork out overnight, but if one of the raiders happened to have a bayonet, or even a saber . . .

He'd almost decided to give himself up. They might kill him, but maybe they'd spare a child. But just then, a shift in the gentle night breeze brought a new smell. The musky scent of a distant skunk is not at all unpleasant, if indeed it's distant enough. Somewhere down along the creek, a black-and-white-striped hunter had encountered a larger predator, maybe a raccoon or bobcat, and had responded with his well-known defense. The faint yet unmistakable scent reached John's nose just as an exclamation came from one of the raiders.

"Say! Smell that? A polecat! I'd bet its mate's in here!"

In a few heartbeats, the shuffling sounds of retreating footsteps were moving away from the haystack.

"Come on, Esau, you don't want to tangle with no skunk!" someone chided.

In the hay, John whispered a silent prayer of thanks for skunks. He'd always wondered why the Creator had put certain nuisance creatures on this earth. Now, he knew the reason for at least one of them.

He lay there as darkness deepened, trying to ignore the tickling scratch of the hay on the back of his neck. He also tried to forget that in all probability there was an assortment of ticks, fleas, and spiders crawling through the hay, over their bodies, maybe in their clothes. He shuddered a little. He'd try to think about something else. . . .

Nancy would have fed the boys, now, and they'd be trying to let on like they'd expected him to be gone for the night. They'd have prayed a bit. He'd done that, too, here in his hiding place. He'd do more before morning.

Ezra stirred restlessly, and John gave the child a reassuring hug, patting him gently. Another thought struck him. . . . Had the raiders noticed *how many* youngsters there were at the Willett place? If they'd paid any attention, they'd see one was missing. . . . Of course, they might *not* have seen Ezra at the house. Well, Nancy'd think of that, too, likely. Maybe she could put a roll of blankets and such in one of the beds, and say her youngest was sick and had to have rest and they'd best not look. Or, that he had smallpox or . . . No, they'd know better. . . .

That line of thought was making him feel worse. He'd listen to night sounds awhile. . . . A hunting owl, down by the creek, sounded his hollow song. Another answered. Horned owls, likely, by their call. Then the other owl that was common here, the one Nancy called a hoot owl, chimed in.

Farther down the creek, he heard the bark of a fox. Not much different, he'd always thought, than the watery *sqwonk* sound that the little green heron calls to his mate.

A 'coon whickered upstream in the other direction. . . . Or could that have been a screech owl? Maybe. The coyote's chortling yodel from the ridge yonder was unmistakable. He'd never understand how one of those critters could sound like half a dozen.

·   ·   ·

Toward morning, he dozed off for a little while, and scared himself some as he fought his way up out of a dream. He was being chased and couldn't run, and was glad to wake up. He hoped he hadn't cried out.

Ezra was sleeping, and John comforted him, moving cautiously to limber up his own stiff body. His left leg was numb, useless and wooden if he'd have to jump and run. His right arm was asleep, too, where the boy had lain in its protecting circle through the night.

He considered creeping out of the stack and trying to escape. But there was a bright half-moon. He'd be easy to see, crossing the open meadow. And there'd surely be sentries, who'd be watching. . . . Anyway, where would they go if they left the stack? The house might be watched. The fort? That was nearly four miles away.

He finally decided that the best course of action was to take no action. . . . Stay right here, in the stack . . . The raiders would move on in the morning. It bothered him some that they might burn the hay as they rode out, just to thumb their nose at the army. But, he thought not. If he were a raider, he wouldn't want to advertise that he was in the area and have a platoon of dragoons after him. He'd have to take the risk, he guessed.

There *was* a considerable risk, he reckoned. Some of those riders weren't the smartest he'd ever encountered. A man who'd consider poking a skunk with a pitchfork might not even be thinking about dragoons and pursuit. It would be risky, no matter what.

It eventually began to come morning. John could see the ghostly yellow-gray of the false dawn begin to lighten the meadow. He woke little Ezra, so as to have him ready in case they had to make a run for it. They waited some more.

Finally there came sounds of activity as the raiding party began to stir and move around. He caught the scent of coffee. . . . They probably stole it somewhere, he figured.

It seemed like hours elapsed until he heard the squeak and jingle of saddles being tossed on horses, and horses being ridden at a trot to loosen them up for travel. Finally, those sounds died, and he could hear nothing but morning birdsong as the creatures of the day succeeded the night creatures in the never-ending circle of living. And he and Ezra were still living, too. . . .

With a silent prayer of thanks, he crawled from the stack, almost stumbling as he tried to stand on cramped and tingling legs.

"Come on, Ezra," he said. "Let's go to the house."

Nancy ran to meet him, and flew into his arms, tears streaming down her face.

"They're gone," she said. "The boys watched them for a mile or so. Oh, John . . ."

He held her tightly, and Ezra clung to her skirts.

"Nancy," he muttered, "this is *it*! We're goin' to Iowa till all this is over."

It was later that day when they discovered that the raiders had driven away at least thirty of their young pigs.

5

It was painful to leave the farm.

"You've worked so hard on it, John," Nancy said sadly, watching him load the wagons.

"It's all right, Nan. We're alive. So far, anyway. I hate to give it up, too. But we're not really admittin' we're licked. And we'll be back. Into Kansas, next time, maybe."

"I know . . ."

Some who were stubborn and had ignored warnings to leave had been killed. Mostly, though, families who appeared to be leaving were allowed to do so. She thought of an old jingle she'd heard once, maybe from *Poor Richard's Almanac* or somewhere.

> He who fights and runs away
> Lives to fight another day.

Well, it was time to run. They'd find a place in Iowa, plant next spring. In a couple of years, they'd come back. John was a good farmer. He saw things that others didn't. Like the seed corn . . . Most folks just shelled out their corn and saved back a part of it for seed next year. Not John. When they were picking corn, tossing it in the wagon in the field, he'd always have a big box under the wagon seat. Whenever he'd run across an ear of corn that was a little bigger and better than the rest, he'd toss that one in the box for seed instead of in the wagon bed with the rest. Back where they'd lived in Indiana, the neighbors all admired John Willett's corn, and wanted some of his for seed. He'd give it to them, but not out of his selected seed box. Their corn would be a little better, but still never held a candle to his. It amused her to see that they never seemed to think of selecting ears for seed from a *stalk* that produced well. Even now, the box with the seed corn was already under the wagon seat. It was a hard job to get ready for the move. They'd sold the stock, rather than butcher. John hated that, because everybody was selling cattle in the fall, and prices were low. Folks didn't want the work and expense of wintering them. He'd rather winter them through and sell in the spring when things greened up and folks wanted to buy.

The milk cows . . . They'd take one, sell the other. Which one would they take? Bossy, or Buttercup? Bossy, named because of her horn-less, or "bossed" poll, usually had good calves, and they seldom had horns. But Buttercup gave more milk, and richer cream. John chose to take Butter-cup. He'd try the idea of hornless cattle some other time, maybe.

They sold the remaining hogs. There was simply no time to butcher, smoke the hams and bacon, render lard, and all. There'd be pigs to buy in Iowa.

They'd keep both teams of horses, of course. They needed them to pull the wagons. One wagon for the household goods, the other for tools and grain for the horses on the trip, and a crate with a few hens tied on the back. The big wagon with the furniture was fitted with bows and a canvas cover. The other was open. Sam would drive it, and the older boys would ride with him. Ezra would ride in the big wagon with his folks.

The attempted sale of the farm was a disaster. They knew its value. So did everyone else. But people knew they had to sell and wouldn't pay what it was worth. John finally negotiated a price, far too low, with a banker in the town of Deerfield, but then decided he couldn't do it. They'd come back and sell later.

A little money in gold coin for necessities of the journey would come from the sales of cattle and hogs. . . . The rest in paper bills. He'd turned that over to Nancy for safekeeping.

It was a bright day in early autumn when they were finally ready to depart. Despite the warm sun, it was a time of gloom and disappointment. Nancy's heart was heavy, and she refused to look back at the house. She'd longed for the day when she'd be able to leave it and move on, but not this way. She wanted to move forward, not back.

Her flag, still not finished, was carefully folded and hidden among their clothing in a box in the wagon. She'd finally figured how to arrange the stars. . . . A circle of thirteen for the colonies, then five along each side of the square. That made twenty more. . . . Thirty-three, and the bigger and brighter one in the center of the circle. That one represented Kansas, the thirty-fourth. She'd finish it when they got settled in Iowa. Then in a couple of years they'd be back, with her flag flying. . . .

They'd chosen to go west, the few miles into Kansas, to pick up the Military Trail at Fort Scott. There would be more traffic, and it should be safer than traveling north on the Missouri side. John was concerned that their Southern-sympathizer neighbors knew of the sale of the livestock. Rumors could and did spread like wildfire along the border. News of a family of Yankees traveling through territory of primarily Southern sympathies, and carrying money from the sale, was bound to bring trouble. It would be safer on the military road.

They passed the fort and headed north on the well-traveled pike. Nancy was pleased to have caught the eye of some of the men around the post. She'd dressed in her finest for travel, and had carefully combed and pulled her long auburn hair up in a neat bun at the back of her head. She'd keep her dignity.

"You're dressin' up to travel?" John had asked in amazement.

"Of course! They may run me out, but I'll go with pride. I'll show 'em what a lady looks like!"

"This ain't like you, Nan."

"Maybe not. But don't you think it's safer? Even Ruffians might show a little more respect to a lady."

She was still pretty, she knew, even at thirty-five, and her shining glory had always been her hair. It had never been cut. She had bestowed its color, to some degree, on all her boys. All had hair that ranged from sandy to outright red. She even thought that might be what had caught John's eye in the first place. He'd never said so. . . . John wasn't much for compliments. But now, she'd fixed herself up a bit for just the reason she'd told him. She wanted to look like a lady to any passersby whom they might meet on the road. She had an idea that a woman who behaved like a lady was more likely to be treated like one. And of course, it was always nice to be admired.

It was late afternoon and they were nearing the Little Osage River. There wasn't much traffic here, a half-day's travel north of the fort. Then suddenly, riders ahead on the trail. Armed men, not in uniform, had drawn up and sat blocking the trail.

"Oh, oh . . . ," whispered John. "This is bad. . . ."

He kept the horses moving, though. It would be useless to stop.

"Where's our money?" he asked.

"Never mind. It's safe."

John nodded, tossing only a quick glance as he flapped the lines on the mares' rumps to keep them moving. He pulled to a stop, face-to-face with the riders. Five, he counted in the road, but he saw other figures among the trees.

"Howdy," said the leader. "Have to ask you to step down, folks. We're checkin' for contraband."

Contraband . . . A term being used as an excuse to stop and search anyone.

"What sort of contraband?" demanded John.

"Never can tell . . . Weapons, powder and ball . . ."

Yes, or money, thought Nancy, fuming inside.

The rider now drew a pistol. . . . He did not point it, but held it threateningly in the air.

"I said, step down, and nobody gets hurt."

"We don't want trouble," John said carefully. "We're leaving, heading to Iowa, and—"

"Down!"

The pistol's muzzle swung suggestively.

"Now!"

John looked helplessly at Nancy and wrapped the lines around the brake lever. He stepped to the ground, calling to the boys in the wagon behind.

"Do what they say, boys. We don't want trouble."

A rider motioned to Nancy, indicating that she, too, should alight. He had an ugly leer, and was missing his front teeth.

"Get down here!" he snarled.

Nancy spoke now, to the leader.

"Must I, Captain? Surely, you do not make war on women!"

The leader seemed confused for a moment, and then turned to the man with the broken teeth.

"Let the woman alone. Search both wagons," he called to the others.

Men were already pawing through the wagons, tossing out the contents of bureau drawers, pocketing small items of jewelry, of which there were precious few anyway.

Nancy sat primly on the wagon seat, head high, her hands folded, looking straight ahead. She heard a crash of breaking china, but did not turn.

"Aha!" shouted a man. "Here it is!"

Now she turned to look. The man was waving John's long rifle.

"Contraband!" the Ruffian chortled.

"But I'm not a combatant," John protested. "I'm just a farmer. That's—"

"Shut up!"

Now the search became really intense. They found the supply of powder and lead for the rifle, and took the powder horn and bullet mold, too.

"Here's a box of corn, Captain," called one of the searchers.

"Find a sack or two," the leader instructed. "We'll take it for the horses. That's military supplies. And make sure nothin's hid in it."

So, they ARE looking for money, Nancy thought.

"That's my seed corn, Captain," John protested.

"You got nowhere to plant it," the leader sneered. "You're lucky we don't execute you for treason, carryin' weapons like that!" He motioned to the rifle.

"How about a chicken dinner, Cap'n?" somebody yelled.

"Bring 'em."

The hens were trussed in pairs, legs tied together, and the squawking birds draped across saddle horns.

"Shoot the cow?"

"No. We'd have to butcher it."

"Just a steak or two?"

"*No!* No shooting. Mount up, now. It's about time for the patrol to come by."

And the riders quickly disappeared into the trees.

They were still picking up scattered possessions when the patrol from Fort Scott approached.

"Sorry, folks," the platoon leader said when they had explained. "This happens. Too often . . . Good you didn't resist. They were probably looking for a chance to start a fight. What will you do now?"

"Camp here tonight, I reckon," said John. "We got to repack. We'll head on toward Iowa."

"Good. Best of luck!"

The lieutenant waved his dragoons forward, and the patrol moved on toward the fort.

They continued to assess the damage.

"Most of your seed corn, John!"

"Yes. But the chickens, too. Oh, Nancy! They broke the mirror on your dresser."

She smiled sadly. "Seven years' bad luck!"

"But for them, not us, Nan. Oh! The money . . . ?"

"It's safe. And we're all alive. It could be a lot worse, John."

6

John was seething with anger. Nancy knew how frustrating it must have
been for him. The only way that he could have protected his family was
to do nothing at all, to stand and watch while the riders robbed them.
She knew that any sign of resistance would have been an excuse to kill him.

Methodically, she shook out and refolded their clothes, repacking
carefully. This had been only the first day. It would take nearly two weeks
to reach anywhere in Iowa. Then, they'd be trying to find a place to winter,
as well as somewhere to settle for a couple of years.

Her heart went out to John. He'd lost his precious seed corn, improved over a period of years by his skill in selecting special types. He'd lost
his rifle, and that was important. It had been no defense against the marauders, but would have been mighty handy to furnish game for food now that
they'd no chickens. That riled her to think about. She'd sure miss the eggs,
too. Well, there were more chickens in Iowa, she figured. And, they
wouldn't have to feed them as they traveled, now.

At least, nobody had been hurt. They even had a few gold coins left.
John had distributed coins among the boys, and they'd scattered those in
various pockets, and in their boots. Nancy had sewn special little pouches in
the waistband of John's jeans, where a goodly portion was hidden. He had
let the raiders find a few coins in his pocket to pacify them. And most of the
money was safe. . . .

·   ·   ·

The next morning they traveled on. They nooned near Pleasanton, let the horses rest and graze a little, and moved on.

They were stopped again, as they neared the ford at the fork of the Marais des Cygnes River, by some of the same riders. Nancy recognized the one with the teeth missing.

"Where's the money?" one of the men demanded of John. "We know you sold your stock. Now, cough it up!"

"There isn't any," John insisted. "Look, you found the gold in my pockets. We had a lot of debts to settle before we could leave."

Nancy figured that under the circumstances, stretching the truth was forgivable. But she'd have to explain it to the boys, especially Ezra. Lord, it was hard to teach right and wrong in times like these!

Again, the riders dumped their belongings into the road and searched the wagons while Nancy sat primly on the seat. They camped, repacked again, and moved on the next day. The robbers had been frustrated and had stolen a few more small items as they rifled through the wagons.

"If this keeps up," John observed, "we won't need but the one wagon."

It was an attempt at wry humor, but Nancy was in no mood to appreciate it.

They passed the turnoff to La Cygne, but before they reached Louisburg were stopped again and searched. And again, Nancy sat unmoving on the seat while the Ruffians plundered through their household goods and personal belongings. They crawled under the wagons, looking for secret compartments. Their search was quicker this time, though. The traffic on the military road was heavier here.

"Somebody's comin'," called a lookout. "Hurry it up."

In a few moments the raiders were gone, disappearing into the timber.

"My gawd! What happened?" asked the driver of the approaching team as he pulled to a stop, staring at their scattered goods. It was a useless question. It was apparent that they'd been robbed.

"Anybody hurt?"

"Reckon not. Just our pride," said John ruefully.

The other nodded. "Hard times. Where you headin'?"

Both Nancy and John were trying to catch a hint of the man's loyalties from his talk. Not much of an accent either way. But he seemed to pose no major threat. John decided to be perfectly frank.

"We're headed for Iowa, till things settle down some. We've been tryin' to stay out of it, but folks where we been are bein' raided by both sides."

The man shook his head sadly. "Hell of a thing, ain't it? Where was you?"

"Near Fort Scott."

"You'd think that'd be some protection, no? Not hardly! But I reckon it's worse up toward Fort Leavenworth."

"How so?"

"Lots o' privateer companies. Even a couple of cannon batteries."

"Which side?"

"Both. A Confederate battery, a couple of Union infantry companies." He removed his hat and scratched his head. "I'm thinkin' a lot of 'em are mostly out for the raidin' and lootin'. Not all, of course. There's some whose hearts are right, I reckon. It's just figgerin' *who's* right. Well, I got to be movin' on. Any way I can help ye?"

"Don't reckon so. Louisburg a day ahead?"

"Yep. A purty long day." He shifted his reins, and then paused. "Say, you're gettin' into some dangerous country, the way you're headin'. You'd do better, maybe, goin' straight east from Louisburg. Off the military road, and over into Missouri. It's calm there. Harrisonville's about a day east of there. Then you go on north. Takes you into Independence, in a couple of days. Northern town, it be pretty safe country."

He lifted the reins again and clucked to the team. They watched him go.

"What do you think, John?" Nancy asked.

"Well . . . Anybody's guess. He's prob'ly right, though. Most of the trouble has been in the border counties. If we get over into Missouri . . . It's declared for the Union, of course, so there's bound to be more Northern sympathies somewhere, if we can find 'em."

Nancy had another thought as she started to pick up and repack yet another time. It must be hard for somebody with a states'-rights leaning living in a Union state. . . .

No excuse to be raiding and stealing, of course, she thought irritably as she folded soiled clothing yet another time. At least, they hadn't found her flag. Or the rest of the money.

It rained before they reached Harrisonville. A cold drizzle, working itself into a downpour. They pulled off the road into a grove of hickory trees and made camp. John took a canvas tarpaulin out of the open wagon and used it to rig a lean-to tent for shelter.

Nancy watched the water sluice down the tarp and onto the ground for a while, and then brought a wooden bucket from the other wagon. She had changed her clothes already, to save her good things from the rain and mud.

Now, she placed the bucket beneath a rivulet that trickled from a fold of the canvas.

"What you doin', Nancy?"

"I want to catch a little rainwater, wash my hair. I intend to remain civilized, John. No water is as good for the hair as rainwater."

He did not argue. He'd learned long ago what it meant when she used that tone. When the sun came out, she'd wash her hair, come hell or high water, or both. Come to think of it, they'd come pretty close to both already, John mused.

Nancy reentered the makeshift shelter and they waited while the rain pelted down and drummed on the wagon cover and the canvas tarp. From time to time there was a flicker of lightning and a roll of distant thunder. The boys amused themselves by estimating the distance to wherever the lightning strike might have occurred. The flash, then start to chant . . . "One steam engine, two steam engine, three steam engine, four . . ." *Boom!* A little more than three "steam engines" in the count before the crash of the thunder . . . A little more than three miles away.

Gradually the space lengthened until the lightning's flicker could not be seen at all. There was only a low muttering roll to the thunder, barely audible. But rain continued to fall. Not a downpour, but a slow, sodden drizzle, as the sky drew darker with the onset of evening. John had managed to get a fire going. He'd kept a small bundle of tinder and dry twigs in the big wagon, carefully wrapped, for just such an emergency. Once started, wet wood could be added, small sticks at first, then larger fuel. It made a lot of smoke and steam, the wet fuel sizzling and hissing as it dried, before igniting.

By dark the fire was going well, and a supply of wood to last through the night was propped near the heat to begin to dry. Even so, it was a cold night. John, Nancy, and Ezra slept under the shelter of the big wagon's cover, while the older boys made their beds under the tarpaulin and the other wagon, next to the fire. They did not even post a watch. No raiders would be abroad on a night such as this.

Morning dawned crisp and clear, the sun beginning to warm the day quickly. John announced his decision about travel.

"We'll let it dry a bit. The road will be muddy, anyhow. So . . . We'll build up the fire, dry our clothes and the tarp. Let the horses graze. They could use a day to eat instead of travelin' anyway. They're gettin' a bit ribby."

"Good," said Nancy brightly. "The sun's warm. I'll bathe and wash my hair!"

Several days had passed since they had been able to afford such a luxury. The boys quickly found a grassy area where the horses could graze, and a bend of the creek with a white gravel beach and clear water.

"Sam, you look after Ezra!" she instructed.

She selected a more secluded area for a bit of privacy, and took soap, towel, comb, and brush. . . . She could do her hair first, then bathe while it dried. She'd not take off all her clothing at once, of course. Most of her bath would be with a cloth, and inside her dress, anyway.

She could hear the boys laughing and splashing, and the sun felt warm through her dress. She took the pins out of her hair, carefully removing the "rat," a tight roll sewn into a sock, around which to wrap her hair into a bun at the back. She tucked the rat into the front of her dress, between her breasts, for safekeeping. Her auburn hair billowed down, shining in the sun as it cascaded to her knees. She'd wash it with soap in water from the stream, then rinse with her bucket of rainwater, and comb it out as it dried. John would help with the rinse, pouring from the bucket.

She lifted her long skirt and tucked it into the belt of the dress, revealing shapely legs. Kicking out of her shoes, she peeled off her stockings and tossed them, too, aside. The water was icy as she stepped in to fill her extra bucket. No wonder the boys were hollering so! She hoped they wouldn't all catch their death of cold. . . .

7

They reached Harrisonville the next day and bought a few provisions to replace those stolen by the raiders. It was good to see a Union flag fluttering proudly over a recruiting table on the boardwalk in front of the city office. A mustached lieutenant in blue was talking to several young men.

A merchant where they bought bacon, beans, and a little sugar talked of the war. There were organized Missouri troops, he said, going to fight for both sides. The Union recruiter was in town trying to raise more federal support.

John inquired about the road to Independence.

"Independence? Two days. Lots of traffic, but the road's pretty easy."

John didn't ask about safety, but there was a more comfortable feeling here. Still, he had the sense that he'd not rest easy until they crossed into Iowa. There, they wouldn't have to fear everybody who came down the road. He had mixed feelings about it. He longed for new land in Kansas, but safety for his family, too. And for now, there seemed to be very little safety with the bitter war continuing to flare up along the border. Maybe someday . . .

A thousand miles to the east, eight men had gathered in a room for a meeting of utmost secrecy. Their leader, a tall, ungainly man, paced the floor a step or two and let the small talk subside. Then he cleared his throat, grasped the lapels of his coat with both hands in a familiar mannerism, and began to speak.

"Gentlemen, we gather today that I may tell of a decision I have made, after due deliberation."

Every face was alert, every ear listening.

"You will remember, of course, that I have always been opposed to the view of the abolitionists."

The others waited expectantly. There were nods of agreement, but also some grim and determined looks.

"I have insisted," the speaker went on, "that there be no attempt to destroy slavery where it now exists, but only to prevent its spread. Allow it to fall under its own pressures . . . Our goal in this war is not to destroy slavery, but to preserve the Union."

He turned his craggy face to each of the others for a moment, but there was no marked reaction. He took a deep breath, more like a sigh.

"Now," he went on, "I feel that it is time to change my position."

There was a buzz of response, even a gasp or two.

"But Mr. President . . ."

He held up a hand for silence. "Let me go on. In this war, we must have the wholehearted support of the people. On this I think we all agree. We have had this unity, but I fear it is now slipping. Union forces have suffered some defeats. The public is shocked by the fact that war begets dead and wounded. It is no longer a picnic."

"Mr. President, our forces will prove themselves!" blurted the Secretary of War.

"I know, Mr. Stanton. When we find the right generals . . . I would that Mr. Lee had chosen to accept my appointment. Instead, he felt that he must fight for *his* country, Virginia. His leadership at Bull Run was brilliant. But let me go on. . . . We need a pronouncement of some sort. Something that will warm the cockles of faint hearts and unite us in the cause of preserving the Union."

He looked around the room, pausing just long enough for effect, and spoke again.

"Freedom!"

There were nervous glances from one to another of the assemblage, exchanges of puzzled looks, as the President continued.

"I have prepared a proclamation freeing the slaves."

Now there was a flurry of talk.

"But . . ."

"Free the *slaves*?"

"But you . . ."

He waited, and spoke again when the room had quieted somewhat.

"A proclamation of emancipation . . . There is much sympathy for abolition in the North, and this will unite even such radicals to the cause of the Union."

"But sir," spoke the Secretary of State, "there are slave owners in the Union."

Lincoln smiled sadly. "Yes. No slaves in areas of loyalty to the Union will be included in the proclamation. Only those in areas of secession. West Virginia, for instance, remains loyal, as do some parishes in Louisiana."

"Good!" exclaimed Stanton. "Punish the Rebels!"

"With all due respect, Mr. President," said the Attorney General, "as a matter of law, you are on shaky ground. You have no legal authority over citizens of another sovereign power."

"I have considered this, Mr. Bates, and agree in theory. But we have not recognized the legitimacy of the Confederate States' union. Therefore, our government still reigns. We cannot exist except through the strength of unity. As you have heard me say, half slave and half free. I had hoped to accomplish this in other ways, but now I feel that we must move."

"But why not *all* slaves? Why only in Rebel territory?"

"To protect the property rights of those who are loyal to the Union. We can reimburse slaveholders for their losses at a later date. It is possible, perhaps, that freed slaves from the Southern states may wish to fight for the Union."

"Could they be made into soldiers?" asked Secretary Stanton. "John Brown failed to do it."

"But that was a special case. Brown was clearly outside *any* law, and was guilty of treason." There were nods of agreement. "In this case, it does not matter. If freed slaves wish to fight, let them, or not. That is not the purpose of this proclamation. Its purpose is to spur the emotions of our citizens, to unify them."

"May I make a suggestion, Mr. President?" asked the Secretary of State. "The timing of such a proclamation is critical. It must not appear to anyone as an act of desperation."

"Then what do you suggest, Mr. Seward?"

"Postpone the announcement a little. The public is saddened over Bull Run. At this time, the proclamation might give a wrong impression. Wait for a victory, even a minor one. Mr. Stanton assures us that there will be one."

Stanton's face reddened, but he said nothing.

"Your suggestion merits consideration, Mr. Seward," Lincoln mused. "To ride the crest of a victory with another . . . Yes! I will prepare the proclamation. My thought is to allow any state to return to the Union at this time if they wish. A time limit . . . The proclamation would take effect at an announced time, and would include only those states who have not yet rejoined the Union."

"Do you expect any to do so?" someone asked.

"I could not say. I would hope so. They should at least have the opportunity. There is much sympathy toward the Union throughout the South, I am told. This may nurture it."

"Might this not change the perception of the war's purpose, sir?" asked Secretary Smith. "From preservation to abolition?"

Lincoln nodded, again with a great deal of sadness. "Possibly. But it takes heart to fight a war. The goal of abolition of slavery is a more pressing one than that of preservation of the Union, to many citizens. At least, it seems so. Now, as to when the proclamation will be. Mr. Welles, is our naval blockade sound?"

"Yes, Mr. President. Our control of New Orleans has been a great help. We have a fleet of ironclads plying the Mississippi, and controlling the shipping there. A few blockade runners from Europe are reaching the Carolinas, but the situation is improving."

"Mr. Stanton, what of the border states?"

"Settling down some, Mr. President. Our March victory in Arkansas served to secure Missouri. Some privateer activity by Southerners, but this presents no tactical problem."

"And what of McClellan in Virginia?"

"We expect him to engage Lee and Jackson again soon, sir."

"Successfully, I trust?"

Stanton flushed. "I have every confidence, Mr. President."

"Very well. I shall be in readiness to make the preliminary announcement when that, or some other major victory, occurs."

The hoped-for victory took place on September 17 at Antietam Creek, near Sharpsburg, Maryland. It was one of the bloodiest engagements so far, with the loss of more than twenty-five thousand lives. General Lee retreated into Virginia to regroup. On September 22, 1862, President Lincoln announced his Emancipation Proclamation.

That on the first day of January, in the year of our Lord one thousand eight hundred and sixty-three, all persons held as slaves within any State, or designated part of a State, the people whereof shall then be in rebellion against the United States, shall be then, thence forward, and forever free; and the Executive Government of the United States, including the military and naval authority thereof, will recognize and maintain the freedom of such persons. . . .

This proclamation applied only to slaves held in states that had seceded from the Union.

. . . the following, to wit: Arkansas, Texas, Louisiana (except parishes of St. Bernard, Plaquemines, Jefferson, St. John, St. Charles, St. James, Ascension, Assumption, Terrebonne, Lafourche, St. Mary, St. Martin, and Orleans, including the city of New Orleans), Mississippi, Alabama, Florida, Georgia, South Carolina, and Virginia (except the forty-eight counties designated as West Virginia, and also the Counties of Berkeley, Accomac, Northampton, Elizabeth City, York, Princess Anne, and Norfolk, including the cities of Norfolk and Portsmouth), and which excepted parts are for the present left precisely as if this proclamation were not issued.

The proclamation would take effect on the first day of January, 1863. A paragraph was included inviting any newly freed slaves to fight for the Union.

. . . persons of suitable condition will be received into the armed service of the United States to garrison forts, positions, stations, and other places, and to man vessels of all sorts in said service.

By virtue of the three months' time until the proclamation would take effect, any state wishing to renew allegiance to the Union might do so. Such states would not be affected, and would remain slave. None of the Confederate States took advantage of this offer.

When the news reached the border state of Kansas, it led to some odd situations.

Jedediah Sterling, of Sterling and Van Landingham, hurried home to tell his wife the news.

"Suzannah, the President has freed the slaves."

There was doubt in her face. "*All* slaves?"

"Well, no . . . Those of states in rebellion." He handed her the newspaper, fresh from the press, and they studied it together.

Suddenly, Suzannah's expression changed.

"What is it?" Jed asked.

Suzannah looked around to assure herself that no one was within earshot, especially the children.

"Jed," she said, "you realize that under this proclamation, I'm still legally a slave?"

"*What?*"

"Read it! We're in Kansas, loyal to the Union. If we were still in the South, I'd be free!"

Jed put an arm around her. "Well, I guess for the present, it won't make much difference, then. But nothing will, you know, if we're together."

None of it made much of a difference to John and Nancy and their sons, on the road to Iowa and safety from the raiders.

8

They were camped for the night near Independence, now feeling much safer. For one thing, they weren't known by name here, as they'd been on the farm near Fort Scott. Here, there were many more travelers. They and the boys and the two wagons could mingle with all the others, becoming part of the shifting mass of humanity.

There was a different atmosphere. Most of the people they encountered were merely passing through, en route to somewhere else. No one knew their reasons, their destination, or their political views, and few really cared. A family with young sons and two wagons was hardly noticeable. The other traffic included not only similar families, moving in various directions, but military and commercial wagons. Big freighters, smaller farm wagons pressed into service to haul goods . . . Passenger coaches . . . Light buggies with well-dressed people, moving on more local errands . . . A traveling trader, his wagon hung with pots and pans . . . A few travelers on horseback, and an occasional military unit, seldom more than a dozen, sometimes mounted, but often on foot. It was reassuring that the uniforms were blue.

They had stopped for the night now, and the boys had scattered to look for firewood. There were plenty of trees, but it was apparent that dead wood for campfires had been depleted by heavy demand.

"How far to Iowa now, John?" Nancy asked.

"Not sure . . . Four, five days, maybe. Depends some on the weather. We'll reach Liberty tomorrow, I figure."

"Do you think there's many raiders north of here?"

"I don't know, Nan. It's risky to ask about it, even. But we do know not to get too far west after we pass Liberty. There's places near Fort Leavenworth, in both Kansas and Missouri, that are Rebel towns. I've heard mentioned Weston, on this side of the river, and Atchison over in Kansas. But no matter. If we head north from Liberty, we'll stay well away from trouble, I think. It's the border counties that are in contention, and we'll be farther from the state boundary every day we travel. And, safer."

At least, he hoped so.

It was a long speech for John, and Nancy knew that he was uneasy about it. She, too, was concerned. But as he'd said, it was unwise to ask too many questions. A person could never be quite sure of the political position of a stranger. Or, even more serious, his intent. Otherwise rational people were swept up in the emotion of the conflict and might easily react with reckless and irrational behavior. They had seen it.

Now, a wagon was approaching, a vehicle of moderate size. . . . Canvas top, a young man and woman on the seat. The outfit was fairly new, drawn by a good team of horses. Young settlers, likely fresh from the East.

"All right to camp here?" the young man called.

"Reckon so," John answered. He had started to add "It's a free country," but thought better of it. Things were really bad, he thought, when just to pass the time of day might be taken as a political statement.

"Wood's a little scarce," he called. "Our boys are lookin' for some sticks in the timber, yonder, 'fore it gets dark."

The young woman turned and called toward the back of the wagon. "Will, best you try to find us some firewood."

A lanky youngster dropped from the wagon and shuffled toward the woods. He looked to be in his early teens, not much younger than the girl on the wagon seat, who now swung to the ground.

"My brother," she explained.

Nancy nodded. "He's about the age of a couple of ours, it appears."

"I'm Mary," said the girl awkwardly. "We just been married a short while. . . . Comin' west to homestead, and my brother was pinin' to come with us. Our folks wouldn't let him. Well, we weren't too eager to have him with us, either." She blushed and giggled. "Just married, and all. Well, we were three days on the road before we found him hidin' out under some furniture in the wagon."

She glanced at her husband, who was beginning to unhitch the team. "Reuben's still not very happy about it. It was too far to send him back, of course."

"Do your folks know?" asked Nancy in amazement.

"Well, we sent a letter back. . . . Reuben can write, and even cipher a little. We've been travelin' ever since, but I s'pose they got it, so's not to worry about him. About Will, that is. But he'll be all right. He's a good boy, though I was surely aggravated with him for a while."

"Where did you come from?" asked Nancy.

"Pennsylvania. You?"

"South of here, a ways." Nancy was intentionally vague. "Missouri's got a lot of strife, with the war on, and all. We thought we'd head to Iowa for a while, where it's quieter."

"You've seen some fighting?" asked the girl in alarm.

"No . . . Not really." Nancy was afraid that this conversation was getting out of hand. "There's some feeling on both sides of the war, along the border. Missouri's Northern, you know, but there's some Rebel sympathies. We try to stay out of trouble."

She glanced at John, whose face held a mixture of amusement and mild concern. He must think that she was bordering on giving too much information. No real threat, though, from this young couple. They carried enough problems of their own, and she knew that John was aware of that.

"How many boys do you have?" asked the girl.

"Four. Ezra's with his daddy, there. He's six. The others are older."

"Gracious! You don't look old enough to have such a family. And so pretty! I've always been so plain. . . ."

Nancy warmed to this girl. Such talk was good to hear, whether or not it was actually valid. But she knew that she did look pretty good, especially having been on the road. She had spruced up a little when they began to see more local traffic again. It was part of her plan.

"Your hair is so pretty," Mary went on. "Mine is so plain and dishwater brown."

And pulled back so tight it makes your eyes bug out, thought Nancy.

Aloud, she took a different tack. "Oh, not really," she said, touching her auburn crown self-consciously. "Maybe we can try something with yours after supper. Have you tried it a little looser around the sides? You use rainwater, I suppose?"

"Yes, when I can. But we've been traveling. . . ."

"And rain is a mixed blessing, no?"

Both laughed, and it was good.

The families parted the next morning. Nancy had enjoyed the female companionship, the sharing of hardship stories. Just being able to talk to another woman . . .

Nancy had great sympathy for Mary, the young bride. It would be hard enough to be starting out on a new marriage with the exhausting struggle of a trip across country in the wagon. But, add to that the nuisance, the irritation, and the responsibility of caring for a younger brother.

"But after all, he's a good boy," Mary had insisted.

That might be, but Nancy was not completely convinced. She knew that surely there must have been times when the young bride had felt like dissolving into tears. . . . Probably *had* done so. It was quite likely that young Mary would have fled back to the protective arms of her own mother if it had been possible. But here she was, struggling to establish a home on the inhospitable frontier in wartime.

"It makes me see how good I really have it," she told John. "We never had the problems those young folks do."

John smiled. "And you have none, Nan?"

"Well . . . None we can't handle!"

Now he chuckled. "Nancy, look at yourself. We've been run off from our farm, had our lives threatened, we're still on the run from trouble, don't know where we're headed, or how we'll manage when we get there. And here you are, feelin' sorry for somebody else. You are truly a remarkable woman!"

She made a face at him.

"I don't reckon so, John. We do what we have to. A body can't do less, can we?"

They came to a town a few days later, one which looked exactly like any of a number of such towns, sprawling settlements with any and all sorts of shelters and buildings in all stages of construction. There were even tents, sometimes with a skeleton of poles or rough lumber framing to lend a little stability against the wind. John wondered how these people would weather the winter. After all, they were quite a few miles north of the farm they'd been forced to abandon. Winter might be harder here. Then he remembered. He and Nancy had even less, at present, to help them prepare for the cold. A couple of wagons, with a canvas top on one . . . And, they'd be traveling even farther north before looking for a place to winter, a place to plant in the spring. . . .

"What's the name of this place?" he asked a young urchin only a year or two older than Ezra.

"This here's Lamoni, mister."

"Lamoni, *Iowa?*"

" 'Course! What did you think? Missouri or someplace?"

"We're in Iowa?" asked Nancy.

"Yep. We're here," John smiled. "Now . . . Well, maybe another day or two north wouldn't hurt. Let's camp tonight and go on a ways tomorrow."

They sought directions at Lamoni.

". . . It'll appear that the road turns east, a ways out of town, here. Just foller it, though. That takes you to the best crossin' at the river. The

Thompson. Then you'll be headin' north again. Where you say you're goin'?"

"Not sure," John answered. "I'm lookin' for a place to farm."

"To buy? There's not much unsettled land hereabouts."

"I figured that. Someplace we can rent or work on shares."

"Well, you can find somethin'. There's a lot of folks gone to the war. Or, on account of it."

"Been much trouble here?"

"Naw. Enough, I reckon. Mostly, them as wants trouble finds it a few days west of here, along the border."

John nodded. The man was curious, but refrained from asking questions of a more personal nature. In these troubled times, too much probing was not only impolite but could be downright dangerous. He returned to the wagons, where the routine of camping for the night was in progress.

"He says we'll cross the Thompson tomorrow. The road winds around some, but still leads north. I guess it's been pretty quiet hereabouts."

"That's good to hear," Nancy observed. "How far north do you figure we should go?"

"Hard to tell, Nan. Reckon we'll know when we get there. Oh, yes. I was warned Iowa's dry."

"Dry? But . . ." Then she noticed a twinkle in his eye. "Prohibition?"

"Guess so. That feller offered me a jug, on the sly."

"Did you tell him we're churchly folk and don't drink?" she asked primly.

"No, I didn't bother him with that, Nan. I just told him no, thanks."

"This may be good, with the boys comin' up," she mused. "But, maybe we won't be here long enough for it to matter."

9

They crossed the Thompson River the next day, and the road wandered on northward through rolling hills and good farmland. Yet another day brought them to a smaller stream.

"What's this river called?" asked Nancy.

"Well," said John hesitantly, "the fella at Lamoni called it Whitebreast Creek."

Nancy blushed. "Really? Why, John?"

"I didn't even ask."

Now her eyes were teasing. "You must have wondered."

"I . . . Well, I reckon . . . Jest didn't want to talk about it. It wasn't fittin'."

"What wasn't fittin', Daddy?" asked Ezra.

"Never mind, son. Jest grown-up talk."

Another day beyond the creek with the indelicate name they reached another town. Towns were strung along the old road like beads on a string, a day's travel apart. Osceola, this one was called. They made camp, and John walked back the short distance into town to make a few inquiries about the road and the area.

At the general store, he bought a couple of staple items. . . . Sugar, tea . . . He saw a basket heaped with large brown eggs and bought a dozen. Nancy'd relish them. They'd all missed fresh eggs since the loss of the hens. These looked exceptionally nice, and he commented on them to the storekeeper.

"Yep. Fresh, too. Just come in this morning."

He took John's coin and began to make change.

"Seen you come through earlier," he went on conversationally. "You headed north?"

It was not really a question. If the storekeeper had seen them, he was well aware of their direction of travel. John nodded noncommittally, and the storekeeper studied him a little longer. Finally he spoke again.

"You lookin' for a place?"

John was startled. "Why would you ask that?"

"Well, you appear to have everything with you. Wife and kids . . . Two wagons, purty good teams. What else would you be doin'?"

John was quite uneasy. The man was asking too many questions. . . . He was probing, curious, and John felt an irritated resentment growing. Still, he did not want to anger this man by failing to answer. The political mood of the town was completely unknown to him, and some areas were potentially dangerous to those with Northern sympathies. At least, it had been so in Missouri.

"Well, I . . . ," he began cautiously.

The storekeeper smiled. "Settle down, son. It's all right. Let me guess . . . You been down in Missouri, and it's pretty uncomfortable with Quantrill and them, raidin' and killin'. Both sides jayhawkin', robbin' settlers. Am I right?"

John smiled, still cautious. "Well, pretty close."

"Look," the storekeeper said confidently, "you're in Ioway, now. You're Northerners, or you'd be headin' south. I figger you're tryin' to get the family out of danger. You left a farm in Missouri or Kansas, mebbe?"

"Maybe." John was still cautious. The man was too nosy.

"Look, son," the other finally said. "I'm tryin' to *help* you. Reckon I see why you can't trust no one, seein' where you been. You don't have to trust me, either. But here it is: There's a young widow woman with a couple of small ones, lost her husband to pneumonia. Neighbors got her crops in for her, but she can't hang on. Wants to go back to her folks in Ohio, but farms ain't sellin' well. You know why, I reckon. She'd prob'ly lease it, if you can't handle buyin'. Talk to the banker. He's handlin' it for her. Ask about the Campbell place."

John relaxed a bit now. He grinned. "Thanks. I'll think on it."

The bank would be closed, but he'd talk it over with Nancy tonight. Wouldn't hurt to inquire, anyhow. They couldn't afford to buy, of course, but maybe something could be worked out. . . .

.   .   .

The banker appeared grim, tight-lipped, and suspicious. He gestured to a chair across the desk from his own. His demeanor brightened somewhat with John's inquiry regarding the Campbell place.

"You're interested in buying?"

There was still a great deal of doubt in the banker's attitude. John realized that in his trail-worn condition, he did not present the picture of a well-funded buyer of real estate.

"Maybe," he began, "but it's not likely we could handle it all at once. We still own a farm in Missouri, too. I wondered about a lease for a year or two. I'd want to look at it first, of course."

Now the banker seemed considerably more interested. "Of course. We can arrange that. Where are you staying?"

"Camped just out of town. My wife and four boys. When could we look at the place?"

"Well . . ." The banker pulled a large gold watch out of his vest pocket by its large gold chain. "Let's see," he continued, glancing at the watch and dropping it casually back into the pocket. "I have another appointment, and . . . Would early afternoon be satisfactory? I can have someone take you then."

"Fine. I'll be here, then."

They rose, shook hands, and John turned to leave.

"You are a Union man, I presume?" asked the banker.

John's temper rose for a moment, and then he realized that under the circumstances, the question was quite legitimate.

"I presume so," John answered. "Would I be here otherwise?"

"I . . . No offense, sir," mumbled the banker. "It's just . . . You know, sir, we have to be careful. In these times . . . Why, you might be Quantrill himself."

John smiled. "I might be, but I'm not. Has Quantrill been active this far north?" Maybe this was not far enough for them to travel before trying to settle.

"No, no! I meant no offense, Mr. Willett. You can understand, however, that I have to be cautious."

"Of course. And I, too. Now, I will return shortly after noon. Oh . . . May my wife accompany us?"

"Certainly. But let my assistant, Mr. Brooks, come for you in the buggy. You are camped at the edge of town? I know the place."

"Oh, John, it's a beautiful place!" Nancy said as Brooks turned the team into the barnyard.

"Needs some work on the barn and the corrals," John noted.

"That's true," agreed the young banker. "Mr. Campbell passed on in July, and there's been no one to keep things up."

"Mrs. Campbell is still here?" asked Nancy.

"No, ma'am. She's been gone only a short while, though. She left the place for the bank to manage or sell."

"May we look at the house?" asked Nancy.

"Yes, ma'am. I think you'll find it in good shape."

It was a simple log structure, a single large room with a lean-to addition, and a loft above where the boys could sleep. John noted the precise fitting of the corners, in contrast to the overlapped "hog-pen" corners of cabins on the frontier. The builder had been a skilled workman with the ax.

"Mr. Campbell built this?" he asked.

"I believe so, sir," Brooks answered. "I can inquire if you like."

"No, don't bother. I was just admiring the work."

A man who would be so precise in his construction would also be likely to have well-kept fences and outbuildings.

"There's a stove!" Nancy exclaimed as they entered the cabin. "An oven!"

"Yes, ma'am. Mrs. Campbell took most of her furniture, but didn't want to transport the stove. Too costly to ship, and worth more here. But it goes with the house."

"How much acreage?" asked John.

"Forty acres, I believe. About ten or twelve in pasture, the rest has been in corn and oats. A few apple trees, a good well. You saw the barn, coming in. There are a couple of milking stanchions, a hog pen and shed, chicken house over there. . . ."

"I hate to ask about price," John said. "We surely couldn't afford to buy, but something was said about a possible lease?"

"You'll have to take that up with Mr. Arnold, sir. But he should be back at the bank by now. Shall we go and see him?"

"I could loan you money on your first crop," the banker offered. "Or, on your land in Missouri. You have a deed, I presume? Of course, it's not worth much in that area, with all the trouble."

"But worth much more after things settle down," John observed. "But, let's forget about loans if we can agree on a lease. How about a simple lease, renewable in a year, with option to buy at that time?"

The banker hesitated. "I'd hoped for a longer contract, Mr. Willett. But . . . You'll have cash in hand at signing?"

"I hope to, sir, if the price of the lease is right. I'll have other expenses, of course. The lease is no good unless we have money enough left to buy chickens, some livestock, seed corn for next spring. . . ."

"I understand. Now, let us get down to figures. Then we can prepare the papers, and consummate the contract tomorrow morning."

.   .   .

Nancy rose in the morning, combed her long hair, and then took the ratted sock and her embroidery scissors, to sit on the seat of the wagon. Painstakingly, she clipped each tiny stitch until she could reach inside the sock. She drew out a tight roll of paper bills and handed them to her husband.

"Here's the money, John."

"Thanks, Nan! That was some idea of yours, carryin' the money in your hair. None of 'em ever thought to look there."

She smiled, giving a coy sidelong glance. "Sometimes brains beat brawn, my mama used to say."

"Well, it sure worked this time!"

Nancy replaced the roll with a wad of clean rags, stitched the opening, and rolled her freshly combed hair around the rat, pinning it up with care at the back of her head.

John pocketed the money and prepared to leave for his meeting at the bank.

Back along the border, from the abandoned farm to the area of Kansas City, conditions worsened rapidly. Guerrilla bands raided back and forth across the border. On the Missouri side, officially Union, a great many still held Southern sympathies. Some formed military companies to join the Confederate cause. Others, with little regard for political orientation, raided indiscriminately, killing, looting, and plundering. Some settlers were raided by both sides.

Many Northern sympathizers on the Missouri side crossed into Kansas to enlist in Kansas regiments and fight for the Union. This allowed more freedom for the guerrilla bands to move unchallenged.

In 1863, a "Military District of the Border" was created under the command of General Thomas Ewing. It would include eastern Kansas and a thirty-mile strip of Missouri where it adjoined the new state. Command posts were set up along the state line, from Kansas City to Fort Scott. This, it was hoped, would prevent the marauding bands from crossing the border into Kansas to raid, and then retreating back to the protection of Missouri's Southern sympathizers.

General Ewing, when he assumed command, was appalled at the conditions he found. On August 3, he reported:

> About one-half the farmers in the border tier of counties of
> Missouri in my District, at different times since the war began,
> entered the rebel service. One-half of them are dead or still in
> service; the other half, quitting from time to time the rebel

armies, have returned to those counties. Unable to live at their homes if they would, they have gone to bushwhacking, and have driven almost all avowed Unionists out of the country or to the military stations. And now, sometimes in bands of several hundred, they scour the country, robbing and killing those they think unfriendly to them, and threatening the settlements of the Kansas border and stations in Missouri.

10

General Ewing estimated that about two-thirds of the families on farms still occupied were related to some of the guerrillas and were engaged in feeding, clothing, and generally supporting them.

He asked and received permission, by Order No. 11, to arrest and deport to Arkansas some of these families. In the course of this activity, it was inevitable that some of the women of such families would begin to act as spies, and some were arrested and accused.

Abigail watched the blue-coated federal soldiers ride into the yard. She was glad that Hiram wasn't here. He'd been gone for a couple of weeks.

Abbey hated it when he rode off with those men. She didn't like some of the people who stopped at the house from time to time to eat, drink corn whiskey, and curse the Yankee invaders. Some of them told pretty grisly stories about scrapes they'd been in and how many people they'd killed.

They'd gotten pretty drunk sometimes, and bragged a lot. They told tall tales of the exploits of some of their leaders.

Captain Quantrill, it was said, had actually lived in Lawrence for a couple of years, pretending to be an abolitionist, under the name of Charley Hart. He'd managed to worm his way in among New Englanders who were helping runaway slaves escape to the North. He'd even helped escort a few to safety through Iowa. But when he was ready, he set out with a bunch of fugitives, and instead of taking them into Iowa, crossed into Missouri. There, he'd sold the niggers to some plantation owners. It was a big joke.

Then there was that Bill Anderson. His attitude bothered even some of the raiders. He'd raid a family he *knew* had Southern sympathies, sometimes, if it looked like easy pickins, and then blame it on Yankee jayhawkers. Quantrill had actually arrested him one time, it was said, but they'd talked out their differences somehow.

Anderson had stayed at the house once, and he really gave her the creeps. She'd happened to notice him while he was shaving, talking to himself in the mirror. It was spooky to see and hear him, carrying on both sides of a conversation.

"And are you well this morning, Captain Anderson?"

"Doing quite well, sir, thank you."

Abigail had withdrawn quietly. For a moment she'd thought there was somebody else there, around the corner, whom she couldn't see, but she quickly realized the truth. Then, she couldn't get it out of her head.

She didn't like the way some of them leered at her. None had ever really gotten out of line, but the suggestive glances sometimes made her skin crawl. Still, they were bravely defending their country, and she owed it to them to feed and help them when she could. But that would be all.

She wished she could talk to her friend Nancy, who'd left with her family last fall. The two of them had always gotten on pretty well, though their politics differed. They'd just agreed not to talk about that. She should have found a way to say good-bye when they left. It saddened her to hear the men brag about how they'd run the Willetts out. They'd followed the wagons halfway to Iowa, and robbed them a couple more times. As far as she could find out, no one had been hurt. She hoped that they'd reached Iowa safely.

Lately, though, there had been more federal troops passing through. A time or two, Hiram's raider friends had questioned her closely about who had passed on the road, and when. Once, she had been asked to watch from a hilltop, and to hurry back to the house where the men were resting as soon as she saw the Yankee patrol. She was glad to help in these ways if it would avoid any bloodshed.

Hiram's mother hobbled into the room, wheezing a little from the exertion.

"What's happenin', Abbey?"

"Bluecoats on the road. They're comin' in."

"Confounded Yankees! They're *so* aggravatin'. Prob'ly rob us blind."

"Probably. But aren't you glad Hiram isn't here, Mrs. Botts?"

"He'd stop 'em!" Irma insisted.

Abigail didn't try to argue. That was always useless. Her mother-in-law constantly criticized everything Abbey did or said, no matter what. Her cooking, her sewing, the way she kept her house. In the guise of helping, Irma would rearrange things in the cupboards and drawers. Worst thing was, Hiram always took his mother's side. . . . No, that wasn't the worst. The worst was that the woman was always making snide remarks about having no grandchildren. Sometimes even blunt questions about *why*. Abigail was offended by that. It would be nice to have a child, of course. She hoped to have one someday, and envied Nancy her four strong sons. But it had been nearly five years since they wed. She didn't know why she hadn't conceived, but it was almost a pleasure to not do so if it would irritate old Irma. Abbey had a private theory that no child would want to be conceived in a house with that old woman. She'd lived with them almost from the first.

Now an officer dismounted and knocked firmly, flanked by a couple of soldiers with rifles at the ready. She opened the door.

"Mrs. Botts?" the officer asked, touching a finger to his hat brim in a gesture of salutation.

"One of them," Abigail said flippantly. "Which one do you want?"

The officer smiled. "How many are there, ma'am?"

"Just two that I know of. My husband's mother is here."

"And your husband?"

"He's away on a trip."

"So we understand," said the officer wryly. "To *where*?"

"I don't know. Or how long he'll be gone."

Irma shuffled up behind her daughter-in-law.

"Ef he was here, he'd show you Yankees what!" she yelled.

The officer smiled again. "Yes, ma'am, I'm sure he would. But I think this answers some of my questions."

He turned and spoke to a sergeant. "Search the barn and outbuildings," he ordered. "Confiscate what's appropriate." Then, to another . . . "Corporal, take two men and search the house. No violence." He took a long breath and spoke directly to Abigail. "Ma'am, I'm afraid I have to place you under arrest."

"Arrest? Me?" Abigail was astonished. "What for?"

"Spying, ma'am. You've given aid to bands of Ruffians engaged in guerrilla activities."

"But, I . . ."

"I know . . . Loyalty to your husband. But he's been—"

"Is he all right?" she demanded. "Has something happened to him?"

"No, no. It's not that, ma'am. He's in danger, of course, running with the Rebels, but that's another problem. My duty is simply to arrest spies today."

At this point Irma let loose a string of profanity at the officer, the most gentle of which was "Yankee bastards." Abigail was shocked. She'd heard Hiram's mother swear before, but nothing like this. She didn't even know the meaning of some of the words.

"You want her, too?" demanded Abigail indignantly.

"No, ma'am. She's not accused of any wrongdoing."

"You'd leave her here alone?"

Abigail was viewing this with mixed emotions. Nobody could be accused of wrongdoing if they were never doing anything at all. Irma never turned a hand. That part was rather amusing. What was not amusing was that she herself was about to be carried off and Irma left alone.

"We'll take Mrs. Botts . . . the other one . . . where she'll be safe, if she likes," said the officer.

"I ain't goin' anywhere!" Irma screamed at him. "I'd be safe, if it wasn't for you bastards!"

"As you wish, ma'am." He turned back to Abigail. "You'll want to gather some things, I suppose."

She hesitated. "I . . . How long will I be gone?"

"I'm sure I don't know, ma'am. For some time, probably. Maybe until the war's over." He softened a little. "It will depend on the nature of the charges. Assisting the enemy is one thing, spying quite another. Treason is possible. But, it brings me no pleasure to make war on women. It's likely that this will be only a move to place those in custody who might be helping the guerrillas. Now, let us move!"

She gathered a few things and wrapped them in a bundle made from a square of cloth she used on the table when she felt like being fancy. The men had finished their looting, and there was a short discussion.

"Do you have a sidesaddle, ma'am?"

"I do not. Am I to walk, then?"

"If you prefer. But you may sit behind my saddle, sidewise, and hold to my waist. Here, Sergeant, take her bundle."

They helped her to the horse's back, and she gingerly clasped the belt of his uniform.

"It's only a short distance to the fort," he reminded her.

They moved out of the yard, with the curses and threats of Hiram's mother echoing after them. Abbey was glad there were no firearms in the house. Her mother-in-law might have done something really stupid.

"You mentioned the fort," she said after a mile or so. "I am to be held there, then?"

"Only temporarily, ma'am. You will be transported to Kansas City, I believe, with the rest. I regret the necessity, Mrs. Botts, but I—"

"The rest?" Abigail interrupted. "There are *more* women being abused like this?"

The lieutenant seemed flustered.

"I have my orders, ma'am," he protested. "You must realize that a spy of whatever gender is a danger to the other side. We have no recourse but to eliminate that risk. I shall insist, however, that you be treated well."

"How generous of you," Abigail said sarcastically. "My house has been violated and ransacked, I have been tossed on the back of a horse like a sack of meal and jostled until my teeth rattle. And *you* will see that I am well treated?"

He did not answer, and both maintained silence until the fort was in sight.

11

Several other women were in the room to which she was ushered. These appeared to come from all walks of life. Two were hard-looking girls, their faces heavily painted with rouge and lipstick, who sat apart from the rest, sneering at the reactions of the others. One of them yelled at the young soldier who had unlocked the door for Abigail.

"Hey, honey, you're cute! Come back after dark." She crossed her legs slowly and suggestively.

The blue-coated young man blushed furiously and tried to back out the door, almost stepping on the boots of the lieutenant, who now entered and glanced around the room. There was concern in his face as he turned to Abigail.

"Again, my apologies, ma'am, but we are engaged in war. I shall return tomorrow to see that you are properly treated. Meanwhile, if dire need arises, ask that I be sent for. Lieutenant Smithers."

It was the first time she had heard his name. He did seem genuinely concerned for her welfare, and he had a kind face. Unexpectedly, she felt attracted to him. As a friend, of course . . .

"I thank you, sir," she stammered, slightly confused. Again, that was a reaction she had not expected in herself.

Now a dignified, well-dressed woman of middle age stood up from her straight wooden chair and spoke haughtily to the officer.

"Lieutenant . . . 'Smithers,' is it?" She pronounced it as if it were a dirty word. "I demand to speak to someone with some authority! I will not be subjected to such outrageous indignity!"

The officer reddened. "Ma'am," he began firmly, "you are a prisoner of war. You will be treated no different than the rest. You will have opportunity to speak with an interrogator later, in your own turn."

"My *'turn'*?"

Obviously the idea of treatment on an equal basis with everyone else was completely foreign to this woman.

"I'll have you know, young man," she sputtered, "that you are speaking to a *lady*!"

"Ain't that fancy?" sneered one of the prostitutes. "Where's this here lady at, ma'am?"

The woman's nose elevated even a trifle higher as she cast a withering look of scorn at the painted pair.

"Come down off it, your ladyship," the girl said sarcastically. "We're all in this together. We all make our living the same way, don't we? On our backs? You're jest paid in different coin than me and Sally here."

Abigail had never heard such talk. Possibly, the self-impressed dowager hadn't either. She looked as if she might swoon, or explode. Whichever came first, it might be interesting.

"You look like you might've fetched a pretty good price once," the prostitute taunted. "A right handsome woman . . . Of course, that was a long time ago, wasn't it?"

"Ladies, please," pleaded Lieutenant Smithers, "there is no reason to abuse each other."

"You aim to do all the abusing, Lieutenant?" asked the girl flirtatiously. "You *are* kinda cute. Want to abuse me awhile, a little later?" She ran her tongue along her lower lip and arched her left eyebrow at him.

"No, thanks," he smiled. "Behave yourselves, now!"

He closed the door, and Abigail heard a key click in the lock. She took a step in that direction, and then stopped, a little frantic.

"You been beddin' him, honey?" asked the trollop. "He seemed sorta sweet on you."

"Of course not!" snapped Abbey. "I'm a married woman."

"So?" said the one called Sally. "What's your point, honey?"

Both prostitutes laughed loudly, and several of the others drew away in disgust.

"Look," the other hussy went on, "we're all in a spot, here, because of our spyin'. I don't know what they call spyin'. . . . More like helpin' our men or our friends, I figger. But I'm wonderin' what they do to spies. It don't look good, and we're all in the same boat, here. No cause to take it out on each other."

It was plain that her offer of cooperation was falling on deaf ears. No one answered her. Soon quiet conversations began among some of the other women.

Abigail felt alone. She wished she could talk to Nancy. She missed her neighbor. Nancy had always seemed to be in control, calmly efficient. Dignified, yet a good friend, and a real person. *Nancy would know what to do now,* she thought.

She put down her bundle and sat in the chair beside it, feeling like a trapped animal. She tried to put out of her mind the stories of people accused of spying, tried for treason, and shot. Would the Yankees treat *women* this way?

In the morning, after they had been given bowls and spoons, a corporal came in with a kettle of watery, grayish mush and ladled some into each bowl. It was steaming hot, and she found that after the first bite, it tasted somewhat better than it looked. She knew that she must keep up her strength. There might be need for it if she had a chance to escape.

A little while later, the door was opened and they were herded outside to a boxlike ambulance wagon. A sergeant stood there with a number of short pieces of chain draped over his arm, iron cuffs dangling at the ends.

"That won't be necessary, Sergeant," said a firm voice.

Abigail turned quickly to look directly into the eyes of Lieutenant Smithers. She found herself glad to see him. He was one apparently predictable element in a world that seemed to have gone mad.

"Are you being treated well?" he asked gently.

"Well enough," she answered. She chose to overlook the fact that the blankets they had been given were dirty, and that corn husk mattresses on the floor were hardly suitable for women who had known better.

"I'll be escorting you to Kansas City," he told her quietly. Then he spoke more loudly to the entire group.

"Please seat yourselves in the ambulance. You will find benches to sit upon."

"I will not ride in such a conveyance!" stated the well-dressed matron who had confronted him before.

The lieutenant heaved a sigh of exasperation. "Very well, madam. You may walk behind in irons if you choose."

"Climb in, your ladyship," called one of the prostitutes sarcastically. "Our carriage waits."

Furiously, the woman complied, followed by the others. The ambulance moved northward on the military trail, flanked by mounted troopers.

Abigail found herself seated next to one of the "fallen doves," who reeked of stale perfume and alcohol. Abbey was shocked at the length of leg that the girl casually displayed. It was not seemly to show more than an inch or two at the ankle, and that only in coy flirtation.

They bounced along for a few minutes, and finally the girl spoke to her. The voice was quiet this time, a trifle hesitant. It was a marked contrast to the bawdy, raucous tone that she had used earlier.

"The lieutenant *is* interested in you, you know."

Abigail was startled. "I . . . No, I don't think so."

Even as she said it, she realized that he *had* given her a little extra attention, had promised her protection, and asked about her welfare.

"He's just being nice," she added clumsily. "He knows I have a husband."

"But just nice to you," reminded the other. "Be nice to him, honey. It will help us all."

Abigail flushed, not completely understanding.

"I know men," the girl continued. "I'm in that business. Our hold over them is, we have something they want, and need. Or *think* they do. How we handle the bargaining gets us where we want to go."

"But he doesn't—"

"Yes, yes, I know. He's a gentleman, or so it seems. But listen . . . If you were single, and met him at church, you'd be interested, no?"

"Well, yes . . . But I *am* married, and it's *not* church."

"It sure ain't. But your husband . . . Where is he?"

"I . . . I don't know."

"Thought so. He's ridin' with Quantrill or Anderson an' them, right? That's why you were picked up."

"I guess so."

"So . . . This will all be over someday. And honey, none of us knows whether our men will be back or not. Sally, there, already lost hers."

"I'm sorry. I didn't know."

"No matter. It happens. But all I'm sayin' is, don't close any doors in times like this. Your husband a good one?"

"I think so. . . ."

She was feeling strangely as if she had to defend Hiram. Well, he'd never beaten her. Not much, anyway. He was hardly the husband that Nancy had, but . . . Of course, he did drink quite a bit, and was gone a good part of the time. That was just on account of the war. . . . *Wasn't* it? *Of course,* she told herself fiercely.

"That's good, honey. But like I said, don't close any doors. We don't really know who's comin' back."

"But I have to *believe* he is!"

"Of course you do. And I'm not suggesting you *bed* with your lieutenant, though he is pretty handsome." She giggled. "But, just be nice to him. Does *he* have a wife?"

"I don't know."

"Wouldn't hurt to find out, though. He ain't likely to take up with Sally or me, it appears, but *you* could ask him."

Although she hadn't even thought about it before, now Abigail was curious. *Does* he have a wife? she wondered. If she knew that, it would make a big difference in how she interpreted his actions.

Yes, she thought, *I could ask him.*

They stopped that night at another of the military border stations and were quartered in a small house nearby. Here they were joined by two more women prisoners. These, like most of the others, seemed to be farm wives. The two prostitutes and "Her Ladyship," as the others called her, were the exceptions.

Abigail noticed that there was a tendency for the women to separate into groups. A few, impressed by Her Ladyship's affluence and dignity, tried to ingratiate themselves to her. Possibly they hoped to benefit when all this was over and things were made right. Abigail didn't cotton to that sort of thing. She'd talk with whom she wanted and not expect anything in return, and she didn't care who knew it.

She was a bit in awe of the two "fallen women," but didn't mind talking to them. After the rouge and paint were washed off their faces, they looked much like anyone else. Except, of course, for their revealing dresses and short skirts. They'd even changed those for more conventional dress before leaving Fort Scott, though.

The one she'd chanced to sit with that first morning was Big Etta. She wasn't really all that big. No bigger than Her Ladyship, actually, except in the chest. There, she was big. Abbey decided that her name must be a sort of inside joke connected with her work. She supposed it was considered work, though the whole idea was completely foreign to her. But these girls were people, with problems much like her own at the moment.

In fact, just before the lamp was extinguished that night, she noticed Sally, crying softly as Big Etta tried to comfort her.

12

"I'm not goin' in there!" Big Etta insisted.

The entire group stood in the street in front of a large brick building. Men peered from barred upstairs windows, hooting and hollering lewd remarks. A newly painted sign next to the entrance proclaimed that this was a military prison.

"But, ma'am, your quarters will be separate from those of the men," explained Lieutenant Smithers.

"I don't care. I know about jails!" Etta stated flatly.

Others joined in the protest, and the clamor of feminine voices rose. Finally the lieutenant threw up his hands.

"All right, ladies. I will see what can be done about other quarters. Meanwhile, we shall return to headquarters."

They turned and walked back to the command post, the party of women flanked by uniformed armed guards. Their number had grown with the addition of several other women, who were transferred from Leavenworth. Three of these were said to be sisters of Bloody Bill Anderson. They were haughty, demanding, and loud in their criticism of the Union troops. They kept aloof from most of the rest, but seemed very friendly with two other women, also sisters, by the name of Munday. There was a third Munday sister who went by her married name, Gray. It was whispered that in one way or another, these six were closely involved with several of the top leaders of the border raiders. Abigail decided to avoid them as much as possible. She wondered if the Anderson girls talked to the mirror too, like their brother.

It was several hours before the tired and impatient women were addressed by another officer.

"Ladies, I am Major Plumb. I can understand your concern regarding the men's prison. We have located a frame house which will be your temporary quarters until a more suitable structure is arranged. Be assured that we shall treat you with respect and dignity, insofar as is possible under difficult circumstances. I trust that you will do likewise."

He turned on his heel and left them.

Again, they walked under guard to a white frame house, which would be their place of confinement. At least it was better than the men's prison.

"How long will we be here?" Abigail asked the lieutenant.

"I can't say, ma'am. There are arrangements under way. . . . A few days, perhaps."

Again, there was genuine kindness and concern in his voice and manner. She was beginning to look forward to the brief contact and the words exchanged with Lieutenant Smithers in the course of daily routine. This, in turn, puzzled her, and excited her a little.

Don't be silly! she told herself fiercely. She wasn't looking for excitement. And after all, the man was a *Yankee.* . . . The enemy . . .

She could hardly believe it, then, when she found herself asking him the question.

"Have you a wife, Lieutenant?"

Then, at the startled look in his eyes, she found herself blushing furiously.

"One of the girls wondered," she mumbled. How could she have made such a fool of herself? And why should it matter to her that she must now appear such an idiot to the lieutenant?

Lieutenant Smithers was still looking at her in surprise. He smiled, embarrassed.

"I am a widower, Mrs. Botts."

"Oh . . . I'm sorry . . ."

He shrugged. "Such things happen. It was some time ago."

The next logical question fluttered through her mind, but she dared not ask it. She had already embarrassed herself enough. If there were only some way to change the subject . . .

"Fortunately," the officer went on, "we had no children yet. That would have been worse. My loss was hard enough as it was."

Let it go! Abbey wanted to scream. She was embarrassed that she'd asked, and now he wouldn't even get away from the subject. What ailed the man?

She did not answer him, and they walked in silence for some time. She thought of trying to edge away, but was afraid it would seem too obvious. He continued to walk beside her.

•   •   •

A day or two later, the lieutenant arrived at the temporary quarters with a squad of soldiers to escort them to a more permanent location. The women were again lined up in the street, carrying their belongings, and marched in a loose column through the streets of the growing city.

After what seemed an eternity they stopped in front of a brick building, flanked by other similar structures. Smithers checked some papers, seeming a bit confused. There was obviously a store here, with the door opening on the street.

"A moment, ladies," he said as he strode across and into the store.

Soon he emerged and spoke again to the group.

"This is it. Our entrance is at the rear."

He led the way around the side of the building, where an outside stair led to the second floor.

"Well, I'm used to usin' the back door," said Big Etta grimly.

The Women's Prison, when arrangements were completed and they moved in, was not at all uncomfortable. It was a three-story brick building on Grand Street in Kansas City, Kansas. The first floor was occupied by a Jewish merchant who sold liquor and assorted cheap sundries to the soldiers, and operated also as a pawnbroker. Access to the upper floors from inside had been sealed off from the store as a security measure. The second floor was reached by the outside stair.

The women were billeted in three rooms on the second floor. Sally and Big Etta were assigned the smallest of the rooms to themselves by Frank Parker, the captain in charge of the prison. Apparently they were considered unfit for association with decent women. The others were allowed to choose between the other two rooms, which were large and airy.

"Etta, I . . . ," began Abigail apologetically, but Etta interrupted.

"Forget it, girl. We're used to such. It don't matter none."

It was apparent, of course, that it did matter. Etta, who could be soft and caring, had again assumed the hardened role of a whore. Sally, a bit more vulnerable, said nothing.

"Thank you, Etta, you've helped me a lot," Abigail said softly.

"I said, forget it. Anyhow, nobody's leavin', are we?" She laughed her hard, raucous laugh.

"I guess not. . . ."

The other women had informally sorted themselves into two groups. The more dominant party was composed of the Anderson girls and the Mundays, Mrs. Gray, and a few others like Her Ladyship. These seemed to consider themselves a cut above the general run of farm wives, sisters, and sweethearts of the raiders. They continued to dominate, moving into the better of the two rooms. They had also managed to insist on bringing their own blankets from the Munday home. This was welcomed, of course, by the army, already short on all supplies.

They had been there only a day when Lieutenant Smithers stopped by to check on their welfare. Again, he was kind and courteous, and politely inquired about their well-being.

He was not actually assigned to the prison detail, it was learned, but was temporarily stationed in the area as an officer in the border guards. He had ridden in just for a visit, he said. It was plain that his concern, though for all of the female prisoners, was primarily for Abigail. This was quite embarrassing for her, but also quite flattering. She could not forget that her mother-in-law had cursed him profanely at the time of her arrest. He seemed to hold no grudge.

Their main problem, the women told him, was boredom. All had had busy lives, even without the activities now considered spying. With no work to occupy them, they were completely at a loss. Their first few shifts of guards had been quite obnoxious, but Major Plumb, whom they had seen only once, had assigned a different unit as prison guards. These were more polite and helpful. Still, it was boring.

"What would you like to do?" the lieutenant asked.

"Get out of here!" yelled one of the Andersons.

"Of course. But within reason," he told them. "Books?"

"Yes, that would be good," answered Abigail quickly, trying to smooth things over.

"I suppose that my violin was stolen by your Yankees," observed one of the others.

"Violin? I'm certain I don't know, ma'am, but I'll see if I can find one."

"You'd do that?"

"Of course. Any other requests . . . other than release, of course?"

There was a smattering of laughter.

"I . . . I can play a flute," said another.

"How about a deck of cards?" asked Big Etta.

"Good idea," noted the lieutenant. "Let me see what I can do. . . . Would you be amenable to some company? A few junior officers, just to visit, sing a bit, perhaps?"

"No strings attached?" asked a suspicious woman.

"None. My word on it. I'll talk to Major Plumb, and report back to you."

"Thank you, Lieutenant!" Abigail smiled.

She did not fail to notice the sidelong glance of approval from Big Etta.

·　　·　　·

The lieutenant was true to his word. He returned the next day with a flute, a violin in a case, and a banjo. There was also a dulcimer.

"I don't know whether anyone can play these," he apologized, "but someone mentioned a guitar. I couldn't find one."

He also brought a box with several books and two decks of cards.

The women were overjoyed. These things would break the monotony of their imprisonment. They rifled through the box, finding copies of *Pilgrim's Progress, Aesop's Fables,* and a couple of adventure stories by James Fenimore Cooper. There was a Bible, classics by Plato and Homer, and a copy of *Uncle Tom's Cabin,* which was totally ignored by the prisoners and disappeared completely in a few days.

Smithers told them that he would be out on patrol for a few days and would come to see them when he returned. He would also request permission to bring another junior officer or two to socialize, as he had previously suggested. He made it a point, before leaving, to take Abigail aside for a moment.

"Are you being treated well?"

"Of course, Lieutenant." She was embarrassed, but flattered by his attention. "We are grateful for your concern."

She watched his broad shoulders as he descended the stairs, and for a moment wished that . . . No, she must not have such thoughts. . . .

13

The first of the evenings of socialization with the Yankee officers was somewhat strained. The women had rehearsed several familiar songs, old favorites to be sung together with the men. There were hymns, ballads, and popular songs like "Wait for the Wagon" and "Sweet Betsy from Pike."

They teased the Yankees a bit with a well-rehearsed rendition of "Bonnie Blue Flag" and "Dixie," and the men responded with "Rally Round the Flag, Boys" and "John Brown's Body." This led to a popular parody used by both sides. . . .

> John Brown's baby had a cold upon its chest,
> John Brown's baby had a cold upon its chest,
> John Brown's baby had a cold upon its chest,
> So he rubbed it with camphorated oil. . . .

This was followed by the sentimental "Lorena," familiar to both. There were a few tears, but there were stories and laughter, and a good feeling, and Abigail could not remember when she had had such a good time. Nobody mentioned the war, except in a teasing way. A few of the women did not choose to participate, apparently convinced that *any* decent conversation with Yankees was suspect. The Andersons withdrew to their private domicile with a few others to verbally abuse the participants for days afterward.

.   .   .

The summer of 1863 dragged on, the heat and boredom relieved by the social visits of the young officers. Abigail found herself confused. She was treated with kindness and consideration by men whom she had been taught were ruthless aggressors. Meanwhile, her own husband, she was sure, was out raiding farmsteads like their own, and probably killing men like the husband of her friend Nancy. The world made no sense.

She did not want to think about it. It was easier to withdraw into the protection of her captivity, to escape into a book. . . . Her reading, which had been rudimentary, was improving with practice. She loved the fanciful fables of Aesop, where animals talked and exhibited the errors or wisdom of human ways.

The improved human relationships at the prison were aided considerably by the visits of the officers. One evening, a young lieutenant asked a question.

"What would you like to do tomorrow? Except for immediate release, of course."

"I'd like to go shopping!" one of the women responded instantly.

There was general laughter.

"No, really. Be serious."

"Well . . . Better food, maybe."

More laughter. It was apparent that the women were already receiving better rations than the army. Besides, the officers would, when they were able, bring candies and sweetmeats to the "socials," as the gatherings were now called.

"Wait a moment," said Lieutenant Smithers. "It seems that the shopping might be a reasonable request. There are things you need. Possibly, two or three women at a time, under guard, of course . . ."

He was interrupted by a chorus of hisses and hoots.

"No, let me rephrase. . . . Under *escort*. The soldiers could stay far enough away to allow private talk, yet with a pledge not to attempt escape."

This time there was silence, finally broken by a quiet question.

"We could really do that?"

"I don't know," Lieutenant Smithers admitted. "We can try. Let me work on it."

There were more hoots of derision, but there was also a possibility. Who would have thought that there could be the pleasantry of the socials they now enjoyed?

It was easier than expected. Before long it *was* possible, by requesting a shopping trip in advance, to take one. Basically, the rules were much as Lieutenant Smithers had outlined originally. Two or three women, an equal number of escorts. The soldiers were to keep a respectable distance and to allow conversation among the prisoners, as well as private conversation between prisoners and store clerks.

Lieutenant Smithers . . . James Wesley Smithers, they had learned, was held in increasing esteem by the prisoners as a friend. He seemed to demand nothing in return for helpful friendship. It was plain that much of this friendship was directed toward Abigail, which further embarrassed and confused her. She tried to visualize her life after the war, and could not. There was also the guilt that she felt when she occasionally compared her feelings for Hiram with those that were growing for Lieutenant Smithers.

Besides, when would the war ever be over? News filtered in from time to time. . . . Yankees under General Hooker had been defeated at Chancellorsville, Virginia, in May, by the skill of General Lee. But shortly after, Grant laid siege to Vicksburg, Mississippi.

In July, word was received of the greatest Southern losses yet. At Gettysburg, in Pennsylvania, General Lee had suffered over twenty thousand unnecessary casualties. There was great concern among the prisoners, although most of their men were not directly involved. Their activities were more limited to the West and the border states. Still, it cast a dark shadow over the next "social," which adjourned early after an uncomfortable evening.

A more tangible concern was of a quite different nature. It had been noticed for some time that the building was noisy. That is, it creaked under the footsteps of people walking down the hall. No one was billeted on the third floor, but occasionally noises from above came to listening ears in the dead of night. There was even a rumor that the building was haunted.

The women complained, and the captain of the guard brought in a squad of troops for a thorough search of the third floor. Nothing was found, and they settled back into routine boredom.

Their uneasiness continued, however, and early in August, the women called the attention of the guards to cracks in the walls, which appeared to be larger than before. A lieutenant of the provost guard arrived and noted the cracks and also mortar dust and fragments on the ground outside. He reported this information to General Ewing, who sent his adjutant to inspect the building, and it was declared safe and sound after a cursory visit.

Captain Parker was still uneasy, and after the noon meal asked a member of his unit to accompany him to carry out a more complete examination. The two men climbed the stair to the third floor, and to their horror watched the wall slowly *moving,* separating from the ceiling.

"We must get them out," the soldier told Parker in awe.

"Get out of here!" Parker yelled to the women below. "This building is going to fall!"

They thundered down the stairs and joined the fleeing women and a couple of the guards on the outside stair to the ground, just as the building collapsed inward on itself.

Abigail half fell, half jumped from the stair as it fell from under her. She landed heavily, knocking the breath from her lungs, and the next moment, she was blinded by a choking cloud of dust that rose to blot out everything in sight. She could hear the screams of women trapped in the rubble, and of their friends outside, who had managed to escape.

Abigail watched the unfolding scene with a numb detachment for a few moments. It was a dreamlike sensation, and there was a short space of time in which she assured herself that she'd wake up pretty soon and this unspeakable horror would be over. Her eyes were burning from the dust, lending a blurred unreality to the whole panorama.

Through the smoky dimness she saw survivors crawling out of and over the tangle of shattered timbers and bricks. To her horror, a bloody arm protruded through a pile of broken stone and mortar. The fingers grasped in a futile effort to hold to the life that was slipping away.

Soldiers were helping the injured out of the debris. Captain Parker was calling orders, dispatching a messenger to headquarters for help, organizing an area where the injured might lie. A crowd was gathering in the street.

"You planned this," screamed a woman, confronting the officer. "You'd kill us all, you Yankee bastards!"

"You make war on women now, Yankee?" someone in the crowd yelled.

More people were running to the scene.

"What happened?"

"The Yankees bombed the damn prison to kill the women!"

The situation was turning even more ugly. The soldiers who had laid aside their arms to rescue the injured were now threatened with mob violence themselves. Soldiers from headquarters arrived.

"Platoon, fall in!" yelled Major Plumb. "Fix bayonets! Cordon off the area!"

Then he strode toward a cluster of the more vocal citizens who were threatening.

"You, you, and you . . . Close your mouths and get in there to help the injured. Yes, *you,* too!" He turned to the sergeant. "Sergeant, if these men try to make trouble, shoot them!"

By this time Abigail had recovered to the extent that she was helping other women out of the rubble. Some were bleeding, and she began to tear strips from her petticoat to bandage the wounds. She could hardly recognize some of the faces through the coating of black dust. One buxom figure was unmistakable, though.

"Etta! You hurt?"

Big Etta shook her head. "Don't think so . . . But . . ."

"Is Sally . . . ?"

Etta nodded, tears streaming down her face and creating little rivulets of clean skin through the dust.

"Sally's dead."

Abigail burst into tears, all the pent-up emotion finally breaking out into the open. Big Etta took her by the shoulders for a moment and then spoke, firmly yet gently.

"Come on, honey. We got work to do, helpin' the living. We can cry later."

She turned and plunged back into the rubble, offering a hand to a staggering figure that Abbey now recognized as Her Ladyship.

The crowd in the street had grown to hundreds now. There were still some derisive hoots and verbal abuse of the soldiers, but it was more subdued. The rumor still filtered through the crowd that there had been a bomb. This spark was fanned by the continued talk from the Andersons and Mundays.

"I know the building was mined," one kept saying. "I saw soldiers going in and out the front door all morning."

"For God's sake, woman," Big Etta muttered an aside to Abigail, "of course they went in and out. It's a damn store. Or it *was.*"

Someone helped to carry out the injured pawnbroker, whose store was completely destroyed. This helped to discredit Mrs. Gray's theory of a bomb or mine planted by the soldiers. It could hardly have happened without his knowledge, since it would have been in his store. The question of *why* the army would want to do such a thing was entirely ignored.

In the midst of all the confusion, Abigail heard someone call her name. She turned, to see a familiar face.

"Abigail . . . are you all right? Are you hurt?" asked Lieutenant Smithers. It was the first time he had used her first name.

Her emotions gave way again, and the tears came. At the moment, it did not matter what anybody in the world might say or think. He was here when she needed him, and she ran to his arms.

"Oh, James," she whispered as her tears poured forth on the shoulder of his blue uniform.

14

The injured were taken to the military hospital for treatment. The uninjured were moved to new quarters.

Abigail was feeling better and was somewhat embarrassed by her emotional display at the demolished prison site. Still, it gave her a sense of satisfaction that the lieutenant's reaction had been very similar to her own. She knew that he understood, and it made no difference what anyone else might think. Part of the time she tried to convince herself that he was only a friend and no more. That in itself was true, the part about his friendship. She had never had a better friend.

In her own introspective moments, she admitted to herself that there was more. There had been such a good, safe feeling in his arms for that little while. There was safety, security, and protection in those strong but gentle arms, a sense that no harm could come to her, and that was good. What she felt was wrong was that she'd been physically stimulated, too, in a sweet romantic way. The way she felt was *different* than she'd ever enjoyed. It delighted her and at the same time caused her guilt and embarrassment. They had not spoken of it since. Their few contacts had been short, somewhat formal, and a bit distant. Apparently James, too, had felt an uncomfortable reaction that embarrassed him. Either that, or the other possibility she hated to consider. It *could* be that he had lost some respect for her because of her behavior. She had completely forgotten her dignity and her sense of propriety for a little while there. She cared very little for what anybody might have thought of her. Except for Big Etta, nobody really seemed to have noticed. But Abigail was very concerned that she retain the lieutenant's respect. She would not have been surprised if he never came to see her again, but he had. Still, their friendship was quite forced.

The death count after the collapse was a bit uncertain. Some of the prisoners were missing, but it was unknown whether they had escaped or were buried under the rubble. Several were known to be dead, as their bodies had been found and identified. Among these were listed a Mrs. Vandiver, Mrs. Selvey, Nannie Harris, Josephine Anderson, a sister of the guerrilla Bill Anderson, and Charity Kerr, who was a cousin of Cole Younger, another of the guerrillas. It was learned later that Nannie Harris was alive and well and living in Missouri.

A more immediate reaction to the tragedy was the response of the public. Despite the obvious facts and the utter lack of motive or purpose, rumors persisted that the destruction of the Women's Prison had been intentional, carried out by Union troops. The building had been undermined and explosives planted, it was whispered, to kill the wives and sisters of the border raiders. Sue Anderson truly believed this until her dying day, decades later.

There is always a need following such tragedies for friends and relatives of the victims to seek comfort in their grief. Many times this emerges as an irrational need to place blame and to seek revenge. Rumors continued to spread along the grapevine communications system of the border guerrillas, and there came a groundswell of demand for retribution.

It was only a few days after the collapse that William Quantrill, the acknowledged leader of the guerrilla forces, sent out word. All who followed the Southern cause as border raiders would gather at a rendezvous on Blackwater River in Missouri, a day's ride from the Kansas border. There was extensive scouting and intelligence, and it became apparent that a major raid was intended. Excitement mounted as more and more riders joined the encampment on the 19th of August. Quantrill led his raiders several miles toward the Kansas border, and during a rest stop, revealed their purpose. The hotbed and the headquarters of the hated abolitionists, he reminded them, had always been the city of Lawrence, Kansas. It was located just south of the Kansas River and a few miles north of the old Santa Fe road. It was some fifty miles west of the border. By riding steadily through the night they could cross the heavily patrolled border the next day and head northwest toward Lawrence. He proposed to completely destroy the town and to kill every abolitionist who resisted.

A cheer went up from nearly three hundred throats as the raiders remounted to travel on. Later that day they encountered a unit of 104 Confederate troops under the command of Colonel John Holt, who elected to join the raid. The next morning near the border they were joined by fifty more privateers. When they crossed the border near Aubry, Kansas, and stopped for an hour to rest and graze the horses, they were nearly 450 strong. They moved on.

They had been seen by the Union patrols, but Captain Pike, commander of the border post, having only a hundred troops, elected not to pursue. Instead, he sent a courier to headquarters to report the movement of guerrilla strength.

Passing through the towns of Spring Hill and Gardner, Quantrill headed directly northwest toward Lawrence. They were now in unscouted territory, and adopted a new technique as they traveled. A local farmer would be captured and forced to guide them until his knowledge was of no further use. Then the captive would be shot, and another seized. In the rolling hills between Gardner and their goal, ten conscripted guides were killed in one eight-mile stretch.

By this time, it was reported that they were followed. They rode through the night again, and at dawn on August 21, exhausted men and horses stood on high ground overlooking the town of Lawrence. Captain Gregg and five men rode toward the town to evaluate the situation. It was so quiet that they feared an ambush, and withdrew to discuss the situation.

"Well, I'm going in!" proclaimed Quantrill. "Alone if I must." He spurred his horse toward the sleeping town. The rest followed.

Lawrence was defended by two groups of new recruits, no more than thirty in all. They had only recently been issued weapons, and were quickly run down and killed. Some escaped to a brushy ravine outside the town.

The raiders galloped through the streets, firing indiscriminately at anything that moved. Unarmed civilians, stepping outside to see about the commotion, were shot down. There was virtually no resistance. Those who did not come out or were able to retreat back inside were no better off. The raiders began to burn the houses, shooting people who fled the flames. Many were trapped in the flaming inferno of their own homes.

The raiders smashed store windows, looting as they went. Several men entered a liquor store and began to celebrate, entering other stores to plunder small and easily carried valuables such as jewelry. Women who were unfortunate enough to be caught outside were accosted and stripped of jewelry and any other valuables. Wounded men were thrown bodily into the flames of burning buildings.

Nearly two hundred people had died by the time the thirst for vengeance was satisfied. As they prepared to leave, their horses heavily laden with loot, lookouts reported from Mount Oread above Lawrence that a pursuit column was approaching. Quantrill's force retreated to the south, systematically burning houses and farmsteads as they went. The progress of these columns of greasy black smoke allowed the pursuers to guess the direction of retreat and to try to intercept.

It had been intended to burn the towns of Prairie City, Palmyra, and Baldwin, where the Methodist Church had established Baker University five years earlier. The approach of a Union force under Major Plumb saved the towns and the school, as Quantrill altered his course and moved on southward.

Colonel Sandy Lowe of the 21st Kansas Militia mustered his troop, mostly from the Baldwin area, and joined the pursuit. Lowe held a smoldering hatred for the raiders because of mistreatment of his wife and child some years before. He had carried out many grudge killings already, and was eager to continue his program of vengeance.

The guerrillas were beginning to straggle, but so were the pursuers. The fierce August heat and the merciless pace were causing horses and men to drop.

Hiram Botts, somewhat drunk and his head swimming from heat and whiskey, found his horse stumbling. He stopped at a stream, and slid to the ground to drink while the horse did likewise. He wasn't sure, when he lifted his head, how long he had been there on his knees in the shallow water. None of his companions were in sight. Somewhat alarmed, he stood and looked around.

Then he saw a horseman approaching, in rough clothing like his own. Hiram grinned.

"Hell of a party in Lawrence, wa'n't it?" he offered.

The other man dismounted, drew his pistol, and pointed it at Hiram.

"I reckon so, bushwhacker. You are my prisoner. I'm taking you to Colonel Lowe."

The militiaman disarmed him and escorted him to a cluster of men who had stopped to water horses.

"Here is one of the guerrillas, Colonel Lowe," he reported. "You may wish to question him."

"Ah, yes!" answered the colonel.

He drew his own pistol, casually pointed, and fired directly into the chest of Hiram Botts.

"That makes forty of them I have killed," he remarked as he reholstered his pistol. "I had killed thirty-nine before."

The expression of surprise on the face of Hiram Botts faded to a glassy blank stare as he slid to the ground.

Quantrill managed to evade the pursuit, though he was followed into Missouri by federal troops. By this time the guerrillas were scattering, and the raiding force disappeared. The pursuers came up empty.

There continued to be sporadic raids on a smaller scale, but Quantrill moved farther east. He was fatally wounded in a raid in Kentucky in 1865.

Bloody Bill Anderson continued to raid and pillage. In October 1864, his guerrilla force of seventy men was ambushed near Albany, Missouri, by a Missouri State Militia unit. Anderson fell in the middle of the road with a pistol in each hand. His body was publicly displayed on a pole in the town square in Albany.

15

"Mrs. Botts, you have a visitor," the guard said from the hallway. Abigail rose and walked to the reception room at the end of the hall. It was jokingly called the "parlor" by the women prisoners.

They were treated well, but life was boring in the prison. It had become routine, in the month they had been here. She had made few friends. Big Etta had been released. Abigail had had no visitors at all. Visitors were an important event at the newly designated Women's Prison.

She had been officially notified of Hiram's death some weeks before, and had received that news with mixed feelings. It had been a long time since she had seen her husband, or even known of his whereabouts. She had written to her mother-in-law, but received no answer. Maybe Irma had come to visit.

Now, she realized that she had gradually lost any remaining feeling for Hiram. At best, he had been abusive. When drinking, even worse. There were times since she heard of his death that she felt something like sorrow, but not for herself. For Irma, maybe. But that part of her life was behind her.

Lieutenant Smithers was standing at the window as she entered the room. She had not seen him for several weeks, since he had been on detached duty. He had sent her a note to that effect after his sudden departure.

Now, she resisted the impulse to run to him as he turned. The uneasy tension between them was still there. Abigail attributed that to her unladylike behavior at the collapsed prison. She tried to smile.

"I . . . I thought you were gone for good."

He shook his head. "Sometimes I thought so, too." He took a deep breath. "My condolences for the death of your husband, ma'am."

She wished now that Lieutenant Smithers would understand her feelings. Instead, he seemed cold and formal. As much so, in fact, as he had on that day when he had arrested her for spying. She wanted to cry out to him, *Don't you see how I feel?*

Instead, she demurely dropped her eyes.

"Thank you, sir, for your concern."

"May we sit?" he asked, gesturing toward two chairs.

"Of course."

They seated themselves, and there was an uncomfortable silence. Finally, both tried to speak at once.

"Mrs. Botts . . ."

"How have you . . . ?"

Both laughed nervously.

"You first," she suggested.

The lieutenant nodded. "I have been in the area of Fort Scott," he began. "I took the liberty to look at your property. . . . The farm east of the fort. The house and buildings are still there. Your husband's mother had departed."

"But . . . Where . . . ?"

"Back to Carolina, I was told."

"Did she know?"

"About her son? Yes, she had been informed by the army. I was unable to determine what had happened to the body. There have been so many. . . . I fear some will never be located."

"Yes, I know. . . ."

"Your title to the property should be valid, I'm led to understand, when hostilities are past."

Lord almighty, she thought, *he came to talk about that?*

"Mrs. Botts," he went on, "Abigail . . . I hope you won't think me presumptuous, but . . ." He paused, embarrassed.

"Yes?" she prompted.

"Well . . . I know that you must have a decent time for mourning, but times are unpredictable, and I must let you know . . . That is . . ." He paused and shook his head. "Good Lord, this is clumsy. . . . May I have your permission, ma'am, to come courting . . . when possible, of course, and after a decent period for your grief?"

She nearly interrupted him with her answer before he finished, and tears filled her eyes.

"Why . . . yes, Lieutenant, I would consider such to be entirely appropriate. After a decent period, of course."

She smiled. This would make all the difference in her world. She was sure that Big Etta would have approved.

BOOK IV

✵

WOUNDS OF
WAR
1863

1

Jedediah Sterling strolled down the gangplank and up the slope toward the town. It was barely daylight, but he'd always been an early riser. It was a good time to spend a little while alone, to loosen his joints and muscles for the day, and a time to be alone to think.

There were few signs of life yet on the packet steamer *Prairie Queen,* behind him. A couple of sleepy-looking deck passengers had glanced at him as he passed. A fireman, stoking the firebox to start building up steam for the boilers, nodded to him. The town appeared even sleepier. The streets were empty. . . . A good time to walk.

His thoughts turned to the troubled times as he reached the street. Sometimes it seemed to him that life had been much simpler when he was young. But had it really been? He wasn't sure. There was all the confusion of this damnable war. . . . *That* was certainly more complicated than the old days on the prairie had been. Yet maybe not. There had never been much assurance, when meeting a party of Indians, whether they'd be friend or foe, a hunting party or a war party, or what their mood might be that day. But a man could meet that sort of threat head-on and deal with it. The frustration of the war, of having no control over his life and the lives of his family, was a constant worry.

He reached the street and looked south along the business district. . . . Massachusetts Street . . . The very name was an ever-present irritation for the sympathizers of states' rights and the Confederacy. Thousands of New England Yankees had poured in to vote the Union cause. He turned west and walked along Sixth.

He had accomplished a lot, he reckoned. He treasured some of the memories. The fur-trapping days . . . Now, he realized that he'd just gotten in on the tail end of the fur trade. At the time it had seemed it would last forever.

He couldn't figure exactly when life had changed. One day, somewhere, there must have been a time when he wasn't looking ahead anymore, but back. Yet, he couldn't for the life of him figure when that day had occurred and why he hadn't noticed it. It just seemed that one day he noticed that he was getting old. Well, older, anyway.

He'd never really understood when the old Pawnee men of his wife's town had mentioned it. *My bones tell me of a storm.* Jed had not taken it seriously. A figure of speech . . . Raven's people, like most of the Indians he'd known, had strange ways of expressing the relationship of body and spirit. Part of the time he thought he understood it. Part of the time he didn't even want to try.

After Raven's death he had rejected it entirely. Those were his bad times. Some of his period of grieving he couldn't even remember.

But now, he knew what the old men meant about the weather. The snows of quite a few winters showed their frost around his own temples now. The chill of forgotten nights on the prairie or in the mountains now returned in the stiffness of his joints on cold mornings when he swung his legs from the bed. Just a reminder, maybe, that time moves on.

The business had prospered, even with the war, and without Ben. He wished that young Ben, his partner in business, had not felt obliged to enlist. It was not easy to assume the responsibility of directing the company. And in spite of his feelings about slavery, Ben had joined the Southern cause. Well, if he were younger, he might have . . . No, no sense in that line of thought . . . He doubted that he'd have known which side to support, though. Probably the North, because of Suzannah. Slavery had to stop, though he didn't think the war was the way to do it. It would soon collapse because it wasn't practical economically. You couldn't feed a man for a whole year just to have him work a seasonal crop that took only a few weeks to harvest. Overstated, of course, but that was the problem, he thought.

He reached Tennessee Street and turned south, away from the river. He'd loop back by way of Massachusetts, he figured. He didn't want the steamer to have to wait on him. They would, of course, but it would not be good business to have it happen. After all, this trip was to check on the efficiency of the operation. Sterling and Van Landingham was still a conservative freight line. Their safety record was the finest, partly because of their caution. They'd tie up for the night or in bad weather rather than take risks. That was how the *Prairie Queen* happened to be at Lawrence, on the trip upriver to the docks at Junction City, with military freight for the fort.

His thoughts turned to Suzannah and the children.

Suzannah had kept him young in several ways. There was the physical part, of course. That was marvelously romantic and fulfilling. The yearning lust of her young body called for fulfillment. But it was not only that, or the warmth of their shared bed, which soothed his stiff joints on cold nights. As much as anything, it was her attitude. It was fresh and vibrant and compelling. It was as if she simply would not allow him to think himself old.

There had been a time for them, at first, when he wondered if his love for his lost Raven would contaminate his rapidly growing love for Suzannah.

It had not been so. Initially, he *had* been attracted to Suzannah because of her resemblance to Raven. Soon, that was behind him. The charm of his new love was, perhaps, her very difference. Her shy dignity balanced beautifully with her deliciously unpredictable sense of humor. Their love continued to grow even now.

There *was* a great deal of difference in their ages, of course. It startled him to think of it. When they met, he had still thought of himself as a young man, and she, a young woman. But he had been past fifty then, he realized. Incredible! Still, he had trouble accepting that he was in his mid-sixties now. *I don't feel any different than when I was forty,* he told himself fiercely. Well, maybe on cold mornings . . .

Suzannah, as far as he could tell, had not changed at all. She had been only half his age when they met, he realized. It had never seemed important, they had so many other concerns. Her status as a woman of mixed blood, and consequently a "person of colour," had been much more important than her age. That had never become a problem, though he still worried about it occasionally. Everyone seemed to assume that Suzannah's dusky coloring was from Indian blood. Both their children were light-complected. Odd, he reflected. . . . In some times and places intermarriage to Indians had been perfectly acceptable. In others, in "polite society," strongly criticized. It was still that way, to an extent, but more tolerated now. Suzannah was accepted among their circle of acquaintances.

They had few close friends. For those who must do business with the public, it was not good to become associated with any specific political faction. Since feelings about the war and the Union had been so extreme in this area, it was dangerous to express an opinion in public. Besides, Jed still had mixed feelings about it. He felt strongly that the states had certain rights as individual republics. In that respect, the Confederacy was right. *That,* he still felt, was the cause of the war. He deplored the fact that most people now considered it to be over slavery. *That's not the point!* he wanted to yell sometimes. But he kept quiet. He wondered what his father would have thought now, were he still alive. They had received word of his death from a sudden stroke during the riots in Baltimore at the start of the war. Jed had a strong suspicion that the Judge's demise was caused by the failure of his country, his beloved Maryland, to join the Confederacy.

The war had prevented him from returning to visit the family, and communication was unreliable. He and young Ben had continued to operate the shipping company as a separate entity from the business interests back east. Business was good, with all the moving of military supplies as well as population. So far, there had been no major threat to Sterling and Van Landingham's assets.

At Ninth Street, Jed decided he'd better turn back toward the docks. It was nearly full daylight now, and the captain would be wanting to start. Captain Brighton was a capable riverman, but logically concerned with the war and with the vulnerability of a riverboat. Several packet steamers had been seized and the passengers robbed by armed terrorists over on the Missouri side.

The progress of the war was the important concern of everyone. Jed was sure that, right or wrong, the South must eventually run out of armament. They lacked the production facilities of the Northern states. Already there was a report out of Macon, Georgia, that indicated the severity of the shortage. The gun factory at Griswoldsville was using the bronze from the church bells of Macon to cast the frames for revolvers to fight the war.

Many church denominations had split over the conflict. There were now national organizations of Methodist, Baptist, and Brethren churches designated as "Northern" and "Southern" conferences.

It had been expected that France, and perhaps even England, would come to the support of the South, but it had not happened. There seemed to be a hesitancy, a policy of waiting to see if the Confederacy would actually mount a realistic campaign. Yet, Southern victory would be followed by another for the North, and the military advantage seesawed continuously.

He was approaching Massachusetts again now, and a movement ahead caught his eye. On Ninth, farther to the east, he saw several riders. He stepped close to a building to watch them for a moment. No reason, except for their manner and his own instinct. Five of them . . . They rode slowly, casting furtive glances ahead and to both sides. They were heavily armed. Somewhere in the darkest corner of his mind, a tiny whispered warning . . . It had saved him before, and he had learned to listen. These men clearly had the attitude and mannerisms of scouts, those who travel in advance of a war party. Or, a military unit . . .

Moving slowly so as not to attract attention, he slipped around the corner onto Massachusetts, and then sprinted northward. They must get the steamer under way.

He was running when he reached the gangway and practically collided with the captain.

"Captain Brighton! Do you have steam?"

"Well . . . I . . . Almost. What is it, sir?"

"I'm not sure. But there are riders in the streets. They look like scouts for a bigger force."

The captain appeared concerned. "Federals wouldn't send in scouts. Let's move the ship!"

He hurried to where the fireman was working and quietly spurred him to faster preparation. Then he turned back to talk to Jed.

"It will be only a few minutes, sir. I would suggest that we cause as little excitement as possible. We can do without a panic."

"My thoughts exactly, Captain," Jed agreed.

"Thank you, sir. Maybe we can avoid any trouble."

The *Prairie Queen* started majestically into the current and was about to nose westward when the first shots began to sound. Then screams, more shots . . . *Many* shots. It was like a tattoo of distant drums.

"It would be quicker," the captain suggested, "if we go downstream with the current rather than continue our intended course."

"Do it!" Jed agreed. "We can make it up later, but not if they burn the ship at the dock. Let's get away from here."

The helmsman swung the wheel, and the ship responded, ever so slowly. Or so it seemed to Jed . . . Passengers were beginning to realize what was happening. There were screams and shouts of alarm.

"Look!" someone yelled. "They're burning!"

An ugly smudge of black smoke rose from somewhere in the town, and then another. . . . A squad of horsemen spurred down Massachusetts Street toward the river, firing random shots.

"Get down!" Jed yelled as bullets splattered against the stacks and the big engines. He had drawn his own pocket pistol instinctively, but realized that it was virtually useless at this distance. For a moment he wished for the old Hawken that now graced the mantel at home. *That* would let him teach the marauders a lesson.

The *Queen* was picking up speed now, her paddle wheel laboring as she began to draw out of range. There were a few more shots, but now they could see the plop-splash of the lead balls as they fell short into the river. The horsemen turned away.

"The whole damn town's afire!" said Captain Brighton in awe. "This is a major thrust, sir."

"I'm afraid so," Jed agreed.

Privately, he wondered if it was a major shift in the tactics of war. Were there Confederate units also attacking in the Kansas City area? The hurried trip downriver seemed painfully slow, as they looked back at the dark smoke that was visible for hours, rising from what had been the city of Lawrence.

.   .   .

It was the next day before they learned more of the story. Quantrill and his 450 raiders had escaped back into Missouri, eluding Union troops at Baldwin and Ottawa. The dead in Lawrence numbered more than 150, and the town lay in ruins.

But at least, Jed reflected, he was back home, and his family was safe for the present.

2

It was now several months later. The destruction of Lawrence had apparently been a random attack involving mostly volunteer raiders and only a few regular Confederate troops. Things were somewhat more quiet here, but still active in other areas.

Jed was seated at his desk, struggling with the paperwork that he hated, when a gentleman entered the office door.

"Mr. Sterling?" the gentleman inquired.

He was well dressed, and there was something about him that stamped him as an easterner. An abolitionist, probably. Jed stiffened a little. Although he sympathized with their cause, he thought they were going at it wrong. They'd certainly raised hell with their emigrant programs, trying to bring in voters. Even worse, the New Englanders who were in the emigration business for the money.

"I'm Jedediah Sterling," he acknowledged. "Can I help you?"

No matter if he agreed or disagreed with a prospective client, he *was* in the shipping business. They often carried cargo for people with whom he disagreed politically. It was part of this complicated way of life.

"I'm not certain I have the right man," the other said, some doubt in his voice.

His accent said no, not New England. . . . Ohio, maybe . . . He was possibly forty, fairly tall and capable looking, about the right amount of self-confidence. Jed felt that he could like this man.

"What is the nature of your need, sir?" he asked. "Shipping?"

"No . . . Well, yes, in a way. The war has created a problem. . . ."

He seemed hesitant, but then spoke again.

"My name is Adams, Mr. Sterling. We . . . I have carried on trade from New Orleans in the past, and still have connections there. Now, with the threat of blockade on the Mississippi, I have been forced to move my . . . ah . . . goods, through Texas, by land. I am seeking land transport, into Nebraska Territory or into Iowa. Can you help me?"

Jed's mind whirled. He knew of only one commodity that might be moving from New Orleans into the Northern states at this time: slaves. He did not answer for a moment. What was this stranger trying to do? Was the man a Northern spy, trying to . . . *My God!* Was Sterling and Van Landingham suspected of smuggling runaway slaves? Was this a trap? Or was this Adams attempting to *recruit* him to help with the rumored "Underground Railroad," the secret escape route for fugitive slaves? He was sure that it existed and had tried to avoid all thought of it. It was a cause for which he had sympathy, but for anyone to know his sympathies might draw attention to him, and to Suzannah.

His thoughts were interrupted as Adams spoke again.

"I was referred to you . . . that is, if you are the man . . . Do you know a Mrs. Thorpe in New Orleans? She runs a boardinghouse. . . ."

Jed could not make the connection for a moment, but then a chill of fear gripped his stomach. The boardinghouse . . . Yes, Mrs. Thorpe had helped him get Suzannah out of Louisiana, where her status was that of chattel property. He had wondered at the time, so long ago . . . Mrs. Thorpe had yelled at him indignantly when he had appeared with a newly purchased slave. But then the woman had changed completely, had helped them find clothing. . . . Yes, this man *was* a representative of the secret escape route. So was Mrs. Thorpe, even back then, and he had not realized it until this moment.

Now what? He could not help them without endangering Suzannah, who was technically still a slave. Quickly, he ran the options through his mind. First, he must deny that he was the man whom Adams sought. Then, to avoid suspicion . . .

"No, I'm afraid not," he said calmly. "I'm not familiar with New Orleans. Your Mrs. . . . Thorne, you said? She must have me confused with some other Sterling. It's a common name."

"Well, yes . . . ." The look on Adams's face was one of disappointment. "But she seemed so sure. Mrs. *Thorpe.*"

"Yes . . . Well, she's mistaken," he said curtly. "Now, about your business . . . Afraid I'm not interested. That sort of blockade running could be dangerous, could it not? I have to be careful of my reputation, you know. I don't know what your commodity might be, but I'd prefer to avoid any illegalities. I'm sure you understand."

Adams nodded. "Of course, sir. I certainly understand your position. Sorry to have bothered you."

He tipped his hat and stepped out the door. Jed could see him for a moment as he looked both ways and then set off down the street, jauntily swinging his gold-headed cane.

But now, fear gripped Jed. *The fellow knows,* he thought. *I didn't fool him a bit.* Could it be that they would try to blackmail him into helping the Underground Railroad? Not likely. *They* would be vulnerable to blackmail, too. He must talk to Suzannah about this!

Suzannah was calm about the threat, although he could see the fear in her eyes.

"Did he specifically *say* anything about the escape route?" she asked.

"No . . . Not that I recall . . . No, I don't think so, Suzannah. But what commodities are moving from South to North, except slaves? I think they're using the old Lane Road through Nebraska Territory into Iowa."

"Yes, I think you're right, of course. That Mrs. Thorpe . . . Even then, she seemed to know a lot about helping us. She's probably a key station on that end of the Underground Railroad. Maybe we should help—"

"No!" Jed interrupted firmly. "It would be too dangerous for you and for the children. We must deny everything, claim it's mistaken identity. If necessary, we'll move on west and change our name."

"No, no," she said, smiling. "It won't come to that, Jed. Those people are exposed to more danger than we are, if their activities come to light. *That's* our best protection."

He nodded. "You're probably right. Well, nothing to do but wait and see . . . *Say!* What about the children?"

"What about them? They know nothing. . . ."

They had decided during Suzannah's first pregnancy that they would never under any circumstances let their children know the manner of their meeting, or of their mother's status at the time. How would a child respond to the news that her father had purchased her mother on the block at a slave auction?

"Jed . . . ," she continued, "*they* would be classed as contraband, wouldn't they?"

He pondered for a moment. "Under some circumstances, I'm afraid so. I was thinking maybe they *should* know. In case of trouble, they'd be informed."

"No, Jed. In that case, their word would be more convincing if they have no idea at all. They must know nothing. Maybe when they're older. But by that time things will be better."

She kissed him softly.

"Maybe so," he agreed. "Suzannah, I can't tell you . . . This is my fault, for thinking you'd be safe here."

She smiled. "Jed," she whispered, "don't be silly. Look at what I was when we met, and what I am now. You've been nothing but good for me!"

He gave her a little hug. "And you, for me!"

They saw no more of the man whom Jed had believed to be an agent for the underground. He still believed so. But gradually they began to relax a little.

The children still knew nothing of the event that had caused Jed and Suzannah such a shock. Jed worried about them and what influences the war was exerting on their young lives. Still, on a day-to-day basis, there seemed to be little personal danger. And of course, these two had never known anything else. The unpredictable violence of the border had been going on since before the war, virtually all of their lives. They had been born into it, as a way of life. Suzannah struggled to teach them the niceties of civilization, and a solid background of reading, writing, and ciphering. In a way, they were protected by this veneer of gentility, and by the fact that their father was a reputable businessman without political extremism.

He was uneasy, however, over a parallel he saw. The children of his first marriage had been in a similar situation. Their world, among the Pawnees, had been one of violence. Raven's people were usually at odds with their neighbors. There were constant skirmishes, fights over hunting grounds, random killings. He had always considered their children safe from all of this because of the reputation and strength of the Pawnees. He had been right, until the fateful attack by Delawares, who had moved in to destroy the entire village and its occupants.

Jed had barely survived his grief and guilt that he had been absent at the time. Suzannah had helped him forget.

But now, an alarming analogy . . . What if he and his family had been living in Lawrence instead of Shawnee last spring? Quantrill's raiders had destroyed *that* town, much as the Delawares had destroyed his former home. . . . His and Raven's . . . *No one is ever safe,* he decided reluctantly. This was obviously even truer in time of war. His regret was that his children with Suzannah had known little else.

Neosho . . . How marvelous, yet how frightening, to see their daughter maturing into young womanhood. Jed realized that she was quite attractive in the bloom of her maturity, with her mother's dark beauty. But a part of him wanted to keep her a child forever. Her childhood had passed so rapidly. . . . Her breasts showed a ripe, curving fullness. . . . Now her once spindly legs were long and trim, with attractively curving calves. Now, of course, Suzannah had impressed on her the propriety of keeping female limbs covered. How different, in this civilized setting . . . Among Raven's people, a well-turned leg was to be admired.

He paused, startled at the thought. Raven must have been about this age when he met and married her. Sixteen or seventeen . . . This he found doubly alarming. How could he have a *daughter* of such maturity? He mentioned it to Suzannah, who laughed at him.

"How can *I* have such a daughter?" she teased. "*You* may be old enough, but not *I*!"

At any time, he knew, there would be suitors interested in the graceful and intelligent young woman. It could not be otherwise. Probably it would have happened already, except that many of the young men were away at war. That might be the one good thing about the war. The bad side was that the young men who were still around were not the best. The afflicted, unhealthy, shiftless, not to mention the renegades. One good thing . . . In this setting, at least, a young woman did not have the option of initiating the courtship, as Raven had had among the Pawnees when they met. In the setting in which they now found themselves, it would be appropriate for a prospective suitor to approach Jed, the young woman's father, and ask permission to call. It was almost amusing by comparison.

He was less concerned about Daniel, now ten. . . . No, eleven! They had named him for Daniel Boone, who had so long ago taken Jed under his protecting wing. It had been for only a few days, but probably the most important few days of his life as far as survival on the frontier was concerned. He had never been able to repay the kindness, or even thank him properly, yet he believed that Boone had understood.

The boy Daniel was quick and intelligent and fascinated by all things. Especially the prairie, the wide-open spaces of the big sky. This pleased Jed immensely, but worried him some, too. There might come a time when young Daniel would yield to the urge to see the great West, and would leave, as he himself had done. There really had been, he decided, a simpler time. It was a time, of course, when he had been able to carry everything he possessed on his back and in one hand. He was not prepared to do *that* again.

3

ꙮꙮꙮꙮꙮ

"M r. Sterling?" asked a man on the street one day.

"Yes. Jedediah Sterling," he acknowledged, a bit puzzled. The man was a complete stranger to him. A warning flitted through his thoughts. Was this another attempt to involve them in aiding runaways?

"Sir, I have a letter for you," said the other.

He was well dressed, in much the manner of Jed himself.

"A letter? What . . . ? How?"

The stranger reached into an inside pocket of his coat and produced an envelope, which he extended toward Jed.

The handwriting was familiar. . . . *Ben's!* But how could this be? Ben was fighting for the Confederacy. There was no mail service between . . .

"There are still some means of communication," the stranger was saying in a soft, slightly Southern accent. Virginia, maybe . . . "I am not at liberty to tell you how, but it is my pleasure to deliver it. Good day, sir!"

He tipped his hat with a pleasant smile and turned away down the street. Jed watched him for a moment, the determined stride and confident air. He was uneasy about this. It was good, of course, to have word from his nephew. Communication with someone in the Confederate army was next to impossible for one in Northern territory. Still, there was underground communication, he knew. Was this another attempt to involve him and Suzannah? Or, he wondered as he had before, was this man a spy, looking for evidence of treason against the Union?

· ——————————————————————— ·

There were spies and counterspies, and no one could be completely trusted anymore, he sometimes felt. He knew that there were others like himself, who saw the need to continue trade and communication, no matter what the outcome of the war. Yet, such people constantly ran the risk of being accused of treason. And in the border areas, such an accusation might be brought by either side.

He hurried to the office and nervously opened the envelope. A quick glance was somewhat reassuring. There seemed to be no urgent crisis in Ben's current situation at the time the letter was written. But that was many months ago, he noted by the date at the top. He adjusted his spectacles and prepared to read.

There were, in fact, two letters. One was addressed to Ben's wife, Lorena, and was sealed with a small blob of red wax. Jed wondered how Ben had managed that in the often primitive conditions of the military. He replaced that letter in the envelope and turned to the other, somewhat fatter letter. It was unsealed, but had been in the glued envelope, addressed to: Jedediah Sterling, Sterling and Van Landingham, Kansas City.

October, 1862

My Dear Uncle Jed,

I know not when I might have opportunity to send this letter. I shall begin it now, and add to it from time to time. If opportunity affords, I shall send it. It may never reach you, or may never even be finished. But, dear Uncle, I must try to convey to you my feelings about the War and about what I am doing here. Do I regret having enlisted? Sometimes. Would I do so again? Of course! Most of us would. There are some, of course, who enlist and then desert. We have some problems with these "repeaters," though not so many as there must be in Yankee regiments, where they collect the enlistment bounty and then "beat it," to enlist again later. They are poor soldiers anyway, with no scruples. They are called "beats" by both sides, and are despicable creatures, with no loyalty.

We often discuss politics in camp. Most of the men here can read and write, and have some degree of education. We are well-informed as to news, having access to several newspapers, which are read and reread and passed around until they wear out. We have formed a debating society, which argues such Resolutions as the cause of the war, much as you and I have done.

Is it over the rights of the individual Republics, the right to secede, to preserve the Union, or to free the Negro? I am not sure. When some of our troops talk of Freedom and Liberty they see no connection with slavery. Old Abe really raised Hell, with the Emancipation Edict. That pretty well makes it an Abolition war, much to my regret. A man said to me yesterday that Abe Lincoln should "have to sleep with a Negro every night of his life, and kiss one's ass twice a day." I don't like to hear such talk, Uncle Jed. I didn't think when I enlisted that I was fighting against Abolition. I still don't think so. But I wonder sometimes what I am fighting for.

Here, there was a space, before the letter continued in a slightly different ink. Jed removed his glasses and wiped his eyes.

The letter continued:

September, 1863

Much has happened since I wrote the foregoing.

I cannot believe that it is more than a year since I departed. I sometimes feel guilt that I have left you with the business to run, but I know that you will understand. I must answer the call to defend my country, right or wrong. Yet, what is my country? I once thought Maryland, yet she abandoned the cause of the Confederacy to become Yankee. I had come to think of myself as a Kansan, yet cannot see eye to eye with the Abolitionists. I do not . . . Could *not own slaves, but this should not be a matter for the Federation. It has virtually destroyed the Union.*

The newspapers we get from the North blame us. "Johnny Reb," we're called. Rebels! *Well, Uncle, I take pride in the title "rebel," when it means one who fights oppressive tyranny. What difference, now, from the oppression of King George a century ago, and that thrust upon the South today by Old Abe? George Washington was a rebel . . . Thomas Jefferson . . . Patrick Henry, "Light Horse" Harry Lee . . . All Rebels. Even Christ was called "seditious," was he not? Yet . . . I have begun to think that the war will never end until we do away with slavery. I hate to say so, but it has truly become an abolition war. Most of the men I know feel much the same. There are some of them who still can't see it. One has written his wife to urge her to* buy *slaves as an investment . . . Women and children, especially girls, to breed more slaves* after *the war.*

Many of us cannot see why the Yankees want to keep fighting, though. They could go home and let us be. Their homes and families are still there. Many of those in the South are destroyed. At least, our "Rebels" showed them a thing or two at Chickamauga.

Gettysburg must have been a terrible time, Uncle Jed. We read about it later . . . And Vicksburg has fallen to the Yankee siege! I've not been faced with a battle of that sort. Not yet, anyway.

We've been in some "skirmishes," as the newspapers call them, as distinctly apart from a "major battle." I have decided one thing: For the man being shot at, there are no "major" and "minor" fights. All are major *for those involved. The dead are just as dead, the injured still bleeding and hurting.*

November, 1863

Well, Uncle, here I lie in a hospital. No, not wounded. Pneumonia, the doctors say. Many of those here are sick, rather than wounded. Typhoid, pneumonia, and some injured, still recovering. The coming winter will bring more sickness, I fear.

At least, I still have all my limbs, and am improving, although very slowly. One good *thing . . . The food here in the hospital is far better fare than that of the soldiers in the field. Hot meals certainly surpass hardtack in every way.*

December, 1863

Still in the hospital. This is slow duty, Uncle. Had I known how slow, I doubt that I would have bothered to catch pneumonia. Mayhap I could have outrun it.

Christmas is coming, and there is little for which to be thankful. I shall spend it here, among the sick and dying, who miss their loved ones as I do. But, let me not be glum, I am alive, and many are not.

There are some interesting fellows in the ward here. We talk much about the war, and share our experiences. One man, an Arkansawyer, tells of the battle at Pea Ridge last year. Some of the men from Kansas were fighting there for the North, he said. There were Missouri units for both *North and South. A strange situation! His story, though, is of the valor of a troop of Indians from the Cherokee Nation. They were fighting for the South, as a result of their mistreatment and "removal" from their ancestral lands by the Yankee federal government, a generation ago. But according to him, a platoon of Cherokees overran and captured a battery of Union artillery! Can you imagine, Uncle Jed, the courage required to charge into the muzzles of* cannon? *And these men had never seen cannon before! But, they watched, and saw that after it fires, a cannon must be reloaded. This, they understood well. Waiting until the battery fired, they then charged the gun positions, and the cowardly Yankee gunners fled in terror.*

They dragged the cannons together in a pile and set fire to them, with dry brush and sticks. But alas! One of the guns had not been fired before the hasty departure of the Yankees. It exploded

*from the heat of the burning wooden carriages, killing or maiming
some of those engaged in an impromptu victory dance.*

*The North went on to win that day, as in so many cases since.
Uncle, I fear the war is going badly. I had hoped that the Yankees
would weary of it and give up their aggression to go home. But, it
seems not. Must we fight until only one man is left standing? If so,
that man will probably be a Yankee, because the North has greater
population. I would not talk so to my comrades, Uncle, but I fear
for our cause. I do not see the* unity *among our Southern states
that we have always felt in the "United States," now perceived as
the Yankee North. We in the Confederacy are pledged to function
as independent States, each to our own. Good in principle, and
would be workable if we were allowed. But the Yankee invader has
managed to turn the Abolition issue to his advantage. Answer me
this: Why did Mr. Lincoln not free the slaves in the* North? *Because he did not want to risk the wrath of* Northern *slave owners,
I'll warrant! And his freeing of slaves in sovereign republics* not *in
his Yankee Union is ludicrous, not to mention illegal under his own
Constitution.*

*Ah, well, this is all talk. Some of my thoughts as I lie here
recovering. It helps to sort out my thinking, to put it down on
paper. May your family be well, and may the coming year bring an
end to this damnable war. I shall write again soon, God willing.*

Ben

4

Sometimes it was better to concentrate on business. Thinking about the war and the condition the country was in was too depressing. In a couple more years, there wouldn't be enough men still around to plant the crops, or to care for and harvest them. Sterling and Van Landingham had discontinued some of the coach routes to the West.

These routes had become dangerous. The army was concerned with the war in the East, and there were fewer men to patrol the wide expanses of prairie. Several of the smaller posts had closed, and their troops were reassigned. As a result, Comanche, Cheyenne, and Kiowas became bolder. Sporadic raids along the Smoky Hill were becoming more frequent.

Other freight and passenger lines were feeling the same pressure. The Leavenworth and Pikes Peak, operating mostly on the Smoky Hill Trail, was in difficulty. Jed had heard rumors of the demise of the L.&P.P. The Pony Express mail service had lasted only a year, but the telegraph, not the war, had eliminated its usefulness. The Butterfield Stage was doing well, carrying passengers and mail throughout the West. The problem felt by Sterling and Van Landingham was not lack of business. Even the danger of attack could be handled with adequate manpower. *That* was the problem. Manpower. There were times when Jed longed to go out on the road again, himself. Those days on the prairie had been the good ones. But he realized that it was only a pipe dream, a memory of smoke from the pipes around long-dead council fires.

These were modern times. He was needed here, anyway, to handle the reins of Sterling and Van Landingham. Their one clerk could not do it alone. What were needed on the road were drivers, packers, escort "shot-gun" riders. And men became more scarce by the day as the war continued.

With reluctance, he finally decided there was only one way to proceed. They must discontinue most of the land routes, especially for passengers. Let Butterfield take the risks. Sterling and Van Landingham could still handle a little freight by joining other freighters on the trails. Coach travel was too much responsibility, with the risks involved to passengers. He'd keep a couple of coaches. . . . Maybe after the war . . .

There was increasing bitterness on both sides, and reports of atrocities were increasing. Vengeance for such acts seemed to create a burning drive. Southerners, frustrated at a series of losses, fought even harder and more viciously.

At Fort Pillow, Tennessee, Confederate forces, finding themselves facing Negro Northern troops, had presumed them to be former slaves. They had reacted to frustration with savage rage. Nearly four hundred surrendering Union troops, mostly Negro, were massacred. Whether the war had originally been about slavery or not was no longer a meaningful question.

Meanwhile, the river business for Sterling and Van Landingham had increased rapidly. Their packet steamers ran regularly from St. Louis to Leavenworth and up the Missouri to new towns in Iowa and Nebraska. New towns needed everything . . . tools, building materials, food and clothing, blankets, guns, powder and lead. . . . Everything. Their steamers on the Kansas River carried much the same kinds of goods to Lawrence, Topeka, Silver Lake, on west to Junction City, Fort Riley, and beyond. Military traffic in supplies and personnel from Fort Leavenworth to Fort Riley had increased considerably.

With increased presence of federal troops on the river, there was less danger of piracy now. Only a few years ago the Border Ruffians had boarded and searched the boats several times, looting them and threatening and robbing passengers. There was little of that now. In a way, some things were better, it seemed.

The new governor, Thomas Carney, was making it plain that he intended to steer Kansas through the troubled waters of her early statehood. Jed had been pleased with his friend's election. Dr. Charles Robinson, Territorial governor, had assumed the responsibilities of governor of the new state when Kansas was admitted to the Union in 1861. Jed had never cared much for Robinson's pompous ways, or for his close alliance with the abolitionist cause.

But Tom Carney was a man Jed could understand. A hardworking, self-made man from Ohio, Carney had come to Leavenworth to open the first wholesale house, Carney, Stevens & Co., only a few years ago. He had been elected to the state legislature in 1861, and to the governor's office in 1863, the first elected governor under statehood.

At his own expense, Carney had raised a force of 150 men as a border patrol to keep the peace along the military road. His guards were instructed to be in contact with each other at least once an hour as they patrolled. This private force had been discontinued at the request of General Ewing's Military District of the Border. Federal troops would take over the patrol duties. Carney had relinquished quite willingly, being involved not only as governor of the state, but at the same time as a captain in the home guard, which was often called to duty.

In Jed's opinion, Quantrill's destruction of the town of Lawrence might have been avoided if Tom Carney's guards had still patrolled the border. Only three days after his patrol's withdrawal, Quantrill had slipped between the federal squads on the military road with his force of 450 men.

But, that was behind them now. There was much more stability, even as the war continued. The legislature, caught up by the sincerity and enthusiasm of the governor, was accomplishing wondrous things. In their first session, they had accepted a land grant from the federal government for an agricultural college to study the farming techniques needed in the unknown conditions of the prairie. It would be located at Manhattan, in Riley County. They had provided for an asylum for the insane at Osawatomie, a penitentiary at Leavenworth, a state normal school at Emporia, and a university at Lawrence, already rising from the ashes. There were several church-supported universities now in operation, and the Methodist university at Baldwin City had already honored its first graduating class. Still, Governor Thomas Carney, with little formal education himself, felt the need of a state university, and donated a $5,000 personal gift for the establishment of the school at Lawrence.

The second legislature under his governorship had been equally productive. A bureau of immigration was established, and provisions made for an asylum for the blind in Wyandotte County as well as a deaf and dumb asylum in Olathe. These would not only provide refuge and shelter but serve as training schools. All in all, it was a good feeling to have a capable businessman at the helm, Jed felt, rather than visionaries with a personal ax to grind.

So, some things were better, or at least on the way to becoming better. The letter from his nephew had depressed him, though. He missed Ben, more than he realized, and not just in the operation of the business. Ben Van Landingham was a quiet thinker, with a droll sense of humor. He was happiest, it seemed, when he was deeply immersed in ledgers and columns of figures. His ideas regarding business were always sound. The details of cost and profit were as totally boring to Jed as they were fascinating to the younger man. Thus they had been a good team. Ben had always been content to handle the office, the books, and the contracts, while Jed saw to the stables, the rolling stock, and the packet steamers. Jed would much rather be outside, with the sun and wind in his face, than cooped up in the office. After all his younger years on the prairie, there was still the longing for the far horizons. He could understand the aversion of the plains-dwelling Cheyennes and Kiowas to a permanent building. Sometimes he felt trapped, himself, by the solid walls of the office. Like a caged animal, he needed to escape.

Ben's presence had helped. Ben would *rather* run the office, and disliked the day-to-day supervision of mules and wagons and teamsters . . . even steamboats. They had made a good team, and would again when Ben returned. Jed hoped that would be soon.

Meanwhile, Ben's wife, Lorena, seemed to be holding up. Lorena and Suzannah were of nearly the same age, and they related well. Probably this was as close a friendship as Suzannah could make. He understood that she would never be capable of deep relationships, except for their own. It would be too much of a threat to the secrets of her past. She could never share the little intimacies of girl-talk, without raising questions about her background. But, the two got along on a more superficial level. They could talk of their children and their husbands and the problems of household management. This, they did well.

Jed also felt that his association with younger people had been a great help to him in staying young at heart. Suzannah, Ben, Lorena . . . All were really of another generation, but he never thought of them in that way. Those with whom we work, we think of as contemporaries to some degree. There is less distinction by age if people have the same duties, responsibilities, and problems.

His thoughts returned to Ben. Surely, the war could not last much longer. Regardless of cause or purpose or anything else, the Confederacy was simply going to run out of men and matériel to fight.

The newspapers told of Lincoln's reelection, amid bitter criticism. Jed had mixed feelings. The President seemed to be taking advantage of the war to assume powers not really allowed him under the Constitution. Yet he seemed to have no aims of personal glory, only the unification of the country under the federation. Jed was not certain whether so much power in a central government was a good idea. Maybe sovereignty would be returned to the states after the fighting was over. . . .

Newspapers from St. Louis carried news that was disturbing.

With winter approaching, Sherman's army was marching through Georgia, heading toward the sea and destroying everything in its path. It was hard to imagine destruction on this scale. Crops, homes, barns, even orchards and trees, burned and utterly savaged in a strip sixty miles wide and three hundred long, cutting the South in two. The methods brought more bitterness.

Confederates under General Hood had made a thrust into Tennessee but were stopped by superior forces. It was not going well for the South.

There were rumors of an attempt at a peace conference to be held early in 1865. Jed hoped that it might lead to something constructive, but had his doubts. There was too much hate over the wanton killing and destruction by Sherman's forces.

Sherman reached Savannah late in December, soon after the complete destruction of Hood's army in Tennessee by Northern forces a few days earlier. The situation appeared bleak for the Confederate cause.

It was four days until Christmas.

5

In the early weeks of 1865, there were stronger rumors of a peace conference. Jed was optimistic. He had observed or taken part in several peace conferences during his years on the prairie. Nearly always it was possible to bring about some sort of agreement. In this case, it seemed the only logical way.

Both sides had suffered immensely. Casualties had soared, now nearing an estimated million of the finest young men of both nations, from battle or disease. The Confederacy's losses in goods and property as a result of Sherman's unprecedented war on helpless civilians were now estimated in hundreds of millions of dollars. Surely it was time to stop the bloodshed.

Both sides also suffered from desertion, as disillusioned soldiers found their ideals shattered in the horrible reality of battle. Here there was no glory, only fear and hunger and exhaustion and the smell of death.

Jed was sure that the time had come to "smoke the pipe" and settle differences. He had seen it end conflicts between warring tribes and nations. He had been present at treaty conferences between the army and various Indian Nations. Osage, Kansa, Kiowa, many others. It was a logical end to the strife that had destroyed the country, for the leaders of the two nations to meet and negotiate.

Word came after the fact. The conference had been held and had failed. President Lincoln and Secretary of State Seward had met with Vice President Alexander Stephens of the Confederacy and his assistant secretary of state, John Campbell. The meeting had been on board the steamer *River Queen,* in the harbor at Chesapeake Bay, on February 3, 1865. Lincoln had refused to discuss any terms that did not include his Emancipation edict and the restoration of the Union. The negotiations had collapsed.

Jed read the report in the newspaper with disappointment.

"They missed a great opportunity," he observed. "Now there will be more killing."

Suzannah was thoughtful. "Maybe it's best, Jed."

"*What?* How could you say that?"

"Well, what would be the status of slaves?"

"I . . . Oh . . . I hadn't realized. My God, Suzannah, slavery would still be legal in the North, wouldn't it? The Emancipation edict only mentioned states *in rebellion*!"

"I'm not sure, Jed, but that's the way I see it. I've been quite aware of such things, you know."

She smiled, a sad smile of wry humor.

Sherman, having looted Savannah, now turned north into the Carolinas. He continued the destruction, leaving in his wake only ashes and scorched earth in a swath sixty miles wide. In the wake of the troops came scavengers worse than the soldiers themselves. There was no authority to keep them in control, and to those who had lost everything came the final tragedy . . . anarchy.

By April, word came that in Virginia, General Grant's forces had captured Petersburg and the Confederate capital at Richmond. General Robert E. Lee moved his forces westward in an attempt to join General Johnston in Tennessee. But it was apparent that the war was over. Lee surrendered on April 9, to prevent further killing.

"Now what?" asked Suzannah.

Jed had finished reading the account aloud and now laid the newspaper aside. He removed his glasses and wiped his eyes.

"I don't know. It was bound to turn out this way, but . . ." He sighed deeply. "At least, it's over."

"Ben will be coming home," she suggested.

"Yes. We'll hope so. How long since we've heard?" he wondered.

"Last fall . . . But, Jed, he wasn't where the fighting's been. At least not then."

"Yes, that's true. We wait some more, I guess. Maybe we can expand the overland routes again. There will be a lot of emigration now, and men coming back who can drive and handle freight. . . . Well, we'll see. . . . I hope Ben hurries home!"

Suzannah laughed, the throaty musical chuckle that he loved. "I think we can count on it."

.   .   .

Jed had gone down to the livery the next day to check on the readiness of one of the wagon teams when a young man approached him.

"You are Mr. Sterling?"

"Yes . . ."

Jed studied the man, trying to size him up. Someone with a message? A letter from Ben, maybe? About thirty years old . . . Dark complexion, maybe some Indian blood . . . A breed? Jed still had contacts among the Cheyennes and the Kaws. Maybe a message from one of them?

"I was told," the young man said, "you might be hiring drivers."

Jed liked the solid, confident tone, the straightforward approach and eye-to-eye look.

"Maybe," he answered. "You have some experience?"

"Some. I been around horses all my life."

"Riding 'em or driving?"

"Both. Pony Express, a little while."

Jed looked over the lanky frame of the other man.

"A bit big for that job, weren't you?"

"A little bit. I did it."

There was a sureness in his voice. . . . *That's the way it was.* No room for doubt.

"You've driven a six-in-hand hitch?"

"Yes. In the army."

Jed noted that he didn't say which army. It did not seem important to ask. But there were quite a few Cherokees among the Confederates . . . a Cherokee general, even. Maybe this was a half-blood Cherokee. No matter. Jed was only mildly curious.

"You live around here?"

"I do right now."

In the past few years it had become a custom *not* to inquire deeply into anyone's past along the border. It could and *did* become dangerous. Jed let that line of inquiry drop.

"Well, we have only a few wagons on the road now."

The young man nodded noncommittally.

"I see. . . ." He turned away, as if he had expected a refusal.

"Wait!" called Jed. "I was about to say . . . we may want to expand. . . . The war winding down and all . . ."

The man turned back, a surprised look on his face.

"You'd hire me?"

"I'd try you. Hire you if you're any good. And provided I can get wagon contracts."

Just then, an idea occurred to him, a way to learn more if his guess was correct. He would toss out a couple of hand signs and see what sort of response it might produce. He signaled for attention, the sign that might mean either *"look"* or *"listen."*

Then, *"Are you hungry?"*

The response was quick and without thinking.

"Yes, hungry. Cut in two."

Then the younger man realized what he had done. . . . Revealed his Indian background without thinking.

"Better get something," Jed told him with no change in expression. He fished a couple of silver dollars out of a vest pocket and handed them to the still puzzled young man. "You know where my office is?" He spoke this question aloud.

"I can find it."

"Good. In the morning, then. Oh, yes, the café on the corner will have good food." *And they'll serve you, too,* he thought. Some restaurants wouldn't. Jed had a hunch that this man would understand his hidden meaning. The other nodded.

"I thank you, sir."

Walking on, Jed realized that he might have done a very stupid thing, giving money to a stranger whose name he did not even know on the slim chance of wanting to hire him later.

On the other hand, the young Indian had not *asked* for money. He'd asked for a job. There was a chance he'd be drunk in the gutter by evening. If so, Jed had lost a couple of dollars by poor judgment. He'd bet not, though. Somehow, he liked this young man. . . . Should have gotten his name . . .

The next morning, he went to the office as usual and sat at his desk. He shuffled through bills of lading, wishing for Ben's return so that he could resume attention to the outdoor portion of the company's interests.

His thoughts drifted to the young half-breed who had approached him near the livery stable the day before. The man had not made an appearance yet, but that was not surprising. The concept of time was different in the native customs. He smiled to himself as he recalled his frustration over that when he first lived among them.

When will the council begin? he would ask Raven. She would smile patiently and her answer was always ready. . . . *When the time comes.*

It was so for a hunt, or for any event. The sun rises when its time is ready, and sets in the same way, when it is time for it. The idea of marking time was ludicrous to Raven's people. One might as well paint a picture on the smooth water of a still pool, Swimmer had once told him.

So he was not surprised when the young man had not appeared by midmorning. Jed remained certain that he would arrive, when the time came.

It was nearly eleven, however, when the tall figure stepped through the door and nodded a greeting. The man did not appear disheveled, as he might from sleeping off a drinking bout in the street. Jed nodded in return, but then was completely startled when the other stepped toward the desk and placed a silver dollar on the polished surface.

"What . . . ?" he asked, puzzled.

"This one was not needed."

"But it may be . . ."

The young man nodded. "That is true. But I am not yet in your employ."

"It was a gift!"

"Oh! Forgive me, Uncle. I did not see that. I am grateful. Your heart is good."

With a quick motion, he swept the coin from the desk and dropped it into the pouch at his belt.

Jed understood. Pay for work done, or to be done, was white man's way. A gift was something else. To refuse a gift would be extremely impolite. It struck Jed as amusing that this Indian was trying to go by white man's rules, and he, Jed, had been trying to follow Indian custom. But he liked this young man.

"How are you called?" he now inquired. "I should have asked you before."

"John . . . John Burns."

"Very well, John. I . . . Well, you know my name."

Burns said nothing.

Jed wondered at the white man's name used by the young man. "John" was often a name applied to any Indian by the teamsters. John or "chief." There had been times when he had resented the familiarity of such usage. It was intended to be demeaning. Yet that was likely where this man had acquired it. About the "Burns" part, it was anybody's guess. That could be a corruption of his Indian name, or the name of a white employer, or a completely random choice as John became civilized. No matter.

"Where . . . Where are you staying?"

Jed had almost said "where are you camped." For reasons he could not completely explain, he was uncomfortable in this conversation. He was finding a tendency to slip into native terms and phrases, common among trappers and traders. But would John Burns, attempting white men's ways, be offended? Would Jed appear to be talking down to him?

Jed would have liked to ask which was his tribe, or more properly "nation," but again was unsure how such a question would be received. John Burns might be offended.

"I slept at the livery," Burns was saying.

Jed merely nodded, but so far, his impression of this John Burns was quite favorable.

6

John Burns proved to be a useful addition to the company. He was scrupulously honest, hardworking, and frugal. He was quiet and uncommunicative, except when necessary. . . . A loner . . . Jed wondered about his background and whether he had a family, but did not ask. If the young man wanted to talk about it, he could. Maybe he would when the time was right.

John's most remarkable area of skill was with horses. The operator of the livery stable remarked on it to Jed.

"Best hand with a horse I ever seen!" he declared. "That boy kin *talk* to horses, seems like."

"Where did he come from?" asked Jed.

"Dunno. He just showed up one day, asked to work for a place to sleep. You hired him?"

"Well, yes. I can use him as a driver, I figure. He says he's driven a six-hitch."

"You know where?"

"Army, he says. His business, I guess."

"Reckon so. Glad you can use him, Sterling. I like him."

"I do, too. Is he still staying here?"

"Yes. He was sleepin' in the hayloft, but I've got a cot in the tack room. I'm lettin' him use that. He's breakin' a few horses for me."

"Good. I don't know when I'm going to need him, beyond a run or two to the fort."

"Well, he's a good man, for an Injun!"

"He told you that?"

"No, I just figgered. Dark complected, don't talk much."

"I see. . . ."

"Say . . . You heard anything about railroads?" the liveryman asked.

"What do you mean? They're coming, I suppose, after the war."

Actually, it was a matter of considerable concern to Sterling and Van Landingham. Railroads would furnish major competition in the freight and transport business. Already, there was a network of rails east of the Mississippi. A couple of companies had lines in Missouri. He'd heard rumors of a rail company organizing in the Leavenworth-Atchison area. His friend, the outgoing governor Tom Carney, would know. Maybe he'd ride up to Leavenworth for a visit. . . .

The liveryman went on. "I suppose so. Folks will still need horsepower. Some things the 'iron horse' can't do." He chuckled. "But I meant on the rivers."

"What?"

"Oh . . . Well, you know the legislature declared some of the rivers not navigable."

"Of course."

That had been a joke among Sterling and Van Landingham's steamboat captains. They had been navigating those rivers for years, and took pride in the challenge they presented. A snag or sandbar, a slight change in the channel after a flood . . . All in a day's work. There were reputations at stake, and discussions as to which captain could smell or feel danger. . . . Who had the most skill in the use of the winch and grasshopper poles to slide over a sandbar . . .

"We're still doing it," he told the liveryman with a chuckle.

"I know. I just wondered why the legislature would want to say it couldn't be done."

Jed felt a hint of warning in the dark recesses of his mind. *Why, indeed?* And why hadn't he noticed it? There was a reason, somewhere, and he'd been too busy to notice. . . .

On the way to Leavenworth Jed had time to reflect. It was good to be under the open sky again with a good horse under him.

Thomas Carney would have a better idea than most about what was going on. Carney had a finger on the pulse of the state, it always seemed to Jed. An idea man, with a farsighted eye to the future. He had finished his term as governor, and declining to run again, turned the reins over to Samuel Crawford, also a capable man. There had been those who wanted Carney to run again, but he had refused, protesting that his business interests needed attention.

·   ·   ·

Carney rose from his desk to greet his friend, his hand extended.

"Jed! Good to see you. You came in today?"

"Last night. Stayed at the hotel. It's a bit long for a one-day trip."

Carney laughed. "Yes, if you have business at your destination. What brings you here?"

"Just a visit . . . Checking on the riverboat facilities. I like to know how the packets are doing."

"I know. . . . You stay informed, Jed."

"I try. How is life without politics, Tom?"

"Well, not entirely without . . . Sit down, Jed . . ." He pointed to a chair. "I've been elected mayor."

"Mayor?"

"Well, yes. I've felt needed. There's a lot going on. The war winding down and all. Kansas will open up now. You're in a good field, transportation!"

"I . . . Yes, I think so." He decided to come right to the point. "Tom, what do you know about railroads?"

An odd look came over Carney's face. Surprise, mixed with caution.

"You're wanting to invest in railroads, Jed?"

Jed was startled. That wasn't what he'd had in mind, but he'd play along, at least for the moment.

"Maybe. What do you know about them?"

"That they're the coming thing. One of my goals as mayor, to bring rails to Leavenworth and the fort. Think how easy your trip here from Kansas City would have been. Yes, I can put you in touch with people who are looking for backers."

"No, that wasn't quite my purpose, Tom. Not yet, anyway. My partner . . . You know my nephew, Ben? He's not back from the war yet. He'd have a say in it, of course. I just want to be informed."

"Of course. Well . . . You may have heard about the outfit in Omaha . . . Union Pacific, I think it's called. They haven't laid any track yet, but they want to build straight west along the forty-second parallel. Then there's the Atchison, Topeka, and Santa Fe. . . . Chartered in 1859, but the war's slowing them considerably. And, there are several groups here interested in incorporation. I can't be too specific, you realize. Confidentiality . . . Goes with the responsibility, you know."

"Certainly," Jed agreed. "But how do you suppose this will affect my operations, Tom? I know it will, but we've cut back on the land routes already because of the war. Drivers scarce, the army even scarcer, and the Indians restless. We'll start back up with more traffic, I suppose. Meanwhile, the riverboats are busy. Our packets can carry up to two hundred tons of freight, you know."

Carney nodded thoughtfully. "Yes, I know. And you've had few wrecks. . . . Very efficient operation. But a train of railcars, even more so . . . One steam engine, *pulling* cars on rails, can move even more freight, and *faster*. Did you know, Jed, that some of the trains can approach fifty miles an hour?"

Carney's eyes glowed with enthusiasm.

"I'd heard that. Wasn't there a theory about how fast it's possible to travel? A physical limit to the human body's tolerance?"

"Yes, the 'mile a minute' idea. But don't believe it, Jed. We're pretty close to it now. I think we'll *exceed* it. But yes, I think rail transport is the coming *thing,* both passengers and freight."

"But it requires so much construction. Roadbeds, rails . . . It must be terribly expensive to start up, Tom."

"Of course. And there are also trestles to build over uneven country, and bridges. . . ." Carney paused, as if he'd said too much. Then he continued. "Cost can be handled. A short section of track, then put the profits from that into more track and roadbed. I expect the federal government to subsidize construction, too. It's to the advantage of the Union to connect the continent with rails. You should consider investment, Jed."

"Yes . . . Well, I'll think on it. It's certainly an interesting situation. Thanks for the information." He started to rise.

"Anytime, Jed. Won't you have supper with us this evening?"

"No, thank you, Governor. I'd best be starting home. Another time, perhaps."

They shook hands, and Carney walked with him through the outer office of the wholesale firm toward the street door, visiting about the weather and the end of the war.

As they neared the open doorway, there rose a commotion from down the street. People were running toward the telegraph office. There were shouts and yells, and a woman screamed and fainted in the street.

"What . . . ?" mumbled Carney.

The two of them started toward the scene, but were met by a man who was coming toward them. There was a blank, frozen look on his face, and his gait was stiff and wooden, plodding like one half asleep.

"What is it?" Carney demanded. "What's happening down there?"

The man stopped and slowly turned a blank stare toward them. His eyes seemed unfocused, as if there was no spirit behind the pale face. Finally he managed to look at the two men. For another moment his mouth moved but he seemed unable to speak. Then, in a hoarse whisper . . .

"On the wire . . . The President is dead. . . . Somebody shot him. . . ."

He looked on through and past the two, and moved on down the street, staggering from side to side a bit under the burden of what he had just learned.

.   .   .

The shock was also a heavy blow to Jed. There had been times when he hadn't entirely agreed with "Father Abraham," but by and large, he had always felt that Lincoln had tried to be fair and considerate. He could see no leader on the scene to take over the reins of a fragmented nation. It took him a moment to think of what would happen next. . . . The vice president would succeed to office, he supposed.

It took a while longer to think of that man's name. . . . Johnson? Was that it?

7

The last Confederate troops surrendered within a few weeks of the President's death. Andrew Johnson had been sworn in as the seventeenth president of the United States in his hotel room, after visiting the bedside of the dying Lincoln.

A Democrat from Tennessee, the new President was a complicated man. As a senator in 1860, after Lincoln's election to his first term, Johnson had made a powerful plea against secession by the Southern states. He owned eight slaves himself, and opposed abolition, but his loyalty to the Union came first. He opposed Lincoln. . . .

"I voted against him; I spoke against him; I spent my money to defeat him; but I still love my country; I love the Constitution; I intend to insist on its guarantees."

Tennessee had voted to secede from the Union anyway, and Johnson doggedly campaigned to restore his native state to the Union. In 1862, with Union troops controlling much of Tennessee, Lincoln had appointed Senator Johnson as military governor. Johnson held elections for voters who would take the oath of loyalty to the Union, and by 1864, Tennessee was again eligible to send representatives to Congress as a Union member.

Northern Democrats, believing in the Union, slavery or not, had joined the Republicans to nominate Lincoln for a second term in 1864. The nomination of Johnson as vice president had assured Lincoln's reelection by a large margin.

Now, with the war ending, Johnson inherited an even more troubled country. Most Northern politicians supported Lincoln's plan to restore the

Union as quickly as possible, with no further penalties against the suffering South. But a radical group, led by abolitionists, wanted to punish the states who had been in rebellion, placing them all under military rule. The status of freed Negroes was unsure.

Johnson favored leniency, with the right of each state to decide on her Negroes' status as citizens and voters. This offended the abolitionists in the Senate, who refused to seat the Southern delegates. Johnson had already reappointed Lincoln's entire cabinet.

"I don't know what will happen," Jed confided. "Suzannah, this is a very dangerous situation. There's one faction who would indict every Confederate soldier as a traitor. That's almost everyone in the South. I don't know whether this Johnson can hold the Union together."

"And he's a slave owner?" she asked.

"Yes . . . Apparently he still thinks that's within the Constitution. But, he's willing to be moderate. If the Congress votes against it, he'll probably have to go along."

"Johnson did announce amnesty for Confederate soldiers, didn't he?" Suzannah asked.

"Yes, before the Congress convened. A good move," Jed observed. "It would be hard to undo. I still question whether the President has a legal power to do so, if it's done, now."

"Has he freed his own slaves?" asked Suzannah sarcastically. "Under Lincoln's edict, he can still own them."

"That's true. Lord, it gets complicated, doesn't it? When Tennessee voted loyalty to the Union, I guess their freed Negroes became slaves again. The whole thing makes no sense, does it? It will probably take Constitutional amendments to sort out the status of former slaves."

"If they *are* freed, Jed, where will they go? What can they do?"

"I don't know. . . . I suppose some can hire on, to do what they've been doing, but for pay."

"Maybe. A lot more will want to leave, to get away. And anyway, Jed, who has any money now to *pay* them? The whole South is destitute. They've lost *everything*."

"I know. . . ." He took her in his arms. "But how fortunate we are, to be *here*. For a while there, I wasn't sure. Now, things are much more settled. We're well located for the recovery."

At least, he hoped so.

"Jed, who is the young man who brought the firewood? I haven't seen him before," she noted a few days later.

"John? John Burns, he's called. Didn't I tell you about him?"

"No, I don't think so. He works for you?"

"Yes. Something wrong with him?"

"No, no. On the contrary, Jed. He's clean, polite. . . . Efficient. Where did he come from?"

"Don't really know, Suzannah. He just sought me out to ask for a job. Been in the army, good with horses."

"Which army?"

"I'm not sure. He's quiet, hasn't said much about his past. But that's not unusual, nowadays."

"He's dark. . . . A runaway, you think?"

"What? I hadn't thought of that. I'd assumed he was a 'breed. He knows hand sign. Of course, a great many people do. Does it matter?"

"No. Not really. I just wondered. Our daughter was quite impressed, I think."

"Neosho?" he asked in astonishment. "But she . . ." He fell silent.

"But she's just a little girl? Is that what you started to say?" Suzannah teased. "Face it, Jed. Your little girl is a young woman. Young men are scarce. This one is clean and polite and has a nice smile."

I'll fire him before anything starts, Jed thought. But it was only a passing idea. He was still reeling with the realization that Suzannah was right. Soon Neosho would be ready to leave the nest. *But I'm not ready,* he wanted to say.

"Maybe I can find out more about him," he offered.

"No matter, Jed. But we should be aware. These are unsettled times. And sometimes I wonder if we've overprotected our daughter."

"Probably. But she's still . . ." *A child,* he'd started to say. Yet many girls were married at sixteen and seventeen, he knew. Neosho must be . . . My God! Eighteen, going on nineteen?

Yes, they had overprotected her. He, because of the agony of having lost his family . . . Raven and the children . . . A girl and a boy . . .

Suzannah, too, had been overprotective of their children. Her concerns were for their legal status. They as well as Suzannah herself might under some circumstances be considered "persons of colour" in some places. She was now passing as white, but there was always the underlying threat lurking in the back of her mind that the past would come back to haunt them all. Actually, she had wondered whether her own marriage to Jed would be considered legal. In some states, interracial marriage was forbidden. Their children might be considered illegitimate. Worst of all, they dared not ask. That in itself might arouse suspicion. Absolutely no one in their lives knew, and no one must know . . . ever.

The stranger who had approached Jed and had hinted about the Underground Railroad had upset her greatly for a while. Mrs. Thorpe, who ran a boardinghouse in New Orleans, had been instrumental in their successful departure. Nearly twenty years ago . . . Good years . . . How clumsy and amateurish their efforts had been. . . . Only some lucky accidents and misidentification by the officer on the packet steamer . . . Suzannah had managed to "cross over" almost by accident.

She felt some slight remorse that they had not been able to help Mrs. Thorpe with what was probably part of the underground escape network. But it was simply too risky for the children, who had no idea of any shadow in their mother's past.

Now, Neosho was almost the same age that Suzannah herself had been when Jedediah Sterling bid for her on the block. She had thought *that* the end of her life, and it had become only the beginning. There had been good times and bad, but they had weathered it all together. She smiled to herself, hoping for as good a life for her daughter.

This young man, though . . . He reminded her of Jed in his younger years, when they had met. A bit younger, probably, than Jed had been. It was hard to tell. John Burns could have been anywhere from twenty to fifty. His skin was smooth and tanned from outdoor living, but his facial features suggested Indian blood. Jed's discovery that the young man was fluent in hand-sign language supported that idea. Probably, she guessed, one of the Civilized Tribes, maybe Cherokee. The Cherokee Nation had a reputation for thrift, hard work, and affluence. There was much interaction along the southern Kansas border. To "go to the Cherokee" in marriage was a social step upward. And Suzannah, although she was not certain, believed that she carried some Indian blood herself. A shadow of doubt crossed her mind. . . . Was it possible that a reintroduction of dark blood would combine to produce a *darker* skin . . . ? She shook her head. She could not concern herself with that.

Then a startling thought occurred. She was worrying about the skin pigmentation of her *grandchildren*! *I'm not ready to be a grandmother!* she thought in a wave of panic. Jed would laugh at her, probably, if she told him.

But John Burns . . . He seemed a good man. Probably about thirty, she had decided. A hard worker, able to provide for a wife. And men were scarce, not only on the frontier, but everywhere. The entire nation had sacrificed her young men to the gods of war.

They had read various estimates of casualties and deaths, but no one had an accurate count. Yet it was obvious that at best, hundreds of thousands of women in America would be without husbands. She was aware of some of the possible solutions. Among the Indians, especially the plains tribes, who were frequently warring, there was a heavy loss of young men. Widowed or single women often joined the households of their sisters as second wives. Jed had told her about this. Suzannah did not see how a woman could *share* her husband. At least, *she* would not want to. Yet, it was apparent that a woman had to live somewhere.

The Mormons, who had been hated and feared and sometimes massacred as they migrated westward, had lost many men. There had been killing in Missouri. . . . The massacre at Haun's Mill, and more killings at the Mormon towns of Far West, Missouri, and Nauvoo, Illinois. They had solved the problem of excess women in the same way . . . multiple marriage. And, they had been even more hated and persecuted for it.

Suzannah also recalled Bible stories of men with several wives, probably for the same reasons. But this was too close to home. She wished for her daughter, hers and Jed's, a life with a husband and a family, and if possible, the happiness that she and Jed had found. There had really been no suitors, and it was just as well. But now . . . Well, it might be a good thing to learn a bit more about this John Burns. She'd talk to Jed about it.

8

$$\overline{\text{୩ᘁᘁᘁᘁᘁᘁᘁ}}$$

"I don't want to question him," Jed protested. "John has his reasons for not telling everything he knows, maybe. Or maybe he's just a private sort of person. Most Indians are a little reluctant to trust whites. All that I need to know is that he's a good worker, honest, and acts as a gentleman."

"But, Jed, do you know enough to permit him to court your daughter?"

"Suzannah, that hasn't come up yet." He paused, then went on. "Why? Is there something that I don't know?"

"No, no. Just a feeling. A woman can tell, you know. The way they look at each other when he's around."

"He's around *here*?"

"No, Jed. Just when you've sent him with some errand. Like the firewood last week."

"Oh. You didn't mean . . . He hasn't come calling on his own, then?"

"Of course not," she laughed. "He wouldn't, without asking, I'm thinking. My, but you're nervous about this!"

"Sorry . . . This is a very hard thing for me to accept, a grown daughter."

She touched his hand.

"I know. For me, too. That's why we need to understand what's going on, and to learn more about this John Burns."

.   .   .

Days passed, and there seemed to be no logical way to learn more about Burns. Jed tried to find opportunity to observe the younger man, but even that was difficult. As for questioning him, Jed was still very reluctant. It would simply be a breach of etiquette.

He smiled a wry smile to himself as he thought of the unseen, unspoken rules by which people live. . . . The polite, strict grandeur and pretense of his father's house in Baltimore . . . The simple, rough understanding of the rules of the traplines and the fur trade . . . The Indian Nations, each with intricate, complicated rules of its own . . . Then the trails and wagon trains, requiring an entire set of new customs and more rules, implied or stated.

The border years of simultaneous settlement and impending war stood alone in the development of complicated rules for survival. Among these, one of the strictest: *Don't ask questions.* Even an attempt at inquiry might drive a stranger into a frenzy of murderous activity. Or, possibly, it could mark the questioner for later execution. Even with the war winding down, it would be a long time before the frontier recovered from this necessary secrecy about one's past.

So, Jed waited and watched. He tried to find odd jobs for John Burns to keep him occupied between wagon trips. It also gave him more opportunity to become better acquainted. That, however, was slow. Burns seldom engaged in conversation, and then only when necessary.

Once at the livery, Jed happened to step into the stable to find John Burns rinsing a shirt in a bucket of water. He was stripped to the waist. In the light that filtered into the big barn, Jed was startled to see a huge scarred area across the young man's back and left shoulder. It was typical of the scars left by fire. . . . Shiny, wrinkled, and drawn, puckered like tight-stretched cloth. It reached from neck to waistline, disappearing below the top of his trousers. Jed could see that the scarred area also reached around the left side of the rib cage. He marveled that anyone could survive a burn of this magnitude.

He withdrew quietly, not wanting to invade the young man's privacy. This discovery explained another thing Jed had noticed. Burns seemed to favor his left side a little. . . . The arm not quite so strong, his strength to lift a little less on that side.

Burns . . . Of course . . . In an Indian culture, this was a logical way to designate a person. A specific characteristic, known to all. He thought of people he had encountered, and the names by which they were known. Tom Fitzpatrick, the mountain man, known to the trappers as "Old" Fitz because of his prematurely white hair, but to the Indians as "Broken Hand," due to an accident while loading his rifle years before. One of the Bent brothers, Charles, was called "No-Arm" because of a missing upper extremity. The other Bent brother, William, was "Hook-Nose." Burns . . . Of course. Undoubtedly an accident in childhood. It would be applied to an individual as a name simply as a fact of life, without any stigma. No different than nicknames like Red or Shorty or Slim or Curly among the teamsters on the Santa Fe Trail.

The "John" designation might have been bestowed by a priest or clergyman, or even by an Indian Agent on a reservation. But it was nothing about which to inquire. Jed resolved to simply observe further.

In the ensuing weeks and months there were many distractions. It was apparent that Tom Carney's hints about the railroads were based on reality. Rail companies were organizing quickly to take advantage of the expected surge of civilization into the Great Plains. Kansas City would be the gateway. But the bridging of the rivers for rails would be the end of the river steamers. Jed began to realize why the rivers had been declared "not navigable." This would completely sidestep any legal arguments about infringement upon the rights of the riverboat industry.

Jed pored over maps by the hour, trying to fathom what plans to make. He wished that Ben would hurry home. He hated to make momentous decisions such as they now faced without consultation. It had been a long time since Ben's father, Peter, had shown much interest in the western branch of the company. In fact, they corresponded quite rarely now since the death of Jed's father, the Judge. The legal structure of the corporation had been separated at that time into eastern and western branches, with no real accountability. It had seemed best with the impending border problems. Each branch of the family operated that portion of the business with no input from the other.

But now, Jed hesitated to make the major decision. What should be done with the riverboats? He sought Suzannah's advice. She always seemed to be able to cut through to the heart of a problem. He spread the maps on the table.

"Now here's the problem, Suzannah. Our packets run from St. Louis to Kansas City, and probably can still do so. I doubt that many low bridges will cross the Missouri, at least for a while. Now, we have a few boats on the upper Missouri. But it appears that our Kansas River run, from Fort Leavenworth to Fort Riley, is about over." He pointed to the map. "The military will use rail or ground transportation. Our docks at Lawrence, Topeka, and Silver Lake will have to close."

"What are your choices, Jed?" she asked.

"Well, one would be a legal fight in the state legislature. But I'm afraid that's too late. They've already declared that the rivers can't be navigated, and it's the law. Getting a law *off* the books is next to impossible, I suspect. So, we still have the Missouri from St. Louis and on upstream past

Leavenworth into Nebraska and Dakota Territories. The Platte's not navigable, even without the legislature's say-so, for very far."

"So . . . ?"

"Well, we could expand more runs on the Mississippi, or more on up
the Missouri, which seems a better move. We could limit our runs upstream
to Leavenworth, or to Council Bluffs, here, or on north. There are towns
growing on both sides of the river, in Nebraska and Iowa. Omaha's almost
as big as Council Bluffs now, and Sioux City is a good market. On up into
the Dakota Territory . . ."

His narrative trailed off with a sweeping gesture to the northwest
portion of the map.

"Did you want to go there?" she asked bluntly.

"What? Oh, you mean . . ." He smiled. "No, no, Suzannah. At one
time, yes. Maybe I even envy those who *will* settle there. But I've seen it,
some of it, anyway. Good country, but no, we've put down roots here, now.
Why . . . did *you* want to go?"

She stepped close and put an arm around his waist, snuggling against
him. "No, no. I love wherever you are, but I'm very happy here, Jed, troubles and all. But it will be better now. . . . Won't it?"

"It should. But back to the maps. What should we do? I doubt that
we should wait for Ben. It might be months before he can get home. Has
Lorena had any letters?"

"I don't think so. That may mean he's traveling. You should go ahead
with planning."

"So I thought," he nodded.

"Jed, you asked what I think. It seems to me that you have several
choices, but let's look at one at a time. One would be to sell all the riverboats
and expand our land transport. The other extreme, to keep all the boats and
expand on the upper Missouri. In between, sell part of them, keep some, and
just choose where you want to operate."

Again, he marveled at her ability to cut to the heart of a problem. He
smiled at her.

"What would *you* do?"

"If I were you?" she teased. "Well, if I'd decided not to explore the
northwest mountains . . ."

"Yes, that's decided."

"Then sell some of the riverboats to companies operating there. Keep
whatever you need to operate from here. Run from St. Louis to Omaha, or
Sioux City, even. Unless you want to run on the Mississippi . . ."

"No, that's a different kind of traffic. I think not. It could be considered later, though, if Ben wants to."

"Good! That makes sense. Now, one more thought: I would invest
the money from the sales in railroads."

"Railroads? Our competition?"

"Of course. Jed, they have immense political power. They've proved that already. That's why we're talking about it now, isn't it?"

"Well . . . yes, I guess so."

"It gives a solid choice to the company's present land transport business. Trains will carry freight, passengers, and mail, and you can furnish stagecoaches and freight wagons for connections where there are no tracks."

"Yes . . . And expand whichever is needed . . . We'd probably need some rolling stock."

"Maybe. You have some not in use, though, don't you?"

"Yes . . . Hmm . . . I could have John greasing axles, oiling wheels. . . . I'll approach some of the Missouri riverboat operators, sound out the market for some of our packets. We don't want to sell too low."

9

Neosho watched the young man as he stacked firewood outside the back door of the house. He was smooth and efficient in every motion. She admired the swing of his shoulders, the ease with which he handled the heavier logs.

It was a sunny day in February 1866. The winter had been cold, with a lot of snow, but here was a day of welcome sunshine. Her whole world seemed brighter. Buds were swelling on the elm trees near the carriage house, bringing at least a promise of early spring. She longed to be outside, but it was baking day, and she'd been helping her mother knead dough. The last loaves were in the oven now. . . .

Maybe she'd step out and talk to him. No harm in that, surely. John Burns was one of her father's trusted employees. She'd spoken to him a time or two. He seemed pleasant enough, very polite and almost painfully shy. Maybe that was only the Indian side of him. The Indians she'd seen, mostly Shawnees, always seemed quiet around whites. Her mother, though, had some Indian blood. It was seldom mentioned in the family. It was just there, a fact of life. Some of the people she knew didn't like Indians much, or were afraid of them. Neosho had never understood that. People are people, she figured. Whites, Negroes, Indians, abolitionists, secesh . . . Some, you have to be cautious about.

Well, at least the war was over now. Men were coming back, by ones and twos and small groups. Her father's partner, Ben, had returned just last month. She'd seen Ben only a time or two since. There was a haunted, faraway look in his eyes, like a lot of them had. And there still weren't very many men who would be of interest to a young woman of her age and upbringing. It was apparent that "pickings would be scarce," Neosho had heard an older woman say to her mother.

But there *was* John Burns. . . . Both her parents seemed to like him. He was a bit older than she, but she found that exciting. What worldly experiences might he have had?

"I'm going outside, Mama," she called.

She drew a light shawl around her shoulders and stepped out the door to stand on the porch.

"Why, good morning, Mr. Burns," she said brightly, as if surprised to find him there.

He looked up with a smile, and his dark eyes twinkled. "Good morning, Miss Sterling! Nice day."

She was embarrassed, and blushed warmly despite the cool air. He'd known, of course, that she had been watching him from the window. Her pretended surprise must have appeared stupid and childish to him. Still, his smile was warm and friendly.

What do I say now? she thought in a panic. What was there to say about stacking firewood? Neosho wished that she could go back inside, watch from the window a bit longer. She'd think of something a little more intelligent to say and begin again. But it was too late. She must think of something. . . .

"Yes, warm for February," she answered his remark. "Do you think it will rain?"

He straightened, pushed the hair from his forehead with the back of his hand, and took a long look at the sky and the distant horizon.

"Mebbe. Always does sometime, I guess."

She knew that he was teasing her. His face was serious, but his eyes lively as he looked straight at her and through her. It was not an insolent stare, like she'd seen a time or two from men on the street. This was a look of deep understanding and insight into her innermost being. The idea that he could see her thoughts was a bit frightening. Still, it was exciting, like being out of control yet kept safe by his strength and understanding. A strange feeling, one that made her heart beat faster. Watching his strong arms and hands as he handled the rough logs made her wonder how it would feel to be encircled in those arms. She shivered a little at the thought.

"Are you chilly, ma'am?" he asked in concern. "You shouldn't catch cold, you know."

Again, she had the idea that he was teasing her.

"No, no," she said, a little too quickly. "I'm quite warm."

She drew the shawl around her shoulders a bit more tightly. Maybe she could ask about his work. . . .

"Are you driving much these days?"

Again, she felt that this must have sounded stupid.

"Some," he answered. "There'll be more as the weather opens up, I expect. Took a load of goods to Council Grove this week."

"Yes, I think my father mentioned that."

John Burns smiled. "He seemed like he'd have liked to go himself. He's a good man."

Neosho was pleased at the compliment to her father. She smiled.

"I think he misses the prairie. They lived there . . . at the Grove, that is, years ago. I was born there."

"Oh . . ." His answer was noncommittal.

"That's how I got my name. . . . Neosho, for the river that runs through it."

"I see. . . . It's changed a lot, I expect. Lots of building going on there."

"I don't remember much of it, I'm afraid. We moved here when I was small."

He nodded, smiling. This was going rather well, she thought. Now, what to talk about . . . ?

"You have a family, Mr. Burns?"

"No."

It was a single crisp word, dropped like a good-sized stone into the quiet pool of the conversation. She had made a mistake, had gone too far. He turned away to pick up another stick of wood, but then straightened again to face her.

"I'm sorry. . . . No, my family was killed when I was small."

"Oh . . . It is I who should apologize. I had no right to ask."

"It's all right." He smiled again.

The embarrassing moment passed as the door opened and Suzannah stepped out.

"Oh, *there* you are, Neosho. Good morning, Mr. Burns."

"Morning, Miz Sterling. Nice day!"

"Yes, it is. Neosho, would you bring a few sticks for the kitchen when you come in?"

She turned toward the door, but then back again, and spoke to Burns.

"You're almost finished there, it appears. Would you come in for some coffee?"

He hesitated only a moment. "Thank you, ma'am, I'd be proud to."

The warmth of the kitchen was pleasant. It served to call attention to the fact that it was, after all, still February, sunny but crisp outside.

John Burns sat at the table, sipping strong black coffee, while the women moved around the kitchen, taking golden loaves from the oven and placing them to cool on the sideboard. The heavenly aroma filled the house.

With a serrated bread knife, Suzannah cut several thick slices, spread them with butter, and arranged them on a plate. While the butter melted into the porous surfaces, she opened a jar of plum jelly and turned it out on a small saucer. Then to the table . . . A knife for the jelly, a small plate for each, and the plate of hot bread. She lifted the coffeepot and brought it to the table, refilling cups.

"Good coffee, Miz Sterling," Burns said. "Thank you."

It was strong and black, in the style of Suzannah's Southern background. There was a bowl of sugar at hand, with a small pitcher of cream. John Burns added a spoonful of sugar, but declined the unfamiliar cream.

"I can't get chicory anymore," Suzannah apologized. "Maybe now that the war's over, trade will improve."

Burns was somewhat ill at ease, but was handling the situation well. Suzannah was quick to note that at some time he had been exposed to table manners. An Indian school, maybe? Well, one way to learn.

"You have had some schooling, Mr. Burns?"

He looked startled.

"Yes, ma'am. Mission school."

"I see. The Shawnee school here?"

"No, ma'am. The Kaw school at Council Grove. A little while."

"You are Kaw, then?"

"No, I . . . I am Pawnee."

"Pawnee?"

"Yes, ma'am. My mother was killed in a raid on our town when I was small."

"And your father?"

"He was a white man. Most of our people were killed, but he wasn't there. I don't know where he went after the town was burned."

The subject was obviously painful, and Suzannah regretted having made him uncomfortable. It was bothering Neosho considerably, too.

"Never mind. I had no cause to ask. But we lived there when Neosho was born. In Council Grove."

"Yes, she told me."

He relaxed a little.

"You know Seth Hays's trading post west of the river ford?" she asked.

"Yes, ma'am. Quite well."

"Our place was north of there a short distance. Mr. Sterling was guiding on the Trail and for the army."

"I'd heard that. I was there some later, I guess."

There was a heavy silence, which was becoming uncomfortable. A welcome interruption came as Jed's boots sounded on the porch and he opened the door to step into the fragrant kitchen.

"Ah! Smells good! Oh . . . Hello, Burns."

"I . . . I was just leaving, sir."

"Sit down. Glad to see you. I wanted to talk to you, anyway. Can you take a wagon to Fort Scott tomorrow?"

"Of course."

"Good. Some goods off the boat."

He hung his hat on a peg by the door and pulled up a chair. Suzannah poured him a scalding cup.

"Well, John, have they been talking you to death?"

"No, sir," the young man answered quickly. "I'd just finished with the wood, and—"

"Never mind!" Suzannah said crisply. "He's just teasing us. Here, Jed . . ."

She had sliced the heel from the other end of the already cut loaf of bread, buttered it, and set it before him. She knew that was one of his favorite treats.

"You're home early," she teased. "You must have known I was baking."

"Yes, I confess," he answered. "And frankly, I *had* hoped to find John still here. I need to talk to him about this haul to Fort Scott. Let's not talk business, though. Tell me about your day, Mrs. Sterling. Wonderful jelly . . ."

"Not much to tell. We've been baking. Last loaves out about the time Mr. Burns finished with the wood. We've been visiting. Did you know he was in school at Council Grove?"

"No! When?"

"After we left there, of course."

The conversation continued with small talk about the weather, and soon John Burns rose.

"I'd better be getting back. There's horses to be fed."

Jed walked out with him to discuss tomorrow's haul to Fort Scott, while the women picked up the dishes from the table.

He reentered the kitchen a few minutes later.

"Nice young man. I'll try to learn more about him."

Neosho hoped that her father would not notice her flushed cheeks.

"Where's Daniel?" Jed asked.

"He's spending the day at Ben and Lorena's, while we baked. Do you want to go after him?"

"Certainly." He took his hat from the peg and turned to kiss Suzannah. "We'll be back soon."

10

The more Jed saw of young Burns, the more he liked him. It had been somewhat of a surprise to come home and find him in the kitchen drinking coffee with Suzannah and Neosho. But, in a way, a pleasant surprise. *This is how it should be,* he told himself. In the end, he had been pleased.

"I hope you don't object, that I invited him in," Suzannah said later as they prepared for bed.

"Of course not. I might have done the same."

"Jed, I think he's seriously interested in our daughter."

"Yes, I gathered that impression. Well, she could do worse."

"Don't talk like that! But really, Jed . . . I think he might be reluctant to make his feelings known. He's shy, and . . . Well, you know the expression. . . . He might think it ain't fittin' to approach her."

Jed chuckled. "He seemed to have no trouble in the kitchen."

"Yes, but I had *asked* him to come in. Once there, he's well mannered, quiet, and polite. But he might be reluctant to act on his own."

"Are you suggesting," he asked teasingly, "that we *invite* him to court our daughter?"

Suzannah made a wry face at him.

"I'm not suggesting anything. But it wouldn't hurt for you to find out a little more about him. It would serve to reassure him, too, if he has nothing to hide."

"You think he *has*?"

"I doubt it. I think he's very sensitive to his own heritage, whatever it may be. I think it's prudent to make sure that he has nothing to be ashamed of, *and* that he knows we don't disapprove."

It was then that she remembered. . . .

"Jed, did you know John Burns is Pawnee?"

"He is? He told you that?"

"Yes. His mother was killed when he was small, he said. His father was a white man. He doesn't know whatever happened to him."

"Hmmm . . . He say what band?"

"No. He seemed very reluctant to talk about it."

"Odd. I don't recall many other whites with Pawnee wives. Maybe just the result of a one-night encounter."

Her face was flushed, and Jed could see that this had become very important to her. She took a deep breath.

"Jed, I want so much for Neosho to have a chance at a good marriage and a family. A lot of women are *not* going to, you know. Too many young men have been killed."

She softened and leaned against him, slipping an arm around his waist.

"I know she can't find anyone like *you,*" she whispered, "but I wish she could."

At that moment, he would have done anything in the world to give Suzannah what she wanted.

"I'll try," he said. "I can talk to him. . . ."

As it happened, it was John Burns who initiated the conversation. He had come to the office to leave a bill of lading from a shipment by wagon, and paused on his way to the door. He turned back. . . . There was no one else in the office.

"Mr. Sterling, may I talk with you?"

The young man seemed serious and concerned.

"Certainly, John. A problem?"

"No . . . I hope not. I wish to know . . . Was it proper, at your house the other day, for me to come in?"

"Proper? Of course! You were invited."

Burns nodded. "I know. . . . But . . . I . . . I am not used to white man's ways. Except for army and a little while in school. Indian school. That is different, no?"

"That is different," Jed agreed. "What do you wish to know?"

"Well . . . Your daughter, Neosho . . . Her heart seems good toward me. At least, I am made to think so."

"And, is your heart good toward her, John?"

"Oh, *yes*! But I know the ways of my people, yet not yours. What does a man do, when his heart is good toward a woman, and he hopes that hers is the same?"

Jed could see the problem. Among many of the Indian Nations, a courtship ritual could be quite complicated. A young Cheyenne might play a courting flute for his intended. Another tribe might require gifts to the parents. In some cases the woman might even be the one expected to initiate the courtship. Jed had once gone through just such agony as Burns now faced, but in reverse. It was a very serious challenge. Even more so, because it now involved his own daughter. Under other circumstances, he might have found it amusing, but this was a sobering thing.

"You want me to tell you how to court my daughter?" he demanded.

"I . . . I wish only not to offend, sir. . . . You *or* your daughter. What must I do, to avoid this?"

Jed took a deep breath. Maybe this could be the desired introduction.

"I see. . . . Well, usually the parents want to know all about the suitor. The young man."

"You know *me*."

"But I know that you are honest, a hard worker, good with horses, yes. I know little else."

"What do you wish to know?"

This was going rather well, Jed thought. Then why were his palms damp and his heart racing?

"First, what is your nation?"

There were some that might be considered more desirable than others. If he had been guessing, he would have said possibly Osage, or more likely one of the Civilized Tribes, until learning from Suzannah that Burns was Pawnee.

Raven's people . . . Jed had *been* Pawnee himself, by marriage. He had not shaved his head like the other warriors, but . . . Yes, that was it. Burns had adopted the white man's ways to the extent that the hairstyle of a man of the Pawnees was missing.

"Pawnee," said John Burns.

"Oh? What band? What town?" Jed asked cautiously.

"*Skidi* . . . Wolf. Not my own, though. My town was destroyed when I was a child." Tension showed in the young man's face. "I don't know where it was."

There had been several Pawnee towns besides his own attacked and the people massacred at about that time, by whites or other tribes, Jed remembered.

"By whites?" Jed asked.

"No. I remember little. . . . Fire . . ." He pulled up his shirt to show the scars. "That is how I got my name. My mother was killed."

"Your father?"

"I do not remember him very much. He was a white man, I was told. My teacher was my mother's brother, as it should be among the People."

"Then *he* raised you?"

"No. Strangers took me. My uncle was killed, we thought, in the raid. Later, we heard he had survived and was taking vengeance by killing Delawares. But, then they killed him. So, I had no one."

Jed was startled. *Delawares?* This was too much like his own story. Surely . . . No, Swimmer had told him that Raven and the children were killed. Swimmer had buried them himself, had he not?

Jed's head was spinning. It had been years since he had wondered about his lost loved ones with more than a warm sadness. Raven . . . It was still a bitter memory, though he had managed to think mostly of the good times in recent years. Time cannot erase the bad memories, but softens them a little by making the good memories more distinct.

Delawares! Jed had tried to forget that he had gone on the terrible path of vengeance with Swimmer, his wife's brother, to kill Delawares. After his first kill, a Delaware probably innocent, he had realized that he could not do it. They parted ways, and Swimmer had been killed the following year.

But how . . . ? Jed recalled the situation. . . . The big earth-bermed lodges, holding as many as fifty or sixty people of the extended family, collapsing as the support timbers burned away. There must have been many bodies, some burned badly. Survivors had fled, taking any living children with them. Swimmer had returned the next day, and buried . . . the bodies he *found* at the lodge. Some had been buried in the fallen rubble, he had said.

"John," Jed asked, his voice husky, "were there other children in your family?"

"Yes, a sister. I saw the roof pole fall on her, at the same time I was burned."

"Where was your mother?"

"She was outside, fighting the Delawares."

That was as Swimmer had told it. He had described the wounds on Raven's body. She had fallen, weapon in hand, defending her people with the other women, a few youths, and old men. At least, Swimmer had been certain of that. But it was possible that he had buried another boy, burned beyond recognition.

Jed swallowed hard. "What . . . what was your uncle's name, John?"

"Swimmer. My mother's brother. Why?"

There, it had been said. Jed had been dreading the moment, and now his mind was trying to grasp the consequences of what he had just learned. His son . . . He took a deep breath, and tried to speak.

"What is it?" asked John Burns.

"John, I have to tell you. You cannot court Neosho."

Anger began to burn in the young man's face, and he rose from the chair.

"Because I am Pawnee, or just because I am a savage?" he demanded. "I would not have thought this from you, Mr. Sterling!"

"No, no, that is not it, John."

"Then *what*?"

"My heart is very heavy with this, my son," Jed began, lapsing into the old way of talking. "It is not easy. . . . Your mother was Raven, no?"

"I had not told you that—"

"I know. Your sister's name was Cherry Flower, and your own, Little Elk."

"How do you know these things?" Burns gasped, his face pale.

"My name was Long Walker," Jed told him.

"You? You are my *father*?"

There was a mixture of emotions in his face, from confusion to doubt to anger.

"You *left* us!" he accused.

"It was not like that!" insisted Jed. "I was away at the time. John, I loved your mother very much. I love her memory, still. The town was dead when I returned. *Gone,* all of our People. I was told that *you* were dead."

He did not mention the lost years when he had tried to drink himself into oblivion, or the fact that his original attraction to Suzannah was her resemblance to John's mother, Raven.

"Then . . . ," the young man said finally, his anger appearing to fade somewhat, "Neosho is . . ."

"Yes," Jed nearly choked on the words. "You can't court her. She is your *sister*."

11

Jed might have expected many things out of the conversation that had occurred that afternoon. This was certainly not one of them. So many problems . . . So much confusion . . . What now? There were moments when he was elated. He had found his long-lost son. . . . His and Raven's. That was all to the good. But it was part of another world, a world that had been and could never be again.

His first impulse was to take John Burns home and to explain the situation to Suzannah and the children when they arrived. That thought was quickly discarded. It would be completely unfair to everyone concerned. "Children" . . . Neosho was hardly a child, and was already romantically inclined toward the handsome young man, who now turned out to be her *brother*.

"John," he said soberly, "this will take some thinking. I've found you, my son. . . ." His voice choked for a moment before going on. "I have thought you dead for all these years."

"And I thought you had left me."

"No, no, son, I could never have done that. Your mother and I . . ." His eyes filled with tears. "But *you* are alive."

He wanted to take his son in his arms, to embrace him, but there was a barrier of custom and convention between them. Besides, he could see a lingering resentment in the eyes of the young man. John Burns still felt abandoned.

"Let us sleep on this," Jed suggested. "We must talk more, but we need to think. And I must tell Mrs. Sterling."

The young man nodded, still numb with all the change in thinking required by this new revelation.

They shook hands, and Jed impulsively added a quick embrace. The two separated clumsily and John hurried out the door.

Jed sat for a long time, staring at the wall as the shadows lengthened in the street. Finally he closed the office and started home. Maybe it would help to talk to Suzannah. . . .

"Supper's nearly ready," Suzannah greeted him. "Wash up."

He did so as she and Neosho finished setting the table. Daniel joined him at the wash basin. A strange sensation . . . Yes, the boys did look quite a bit alike, now that he knew. John, so much older . . . Old enough to be the father of Daniel. Strange thought . . .

"Papa, the calico cat has kittens in the manger," the boy announced.

"Oh?" answered Jed absently as he dried his face and hands on the towel. "How many?"

"Six, I think. I didn't bother them."

"Good. She'll hide them if you do."

"I know."

They gathered at the table, and after grace was said, began to eat. Jed's mind was far away.

"Jed, what is it?" asked Suzannah finally.

"What?" he asked, startled. "Oh . . . Nothing, Suzannah."

"You're very quiet."

"Sorry . . . Thinking about the office."

"Problems there?"

"No, not really. Good to have Ben back, but he was on a trip to Leavenworth today. I'll tell you about it later."

"Did you see John Burns today, Papa?" asked Neosho, her eyes bright.

"Yes, he stopped by."

"How is he?" she asked excitedly.

Jed shrugged. "All right, I guess."

"Did he mention me?"

"I . . . I don't think so, Neosho. We were talking of other things."

Neosho's full lips protruded for a moment in a pout of disappointment, but the moment passed. Her mother did not fail to note that, or the expression on Jed's face.

It was much later, as they prepared to retire, before an opportunity came to talk. Suzannah waited, knowing that it would happen. Finally, he broke a long silence.

"Suzannah, I don't know how to tell you about this."

"It's about John Burns?"

"Yes."

"It must be something bad."

There was worry in her tone.

"No . . . Well, yes, maybe. Suzannah, we have to talk."

"This sounds serious, Jed." There was concern in her voice.

"It is. John Burns is my son."

There was a long silence.

"Did you know?" she finally asked.

"No . . . Not until today. Neither did he."

"How can this be?" she asked.

"He came in to talk about courting Neosho. Hearing his story, I realized it was the same story as mine."

"But *how?*"

"Well, you know about how I lost Raven. I wasn't there at the time of the massacre and destruction. Raven's brother told me he had buried her and the children. But they were all burned terribly. He must have buried someone else's child by mistake."

"Oh, Jed . . ."

"Another family raised him, apparently. He thought his father had abandoned him."

"How sad . . ."

"Yes. He's still a bit angry about it."

"Of course. But he . . . Jed, he's Neosho's *brother?*"

He sighed deeply. "Yes, that's one of the problems."

"Oh, my! She'll be crushed, won't she?"

" 'Fraid so. But she's young."

Suzannah sighed. "He's such a good young man, Jed. I had hoped . . ."

"I had, too." He smiled wryly. "I'd want him for a son *or* son-in-law, but he can't be both."

"Or either, maybe," she observed.

"What do you mean?"

"I don't know. . . . It's so complicated. Well, let's sleep on it."

"That's what I told John. Maybe we'll have some answers in the morning."

"Yes," she agreed. She blew out the lamp, plunging the room into darkness except for a sliver of pale light from a waning moon spilling through the curtained window. "Or, maybe not."

"What shall we tell Neosho?" Jed asked as they rose next morning.

"I don't know. Is the problem any clearer this morning?"

"Not for me."

"Then let's say nothing for a little while. It can't stay this way. Something has to happen."

"But *what?*"

"I don't know, Jed. But we'll see. We'll know and understand, when it does."

He did not understand, but somehow he had the same feeling. All of them were caught up in events over which they had no control. He had felt this before, and it had been uncomfortable at the time. He had adapted to the approach of Raven's people. What will happen will do so. We try all we can, and then we wait. Sometimes the proper course of action is to do nothing, until there is new information or new events occur. Then sometimes, things that seemed to make no sense when they occurred become plain in their meaning. Sometimes not. He had come to the conclusion, though, that eventually, many things make sense. If he had not lost Raven, he would never have met Suzannah, now the light of his life. Still, he could not identify any meaning here.

He had indicated to John Burns that they could talk again after sleeping on it. He knew that the young man had probably not slept any better than he had himself. But, he headed toward the livery.

"Mornin'," greeted the liveryman. "You seen that damn Injun?"

"John? Not today. I came to talk to him."

"Well, he ain't here. I thought you'd sent him out, but your hosses and rollin' stock are all here."

"When did you miss him?"

"Just this mornin'. He said nothin' about leavin'."

"Is his bedroll still here?"

"Don't know. Let's look."

The two men walked to the tack room. The cot was there, but no blankets.

"Gone!" muttered the liveryman. He took a quick look around. "Nothin' missing."

Jed took offense at the assumption that there might be, but said nothing.

"Wait!" continued the man. "He asked last night about a mustang he'd been breakin'. Wanted to buy it. I told him sure, I'd sell it."

They hurried to the corral.

"Yep, it's gone. Nice little gelding."

"He *stole* it?"

"No, no. He bought it. I owe him more pay than the damn horse was worth. I just hate to lose such a good hand."

"Yes," sympathized Jed. "I do, too."

.   .   .

He went home to tell Suzannah.

"John Burns is gone."

She smiled sadly and nodded.

"I thought he'd do that," she said.

"He bought a horse from Jim last night, and cleared out. What shall we tell Neosho?"

"Just that, I guess," Suzannah said sadly. "I'm not surprised."

"You're *not*?"

"No. Not really, Jed. I thought of it in the night. He's a smart, ethical young man. He'd want to do the right thing. . . . Like his father, maybe . . . He figured this would be the least hurt, to the fewest. Jed, you have to give him credit. It was the only way. . . ."

BOOK V

❋

TO THE
STARS . . .
1866

FOREWORD

In the aftermath of the War Between the States, the attention of the nation turned to "Reconstruction." The Southern states were in disarray, defeated republics under military occupation, now considered "provinces" without the rights of statehood. The lives of many Southerners had been shattered, all of their possessions destroyed or stolen by the hated invaders from the North. Poor and homeless, they faced a crisis . . . how to stay alive until the ravished land could be planted and produce food.

Four million Negroes, newly freed, had been granted rights that were poorly defined and often denied. It was completely foreign to the experience of most former slaves. How does one go about being "free"?

The Northern states, by contrast, were riding the crest of a booming economy brought on by the war. Business was good, and expanding with the improvements and expansion of the railroads west of the Mississippi. This, too, caught the attention of the nation and the world. Millions of acres of land for settlement beckoned in the West, which opened through the new state of Kansas.

People swarmed in, in unprecedented numbers. People of all races, religions, and cultures . . . Their stories are different, yet have a sameness: conflict and adjustment with each other, with the climate, and the land. Some were to succeed, some to fail.

The cost had already been high, and would continue to be so. The millions of acres of "free" land were already occupied by American Indians, who had used them for centuries and would resent the incursion.

The bloody experiences surrounding the struggle for statehood and the prelude to the war had prompted a motto for the official great seal of the infant state: *Ad Astra per Aspera* . . . "To The Stars Through Difficulties." The Latin *aspera* can also be said to imply "harsh" or "rough," certainly a well-chosen motto when considered in these circumstances. . . .

In the city of Washington, an informal meeting was about to convene. Perhaps a dozen men were in the room, conversationally discussing the weather. There was an air of expectancy that created an uneasy tenseness in the attitudes of those present.

"Good morning, Mr. Seward. I trust you are doing well?"

"Much better, thank you, Mr. President. It has indeed been slow."

"I would surely think so. May you continue your progress. Your son Frederick is well?"

"Yes, sir. His wounds were not as severe, and he has the added benefit of youth's resiliency."

"Ah, yes. Would that we all had such qualities. It has been a year, now."

On the fateful night of the assassination of President Lincoln, the Secretary of State had been attacked in his own bed by a knife-wielding assassin. Perhaps coincidence, perhaps the tip of an iceberg, a deeper plot to take over the government. Secretary Seward still wondered about that sometimes. He had been recovering from a carriage accident at the time, nursing a broken jaw and arm, and had been virtually defenseless. Had it not been for Frederick's intervention, he surely would have died under the assassin's knife. He still shuddered. . . . As it was, the severity of his several stab wounds as well as the already existing fractures had made healing quite slow. He was grateful to the new President, Andrew Johnson, who had reappointed the entire cabinet of President Lincoln.

There was a great deal of enmity among the members of the cabinet. Stanton, Secretary of War, sat glaring at the President, making no secret of his disapproval. Stanton had disapproved of President Lincoln's approach to Reconstruction, too, and Johnson was attempting a similar approach, one of forgiveness and reconciliation. The radicals were still insisting on punishment for everyone who had fought for the Southern cause. President Johnson, himself a slave owner, still favored a plan much like Lincoln's, which would strengthen the Union. Seward, along with them and more moderate members of Congress, felt that the South had suffered enough. It was time to move on.

Besides, there were matters of great concern, both within the Union and on an international level. The United States, weakened by the war, might be considered vulnerable by potential enemies abroad. Napoleon III of France had already conquered Mexico, appointed an emperor, and must surely be looking toward the vast prairies of the country to the north. Still farther north and northwest, Russia claimed the huge area called Alaska.

"Gentlemen, let us begin," the President was saying.

The buzz of conversation quieted, and the attention of those present was focused on the dour face of Johnson.

"It is apparent," the President began, "that many of us have our own agendas. This, perhaps, is as it should be. However, I would call on you today to concentrate on common goals, not on our differences."

There was a quiet mutter, and then expectant silence.

"Very well," Johnson continued. "You are aware, I am sure, that I have accepted the resignation of Mr. Harlan, Secretary of the Interior. I have not yet appointed a successor. I wish to explain, however, that our differences, mine and Mr. Harlan's, are based on theories of Reconstruction, not on the other problems we will discuss today."

"Such as the Indian problem?" asked the Secretary of War irritably. "With all due respect, sir, the army can be in only a limited number of places at once. We have settlers moving into Kansas, and into Nebraska Territory, demanding protection from Indian attack. We have troops on the Mexican border, facing possible invasion by France. . . ."

"Yes, Mr. Stanton, I am aware of this. However, our sources suggest that France has enough other troubles. I doubt that they have the military strength to hold Mexico. Still, I confess, this is of concern. Mr. Welles, have you any comment?"

"Very little, sir," said the Secretary of the Navy. "We have ships both in the Gulf and along the west coast, and see very little activity. I am persuaded to think, sir, that France is in no position to extend her efforts."

The President nodded. "Let us move on, for the moment. I have received a suggestion, which at first seems to have no bearing, but let us look at it. It also concerns another problem, that of the status of slaves. . . . *Former* slaves, of course."

He paused and glanced around the circle at the facial expressions. These ranged from mild curiosity to silent rage.

"Now," the President continued, "it has been suggested that we have here a sizable population, some four million, I believe. They are accustomed to obeying orders. In fact, several Negro units deported themselves quite well in battle, I am told. Their experience lends itself well to discipline. Secretary Stanton needs troops—"

"Draft them?" blurted Stanton in astonishment and outrage. "With all due respect, sir . . ."

"No, no, Mr. Secretary. Make it possible for them to *enlist.* In the war just ended between the states, both sides used colored troops. In the South, primarily as work battalions. In the North, some combat units. But in either case, under the leadership of white officers."

"A Negro army?" someone asked.

The President did not answer directly but with another question.

"Mr. Stanton, you have spoken of a need for troops to face the threat of Indian attack. Could we not solve both problems at once? Encourage enlistment to serve on the Western Frontier?"

Someone chuckled nervously. "Let our problems solve themselves? Kill each other off?"

The President frowned disapprovingly. "That was not my intention, sir!"

"Of course not, Mr. President."

"Still," said another thoughtfully, "it *would* free up our troops on the Mexican border. . . ."

1

I t was early spring, warm in the sun, but still chilly if you stayed in the
shade very long. Patrick sighed deeply and shuffled over to the big
chair on the porch to wait for the darkies to gather. He'd sent Moses
to fetch them so that he could explain what was happening to them. To
him . . . To the whole damned world. In simplest terms, the Yankees had
won their damnable war of aggression. It was over, and the South was
dying.

Three generations had lived in the big house, had played on this
porch and on the rolling lawn that sloped gently down to the road. The big
magnolias that had been the pride and joy of his mother were beginning to
swell their buds now. In another few weeks they'd sport flowers as big as
dinner plates, and their perfume . . . No matter. It was over, now. There
was nothing left. He was glad that his parents weren't alive to witness the
humiliation, the end of a noble effort, the building of the great plantation.
The end of the O'Connor family line, too . . . Mary was gone, ten years
now, and their three sons . . . Two lost at Gettysburg, and John, the youngest, who had tried to stop Sherman's bloody destruction. John had run off
to fight without his father's knowledge. Only fifteen. Maybe if he still had
John . . . No, that wouldn't have made any difference. It was over, anyway. It would have been better, maybe, if he'd tried to fight them, himself,
and gotten himself killed in the process.

He could still see, in his mind's eye, the horde of bluebellies marching
in loose route step down the road, singing their taunting song . . .

> "Sherman's dashing Yankee boys
>   will never reach the coast."
> Or so the saucy rebels said
>   and 'twas a handsome boast.
> But they had forgot, alas,
>   to reckon with the host,
> While we were marching through Georgia.

Sherman *had* reached the coast, of course, taken Savannah, and turned left into South Carolina, burning, killing, and pillaging.

He wasn't sure why Sherman's ruffians hadn't burned the house. They'd leveled the Moores' plantation down the road. The family had fled to Columbia. Hadn't heard from them since, and never would, now. Maybe even Yankees got tired of destruction and looting, he pondered. But, probably not.

The darkies were straggling up from the cabins, now. Nineteen of them left, counting Moses and Molly, the house servants. Ol' Mammy, who had suckled him as a baby, had died last Christmas. He'd had her buried in the family cemetery rather than the slave plots. The Negroes knew what was happening, of course. Not how bad it really was, maybe, but they'd heard gossip for the past two years. They had a grapevine telegraph. Only a couple had run off, though. He could take pride in that. The O'Connors had always treated their darkies well, never sold at auction, and never broke up a family. It had paid off in loyalty, but had now become a liability. They *hadn't* left, and as long as they were here, Patrick felt a responsibility to feed them. What they didn't know was that he could hardly feed himself any longer. There was no money left, and the Yankees had taken everything of value. The silverware and the silver tea service that were his mother's pride and joy . . .

The sheriff would be here this morning to officially take over the place. *Damned Yankee puppet . . . No-'count white trash, never done a day's work in his life, nor his pappy, either. Now thinks he's a big man . . .*

Boggs had been appointed by the military authorities, and now actually seemed to enjoy giving orders to his betters. He especially relished foreclosures, in which he had the duty to formally order the occupants off their property.

Patrick took out his gold watch, checked the time, and snapped the cover shut to replace it in his vest pocket. Timing was important, and he had tried to think of everything. He'd confided in Moses, who could read and write. Hadn't told him everything, of course. That was part of the plan. But he'd already given Moses, Mammy's youngest boy, the paper, to use if anybody stopped them or questioned their possession of the goods. . . . About all that was left . . . A couple of wagons, two span of mules . . . The damn Yankees had shot the rest, just for amusement. Stole all the carriage horses, killed and ate the milk cows, carried off the pigs and chickens, except for the few the darkies managed to hide.

They were gathering below the porch, now. . . . Yes, all here . . . Five families, counting Moses and Molly, who had no children yet. Big Blue, the head field hand, his skin so black that it had a bluish cast to it . . . That was some African strain that Patrick's grandfather had bought when he first settled here. Blue was strong as an ox, and nearly as stubborn, sometimes, but a good man.

The Preacher . . . A more refined field hand. Actually, more of an expert with the fruit trees and the kitchen garden. Mary had depended on Preacher considerably to see to supplying the table.

Patrick rose from the chair and walked to the edge of the porch.

"Try to keep 'em together if you can, Moses," he muttered, aside. "It'll be safer."

"Yessuh," the tall Negro answered, his voice choked.

"Now," began Patrick, raising his voice so all could hear, "I reckon you all know what this is about. We have to leave here."

There was a low murmur. Even though they knew, there was denial.

"Where we goin'?"

"When, Massa Patrick?"

Big Blue spoke, his deep voice rumbling. "Who gwine plant the crop, ef we leave?"

"Nobody, I reckon," Patrick said irritably. "Damn it, Blue, just listen to me a little while. The sheriff's comin' pretty soon. . . ."

"He takin' us off?" cried one of the women.

"No, no! Now listen! I have to leave, too."

"Where you goin', Massa Patrick?"

"I've a sister in Savannah. . . . Damn, Mandy, let me talk! Moses is in charge. He has papers to show that you own what you're carryin'."

"Freed papers?" asked Preacher.

"No, no. You don't need free papers, Preacher. You're all free already. You can go where you want."

"Then we stay here," rumbled Blue. "Plant the crops."

"No, you can't! Somebody else owns it, now. Some Yankee, likely. You'll have to leave. Let me go on, now. . . . The wagons, mules, plows, all written on the papers Mose has. There's a little money . . . very little. I'm sorry about that. . . ."

Beyond the sloping lawn, and about a half mile up the road, he saw the dust of a fast-trotting horse and a light buggy. Time was running out.

"I reckon," he said tiredly, "that's about it. Listen to Moses, and decide what you're goin' to do. I hope you'll stay together."

"But, Massa Patrick . . ."

"You heard Massa," Moses said with authority. "We take the stuff on the paper I have here, and we leave."

"Today?" asked Mandy.

"That'd be best," said Patrick. "No later'n tomorrow. You'd best start loadin' now. Here comes the sheriff."

The buggy had turned in at the long drive and whirled up toward the big house. The high-stepping sorrel trotter gleamed in the sun. Sheriff Boggs was the driver, handling the reins officiously. Beside him sat a pasty-looking man in a derby hat, gripping a leather portfolio in both hands. His entire appearance shouted *Yankee*. Patrick snorted in disgust.

The sheriff alighted and strode toward the porch, holding an official-looking paper.

"Sorry, Pat," he said, the grin on his sneering face belying the statement.

He extended the paper, which Patrick completely ignored. *Damn white trash, pretendin' to be on a first-name basis . . .*

"I know," he said sarcastically. "Now look, Sheriff, I've given the nigras the tools they'll need, a couple of wagons and teams. It's all legal. Moses has the papers, and a copy for your pet Yankee, there."

The birdlike little man in the derby fidgeted.

"I need a moment to go back into the house, and then I'll be gone," Patrick added.

"Well, I . . . ," Boggs began.

I should have thought of somethin' to distract him, Patrick realized. He turned to the darkies still standing there.

"Simon, is there a horse I can ride?"

"No, suh. Yankees took 'em."

He'd known that. "It's all right, Simon. I can still walk. They haven't stolen my boots yet."

He turned and went into the house, moving more rapidly once he was out of sight. Taking a lamp from the mantel, he splashed its oil over a carefully prepared pile of papers and furniture in the dining room. A sulfur match . . . He waited only to see the yellow and blue flame dart over and around the pile. . . . Moses and Molly knew about this part, and were ready to take their belongings out the back when the confusion started.

Quickly, now . . . He opened the buffet drawer and took out the flat rectangular box. The dueling pistols had been carefully loaded and primed with fresh powder and ball only that morning. One in each hand, he stepped through the hallway and back out onto the porch.

The sheriff chuckled. "Come on, Pat! You ain't goin' to—"

His sentence was cut short by the crack of the pistol in Patrick's right hand. Sheriff Boggs was knocked backward down the steps to land flat, sightless eyes staring at the sun. A small black hole had appeared just between his bushy brows.

Patrick, his expression unchanged, stepped back into the hall and out of sight.

"He done shot him!" stated Big Blue, breaking the shocked silence. "Massa Patrick shot him!"

The stunned Negroes stood a moment longer in shocked silence. The derby-topped Yankee stared in horror, then seized the reins and yanked the flashy trotter's head around. Applying the whip, he and the buggy fled down the drive in a cloud of dust.

Moses sprinted inside, across the hall, and past the stair. He had not known about this part of the plan.

"Massa!" he called. "Massa Patrick?" He had just noticed smoke and flame erupting from the partly open door to the dining room when a dull boom echoed through the house from the same area. A quick look . . . He retreated from the heat and flames and ran back outside.

"Massa Patrick is dead," he announced. "The big house is on fire. We got to get goin'."

"Where, Moses?" asked Big Blue.

"I dunno. Out of here! Let's pack them wagons. . . . Ever'body help, *fast*. We'll decide where we goin' on the way there!"

They were already scattering. *Lord, what a responsibility,* Moses thought. *I hope I kin handle it.*

2

They camped about ten miles northwest of the plantation. They passed a sleepless night, wondering if they were pursued. It had been a mad rush to get the wagons loaded and leave. It had been a real temptation to stand and stare at the fire that was devouring the big plantation house.

Moses was afraid that they would be blamed for the fire, for the killing of the sheriff, maybe even for the death of Massa Patrick. Lord, who'd have figured Massa would do such a thing? Thinking back, Moses was struck with the realization that it had been carefully planned. Massa Patrick had always had a care for his nigras, even at the end. It had been set up with a witness to his shooting of the sheriff. If, of course, the frightened Yankee told it straight. No reason not to, as far as Moses could see. The derby-hatted one had even been handed a copy of the papers that now rested in an oilskin packet in Moses' poke.

He was uneasy about that, too. He knew of incidents where a freed slave, carrying his papers, had been arrested, the papers seized and destroyed, and the man sold again. It was hard to realize that things were really any different now. In some ways, anyway. He understood that now to have former slaves around was a liability. He knew that Patrick O'Connor had impoverished himself to try to feed his people. Some planters had just run them off, or had run away themselves.

He tried to tell himself that his pitiful little band of refugees should be relatively safe as they traveled. They carried nothing of real value, except a few tools and farming implements. Nobody'd likely want to steal a hoe or a shovel from them. He smiled a little. That was an amusing thought. . . . Anyone stealing something that meant nothing but hard work.

How had it happened that he had inherited the responsibility for this ragtag party of refugees? He hadn't asked for it. It had just fallen to him, unwanted. He'd just as soon not have it. Maybe he could get out of it. . . . But not yet. They needed a purpose or goal of some sort. What sort? He didn't know. He still had the money that Massa Patrick had given him to distribute to the others. More money than he'd ever seen, nearly two hundred dollars in gold and silver coin. About five dollars for each man, woman, and child in the party. He'd been entrusted with it, and with the safety of the group. *Keep 'em together, Moses!* Like his long-ago namesake in Preacher's Bible story, his was an unwanted responsibility, but something he was called to do. He hoped he could handle it.

He looked at the children, standing by the fire, waiting for something to eat. The women had set up a tripod over the fire and hung a big kettle from it. Buckets of water from the stream . . . He didn't know what they'd put into the soup, and wasn't sure he wanted to know. But every family carried something. A sack of meal, dry beans, a side of bacon or salt pork. There were greens coming on . . . dandelion, poke, lamb's-quarter. . . . They'd make do somehow.

But where? There had been a need to get away from the tragedy at the plantation. He was still uneasy about pursuit, though he couldn't think why anybody would come after them. Good riddance, the white folks would probably figure. Well, he had to do something, even if it turned out to be wrong. He'd have a meeting and talk about it. After they'd eaten, maybe.

"We got some things to talk on," he told the gathering around the fire.

The younger children had been put to bed on blankets and quilts under the wagons. The rest now sat, waiting and wondering.

"Where you takin' us, Mose?" asked Weasel. "The Promised Land?" He giggled.

There was a humorless murmur around the circle. Some did not appreciate Weasel's ever-present jokes. He'd been named "Wesley" by Miz Mary at the time of his birth, after some churchman. But his pinched nose and close-set eyes changed it to Weasel before he was grown. Miz Mary resented the nickname, and in her presence he had remained Wesley till her dying day.

To Weasel, something was always funny. Children loved him. His wife, whom Massa Patrick had bought for him from the Moores, tolerated him with quiet good humor. They were thirtyish now, with two boys of their own.

"Weasel, it ain't funny!" rumbled Big Blue. "Shut up an' listen."

"Maybe he's right, though," suggested Preacher. "We goin' someplace . . . our own Promised Land, if we can find it."

"But we need a plan," Moses said. "Where are we goin' to look?"

"We don't all have to stay together," observed Simon. "We kin do what we want to, now. We kin pick whatever names we want to go by, too, if we want. And Moses, we got some money comin', Massa said!"

"But Massa told Moses to keep us together," Big Blue stated firmly. "I heard him!"

"Oh, shut up, Blue," Simon retorted. "You're nothin' but a dumb field nigger."

Blue shifted his bulk ominously. "You think you somethin', boy, 'cause you take care of hosses an' hoss shit. *Ain't* any hosses, now. Yankees took 'em. You ain't even got hoss shit."

"All right, both be quiet now," Moses said irritably. "You can argue later."

"But where we goin', Mose? I axe you that, before," said Weasel.

"We got to decide," said Moses patiently. "Yes, Massa thought we better stay together."

"Ain't no Massa now, neither," retorted Simon insistently.

"Let's listen to Moses," said Preacher calmly. "But first, we should pray."

He launched into a fervent prayer to help the party as they prepared to "wander in the wilderness to search for the Promised Land." Preacher's prayers were pretty long sometimes. Moses hoped that the Almighty God had a lot of patience. Right now, quite a number of the mere human beings at this gathering were becoming a bit restless.

Finally Preacher ran out of steam and subsided, among a rustle of heartfelt *amens.*

"All right," began Moses, hurrying before somebody else got a start. "Let's talk about it. Massa Patrick thought we'd be safer if we stay together. I think that's right. Anybody can leave if you want, but that's up to each family, I reckon. You can tell us later if you decide that way. Now . . . Where we goin'? We're here because that's the way the road was pointin'."

"We really don't know about nowhere else, Moses," said Preacher. "You got book learnin'. . . . What you think?"

"Well, a lot of freedmen head north, I hear. I also hear they're not welcome. Seems them Yankees fought over our bein' *here,* but don't want us comin' *there.*"

"Ev'body's got to be someplace, Moses," giggled Weasel.

"Be serious, Weasel," admonished Moses. "That's true, of course. Maybe the West?"

"Among wild Indians?" asked a frightened woman.

"They ain't so wild, Belle," soothed another. "You 'member the Cherokees an' all."

"I ain't as old as you," taunted the other. "But yes, and the Seminoles even took in some of our people. I ain't talkin' civilized Indians, but wild ones, huntin' them buffalo an' all."

"Let's get back to what we know about," suggested Moses. "There's got to be space out there, dirt to farm. We can do that, if we can find a place to do it."

They argued until far into the night, and came to no conclusion. There was simply not enough information.

"Let's go on west a day or so, anyway," suggested Moses. "We don't know how far we're talkin' about. But we can ask as we travel. Anyway, it's more open country, fewer towns that way than toward the coast."

The next morning they traveled on. No one had appeared to follow them. One thing, at least, had been accomplished. Moses was elected as leader of the group. He did not relish the idea, but realized that any of the others were even less qualified. There was a token challenge from Simon, but a threatening growl from Big Blue silenced it.

It occurred to Moses that the people he led were accustomed to taking orders, doing what they were told, and making the best of it. This was both good and bad. Good, because they would likely follow *his* decisions. Except for Simon, of course. Not too bright, but bright enough to challenge authority, now that he had status as a freedman. Maybe Big Blue would keep him in line. It had appeared to happen that way. Preacher would have some influence, too, and might be flattered into becoming useful. And Weasel . . . It was possible, Moses thought, that Weasel was the brightest of the lot. Somehow, he felt that the man's joking buffoonery and foolishness were protection for a sensitive, intelligent man. It drew attention away from any serious suspicion.

It was odd that he, Moses, had been elected their leader, since he was the youngest. But Massa Patrick *had* charged him with responsibility. He was, after all, a house servant, with considerable prestige and status on that account. He had understudied old Peter, who had departed for a better world two years ago. At least, that's what Preacher had said at the funeral. Moses owed Peter a lot. The old man had tutored him, not only in the household tasks, but in book learning.

"A man that kin read and write," Peter had been fond of saying, "has a leg up on anybody else."

Moses and Molly were the only couple without children. Nine children, altogether, though four of them belonged to Big Blue and his wife, Sally. Their oldest was a son, and there was a daughter, coming into womanhood at twelve or fourteen. Weasel was in his thirties too, with three children. Preacher and Simon, a bit younger, had one child each.

The women were all strong and hardworking, except for Esmerelda,

Preacher's wife, who always seemed to suffer from poor health. All in all, Moses was pleased with the capabilities of the group. He had known all of them for as long as he could remember. Now, if they'd only cooperate and not argue too much.

Moses had a vague idea that they could stay together for protection and make their way westward to where there was said to be free land. He didn't know much about how that came about, but figured he could find out when they got there. Where? Out there somewhere beyond the plantations and farms and fields and towns . . . Peter had told him he'd heard of land with nobody workin' it or even livin' there.

"It ain't for me," Peter had said. "I'm an ole man. But you and some of the others, maybe . . . You'll find it some day, boy. Your own Promised Land."

It had become a dream, one that had seemed far away, but now for the first time might become possible. *Where?* He still didn't know. Somewhere out west. *How far?* He'd even less idea. But he figured they'd know when they got there. And they could ask along the way.

They were camping for the second night when three people approached in the gathering darkness. Moses recognized them as some of the Moores' darkies. The young man and woman kept holding on to each other's hands. Probably man and wife, maybe just sweethearts . . . The young woman appeared timid and fearful.

The older man was white-haired and could have been any age. But he moved well and had a relaxed and confident manner.

"Uncle Bolivar?" gasped Molly suddenly. "Is that you?"

"Molly? Yes, child! Ain't seen you since you left to go to the O'Connors' place. How be you?"

"Pretty good, Uncle."

"Is he really your uncle?" asked Moses.

"I don't know," Molly smiled. "Does it matter?"

She flew into the old man's arms.

"Close enough!" laughed Bolivar. "Lordy, it's good to see you, child!"

He turned to Moses.

"You're Moses? She was bought for you, wasn't she? We seen your party pass by yestiddy. Reconnized Blue an' them. We heared Massa Patrick's big house done burned. We seen smoke. He be dead, right? Sheriff, too?"

Moses marveled at the speed with which the news had spread.

"That's true. You hear anything else?"

"Nope. Jest that his niggers was gone an' headin' west."

"There wasn't talk of catchin' us?"

Bolivar chuckled. "Guess not. From what I heard, you all din't do nothin' wrong. Whoever's takin' over the plantation prob'ly thinks good riddance. Now, I got to ask. . . . Kin we go with you? This here's Billy and Ella. I'm their uncle, too, I reckon."

"But . . . you don't even know where we're goin'!"

The old man chuckled again. "Do *you*? West, I figure. I hear tell there's free land. Place called Kansas."

"Let 'em come," rumbled Big Blue.

"Sure, why not?" asked Preacher.

"All right, how many say so?" asked Moses.

There were so many voices of agreement that even Simon was silent when it came time to hear the "no" vote.

3

Some people on the road west were helpful, some hateful. Some answered their questions about the road, others turned away. Some cursed them or spat on them.

Moses realized very soon that it was necessary to judge and evaluate quickly, and to act according to a stranger's expectations. A person with a friendly demeanor might well respond to an educated manner and polite conversation. Just as easily, one who was already irritated by the presence of the newly freed party might be offended by the mere existence of "uppity niggers."

In more than one town, it was suggested that they not even pause in their travels but keep moving.

"We burned a nigger here for stealin' chickens, jest last week," a surly man warned at one stop.

They did not doubt that such mob violence had been carried out. They had heard of other lynchings.

"Yassuh, we sho' be movin' on, suh. We don' want no trouble, suh. Jes' passin' through," Moses fawned.

"Why do you do that?" demanded Molly angrily when they were out of hearing. "Mose, he probably can't even read and write as well as you."

"I know, honey, but it's safest. That man wants us to be ignorant darkies to make *him* feel better about it. I don't want to argue with a man who's proud of a lynching, so I'll tell him what he wants to hear."

"But it isn't right!"

"Of course not. But a man like that kills us just as dead, right or wrong."

It became a choice with everyone with whom they had more than fleeting contact. Would Moses, their acknowledged spokesman, assume his educated role, or revert to plantation darkie talk?

"Mose sho' kin talk dumb when he need to," giggled Weasel. "I couldn' do no better mah own self!"

"You don' have to try berry hard," said Big Blue. "Seem it come natural to some."

The others laughed. It was good to hear laughter.

They met with some kindness. The rumor of free land was true, an old gentleman assured them.

"Forty acres an' a mule. The government gives it to settlers."

"To every person, or to a family?" asked Simon suspiciously.

"I dunno. I just heard tell," the man admitted.

"Where?" asked Moses.

"That there Kansas land. That's what I heard, anyhow."

Much later, they learned that such a rumor had little basis in fact. Yes, there was land, a knowledgeable, educated Negro told Moses. He had joined them at their evening campfire for a visit. Not the "forty acres and a mule," but homestead land, which must be lived on, farmed, and improved.

"How much land?" Moses asked.

"It varies, I hear. Up to a quarter section, I understand, one way and another."

"I'm afraid I don't understand the terms," admitted Moses. "How big is this 'section'?"

"Oh . . . Of course . . . A section is a square, a mile on each side. It's six hundred and forty acres. A quarter is a hundred and sixty. I'm not sure of the rules to qualify, or the time it takes to prove out. Seems like you can get extra credit for building stone fences, or for planting timber."

"Planting?"

"So I heard. The fences . . . You can get pay for building them . . . By the rod, apparently. The planting . . . All this is hearsay, but you can homestead more acres if part of it's in trees instead of row crops."

"You're sure this ain't like the 'forty acres an' a mule' story?" Moses asked.

Both laughed.

"Don't think so. That was to get darkies *out.* The homestead laws are to bring folks *in,* to work the new land."

"Have you been out there?"

"Just as far as Kansas City. It's been settled a while, there. You'll want to go on west a few more days. Are you goin' to split up?"

"Don't know. I'd thought we might build some houses close together . . . like a town, maybe. Then homestead the land around it."

"Some of you have varied skills, it appears?"

"Never thought much about it. But yes . . . Simon, there, is a pretty good smith, and he knows animals. Preacher has experience with fruit trees and the kitchen garden."

"You worked in the house?"

"Yes. Molly and I."

The other man nodded. "In a way, you *were* operating as a town. A big plantation has the range of people with skills needed for a community. You're just moving the town west."

"But on our own!" Moses smiled.

"Exactly. Another thing . . . The railroads will be building west across the area. Some of your men can hire out as hands to build the grade and lay track. Bring in some money as they build through. Big Blue, there, looks like he could swing a maul."

"I'd expect he could."

"One other thing . . . I'd suggest that you all choose names. First and last names. There will be papers to sign and file, whatever anyone decides to do."

"But most of our people can't read and write," Moses protested.

"I understand. But they can make a mark by their name, and have it witnessed. They'll need to recognize their name. And they can *learn* to read. You have children, here. They should have schooling."

"Yes . . ." Moses was thoughtful. "Molly . . . my wife . . . she could teach them."

"Exactly! Now you're getting the idea. Make them self-sufficient. As people, and as a group. But you can pick names now, start using them. You . . . You're Moses, right? What's your last name?"

Moses laughed, embarrassed. "I . . . I guess I never needed one."

"But you will, now, for legal purposes."

Moses thought about it a short while, and then spoke slowly.

"I'd been thinkin' some about this. Some darkies have been choosing names like Washington or Lincoln, some are takin' the name of their owner . . . Former owner. Or their job . . . 'Gardner' . . . 'Smith' . . ."

"Yes," chuckled the other man. "I know of a 'Harness.'. . . And one who figures he's 'White' now."

"He doesn't expect to fade, does he?"

Both laughed again.

"Probably not. He's just announcing his changed status, I think."

"I'm thinkin'," Moses said, more seriously, "that I owe a lot to ol' Massa Patrick. He saw the trouble we'd have, and tried to help all he could. Saw to it I learned to read. I reckon I'll take his name."

"O'Connor?" asked Molly, who had come up to stand beside him.

"You doesn't favor Massa much," giggled Weasel.

"And you don't appear Irish," their visitor spoke again.

There was general laughter.

"I was thinking more of 'Patrick,' " said Moses. "Moses Patrick."

"Mrs. Patrick," said Molly tentatively. "Molly Patrick . . ."

"Still sounds Irish, but it's nice," said their visitor. "I like it."

"Me, too," said Molly.

"What about Preacher?" asked Simon. "That ain't a name."

"My reg'lar name is John," said Preacher. "I can use that, and still go by Preacher, I reckon."

"John Preacher?" snorted Simon.

"It ain't bad," rumbled Big Blue. "Let him alone, Simon. Seems I heard tell of a *Simple* Simon."

"I was thinkin' of John Gardner," said Preacher. "Preachin's somethin' I do on the side."

"That's good," the visitor said approvingly. "Has a nice ring to it. Well, you all don't have to decide tonight. Think about it some."

"We've been wondering," said Moses, "how far we're talking about, here. To Kansas City, say?"

The visitor nodded thoughtfully. "Well, you're wondering how *long,* rather than how many miles, probably. How far do you travel each day? Twenty miles?"

"Sometimes," Moses agreed. "Some days, less. Depends on the weather and the roads."

"About as I figured," the other nodded. "Now, let's see . . . We're in North Carolina. . . ."

"Nearin' Tennessee, aren't we?" asked Moses. He had a general idea.

"That's true. Another day or so . . . Well, prob'ly eight hundred miles to go, to get into Kansas. At twenty miles a day, forty days."

"We can't average that," said Moses.

"Yes, I know. But, say two months, sixty days. That will allow for choosing your area and all."

"It's March now," said Moses. "That puts us there in late May. Too late to plant, Preacher?"

"Don't know, Moses. That's farther north than I'm used to. We don't know their seasons. Depends what we're plantin', I reckon."

"An awful lot we don't know about," Moses observed.

"But you're goin' at it right," said the visitor. "Find out all you can, and keep tryin'. You'll make it!"

"Oh, yes," said Molly, "we wondered about Indians."

"Wouldn't worry about them, ma'am. They have some respect for persons of colour. More so than most whites. And, most of the 'wild' tribes are farther west and north, or so I'm told. Those around Kansas City are pretty civilized. And, the government is trying to limit Indians to the Indian Territory or to Dakota."

The visitor was gone when Moses woke in the morning. He had given them much information, and it was somewhat embarrassing to realize that they did not even know his name or where he was heading.

4

They were approaching Independence now. They had heard about this town for the past thousand miles. The jumpin'-off place, gate to the West. Behind them, they had left footprints in the dust of several states. South Carolina, a corner of North Carolina, Tennessee . . . They crossed the Mississippi on a ferry. Moses hated to spend any money so he had negotiated for the men in the party to load freight for half a day in return for passage.

They had had a bad experience with money already. He had handed out a silver dollar to each adult in the party, at the insistence of Simon.

"Massa Patrick said that's *our* money, Moses! I want mine."

Within half a day, the party had been stopped by a man with a badge and a holstered pistol, who demanded to know whether they were carrying any money. Most said nothing, but Simon had to brag a little, and the peace officer had confiscated everyone's silver dollars.

"Uh-huh!" he leered. "Stole ol' Massa's money, din't you?"

"No, suh, he done give it to us," Moses protested.

"A likely story!" snorted the officer. "I better keep it for y'all. I'll give it back when you need it."

"But we're goin'—"

"I don't want to hear no more about it," snapped the other. "Move on, now!"

They moved on, poorer but wiser. Even Simon understood his mistake, and nothing more was said about distribution of their meager funds.

When supplies were needed, Moses or another selected individual bought and paid for them with funds designated for that purpose.

Across Missouri . . . At Independence they began to really feel the flavor of the West. An excitement in the air, a hurry to travel, to see and do and to experience new sights and smells and sounds and sensations.

They had developed a routine when coming to a town. The little caravan would halt and rest while Moses and maybe one of the other men would go in to get the feel of the place. Would they be welcomed, tolerated, or detested? It could be anything. Sometimes people were helpful, sometimes antagonistic. In one town they were warned.

"We don't want no niggers here! Better not let the sun set on you-all in this town."

Heeding the thinly veiled threat, they moved on quickly. The setting sun found them miles away for that night's camp.

Usually, the scouting party had no trouble learning how things stood in a new town. Their first step was to locate a Negro and ask, point-blank, how it was. This would produce information about areas that might be unsafe, where they might be allowed to camp, to buy, or any other information that might be pertinent to their needs.

If they saw no "persons of colour" at all in a town, the feeling of uneasiness became quite oppressive. In such a case there were only two alternatives. They could move on quickly, to try the next town. Or, if they could spot a frontiersman, a mountain man in buckskins, he would usually talk freely to them. At first this was puzzling, but eventually they began to understand. These men had traveled widely, had lived and dealt with many sorts of people. Some had Indian wives and half-breed children. To them, the hue of a person's skin did not carry the importance that it might to people in more "civilized" areas.

In Independence, they felt much of this easy tolerance, although there were some disapproving stares from individuals. They learned of several other parties similar to their own. In each case, the groups had expressed the intention to settle in an area with land available, to build a town and a farming community where they could feel secure among their own kind. At least two of these, their informant said, were composed of freed Negroes like themselves. Some of the others were of European origin and spoke different languages, such as German and Swedish.

On a busy street in Independence, they saw a table set up on the boardwalk in front of a mercantile store. An army officer sat in a chair behind it, looking handsome and capable in his blue uniform.

"A Yankee," whispered Molly.

"Of course," Moses answered. "What did you expect? You've seen a lot of Yankees."

"But this one seems so . . . well, *official.*"

Moses laughed. "I'd expect he's a recruiter."

Just then another man came out of the store and walked to the table. This one wore the uniform of a master sergeant, and it was a moment or two before the realization sank home to the travelers. *The sergeant was a Negro!* He pulled out a chair beside the lieutenant and seated himself. Then he noticed the travelers and quickly rose again.

"Hello, there," he called. "Where you from?"

"South Carolina," answered Moses, puzzled. Even in the Yankee army, they'd seen no Negroes. He'd heard that there were some, but this man had stripes of rank that suggested some status.

"Good!" the sergeant called. He walked around the table and out into the street in a friendly manner. "Where y'all headin'?"

"Don't rightly know. Someplace to settle. Kansas, somewhere."

The sergeant nodded. He was glancing quickly over the two wagons, the people riding and those walking, sizing them up with a professional eye. He smiled, a broad ivory grin, very friendly.

"I might be able to help you," he offered.

The soldier was coming on just a little too strong, thought Moses. "How's that?"

"Well, you've got some capable-looking men here. We're recruiting a few. . . . Fine opportunity, friend."

"I don't know," Moses said. "Not exactly what we're lookin' for. We've got families. Lookin' more to homesteadin'."

"Course, brother. But you *all* got families? Now, that young buck there. He'd make a great trooper."

The sergeant pointed to the oldest of Blue's sons. Big for his age, young Daniel was pleased by the attention.

"You let him be," snapped Sally, his mother. "He be only fifteen. He jes' a baby!"

"Sorry, ma'am! But he soon be a man. Maybe later . . . His own horse to ride, room an' board, an' cash pay besides. But shorely, *you* not his mama. I 'spect you his sister, no?"

Everyone laughed, and Sally, flattered but embarrassed, pretended to be offended.

"Go 'long, now! I heered about you no-'count Yankee soldiers! This here be my husban'." She put a hand on Big Blue's shoulder. "I 'spect you don' want no problems with him!"

The sergeant looked Big Blue up and down and whistled admiringly.

"I sho' don't, ma'am. *He'd* mebbe make quite a trooper, ef we could find a hoss big enough to carry him."

The entire party was laughing at the exchange now. The lieutenant sat, quietly observing, knowing that his recruiting depended on the considerable skills of his dark-skinned sergeant.

"You said hoss?" asked Simon. "You ain't talkin' a work crew?"

"No, no," said the sergeant quickly, sensing an opportunity. "No laborers. Cavalry . . . Dragoons. Horse soldiers."

"The Yankees are doin' that? Colored folks?"

"Shore, like I said. Smart ones, of course."

"Thet leaves you out, Simon," said Blue.

"You, too, I reckon," retorted Simon.

"Now we're not jes' talkin' Yank or Reb, here," the sergeant went on. "We all one, now. But settlers need protection, an' that's what the cavalry does."

"Wait, now," Moses said. "You're really talkin' Negro cavalry?"

"I sho' am. A few white officers, and colored noncoms."

"What means 'noncom'?" asked Weasel.

"Noncommissioned officers . . . like myself." He indicated the stripes on his sleeve. "Jes' our officers on up is white, like the lieutenant, there."

He pointed to the man in the chair.

"That's true," the officer assured them. "As the sergeant says, a great career. Wives might even come along as laundresses or housekeepers at the post."

"What post, suh?" asked Simon.

"Any post . . . One of the frontier forts."

"I'm thinkin' not," said Sally firmly. "I've done a lot of other folks' laundry, an' I'm ready to do my own. Besides, an army ain't a place to raise young-uns, I expect."

"I doubt that any of us are interested, sir," Moses explained. "But we'll talk about it."

They moved on.

There was one other incident that was both encouraging and puzzling. They had crossed into Kansas and were camped on the old military trail near the Lower Delaware Crossing. A horseman approached and stepped down to rest and allow his horse to graze for a little while.

He was well dressed, an older gentleman, and seemed interested in the party from the Carolinas, their travels and their plans.

"Planning to take up land?" he asked conversationally.

Moses had already decided, from the gentleman's attitude, that he need not resort to darkie talk.

"Yes, sir, we hope to. Maybe find a spot for our own town."

The man nodded. "Lots of good sites. Any of you been out there yet?"

"No, sir. We're just findin' our way. You know the country?"

A dreamy look that told of far horizons crossed the gentleman's face.

"Yes . . . Yes, pretty well. Used to trap it, scouted for some wagon trains, and for the army. That was some time ago."

"You live here now?" asked Moses.

"Yes, near here. In business now. Transportation, freight . . ."

He squatted by their fire, as comfortable as if he had been in buckskins for a moment.

"One of your big problems will be water," he advised. "The farther west you go, the drier it will be. I'd guess a lot of the land near here has been claimed, but keep an eye on the streams as you travel. Think about diggin' wells."

"Thank you, sir. What about crops? What will grow out there?"

The man chuckled. "Afraid I can't tell you. I've never farmed. The Indians grow corn, beans, pumpkins. Beyond that, who knows?"

"Cotton?" asked Big Blue.

"Don't think so. They do, down in Texas, I guess."

"You mentioned Indians, sir," Moses said. "Will they be a problem?"

"Hard to say. Depends a lot on how you treat 'em, mostly. But things are changin' so fast now. I'd say don't go too far west. No more'n ten sleeps, maybe."

The man's speech, too, now seemed to be reverting to an earlier day. Ten sleeps . . . An obvious reference, but one that seemed slightly out of place in a gentleman's conversation. There was also an easy tolerance they had rarely encountered before. It was almost as if the man had not noticed the color of their skins.

Now he rose.

"Well, I'd best be movin'. Need to be home by dark. Best of luck to you-all." He paused a moment. "I rather envy you the experience. . . ."

He swung to the saddle and rode away at a swinging trot.

"Well, *that* was somethin'!" said Preacher. "*He* envy *us*? You reckon he be crazy?"

They watched the ramrod-straight figure grow smaller up the trail.

"No," said Uncle Bolivar thoughtfully. "I don't reckon crazy. . . . I don't know how or why, but I reckon there's a man that *understands*."

5

A hundred miles north, in Iowa, a young man of twelve called to his brother.

"Will, come help me with the yoke, here. Please?"

The older boy looked up from the chopping block, where he was splitting kindling for the cookstove.

"Just a minute, Ezra . . ."

A couple more strokes of the hatchet . . . William picked up the slender sticks and tossed them into the box beside the woodpile. He stuck the hatchet into the block and turned to where his brother had tied the calves.

It had been something of a joke all along. Two bull calves, born on the same day, so much alike. The boys always played with the milk cows' calves, handled and bottle-fed them, weaning them from the cows early so as to use the milk. The Willetts always had extra milk and cream to sell or to make cheese and butter.

These two calves became steers, and when the rest of the calf crop was sold, John decided to hold these over for a season.

"We've got enough hay, and they'll be worth more next year."

Ezra had continued to play with the calves as they grew. An extra ear of corn, special attention . . . The two were so much alike, so inseparable, that they were referred to as "the team" . . . Tom and Dick. What began as a joke was taken more seriously by young Ezra. He'd studied the ox team used by the neighbors down the road, and figured he could make a yoke. . . .

Painstakingly, he had started with a five-foot section of timber. Over a period of weeks and months, using the hatchet, a drawknife, and a spokeshave, he gradually shaped the yoke. A hollow to rest on the shoulders of each steer, smooth and with no corners or rough edges. Boring the holes was a bit more complicated. Sam, the eldest, had helped him with that. Two on each side, to receive the bows of slender second-growth hickory. These, when pinned in place with wooden pegs at the top, would circle the animals' necks and hold the yoke in position.

A bit more difficult was the center hole in the beam of the yoke itself. It required a larger auger to bore the hole, and a lot more effort. "Elbow grease," their father called it.

An even greater stumbling block was the question of how to fasten a chain to that center hole. Ezra rummaged through the assortment of iron in the barn . . . cinch rings, old whiffletree fittings, a stirrup without a mate, heavy bolts, washers, and nuts.

His father had finally come to his aid. John had watched the progress with the calves from the first, with amusement.

"He thinks he's gonna have an ox team," he chuckled to Nancy. "It'll be somethin', to see how it turns out."

"He knows we'll sell the steers or butcher them someday, doesn't he?"

"Sure. But he'll learn a lot while we still have 'em. They'll do better while they're handled a lot. . . . Keeps 'em gentle."

John took a long threaded rod, salvaged from a burned wagon bed back in Missouri. . . . An original nut and washer . . . With a cold chisel, he cut the rod to proper length, and with the forge and anvil, flattened the end and shaped it around a heavy iron ring salvaged from somewhere else.

"There, Ezra. Fit it through the center hole of your yoke. You can use the log chain to pull. . . . Just take care of it. . . . Don't leave it out. It'll rust."

"I won't, Papa."

This was the trial run, and Ezra found that he could not handle the heavy yoke alone. He knew that when he had seen an ox team yoked before, two men had done it. Now, he saw why. It would take a very strong man to lay the shaped timber across the shoulders of the two animals. . . . No, they'd have to approach the team from behind, one on each side, carrying the two ends of the yoke. The only other way Ezra could see to accomplish the job would be to lay the yoke across something and lead the animals under it. He tried that a couple of times, with one end of the yoke propped on the fence and the other tied to a rope dangling from a lower limb of the big oak tree near the barn. The effort was totally unsuccessful. The yearlings refused to walk beneath the yoke under any circumstances. Led, pushed, pulled, or driven, it was no different. Well, so be it, he figured. That was apparently why two men usually did it.

With William on one end of the heavy beam and Ezra on the other the task became simple. The cattle fidgeted for a moment when the yoke was placed on their shoulders, but quickly quieted when Ezra spoke to them.

"Now, Will, put the bow through from below, and fasten the top with the short pin, there."

The pegs slipped into place, and the job was finished.

"What are you goin' to haul?" asked the amused older brother.

"Well . . . Guess I'll try 'em on a few fence rails first."

He half led and half drove the team with a long stick, halting next to the pile of poles, where the log chain waited. The slip-hook end of the chain around the pole, the grab hook through the center ring of the yoke . . .

"Giddap!" he yelled, with a gentle tap of the stick on each rump.

There was a moment of confusion as Tom and Dick shuffled back and forward. Very quickly they realized that the burden on their shoulders was more comfortable if they moved together. It was a great help that they had learned to graze wearing halters tied together with a short length of rope.

Now they stepped out, easily pulling the light fence rail across the barnyard. Once around the chicken house, past the pigpen, and back past the barn to the stack of poles.

"Hooray!" shouted William.

"My word!" muttered Nancy from the porch. "They did it!"

"Of course!" chuckled John. "Didn't you think they could?"

He stepped down toward the boys and the team.

"Good job!" he told Ezra. "Want to try one of the logs up in the grove?"

"Sure! Now?" asked Ezra.

"Why not? Go ahead. You know where they are up there, ready to saw up and split. Be careful."

"Where you want 'em?" Ezra asked confidently.

"Just down by the woodpile. Don't work 'em too hard. They're just calves, you know."

"Yearlings, Papa."

"Well, yes, but they don't have their full weight yet. Size, neither. Don't overdo it."

"I'll be careful. . . . Will, want to come with me?"

"Sure! I gotta see this!"

They moved up the hill to the grove where John had established a woodlot, thinning, trimming, clearing brush. A few logs lay at random, waiting to be worked up into firewood.

"How about that one?" asked William.

"Let's try a smaller one, first. This one, maybe . . ."

Ezra poked the slip hook beneath the log and out the other side, hooking it over the chain on the top. He checked the grab at the yoke end. . . .

"Giddap!"

The team moved out as if they'd done it for years, leaning into the yoke to pull. The heavy log refused to budge at first pull, but with another lunge slid smoothly forward.

"Hooray!" yelled William again.

The log pivoted and lined out for the pull down the hill. Ezra's heart soared as they stopped near the woodpile two hundred paces away.

"Good!" called his father. "That's prob'ly enough for the first time, Ezra. Feed 'em some oats!"

That had been earlier in the spring. With the greening of the grass and the return of warmth, the wanderlust began to stir in John Willett's veins. As always, the cry of the wild geese called to him as they headed to unknown places in the north. But their call to him was not adventure in the north, but in the West.

"Nancy," he said one morning, "I reckon we could go back."

"Back?" She was alarmed for a moment. "Back to Indiana?"

"No, no," he laughed. "Back to homestead. The border's more settled, now. The war's over. I'm thinkin' some of that Kansas land might be waitin' for us."

Nancy brightened. "Where would we go, John?"

He smiled at her eagerness. Sometimes he thought *she* was the one with the restless nature.

"Well, we liked the country where we were, on the Missouri side. We'd farmed it enough to know the seasons. I was thinkin' mebbe across the line in Kansas. Far enough away from the old place so as to forget the touchy parts . . . the raiders and all. If there's no homestead land left, there'll be somebody who'll sell their claim."

"When do we start?"

"Well, we'll have to close out here. Sell some of the stock. Be nice if we could get there in time to plant corn, though."

"Is there time?"

"I'm thinkin' so. Talked to a fellow the other day . . ."

"John . . . You've already picked a spot?"

"Well . . . Nothin's sure yet. But we can go look, find somethin' else if it ain't right."

"Where is it?" she asked, eager as a child.

"Farther into Kansas a day or two. Southwest of Fort Scott. Sounds good to me, Nancy. A homestead claim the feller's quittin'. Filed on it just so's he could sell, I figure. Good water, partly farm, some timber . . . If it's like he says, just what we need. If not, there'll be somethin' else."

"There's somebody to contact, there?"

"Yes, the land office."

"Will you go take a look, first?"

"No . . . That'd slow things. We'll all go. Save time and travel."

Now her eyes were glistening with excitement.

"We'll sell some of the stock," he continued. "Take enough chickens for a start. Hogs wouldn't travel well, but we can buy hogs there."

"When shall we tell the boys?"

"Pretty soon, I guess. Maybe at supper . . ."

It was apparent that John had spent a lot of time in planning. He outlined which of the cows would travel well and which they should cull. Take two milk cows, sell old Buttercup, whose teeth were going bad anyway. Keep the two teams of horses for the wagons, and the saddle horse, to drive the cows.

"What about Tom and Dick?" asked Ezra, his voice a bit tight.

"Better leave 'em, son. They'll sell pretty good, now that things are greenin' up."

Ezra was silent for a little while as the conversation continued around the table. Finally, he spoke.

"Papa, couldn't we take my team along? We'll be herdin' loose stock anyway, and it would help keep 'em together. And, ain't they worth more when we get there?"

"Don't say ain't, Ezra," his mother admonished.

"Ain't no such word as ain't," William giggled.

"Stop it, William!" said Nancy.

"Papa says it."

"I know, but—"

"All right, that's enough," John put in with mock ferocity. "Now, about the team . . . I guess it wouldn't hurt to try it. Ezra, you'll have to do a lot of the herdin' anyway. But I don't want 'em slowin' us up."

"They won't, Papa. Can I take the yoke?"

"If you can find a place in the wagon."

Ezra figured he could. If nothing else, he'd hang the yoke under the rear axle of one of the vehicles. For a little while, he wished they had a third wagon. His team could have pulled that.

That evening, Nancy brought out her flag, to display it prominently by the door. It had been a long time coming. . . .

6

For the first few days, the old chill of fear returned when they met riders on the road. *Friend or foe?*

Gradually, it became easier. The realization sank home that it was over. Hard feelings and resentment might remain for years or for generations, even, but the bloody war along the border was finished, the killing ended. Riders who met the little caravan looked only with curiosity. Some were friendlier than others. A cheerful nod, a smile, a tip of the hat . . . A few faces, especially as they neared the Missouri line, showed a certain stolid disapproval. There was no question in any observer's mind as to the nature of these incoming travelers: a family of settlers, farmers with livestock. And, coming from the North, undoubtedly Union.

Nancy had thought it wise not to flaunt her Stars and Stripes. She had originally planned to fly it on a staff at the front of the big wagon. After due consideration, however, she decided against it. The memory of the real danger they had faced as they fled the area was too chilling. Six years ago, it had been, but there were still nights when she woke in terror. She furled the little flag and stowed it inside the wagon. Later . . .

It had taken some figuring, to choose their route. When they started this trip, they had considered following the old Lane Road, crossing west into Nebraska Territory and then south into Kansas. They studied the map. . . . That would bring them into Topeka, a bit farther west than they wanted. Besides, there would be two major river crossings, the Missouri as they entered Nebraska, and the Kansas, or Kaw, at Topeka. They had finally decided to retrace the route of their retreat six years before. The entire mood of the country was different. It might be well to avoid the area too close to their former home, though. There might be smoldering ill will there. They spent one day encamped, while a chilly spring rain pattered on the canvas wagon tops. John had managed to keep a fire going. They had gathered wood before the rain began and stowed it under the wagons. John fidgeted impatiently, eager to be on the road, but realizing the impracticality. The boys lolled under the big wagon, whittling or playing checkers, and slept there when night came.

The sun woke them next morning, and the clouds were gone. The rolling country was alive with birdsong, and beautifully decorated with blossoms of redbud, plum thickets, and dogwood. Elm trees were festooned with their greenish blooms, and the green of grass matched that of unfolding leaflets of elder, willow, and soft maples.

It will soon be time to plant corn, John worried to himself. "When the leaves of the maples are the size of a squirrel's ear," the old-timers said.

Actually, he'd never taken that saying much to heart. A maple leaf isn't really shaped like a squirrel's ear, so how would a person tell, anyway? The time to plant, he'd always figured, is when the soil is warm enough. Only problem, how to tell *that?*

There was a trick to it, like to most things. It had been told to him years before by an old man who'd befriended him. Old Jake knew all things about the woods and the prairie. At least, John had always thought so. Some of his sayings seemed to make no sense, like that about "birds flying low to the ground means a storm's coming within a day." And the "red sky in the morning, sailors take warning," and so on. John wasn't sure how that translated to prairie country, but he'd learned to listen to old Jake's predictions. Generally, they held true, regardless of how illogical they might seem.

The way to tell about planting corn, though, made good sense. He thought about it as they wound along the road. They were approaching a river, and near the ford there'd probably be a fisherman or two. "Ye look for fellers fishin'," Jake had advised. "Ef they're settin' down to fish, it's time to plant corn. Ef they're standin' up, wait a week or so. . . . Ground's too cold to set on, or to plant corn."

The wagon came around the shoulder of a little hill, and the river stretched before them. Not too wide, a pretty good ford. It'd have a solid bottom, he hoped. They were nearing Kansas now, and he was becoming impatient.

Just below the crossing, two youngsters were fishing with long hickory poles, cut from second-growth sprouts of a stump. And standing up . . . Good. He'd feel better, though, if he'd see somebody older. Youngsters had a tendency to be impatient, standing or moving around anyway. He watched their corks bobbing lazily in the current.

Ah! There, leaning against a sycamore, resting comfortably in the sun, was an old man. He, too, was fishing, and *standing* to do so. If it were warm enough, likely the old-timer would be sitting on the rock shelf, there beside him. John smiled to himself as he nodded a greeting to the fisherman. The old man returned the nod and turned his attention back to his fishing.

Now John studied the crossing. Not a bad one, he hoped. Crossing the streams was one of the worrisome things about traveling. The big crossing, of the Missouri River, had been by ferry, of course. Shouldn't be more than a couple more crossings like this, now, before they reached their goal. They'd turn west and cross into Kansas soon.

They had developed a routine for these crossings. John stopped the team, stepped down, and untied Buck, the saddle horse, from the wagon and reined into the stream, riding toward the slope where the wagon tracks led up and out of the river. Not too steep a slope, and the riverbed itself seemed to be a rock shelf at this point. Good . . .

He waved to Sam, who was driving the second wagon.

"Looks purty good! Hold up till I get across, though."

The big wagon with the family's furniture was usually the first to cross. The wheels were higher, track wider, a bit better equipped for questionable trails. The second wagon was heavy with iron . . . the anvil and forge, the plow and assorted tools. The wheels were broad, but smaller in diameter. It had not been a problem, since most of the stream crossings were well chosen and heavily used.

John rode back and handed the horse to Ezra. "You wait here till we get the wagons across. Hold the loose stock."

Ezra swung up proudly, turning the horse to check on the whereabouts of the cows. Holding them was no problem. The animals were grazing along the grassy slope, taking advantage of the stop.

His father climbed to the wagon seat, whacked the reins on the horses' rumps, and gave a shrill whistle. Fanny and Blue leaned into the collars and the wagon moved forward, the animals settling back into the breeching as they started down the gentle slope.

It was on the far side that the first sign of trouble became apparent. The opposite slope, which appeared quite firm from a little distance, proved to be soft. The day of slow spring rain had deceptively muddied the black, loamy soil. The big mares leaned forward, straining to keep moving. When the iron-shod wheels emerged from the stream and sank into the muddy bank, it looked for a moment as if the wagon would stop dead. John whistled and yelled, whacking the reins and trying desperately to keep the wagon rolling. The horses fought and pulled, laboriously pulling front feet from the deep mud, fighting for better footing. Half the energy used was consumed with the simple act of pulling up and out of the sucking, clinging mud. A short step, another, another . . . Finally, a front hoof found more solid ground, and the wagon moved ahead slowly, up the bank to more level road and firmer footing.

The horses were blowing heavily, and John guided them to a flat, grassy area and wrapped the lines around the brake lever.

"We'll let 'em blow a bit," he told Nancy. "I don't know about the other wagon, though."

He swung down and trotted back toward the stream. Sam had seen the entire process, and was waiting.

"You want to take 'em?" he called.

"No," John yelled back, "they know you. Anyhow, I'm over here on the wrong side. Come ahead. . . . Just try to hit the slope with a bit of a start."

One team was about as good as the other. The handicap here would be the weight of the smaller wagon.

"Want to unload some of the stuff?" Sam yelled.

"Don't guess so. I ain't aimin' to wade across carryin' the anvil, are you?"

Sam laughed nervously and urged his team into motion. The crossing was a little faster this time, and the speed a bit better when they struck the slope. There, the advantage ended. The front wheels struck the heavy mud and seemed to jab downward. The horses fought, slipped, and struggled, with no result.

"Hold it," called John. "Let 'em rest a minute."

"Father, that ain't goin' to do it," said Sam. "They were fresh goin' in."

"I know. The rest is for while I figger, here. If there's some way we could hook the other team in front . . . Maybe . . . Trouble is, the front team will be hock-deep in mud, too. They'll be pullin' the wagon and the other team."

Ezra now came splashing across the ford on the saddle horse.

"Papa, the ox team can pull it out!"

John looked around, annoyed, and then paused. "Wait, now . . . Might be they *could* help. A cow's foot slips out of the mud easier. . . . Folds together, like. Tell you what, Ezra. Gimme ol' Buck, there. I'll go bring the loose stock across, an' then we'll see. You got your yoke?"

"Yes, sir. It's in the stuck wagon. The log chains, too."

"Good!"

John rode into the stream, past the struggling horses, rounded up the cattle and urged them across. That part was not difficult. The animals were accustomed to this sort of crossing and to rejoining the wagons on the other side.

"Ezra, you catch your team. I'll bring the yoke."

Back into the water . . . "Sam, can you hand me the yoke?"

Sam tied the lines and scrambled back over the seat, across and among the implements and tools.

"Feels like it's sinkin' a little, Father!"

"Might be. Hand the yoke."

He kneed the horse over alongside and held out his hand. Sam lifted the beam and shoved it up on the tailgate, swinging one of the bows toward his father.

"Yep. Got it! Now, fetch the chain." John swung the yoke up and carried it in his right hand to higher ground, dropped it in the grass, and reined back into the stream. "Ezra, you and Will yoke up the team. I'll get the chain."

Sam had the heavy chain ready. It was clumsy, heavier than the yoke, and difficult to handle.

"Want me to get down and hook it?" asked Sam.

"No, you get ready to drive. I'll hook up."

Back to shore . . . The boys had the ox team in position now, and John tossed the chain behind the animals. He stepped down, picking up the slip-hook end. On foot now, he waded into the water, carrying the chain's end.

"Too short, Ezra. Circle 'em closer."

The boy led and drove the team around, through the edge of the water in front of the horses. Meanwhile his father quieted the horses and stooped between them to loop the chain around the front of the wagon tongue, through the eye, set the hook, and take up the slack. Back to shore.

"It'll reach, now," Ezra called.

"Good. Hook up your end. You drive. . . . They're used to you. But wait till I get out of the way."

"Wagon's tiltin' some," called Sam. "Water's over the left back wheel."

"No matter . . . We're ready," John called. "Now, go!"

Sam whacked the reins and the frustrated horses struggled against the collars. But now, Ezra popped the oxen with his driving stick, and the log chain snapped tight as they too began to pull. The horses, feeling the assistance, put forth another effort, pawing for footing.

"Hooray, it's movin'!" yelled Will.

It was true. Tom and Dick, bowing their heavy necks, pulled steadily, assisted by split hooves designed more for heavy mud than those of the horses. Slowly, inch by inch, but steadily . . . The tilting wagon righted itself and the wheels began to turn. Water poured from around the tailgate and back into the stream.

John let out a heavy sigh. The wagon had taken on more water than he'd realized.

"Take 'em on up to the clearing ahead, there," he called to Ezra. "We'll camp here, and see what kind of shape we're in."

Proudly, Ezra drove his ox team on up the slope to level ground and halted them. Today, the team had proved themselves, and he had, too. He was a man.

"Anything else, Father?" he called, with a voice that was somehow deeper.

Only two days later, they crossed into Kansas and struck the Military Trail. Now they were in familiar territory, and in much better spirits than six years ago, when they had traced the road north.

This time, Nancy's flag fluttered proudly in the breeze on the front bow of the big wagon.

7

⚜ ⚜ ⚜ ⚜ ⚜

Halfway around the world, another young man, only a trifle older than Ezra Willett, was struggling with similar feelings, but with far less satisfaction.

Karl Spitzburg had known, from the time that he was old enough to know anything at all, that he was destined for something special. It was not a thing to be questioned, for it had been decided. He had heard the story many times, how his mother, after a long and difficult labor, had taken her newborn son in her arms and put him to her breast.

"Is he all right?" she asked the midwife anxiously. "All fingers and toes?"

"Oh, yes," smiled the old woman. "A beautiful child, Anna. You will be proud of this one. Look . . . Even though he is tired too, he looks around the room. He wonders at the world. Yes, he is special."

"Then it was nothing wrong that made him so slow in coming?"

"No, no . . . Maybe an arm around the neck . . . Turned not quite right. *He* knew! When the time came, it went quickly, no? And the caul, still covering the head for a few moments . . . Very special."

The tired mother nodded.

"He *is* beautiful. . . . Yes, this is the one, Anna."

"For the church?" The old woman nodded thoughtfully. "It is good. Yes, in some way, I too feel that this is the one, Anna. It is a good choice."

So Karl was dedicated to the church. Father Bernoulli was pleased, and promised special attention to the instruction of this child, as soon as he was old enough.

"I will give him special mention in my prayers," the priest promised.

Everyone in the village knew of the decision immediately. Many of them made such selections. All had large families, and it was customary to designate the roles of the children. . . . This one, strong and hardworking, one of the older daughters, will be the one to care for the parents in old age . . . Or a thrifty son . . . This one inherits the farm. And somewhere along the succession of children, there was often one chosen to dedicate to the church.

The one given to the church would receive special instruction. The priest would spend extra time with the child. . . . More schooling than the rest . . . Then, at the time of coming of age, the church's child would be taken away to school for further instruction. Father Bernoulli usually chose the place, usually the same. A convent in northern Italy for the young women who would become nuns . . . One of two monasteries for the boys. That depended on whether the priest considered that the young candidate had the potential to become a priest, or the stolid devotion to isolation and prayer required by the monastic life.

For the first few years, Karl's life was very little different from that of the other children. He was the seventh child of a family that would eventually have eleven. Two of the older ones had perished before Karl's birth. Although at his christening he had already been dedicated to the church, the early years were quite similar to those of his brothers. All were assigned tasks in the household. Helping in the kitchen garden, feeding the poultry and gathering the eggs. For the older children, helping with the milking, churning the cream into butter, and the making of cheese.

From the earliest years, however, Karl had spent a little while after Mass on Sundays visiting with Father Bernoulli. The old cleric saw in this one a quick mind, a grasp of knowledge. This one he considered far above any other candidate ever brought to him. Therefore, the priest gradually spent more time with the youngster than with others. He was astonished when he realized that the boy could recite most of the Mass quite accurately. . . . A startling ability to memorize . . .

With this beginning, it was possible quite quickly to teach him a working knowledge of Latin. The tongue used primarily in the region of this village was a Germanic dialect, *Schwyzertütsch*. Father Bernoulli spoke it well, in addition to his native Italian and the French used to the west of the Helvetian canton of Schwyz. He was aware of a remote group of people in the mountains to the east who spoke an ancient Latin dialect, but that was of little consequence as he planned the boy's education.

Starting early, he knew, was the way for a child to master language. With this in mind, he began to teach. . . . Even before he could read and write, young Karl could converse in not only his native *Schwyzertütsch* but in the other Swiss tongues.

"Today," Father Bernoulli would say, as he removed and hung up his vestments after Mass, "we will speak only . . . let's see . . . how about French?"

It was a delightful game for young Karl, who absorbed knowledge like a sponge absorbs water. His mind reached out, yearning for more. . . .

Why is sky blue, and grass green? Why not blue grass and green sky?

Even patient Father Bernoulli would sometimes become irritated. *Why do birds sing?*

Eventually the good priest would reach the end of his patience.

"Because that is the way of it, Karl! That's just the way it is!"

By the age of five or six, the youngster could read fluently, and write as well. He was not so quick with arithmetic, because he found the repetition of endless numbers quite boring. Other studies, however, presented more challenging insights. The priest had a number of interests, including botany and astronomy, and was delighted to find an interested pupil. Increasingly more time was spent in the garden at the rectory, where Father Bernoulli propagated a variety of unusual flowers, herbs, and vegetables. Young Karl learned their common and Latin names, their particular needs and wants. This helped in his gardening tasks at home, too. He was developing a "green thumb."

Another of his favorite pastimes was to scan the starry sky with the aid of Father Bernoulli's telescope. It was a marvelous instrument, of shiny brass, with a tube as long as the boy was tall. It was easy to see the mountains and craters of the moon. Beyond that, it was a matter of curiosity about the stars and planets. He learned the names of the constellations, the courses of the planets in their orbits. . . . (*Why is Mars red? Because it IS, Karl!*)

"If we only had a reflecting telescope, Karl, we could see much more. The rings of Saturn, probably. I've seen them, at the observatory . . . beautiful."

They talked more of telescopes, and why a straight tube with refracting lenses is limited in usefulness. . . . It becomes too long to be practical before reaching the desired magnification.

They discussed the changes in crops in the past few generations. . . . New plant species and varieties from the New World, America. Father Bernoulli gave the boy half a dozen seeds of a special sort of bean, mottled red and white.

"Plant them at home," he urged. "The soil is a little different there than here at the rectory. See how they do."

"These are new?" asked the boy.

The old priest chuckled. "New to us. Very old, probably. The savages in the New World have grown them for many lifetimes. Many kinds . . . Hundreds, maybe."

"We did not have beans at first?"

"No, no, child. Not until a few generations ago. Nor pumpkins, corn, potatoes, even chocolate."

"The New World must be a wonderful place!"

"Likely, it is. And savage, dangerous. Much fighting, there. France, Spain, England, all fighting with each other and with the savages."

Karl said nothing, though the story had a ring of excitement to it. Strange lands, sights and sounds . . . Sometimes he longed for other vistas than the sameness of the village, the mountains, and the distant Alps. He longed for the day he could leave for his continued education.

He watched the long lines of geese as they migrated each spring and fall to winter in southern climes and nest somewhere in the north beyond the mountains.

"How do they know the way?" he asked.

"They are born knowing," Father Bernoulli told him. "God shows them."

The boy wondered about that for a long time. *How do they feel such direction?* Was it perceived as an urge of some sort, a need to go and see and do? More importantly, was it similar to the urges that he felt himself, sometimes? A restlessness of the spirit, stirring in his very being, an urge to *be,* and *do.*

There came a time when this stirring underwent a change in its nature. Father Bernoulli had, through the years, indoctrinated him well in the basic responsibilities of a man of the cloth. He understood the honor of self-deprivation, self-sacrifice, for the church and for the Savior. Karl had sinned occasionally, of course, quarreling with his brothers or evading the wishes of his parents. He was chastised and sometimes even punished at home for these infractions, of course. Yet he always went to confession with Father Bernoulli afterward, after he became eligible for communion and confession. It was easy because of long communication with his teacher. His penance was seldom severe, but merely appropriate to the infraction. An Our Father, a Hail Mary, a Glory Be, and perhaps an extra chore.

There came a summer, though, when his body began to change. He grew remarkably in height in the space of a few weeks. His voice was unpredictable. Sometimes he would start to speak, and the sound would be completely unfamiliar. . . . A high squeak, or an uncontrollably loud bellow. He was quite embarrassed, more so because of the teasing of his brothers.

Father Bernoulli took him aside to explain.

"You are becoming a man. Now is maybe the hardest part for a man of God. You will be tempted."

"Tempted?"

"Yes. You are pledged to celibacy as a novice to the church."

"Not to marry? Of course, but what . . . ?"

"To marry would be a distraction. We are instructed and urged to beware of any distractions. The whole heart, mind, and soul must be centered on the Savior and the Blessed Virgin, not on the temptations of the world."

"Then, is my father wrong to marry?"

"No, no. Some must marry, or there would be no new people, no? But one who is pledged to the church abandons earthly pleasures for the higher goal . . . perfection in Christ. It is by choice one accepts this self-denial."

The thought flitted through Karl's mind that he did not remember being offered such a choice, but he said nothing.

At about this same time, he noticed some other changes. There was a soft growth of downy fuzz on his upper lip and along his jaw. Other parts of his body, too, began to grow hair where there was none before.

Most alarming was the stirring in his loins when he looked at Mary Schmidt, one of the young women who attended Mass regularly. He had noticed a change in her body over the past few months. . . . There was a subtle widening of the hips, with an alluring sway that he had not noticed before. Her breasts appeared to take on a new fullness, pushing against the confining fabric of her dress. Her skin took on a new radiance, too, and seemed to glow, in company with the golden sheen of her hair.

But his hardest temptation that summer was the day when, assisting Father Bernoulli at the altar, he turned to move to the chancel and found himself glancing toward where Mary sat. He was shocked when their eyes met and he found her staring back. Huge, beautiful eyes of clearest, coolest blue . . . He almost gasped.

Even more disconcerting was the expression in those eyes. It was one of admiration, pride, and more. Something like *adulation* . . . The urgent flame in his loins alarmed him, and he almost stumbled as he turned.

Father Bernoulli was right. There were powerful temptations here.

8

Karl was quite disturbed by the event in the church. When he thought about it, which was frequently, the strange exhilaration recurred, the stirring deep in his loins. That was pleasant, which he knew must be wrong. This in turn brought feelings of guilt, and the whole cycle began all over again.

He had not sinned . . . at least, he did not think so. He had felt temptation, had imagined for a few moments how it might feel to touch that shapely young body . . . soft and warm, he was sure . . . to gaze into the azure pools of those beautiful eyes, and experience the affection that he had already seen reflected there. He had seen the suggestive lift of an eyebrow, which had conveyed much more than that. Karl did not understand how so much could be implied with the faintest flicker of a smile and that brief elevation of the brow.

Or was he misreading the whole thing? He thought not. He had seen this ritual happen, all his life, in the tiny village. He had, with the other boys, snorted in scorn, and withdrawn to more manly pursuits such as running, wrestling, and shooting, when they weren't choring. They had watched the older boys go through the change, become enamored of the young females' wiles, and had found it disgusting. One by one, the older ones, whom they had so admired, fell to the blooming charms of the village maidens. The youngsters had discussed these events with revulsion and with denial that it could ever happen to them.

In Karl's case, he *knew* that it could not. He had not only the revulsion brought on by the close-knit brotherhood-of-the-small-boy, but the edict of celibacy through the church. It could not happen to *him*.

Now, he was beginning to realize, it *could*. Temptation, predicted by Father Bernoulli, had crept upon him unsuspected, in the beautiful face and figure of Mary Schmidt. He had thought of himself as armed and prepared for the temptation, in whatever form, and now . . . He had been mistaken. The threat had been cleverly disguised, creeping upon him unsuspected in the form of a girl he had known all his life. Mary, daughter of Konrad Schmidt! As nearly as he could recall, she had never been particularly attractive. Now, even that thought seemed evil, because it implied that now, he *did* consider her attractive. Such an admission would suggest that he had already failed to survive the test of temptation.

What now? Should he ask Father Bernoulli about it? Probably . . . But maybe it would be better to go to confession, clear his conscience, and *then* ask about it. He still wasn't certain that he had sinned, but this way seemed the safest.

But the occasion did not seem to arise for such a confession. His studies, his work at home . . . There was simply not the time. This led to further guilt, further procrastination, and more impure thoughts. In the midst of all this, his mother spoke to the family one evening at supper.

"I have something to share. . . . Father Bernoulli has spoken to me of our Karl."

Panic gripped him. Did Father Bernoulli *know*? But . . . His mother was smiling! It must be something else. His face burned with embarrassment, as all eyes turned toward him.

"He tells me," Anna went on, "that it is time that Karl goes for his studies to the seminary!"

There was an appreciative murmur around the table, and Karl's face reddened even more. He would be taking the step under false pretenses!

"Wh-wh-*when*?" he blurted.

"Soon. Next month, after planting, I guess."

Karl's heart sank. Now, he *must* go to confession, to let Father Bernoulli know. . . . He was not *worthy* of this honor.

He tossed and turned sleeplessly for a long time that night, trying to decide how to approach the dreaded confession. It would be the end of his dedication to the church, he was sure. He had proven himself unworthy. . . . Finally he fell into a troubled sleep, and dreamed . . .

He was mowing hay, swinging the heavy scythe with a rhythmic sweep, step, swing, step. . . . Bright stalks of meadow grass fell with each skillful stroke. He could almost smell the sweet scent of drying hay, cut only this morning. As he approached the end of the swath, he looked up to see the beautiful face of Mary Schmidt before him, waiting at the edge of the meadow. He paused, and she smiled, beckoning.

"Come, rest a minute. . . ." Her musical voice was a siren song.

He knew it was wrong, but he moved like a puppet, walking toward her. He laid the scythe carefully aside, its razor-sharp blade in the fork of a tree at the meadow's edge to protect it. Mary took his hand and led him to a little glen among the rocks, where a quilt was spread on soft grass. She sank to it, pulling him along. The sun was warm.

Suddenly they were rolling in each other's arms on the quilt, and off of it, on the grass. His mind tried to resist, but his being cried out for more. The girl was soft and warm and her body pressed to his, her mouth searching for his kisses.

There was a sudden explosive climax, and he awoke, shaking and embarrassed, ashamed. On the other pallets, his brothers snored softly.

"Forgive me, Father, for I have sinned . . ."

The morning sun shone through the bright stained glass and cast strange patterns on the floor of the confession booth. Karl could feel the closeness of the priest on the other side of the carved filigree screen.

"Yes, my son? How long since your last confession?"

"I . . . I don't remember."

"Then a guess . . . A year?"

"No, no. Much closer than that."

This was strange. He was certain that Father Bernoulli knew precisely who the person was, in the other side of the booth. Yet, it was his duty to make the interview anonymous. It struck the young man that this was a tremendous responsibility. To conduct a session that was both intimate and impersonal.

"Maybe two months," he murmured.

"I see. . . . Go ahead, my son. What is your infraction?"

Now it suddenly occurred to Karl that this might be a completely impossible situation. For any other young man in the village, feelings such as his might even be acceptable. He could not reveal them, then, without also revealing his identity. But he must go ahead.

"I . . . I have lusted after a woman," he blurted.

This time, there was surprise in the priest's tone.

"You have been with a woman?" he asked sternly.

"No, no, Father. I spoke of feelings, not deeds."

"Oh." The tone was calmer now. "Tell me of this . . . these feelings."

Briefly, Karl told of his reaction to the flirtatious glance of Mary Schmidt.

"But," said the priest, "you did not act on these feelings?"

"No, no! I tried to ignore my baser instincts, Father."

"But they returned?"

"Well . . . in thought only. And in my dream."

"A dream?"

"Well . . . Yes, sir. But I have no control over a dream, do I?"

"We must talk further on this, Karl. Let us get out of this booth. The benches are uncomfortable."

"But . . . the confession?"

"Yes . . . Some penance, probably. But more importantly, we must talk of managing your temptations."

Karl felt better as they walked to the small room behind the altar and sat in more comfortable chairs.

"Of course I knew who it was," Father Bernoulli said. "I usually do, you know. It is a small village. Now, about your temptation . . . This is one of the hardest parts, Karl. Our animal nature calls to us. Our ability to overcome it is what separates us from the beasts. Well, one of the things. It must be controlled. *That* lifts us above the animals."

"But—"

"Let me go on. It is useless, I think, to *deny* your urges. The important thing is control. You *suppress* these feelings, you do not respond as your animal self urges you to."

"But *thinking* . . ."

"Yes, time spent nurturing such thoughts is time wasted. A monk must drive out such impure thoughts and replace them with thoughts of purity and devotion. Now, I wanted to talk to you, anyway. It is time to enter the monastery."

"My mother said you had mentioned this."

"Yes, I had intended to speak to you before. Are you ready?"

"When?"

"Next week, probably."

"Yes . . ."

"Good. There is less pressure for temptation there. . . . No female influence. It is easier to concentrate."

"But one still *thinks* . . ."

"Of course. I did not say *easy*. I said *easier*. It is still difficult. But there are fewer distractions."

Karl said nothing.

"You have doubts," Father Bernoulli said. It was a statement, not a question. "Of course! No one is ever completely free of doubt, because the flesh is weak. Through history, monks have had to deal with this temptation. Some, who could not do so, have become eunuchs to remove the distraction."

The young man's eyes widened.

"You—"

"No, no, not I," the priest said quickly. "I can control my urges. And, so can you."

Again, Karl was silent. He had grave doubts about his ability to maintain control over his thoughts. And, they had not even approached the significance of his tempestuous dream. He did not want to bring it up again, but how could something that had seemed so wild and warm and wonderful be evil? Maybe it was more than a temptation. Maybe something was wrong with him, and his bladder and bowel would never work properly again. Maybe *this* was his punishment, his penance for evil thoughts.

Father Bernoulli interrupted this line of thought.

"Well, let us plan to start south on Monday next. You will help me with Mass as usual on Sunday."

The priest rose, and the interview was over.

Karl was halfway home before he realized that his penance had not been prescribed. This led to more doubts. Did Father Bernoulli forget, or did he know that penance *was* taking place in the fear and doubt each time Karl started to empty his bladder?

Just to be on the safe side, he prayed the entire Rosary before retiring.

9

Karl couldn't figure at first how he'd do it, but he knew that he must. He simply did not believe that he could ever have the self-control and denial of his feelings, ever stronger. He certainly was not interested in the possible self-mutilation mentioned by Father Bernoulli. He doubted that the priest had meant to suggest that, anyway. It was only an illustration of the devotion of *some*.

However, it did serve to lay an extra burden of guilt on the already laden shoulders of young Karl. He felt that he was a failure, having betrayed the trust of his family, Father Bernoulli, the church, and God Himself. He hadn't carried out that betrayal yet, but he firmly intended to do so. The decision was not easy. There were times when he had wavered, but always his reasoning brought him back to the same point: He was unwilling to accept the sacrifice required of a priest. He could not forsake the possibility of marriage and family for a life such as that of Father Bernoulli. It must be a flaw in his character, one that he needed to discuss with the priest, his friend, mentor, and counselor. But he could not do so.

Occasionally the thought recurred to him that maybe this was a mortal sin. One dedicated and blessed to serve the church might be doomed to Hell and damnation if he denied such a covenant. He would really like to ask Father Bernoulli, but . . . Maybe somewhere, sometime, he would find a priest to listen to his confession. Maybe, even, help absolve him of this offense against God and the church. He could think about that later, but for now, he must plan. Time was short, and there was much to do, much preparation.

He was still determined not to commit any more sins than he could help. . . . Stay within the truth all he could, not bend any commandments that could be spared. That might partially spare him from the feelings of guilt that were already gnawing at his belly.

He openly made a show of preparing his pack for travel. . . . A tow sack, to hold his few articles of clothing. It would take a bit of doing, to have it handy and at the right place, but he'd figure out something. His mother, anxious about her churchly son's well-being, cooperated more than he could have expected even. She handed him a small wheel of cheese and a couple of round loaves of dark fresh bread to sustain them on the journey. . . . A small bottle of wine . . . He hated to deceive her, and tried hard not to make statements that were actual lies. General observations, such as a remark that Father Bernoulli would probably want to start south quite early on Monday, lessened his guilt only a little.

On Saturday, he finished his chores and calmly remarked that he was to help Father Bernoulli with some duties at the church. This was true. He had promised to polish the altar candlesticks before leaving. The part that was a bit deceptive was that he casually, though unobserved, took his ready-packed tow sack along. If any of the family asked, he'd say he was taking it to the rectory so as to be ready. That wasn't quite the truth, but he didn't have to use it anyway. Nobody noticed as he started for the church.

He didn't carry his pack quite all the way. He turned aside on the path and secreted the tow sack in a thicket near a rocky outcrop on the hill.

There was no one in the church, and he dutifully polished and shined the altar setting and replaced the items, proud of the improved appearance. Maybe for the last time. Someone entered to light a candle and kneel at the altar. . . . Konrad's pretty French wife, Celeste. That one stirred his manly feelings a bit, too. He tried to suppress such a thought. That must be especially evil, right here in church. . . . He wondered if she was troubled about something. He slipped out, unnoticed.

Karl was still proud of his duties as acolyte. He wondered which of the younger boys would now assume such duties.

He had it all figured carefully. After Mass on Sunday he'd stay behind as usual. The family would go on home while he visited with Father Bernoulli and took care of the tabernacle and the elements of communion. Then he'd leave, as usual.

It worked out pretty much that way. Father Bernoulli wasn't very talkative, and Karl wondered if he, too, was thinking about this last Sunday together.

They parted with an informal wave and a "bless you," and a last admonition from the priest: "About daylight, remember!"

Karl ambled along the footpath until he was out of sight, then hurried to his cache and recovered his pack. . . . Over the hill to the main road . . . There wouldn't be much traffic on a Sunday, and he'd as soon not be seen.

He'd not likely be missed until suppertime. The family would assume that he was still at Father Bernoulli's house, and the priest would assume that he'd gone on home to await tomorrow and their journey to Italy. Probably, it would be evening before anybody really became concerned. He regretted not being able to say good-bye to his mother, but did not see how it could be helped. That was, maybe, the biggest sadness, as well as a heavy addition to his load of guilt. He knew this would hurt her deeply, and he resolved to write her a letter as soon as he could. He hoped that she could forgive him.

He tried to shove it aside as he hurried along the road toward the town of Arth, to the southwest of home. Once, he saw a horse and cart approaching from that direction and slipped off the road into the trees until it passed. He didn't think he'd been seen.

Nearing Arth, he headed across the mountain on a footpath to the northwest. He'd never been there, but he knew the path would intersect the old Lake Road along the eastern shore of Lake Zug. At the north end of the lake should be the city of Zug, much larger than Arth, or even than Cham. He wouldn't get as far as Zug tonight but would camp along the Lake Road somewhere. He hurried on.

He had studied some of the maps in Father Bernoulli's library, under pretense of tracing their path on the journey south to the Italian monastery. He had managed to memorize the route he wanted, at least moderately well. Just now, he estimated that he was possibly halfway to Zug. There, he'd turn west toward Cham, traveling along the north shore of the lake. He'd even picked an alternative route, heading north a little farther to Lake Ageri and then west. He'd decide when he got to Zug.

His camp near the road on the lake shore was cold and lonely, even with the bright fire. He ate a little cheese and part of one of his loaves of bread, drinking from a spring that came sparkling from the hillside. He did not open his flask of wine.

He prayed a long time for guidance, and concluded with a Hail Mary, which reminded him of his own mother and brought the return of his guilt. For a brief moment he considered going back, but quickly thrust that thought aside. His major problem would still exist, and it must be confronted *now*. Just the same, he shed a lonely tear as he drew his cloak around him and tried to sleep.

He slept poorly, and rose before dawn to warm himself with the activity of traveling on.

.   .   .

Zug was a wondrous city, composed of more buildings than he could count. The rush, bustle, and confusion were almost more than he could bear. It would be good to be in open country again.

He asked a peddler about the road to Cham and received easy instruction. "Just stay on this road. . . . Easy half-day's travel."

That would put him at or near Cham at nightfall. He searched his memory. . . . Menziken would be the next town, he thought, a day or two west. Then, Zofingen, as large as Zug. He'd cross parts of four cantons on the way to the border, he thought. Schwyz, where he had started, then Luzern, Aargau, and Basel. He rather dreaded the town of Basel, at the western border of Basel Canton. It would be a huge city, maybe ten times the size of Zug, even. That was where he'd cross the border, though, out of Swiss territory and into France. There, he would ask directions to Mulhouse, and make his way to the coast. From there, his ideas were a bit sketchy. But, some of the urgency would be behind him. He knew it might take some time to work his way to America, but he was certain he could do it. . . . Others had, so he could, also.

He traveled, stopping for the night in some haystack or stable, sometimes under the stars. Sometimes he worked for a day in return for a meal or two. The country folk, recognizing a kindred soul, would send him on his way with a bit of food . . . bread, cheese, sausage, a flask of wine. . . .

Karl could have easily taken eggs from the nests of hens in the country barns where he slept, but could not bring himself to do so. It would have been stealing. His rejection of the career planned for him by his family and Father Bernoulli did not include rejection of the church. He prayed, he spent a few moments of solitude sometimes in an empty church along the road, alone with his thoughts and his guilt. That was the hardest. . . . The statues, looking down with expressions of sadness, seemed almost to be *accusing* him. At best, there was disapproval in the marble faces, the painted expressions.

He longed to undergo confession, but could not. Karl was certain that a priest would not only reprimand him severely but send him back to Father Bernoulli as part of his penance. Maybe even worse. Could it be demanded of him to enter some monastery that required that its novices become eunuchs? He wondered. It was safest, he decided, to avoid priests as he traveled. That would avoid the threat of confrontation. Unfortunately, it only added to his crushing burden of guilt.

He traveled across France, generally following the River Seine. He was appalled at Paris, at its beauty and at the crush of people. He might have been

vulnerable to its crime, but since he obviously possessed nothing worth stealing, his innocence provided some degree of protection. Or possibly, some of
his guilt-laden prayers reached their target. . . .

On down the Seine, he reached the harbor at Le Havre. That was one
of his major goals. There he hoped to find a ship on which he could work
his way to America, the land of opportunity.

10

They only laughed at him in Le Havre.

"You are crazy, boy!" a French sailor told him when he inquired. He pointed to a tall-masted ship at her berth. "Think you could climb that riggin' and tie off sails? You probably never saw salt water until today!"

That was pretty close to correct.

"I could learn!" Karl retorted stubbornly.

"You wouldn't *want* to learn what you'd have to on this ship, sonny! Forget it!"

The sailor gave the boy a shove, nearly knocking him flat. Karl regained his balance and stifled the urge to strike back. He would only get hurt if he pursued this argument. He turned away bitterly. This was not the first such rebuff. He was actually considering trying to sneak on board when the sailor turned back, his tone only slightly less antagonistic.

"Do not be tryin' to stow away, either," the sailor warned. "You'd be tossed overboard a day or two out to sea."

Karl turned away, discouraged, and wandered along the wharf. The thought crossed his mind that he *could* go back, but he quickly rejected it.

The foregoing conversation had been in French, and he was startled to hear a deep, masculine voice in a more familiar tongue. Not *Schwyzertütsch,* but German.

"Sprechen Sie Deutsch?"

"What? Yes . . ."

"You have trouble, son?" The speaker was a solid, farmer-looking man, with big callused hands. "Where are your people?"

"I . . . I have none," Karl lied.

It was the first outright lie since he had left home. Before this he had managed by merely being rather vague and skirting around the edges of the truth.

He found that it was not difficult to follow the conversation in this dialect, slightly different from his own. The speech was somewhat slow and heavy, which gave time to interpret any slight differences.

"Too bad," the big man said, in answer to Karl's lie about being an orphan.

Karl only shrugged, but his heart was heavy. He looked up and down the dock, now with a different eye. There were perhaps thirty people, men, women, and children, with piles of baggage. Probably six or seven families . . . Yes, he could see that there were couples, mostly young to middle-aged, lounging on or near each pile of luggage. The children were more difficult to sort out, having a tendency to group together by age and gender.

"Where are you going?" the big man asked.

There was a quiet charisma about the man. It was fairly obvious in an instant that he was the leader of the group.

"America," answered Karl. "I had hoped to work my way."

"*Jah!* I saw your talk with the sailor," the man chuckled.

"Where are you going?" Karl asked.

"America, too. We farm. Some of our things, already loaded. We carry the rest." His hamlike hand swept the scene on the dock with a gesture.

Now he studied the young man. "You look strong. . . . You know how to farm?"

"Yes."

"Goot! You come with us!"

"Hans!" exclaimed a handsome blond woman of motherly proportions who sat on one of the baggage piles. "We can't—"

Hans waved her aside. "We can use another pair of shoulders to the wheel, no? This one wants to work!"

He turned back to Karl.

"Like I said, you come with us. You have a name?" He grinned.

"I . . . I'm Karl Spitzburg."

He saw no reason to conceal his identity, and it would only add to his burden of guilt, to lie again.

"And I, Hans Grossenbach. This, my wife Gretchen."

He pointed to the blond woman, then turned and extended a huge paw to shake hands.

"You be with us now," he said.

Karl experienced a moment of hesitation. *What am I getting into?* he thought.

It passed quickly. These people were looking for the same things he was . . . a place to live and work, with a fresh start in a new land. He could leave them, too, if it didn't seem to be working out. . . . After satisfying his indebtedness to them, of course. He stuck out his hand to meet that of Grossenbach.

Perhaps his judgment was influenced to some extent by the shy smile of an extremely pretty girl about his own age sitting beside Mrs. Grossenbach. She had eyes of purest blue, and hair the color of her mother's. . . . But, there was no time for further introductions. A hail from the deck beckoned them aboard, and Karl helped carry baggage. It was a good feeling, not to be alone.

The first three days on board ship were the most miserable Karl had ever experienced. The swaying motion of the ship made him dizzy and his stomach churned. To stand on the deck and stare upward at the sailors climbing like monkeys among the rope ladders of the rigging was enough to make him vomit. The arc from side to side swept by the tips of the masts was quite alarming. He could not believe that he had actually attempted to apply for such activity. It was little comfort that most of the other passengers were equally afflicted.

Gradually, his stomach settled, and he began to take nourishment. It was only then that he began to learn more about his new associates. They were not Catholic, and he had never before been around anyone who was not. This was puzzling to him, but he did not feel comfortable discussing it. The group held nightly prayers and sang sometimes, and talked of Jesus Christ, but there was no priest. Hans Grossenbach seemed to serve as both spiritual and temporal leader. Karl missed the formality of a ritual liturgy. Maybe he would learn more later.

Meanwhile, he enjoyed the company of these sincere and helpful people. He gathered that for some reason, perhaps political, they had lived in several different places over the past few decades. . . . Various parts of Germany, Austria, most recently northern Belgium. They were, like himself, now seeking a new start.

Karl immediately related well to them, and the homesickness that had bothered him lessened somewhat. His longing for the company of his brothers and his younger sister was helped by the association with the Grossenbach family. Gretchen mothered him, along with her own three, all slightly younger than Karl. That particular relationship, though, was a mixed blessing. He could see in Mrs. Grossenbach many traits and even mannerisms that reminded him of his own mother. This in turn brought forth the burden of guilt that he felt when he thought of the manner of his leaving. He would write at the first opportunity and try to explain his actions. If he could, that is. For now, he did not even have access to paper and pen.

He still had no idea about how serious his default might be considered by the church. Sooner or later he must find a way to plead his case, to learn where he stood. He might be required to do serious penance, or possibly even be excommunicated.

Only now did he begin to realize that there was one other option. He could embrace the faith of these good people who had befriended him. As yet, he had very little understanding of their beliefs. He was curious to know more, but that would come, maybe. Meanwhile, he could see no harm in observing their very informal worship and even in participating. *It is the same God, no?* He continued his own prayers, as privately as he could, and the others did not disturb him. Still, he realized that there must come a time of reckoning. He must go to confession and bare his soul to a priest. Only in that way could he learn what he must know for his troubled soul to find rest.

In the course of the voyage he gradually learned more about the destination of the group he had joined.

"We have heard of this place which needs farmers," Hans told him. "I will show you . . ."

He drew out and carefully unfolded a yellowed handbill. It was printed in German and in another language. . . .

"English?" asked Karl. He could make out only a word here and there that resembled Latin.

"*Jah,* it must be."

The German section of the bill extolled the virtues of free prairie land, "awaiting the plow," and described the magnificent crops that could be produced . . . giant pumpkins, heavy yields of fruit, maize taller than a man could reach, called "corn" in English. There was a sketch of a giant stalk.

"That's for animals to eat, of course," Hans explained.

"What tongue is spoken there in this prairie country?" asked Karl. "I do not know English."

"Nor do we. But, we speak mostly to each other, no? Maybe we learn enough English to get by, sell our crops. We will see."

The handbill was fascinating, and spoke of free land for those who would come to settle and farm in this new state, "Kansas." It was exciting to contemplate.

"What other crops do they have?" he asked Hans.

"I do not know, Karl. Almost everything, it looks. The picture shows that. Grapes, the big melons, there . . . See?"

But, there was still the nagging concern about the language. . . .

11

My dearest Mother . . .

Karl paused, deep in thought. His parents could read only a little, and would probably turn to Father Bernoulli for assistance. Knowing that this letter would be read by the priest whom he now felt he had betrayed, he was at a loss as to what to say. He sighed and laid the pencil beside the paper.

Another, separate letter to the priest? He did not feel that he could be comfortable with that until after he had confessed. The story was too long and complicated. Maybe he could finish the letter to his mother, and save it. . . . He picked up the pencil and started on:

> *First, be assured that I am well. I miss you all very much, and regret the worry that I have caused you, and that I have been a disappointment to you. Some of it I cannot explain, but this was something that I must do.*
>
> *I am in a place called "Kansas" which is in the tongue of the savages who live here.*

No, that would never do. He did not want to alarm his mother with mention of "savages." He sighed again and slowly crumpled the little page. He hated to waste the paper. It was not easily available here on the prairie. He put aside the unused paper and pencil, resolved to try again later.

They were still traveling. It had been established, a specific goal. The party would settle in an area of central Kansas, where small communities were springing up. Nearly every day they passed towns and farmsteads in process of construction. The area was said to be favorable for wheat.

"But," Hans had inquired, "is there enough rainfall?"

"Oh, yes, and there will be more," the land promoter had promised.

"More? How can this be?"

"A scientific fact . . . This virgin sod has never felt the plow. When the sod is turned, it *releases* moisture into the heavens, which returns as rain. Look here at the charts: for five years now, an average that is better, more inches of rain. Now, where you came from, Switzerland, you said? Your land has been farmed for centuries, and you have more rain, no? It's a fact!"

They had to agree. It must be true.

"Can a plow turn this sod?" Hans asked, kicking at the curly buffalo grass.

It had been determined that much of the area in which the tallgrass species grew was too rocky to plow. They had decided to move farther west, into shortgrass country, which was flatter and dryer. It was covered with buffalo grass, seldom more than four inches tall, light gray-green, tough and curly. "Nigger-wool sod," the promoter called it.

"Your first plowing is tough," he admitted. "You have to keep the plowshare sharp and polished. But each season, it's easier. You've got another advantage, too. You can *use* the blocks of sod the plow turns up. Cut 'em like bricks or building stone, to build your first shelter. 'Soddies,' we call 'em. There aren't many trees yet, but you can plant 'em. Good fruit country. Apples, peaches, pears. Nut trees, too. And small fruits . . . Grapes, berries . . ."

They had taken the enthusiasm of the promoter with some reservations, but they did have some direction now, and some contacts at their destination. They had followed the old Santa Fe Road for several days past Council Grove, through rolling hills with cold springs and lush grass. It had been heavily timbered in the canyons and along the clear streams. Now, they were in the dryer shortgrass country.

Still, settlers were building towns, about a day's travel apart. That was logical, Karl realized. He had never thought much about why towns are located where they are. Here, in a new country, it could be seen. Produce must be sold, and at no more than a day's travel, to provide ordinary needs.

Karl had been learning some English as they traveled, although most of the party would rather talk among themselves. They had also encountered small communities who spoke other languages. Welsh, Scottish, Czech, Swedish. Some were familiar dialects, others quite difficult.

Overall, though, he was troubled. He felt that he was growing further and further away from his faith. Day and night, guilt at what he had done gnawed at his conscience. It was no help at all that Helga, the oldest daughter of Hans and Gretchen Grossenbach, looked increasingly attractive to him. She somehow reminded him of Mary Schmidt, back in his own church in Schwyz. She often demonstrated the same sidelong glances and coy smiles.

His guilt gnawed not only at his conscience but at his stomach, too. His appetite was poor, and many times there seemed to be a firm, tender spot just under the V where his ribs met the breastbone. *Maybe this is part of my penance,* he thought, *for the betrayal of my faith!* It was an alarming thought, and one that added an extra burden.

The travelers camped one evening near a cluster of new buildings in the process of construction. There were stacks of lumber and shingles, kegs of nails. . . . A partly completed structure that would become a store . . . Wooden frames covered with canvas, a temporary expedient that was little better than camping. At the end of the street, though, was a frame building which was nearly completed. There was a crowd of people, all working with hammers and saws and, on one side, paintbrushes.

Tears nearly came to his eyes when he saw that at the top of the structure, on the pinnacle of the steeple, was a cross. A *Catholic* church!

As soon as he could, he left the travelers' camp to investigate further. The crowd had thinned now, as lengthening shadows signaled the approach of suppertime. A few men were tidying up the churchyard, and he saw that one of these wore the garb of a priest, with a high clerical collar. He almost rushed toward the man.

"Father . . . I . . . Can you hear my confession?"

Karl spoke in his own Germanic tongue.

The puzzled priest answered in English, with a broad Irish accent. "What? I do not understand. Can you speak English?"

How stupid of me, Karl thought, *to assume that every priest will know my tongue!*

"No . . . Only a little," he said hesitantly. "German? French?"

The priest shook his head.

Suddenly it came to him: *Latin!* "Latin, then?"

"Mother of God! You speak *Latin?*" the priest blurted.

"Yes, yes! I was dedicated to the church! I was to become a priest!"

"Ah! I was told your party was Protestant . . . Lutheran or Huguenot or something. How is this?"

"We are . . . They are . . . I met them during the journey here."

"I see . . ."

The priest's expression said plainly that he did not.

"Will you hear my confession?" pleaded Karl.

"Of course. Let us sit . . . here." He pointed to a small stack of lumber that would undoubtedly be used for the inside finishing work. It was protected by a canvas tarpaulin.

"Bless me, Father, for I have sinned," Karl began.

The priest waved a hand.

"I think we can dispense with some of the formality, my son. Now, I am Father Owens. And you?"

"Karl Spitzburg."

"German?"

"No. Schwyz. The others are German."

The priest nodded. "Go on, then. Tell me."

Karl blurted out the entire sordid story. His early training, his temptation, his failure . . . Father Owens sat still, listening, nodding occasionally.

Finally the young man, exhausted from the emotional effort, collapsed into silence. Tears streamed down his cheeks, and he cupped his face in his hands, sobbing quietly. The old Jesuit waited. Finally Karl managed to look up, wiped his eyes with the backs of his hands, and looked at the priest, who had not spoken.

"What must I do?" he asked.

Father Owens heaved a great sigh. "That is it? No more? You have not *acted* on this temptation?"

"No, no, Father. Only in a dream, once."

The old man nodded thoughtfully. "And you have broken no vows?"

"Yes, I have! I ran away from a promise. I was pledged to the church!"

"But that was the pledge of your *parents,* not you."

"But I have failed to honor it. I have betrayed them and my church."

"Because you feared the temptation."

"Yes, I could not resist even the first feelings. I am weak! A failure."

"I understand. But look. The pledge was not yours, but *theirs.* So you have broken no vows. You—"

"I ran away—"

The priest nodded, but raised a hand to silence him. "So that you would *not* give in to temptation, no? Where is that a sin?"

"But I *will*! Father, I am unable to start something that I know will fail."

"So you want a woman, a marriage, a family of your own?"

"I . . . Yes, that is it. I am weak. I cannot be a celibate. I cannot deny it."

Father Owens nodded, a trace of a smile on his lips. "Yes . . . It is sometimes very difficult, my son. It is not for everyone. I am brought to thinking that you would never be comfortable with it. But it is your choice, not someone else's. Your parents have done their part, with their pledge. Your priest has done his. Your part is decision, and you have made it." He spread his palms and shrugged in a question. "Where is the problem?"

"I . . . I do not have to leave the church?"

"Of course not! Will you go home?"

"I could go *home?*"

"Certainly, if you wish."

"I . . . I think not. Not now, anyway."

"Then . . . you still pray?"

"Yes, yes. Of course."

"Good. Do that. Will you stay with the Germans?"

Karl thought a little while. "I think so, for now."

Father Owens nodded, frowning slightly. "It would be better, maybe, if you find a way to follow your own faith. But you know the rituals, the Rosary. You have Rosary beads?"

"Yes."

"Then follow as you are able. Your heart is right, and that cannot be taken from you. There is need for those who enter the priesthood, yes. But also, need for families loyal to the church. Maybe that is your calling."

He rose, a little stiffly. "Well, I must join the O'Malleys for supper. God go with you!" He took a step or two, then turned. "We have Mass in the morning. Do your Germans travel on Sundays?"

"No. They hold services."

"Good. Will you join us for Mass?"

"I will," answered Karl. "*They* may not."

"Probably not," agreed the priest. "So be it."

He shuffled off.

Karl's spirits soared. He felt that suddenly all of his problems were behind him. He would be able to write now to his parents, to Father Bernoulli. With this great burden lifted from his back, he could face the challenge of the frontier with strength and confidence. He started back toward the camp of the Grossenbachs with a new strength, head high, and shoulders squared. Ahead lay the future, and there by the fire, Helga looked up at him and smiled.

12

"Paper, mister?" Tom asked the well-dressed young gentleman who had just stepped from the door of the club.

The man paused, frowning as he glanced at the fine misty drizzle that was beginning to descend on the streets of New York. He rummaged in a vest pocket, while the boy quickly slipped a dry paper from the center of the stack under his arm.

Tom caught the flipped coin that the gentleman tossed, dropping it into the pocket of his ragged trousers without looking. He knew what it would be. A gold dollar . . . Tiny, but valuable. He'd picked his man, one of his regulars, always a big tipper. The price of the paper was five cents.

"Thankee, sir," he called after the retreating form.

He'd learned that timing was everything. That, and selecting customers. This one . . . Tom didn't know his name . . . always came out of the gentlemen's club at about this time. Shortly after that . . . Yes, here he came . . . An older, portly gentleman.

"Evening, Mr. Brown! Paper?"

"Why yes, Tom. Thank you!"

He took the paper, folded it against the weather, and handed his coin. A nickel, the usual. A talkative man, friendly, but not very generous. Sometimes a dime, with an admonition to spend wisely.

"Where's my carriage? He should be here. . . . Oh, here he comes!"

"Thanks, sir!" Tom called after him.

He glanced at the papers under his arm. Three left . . . They were getting a bit soggy, in spite of his relatively sheltered position against the building. And, it was getting dark. One more sale, maybe, and he'd head for the alley. The boys would have a fire going, and he could toast the chill out of his bones. This sort of weather always made his bad leg act up.

Tom wasn't sure how old he was. He'd tried to keep count. Thirteen, maybe. He must have been seven or eight when his mother died. He couldn't remember much about her. She worked hard, and was always tired when she came back to their tiny room. She coughed a lot, and she always worried about him. The leg . . . He didn't know when it had been hurt. A horse had stepped on him in the street, she'd told him. He'd played in the street since he could remember, with other youngsters. Some of them had fathers who drank a lot of whiskey and could be cruel when they were drunk. Tom figured he was pretty lucky not to have one.

He'd been hawking newspapers since he was about ten, after his mother died and the room they'd shared was rented to someone else.

A handful of newsboys lived in the dubious shelter of a blind alley near the docks. Nobody bothered them much. Nick, a bit older than most, was their accepted leader. They helped each other some, when necessary, but mostly it was each to his own. Food was shared, after a fashion. There was usually a pot of stew steaming over a fire of wooden crates and boxes. It wasn't the cleanest, but nobody got sick very often. Not from that, anyway. Most of them chewed or smoked tobacco, acquired from cigar butts in the street; sometimes there was coffee, boiled in a tin can and shared.

Money was not, except for somebody in trouble. Sometimes an older ruffian would assault one of the boys and take his meager earnings. That called for financial help, to buy his next day's papers. This was usually given freely because it could happen to anybody.

This evening three boys were huddled between the fire and the building wall on the side that gave a little shelter from the drizzling rain. Tom hoped it wouldn't rain really hard, like it sometimes did. That was always very uncomfortable, and they had to split up and seek shelter elsewhere, in the rat-infested catacombs of the city's tunnels. And that was not only scary, but dangerous. There were monsters there, the stories said.

Tom laid his last two papers in the usual place beside his dirty blanket and nodded to the others. Maybe he'd try to read a little bit by the light of the fire, if he felt like it after a while. Or, maybe not. The papers were damp, but by morning they'd probably be burned for fuel anyway.

"Where's David?" somebody asked.

"Haven't seen him."

"Me neither. And John . . . ?"

"They'll be along."

There was silence for a little while.

"What's in the stew?" Tom asked.

"Nick got some meat, an' a few turnips. Hasn't been cookin' long, though. Better wait. And, John may get some purty good stuff in back of the hotels. It's a good garbage night."

Tom nodded, and set aside the can that served as his dishware.

"I'm thinkin'," said Nick seriously, "we'd ought to be wonderin' about Davie. He's purty small. . . ."

"That helps him with beggin'!" observed Ben.

"Sure, but . . ."

The rest went unsaid. The vulnerability that made Davie the best of them when it came to panhandling was also his weakness. He couldn't be more than six, Tom figured, and small for his age.

"Should we go look for him?" Tom asked.

There was silence for a little while, and then Nick spoke.

"I'll go check his regular corner," he said. "Be right back."

He was back, sooner than expected, breathing hard from running.

"There's trouble!" he panted. "We better scatter."

"What is it?"

"Dunno. Somebody got knifed, tryin' to pick a pocket. The law's out bustin' heads an' arrestin' the boys off the street. Let's go."

Tom grabbed his blanket and turned toward the street, but it was too late. The alley's entrance was blocked by two burly policemen, and more were coming into view. They carried heavy billy clubs, and their facial expressions said plainly that they meant business. In the deepening dusk, a paddy wagon with barred sides drew to a stop at the curb.

"All right, now!" shouted one of the officers. "Inta the wagon with ye!"

Ben tried to make a break for it, darting toward the street. An officer caught his arm, swung him into the brick wall, and rapped him sharply with his club above the left ear. Ben staggered.

"Enough o' that! Inta the wagon, now, ye little bastards!"

He gave the reeling Ben a shove that nearly sent him sprawling.

"Ain't no need for that, Sergeant," yelled Nick. "Let him alone."

The officer whirled. "None o' yer smart mouth, boy!"

He raised the club, threatening.

"I'm goin', I'm goin'!" said Nick quickly. He jumped into the wagon. "Come on," he called to the others.

They trooped in, to join a huddled knot of children already there. The iron door clanged shut, and the heavy wagon trundled on down the street.

·   ·   ·

The jail was dark and damp. The boys were herded down a corridor and into a large cell with several older prisoners already inside. There were bawdy and obscene remarks as the youngsters retreated to a corner.

"I'll take that purty one with the red hair, there!" a grizzled old man leered.

"You behave yourselves," the jailer muttered. "None o' that, now." He turned away.

"Sure, sure, Sergeant," hooted one of the prisoners. "We'll look after 'em."

The outer door clanged, and they were alone in the cage. Now, a tough-looking man of perhaps thirty spoke for the first time.

"All right, that's it. Let 'em alone or you answer to me."

"What's goin' on?" demanded Nick of the speaker.

There was silence for a little while as they studied each other. Pale yellow light from the coal-oil lantern in the corridor filtered through the bars and made striped patterns on the stone floor and the bunks along the far wall.

"Trouble," said the burly man finally. "That's what. They're roundin' up everybody on the streets."

"Why? We never done no—" Nick started, but was interrupted.

"Yeah, yeah, sure. But, near as we kin figger, somebody got his pocket picked, and pulled out one of them cane swords. They said he cut up the thief a little, an' somebody tried to stop it. Whacked the gentleman good."

"What's that got to do with us?" demanded Nick.

"Nothin'," the older man shrugged. "Jest happens, I guess, said gentleman was somebody important, didn't take kindly to such treatment. They're sweepin' the streets. There was some street Arabs, like your crew here, around where it happened, so they got drawed in, too."

"What will they do with us?"

"Don't know. Some kind of hearin', I suppose. Reckon we'll see."

"They feed us?" asked Ben. He was gingerly feeling the knot above his ear.

"Too late. We already et. In the mornin', maybe. It's hardly worth the wait, though."

Tom looked around the cage. The only furnishings were benches along the left corner and several bunks with stained straw-tick mattresses against the far wall. Not enough for this many prisoners to sit or lie down at the same time. In another corner a stinking slop bucket, half full of urine and feces and infested with flies, served as a chamber pot.

One of the adult prisoners saw him looking at it and chuckled, exposing an expanse of rotting yellowed teeth. "Time to use that is at mealtime, boy. All the flies move over to see what's for dinner and you can shit in peace." He laughed, slapping his knee gleefully at his sickly joke. Tom had never felt lower.

A little later, another load of boys arrived, shoved down the corridor and into the holding cell as before.

"Nick!" shouted one of the smaller ones.

"Davie! You all right?"

"Sure," bragged the youngster, his voice shaky. His lips were quivering. "I'm okay, Nick."

He ran to the older boy, hugged him around the knees, and broke into sobs.

"It'll be okay, Davie. We're all here."

"Tom?"

"Sure, Davie. It's all right now."

It was several hours later that there were sounds of activity on the stairs and the jailer opened the barred door to the corridor. He was carrying a lantern and was accompanied by two well-dressed men. They marched to the cage, disapproval strong on their facial expressions.

"Such filth!" one muttered. "Officer, what do you have to say for yourself?"

"For *myself*? I ain't the one in there, cap'n. And, it ain't my job to clean 'em up."

"But these are children, man! You can't . . . Well, never mind. We'll take them to the home."

"When? We have to feed 'em in the morning?"

"I should hope not," the well-dressed gentleman retorted. "I shall proceed with the paperwork, if you will authorize transportation."

"Well, now, that might take some doin', sir. Hitchin' up the wagon an' all . . . I'd have to turn out a couple of extra men."

He seemed to be hinting at something. A bribe, maybe.

"Do it, then!"

There was little patience in the gentleman's tone, and no offer of a bribe. This must be someone with a great deal of influence, thought Tom.

Now, the gentleman spoke to the boys in the cage.

"All right, listen to me, now. I am Charles Brace, of the Children's Aid Society. You boys are to be taken to one of our orphanages, where you will be fed and cared for."

"Whoo-ee!" shouted the grizzled prisoner with the rotten teeth. "Kin I go too, cap'n?"

"Shut up, Lonnie, he ain't talkin' to you," snapped the jailer.

Mr. Brace started for the door, and then turned to his companion.

"Mr. Reese," he said, "why don't you take a few moments to photograph these conditions? Don't omit the . . . uh . . . facilities."

Brace pointed to the slop bucket, and the photographer nodded in understanding as he began to set up his tripod.

13

It was difficult at the Orphan Asylum. Rules were strict, a new and different experience for many of the homeless boys of the streets . . . "street Arabs." Some escaped, running away, back to the comparative freedom of the former life, with all its risks. Adults, especially those with power and authority, were not to be trusted.

Most, however, came to understand, if they were not entirely trusting. Here were people who, for no apparent gain for themselves, furnished food and clothing and shelter. Some of the orphans who had been there awhile trusted completely.

There were late-night conversations in the dormitory room.

"They just want to help us."

"But why would they do that? There must be somethin' behind it."

"I don't care. There's food an' blankets an' a roof."

"Mebbe they're fattenin' us up for somethin'."

There was nervous laughter.

"Quiet down in there," called the night supervisor. His tone was stern but not threatening.

There was silence for a little while, and then cautious whispers again.

"Listen," said Nick, older and wiser, "maybe they *do* just want to help us. Like we help Davie, there. 'Cause we want to."

"But he's the best at beggin', Nick. He can look more pitiful than anybody you ever seen!"

"True. But that ain't *why* we look after him, is it? He's little, an' he *needs* help."

"I don't need no help!" boasted John.

"Mebbe it's a church thing," someone suggested. "There's a lot of prayin'."

Tom remembered that his mother had prayed often, asking for help for her son. He'd almost forgotten the familiar words and phrases.

"I'll put up with that for the food and a bed," Nick protested. "It's a good trade, ain't it?"

"What's the talk about a train?" somebody asked.

One of the residents with more tenure answered.

"When they get enough of us ready to move on, they put us on a train goin' west. Learn farmin'."

"That's what they *say!*" protested John. "How do you *know?* You never see 'em again."

Davie began to whimper.

"Stop it. You're scarin' Davie. Let's quiet down, now. We'll be in trouble."

"What's across the street?" Tom asked one of the earlier residents. "There's a lot of women over there."

"That's the girls' asylum. There were a couple of girls in our gang, and they took 'em away. They're over there. We wave sometimes."

"They look like they're well treated."

"I guess so. They're smilin'."

"You s'pose somebody's sellin' 'em?" asked John.

"Dammit, John, you're too suspicious!" snapped Nick. "That's what'd happen if they *stayed* on the street, ain't it?"

"Well, yeah, I guess so. How's one pimp better'n another?"

"I don't think it's that," insisted Harry, their new and more experienced friend. "I don't think Mr. Brace would stand for it."

Mr. Brace seemed to be respected by all. He stopped by in a day or two to see how they were doing and tried to explain the program. There were opportunities, he said, in the expanding West. A boy could learn a trade, learn to farm, find a way to make a life for himself. They'd live with families who wanted to take them in. Train tickets would be provided.

"What if we don't like it?" demanded John.

"You don't have to stay. There will be a committee or a person you can report to, in the area where you are."

"Anybody ever come back?" asked John suspiciously.

The room was still as the gathering awaited an answer.

"Yes, as a matter of fact, a few have," admitted Brace. "Not many. Most are quite happy. Would you like to hear some letters? Here's one from a girl in Iowa."

He drew out some letters from a portfolio and began to read.

"Hold on," John interrupted. "How do we know that ain't just made up?"

Brace held out the sheet of paper. "Read it yourself."

John hesitated.

"Can't read? That's all right, son. You'll get some schooling, too. Anybody who can read here?"

"Tom can, some."

Brace turned and handed Tom the letter. Embarrassed, the boy began to read, more slowly than he could have, so as not to appear to show off.

Dear Mr. Brase,

I want to thank you for the chanse you give me. I am with a kind cupl hear and I like it very mush . . .

"That don't prove nothin'! Anybody could of wrote that!" interrupted John.

"Shut up, John!" Nick exploded. "This man's tryin' to help you. Can't you get that through your thick head?"

The others laughed, and John subsided as Brace continued. In a few days, he said, they would have enough boys and girls for a train car of each. They'd be given a suitcase with a change of clothes. When they reached their designated area, the train would stop at towns along the way. People who needed or wanted a boy or girl to board with them could look them over and choose one.

"Now, it's to your advantage," Brace advised, "to make a good appearance. You might want to show what you can do. Sing a song, recite a poem, a little dance or something."

"Do we *have* to?"

"No, but think. . . . We all want to stand out from the crowd a bit. Anything to make a good impression, no?"

"John's outa luck, then," someone quipped. "He's only good at arguin'."

There was uneasy laughter.

"Any other questions?" Brace asked.

"Yes, sir," Nick spoke. "May I ask where we're goin'?"

"Oh, yes . . . I didn't mention, I guess. . . . Kansas! We leave the day after tomorrow!"

Tom stood in line on the platform, waiting to board the train. His hand was sweaty on the handle of the cardboard suitcase they had each been given. It had an extra suit of clothes. He'd save them, he figured, until they began to

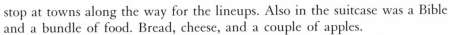

stop at towns along the way for the lineups. Also in the suitcase was a Bible and a bundle of food. Bread, cheese, and a couple of apples.

"Make 'em last!" the supervisor had warned. "You'll be on the train about four days."

There was nobody on the train, Tom figured, that didn't know about making food last. There was quiet conversation as the "caretaker" checked his list, tallying each name. They'd been warned to be quiet and well behaved, and by and large, this was being carried out. Over the gentle hum of talk was the hiss of steam from the escape valve, sounds that would stay in his memory forever.

A couple of trainmen walked along the platform carrying oil cans with spouts two or three feet long, lubricating hubs and pistons and axle bearings on the huge iron wheels. It was a bit frightening.

" 'Board!" the conductor called.

"Come on, lads," the caretaker beckoned, "step up. Remember, stay in our car. Quick, now!"

They hurried up the iron steps and into the passenger car. Tom slid into a seat next to the window, and John joined him.

"What if the boiler explodes?" John wondered.

Tom was impatient. He could always count on John to see the darkest side of any situation.

"Shut up, John. You ain't goin' to ruin this for us all. What if the damn boiler *don't* explode?"

"I dunno. We'd prob'ly live to get scalped by savages, I guess."

"Put a cork in it, John," said Nick from the seat behind. "You're scarin' Davie."

The train moved forward a trifle as the engineer began his adjustments. An explosive hiss of steam from the vent shot a white cloud across the platform. Another turn of the wheels, another rush of steam. Another, and a trifle too much throttle . . . The drivers spun madly for a few seconds, showering sparks from steel rails with an alarming roar, but also moving forward. . . . A bit of momentum, now, the wheels rolling faster . . . The great adventure was under way.

Through the city, across open country, vast fields and forests. Tom had never seen such sights. No buildings, even, just an occasional house with a barn.

"What's all that green stuff?" asked Davie from the seat behind.

"Grass and trees and stuff," Nick explained patiently. "The stuff in rows is crops, I s'pose. Corn and turnips and things. The trees in rows must be apples, I guess, or pears, maybe. Hell, I dunno, I'm guessin'."

"Are we almost there?" Davie asked a little later.

"No, no. You heard the man. Be about four days, he said."

"Four *days*? That's a long time, Nick!"

"I know. Here, eat your apple."

"Maybe I better save it. We et this morning."

Davie curled up in the seat and was quickly asleep, lulled by the rhythm of the big drivers and the double click of steel wheels over the joints in steel tracks. The miles fell away behind, with the life they had known. Ahead, the future, but *what?*

14

On the morning of the third day on the train, the caretaker walked through the car with exciting news. The train would be stopping to take on fuel and water at a country town in Missouri. There would be families there who were looking for an orphan to take in.

"Clean yourselves up a bit," the caretaker urged. "Put on your other suit if you need to. . . . Comb your hair, look as good as you can."

It would be difficult, with no water or any other facilities.

"Stand up straight, walk well. When it comes your turn, you might want to tell about yourself, sing a song, recite a verse, do a little dance, maybe. Show them your talents."

They had been told of this before, back at the asylum. Some of the caretakers had encouraged the exchange and learning of songs and verses. One boy was quite adept at dancing, and had in fact performed on street corners in the city for the coins tossed in his hat by passersby. His crippled brother (or friend, Tom wasn't sure) supplied the rhythm with a set of bones and a battered mouth organ. Some of the stricter supervisors had been a bit critical of this pair of performers.

"They should hear some of the songs we know," the Dancer scoffed in an aside to Tom and Nick. "You ever hear 'Chris Columbo' or 'The Mexican Whore'? We'll sing 'em for you some time."

That opportunity had never arisen, and now, the game was about to begin in earnest. Tom was distressed. He felt that he had no talents, nothing to show his sincerity or his willingness to work and to learn.

"What's the matter, son?" asked the caretaker as he came down the aisle of the train car.

"Nothin'," muttered Tom, a little resentfully. He wanted to blurt *I ain't your son! I ain't anybody's!* But it didn't seem advisable at this time.

"I see," the man nodded. "Have you decided what you'll do for your act?"

"I can't do nothin'."

"Oh . . . I see . . ."

The caretaker squatted in the aisle beside the seat.

"Didn't I see you reading something the other day?"

"I didn't mean no harm, sir. . . . It was a newspaper somebody left on the train."

"No, no . . . It's all right. I just meant . . . Well, how many of the boys on this car do you suppose can read?"

"I dunno . . ."

"Not many, I'll warrant."

"My mother taught me."

"Mother?" The gentleman looked startled. "Do we have the release papers for your custody? I was under the impression . . ." He began to riffle through a sheaf of documents in a leather case.

"No, she's dead now, sir. I'm an orphan. But she wanted me to read. I've been hawkin' papers, and read some if I've got 'em unsold."

"Yes . . . Well, as I was saying . . . It seems to me you *do* have a talent. You can read! Tell them about that. Read a bit of scripture. You have your Bible?"

"Yes, sir."

"Good! Choose a passage, read a bit for them."

Now the caretaker stood up and called for the attention of the thirty-odd youngsters in the car. When the excited talk quieted, he began.

"I've learned a few more details. This is a quick stop, and we'll just line up on the station platform. At some stations, we'll go on into town and put on our show in a church or town hall. There's a committee to organize it in each town."

"What if we ain't treated right?" demanded one youth.

"Then you report to the committee. This is only a trial placement, and will be reviewed in a year, in any case. You can ask to leave if you wish."

Now the train was slowing to the station, and squealed to a stop beside the platform. The crew swung the waterspout toward the boiler, and others began to load firewood into the tender behind the engine.

The boys began to file down the steps of the train car and line up in military precision on the depot platform, backs to the car.

Tom saw that one of the cars ahead was carrying a complement of girls of about their same ages. Other, regular passengers peered curiously out of their windows at the promenade on the platform.

Across the platform along the street or road was a long hitch rail where buggies, surries, and farm wagons were parked. Patient teams of horses or mules waited, tied to the rail or merely standing. A couple of saddle horses drowsed, hipshot and ground-tied, at the end of the row.

The people from the vehicles at the rail now walked along, looking over the orphans. One cluster moved on to the car where the girls were arrayed, and another assembled to confront the ranks where Tom, Nick, the Dancer, and the rest stood. There seemed to be no more than half a dozen families all told, and some forty or fifty orphans.

"Let's begin," said the caretaker of the boys' car. A woman who accompanied the girls was beginning a similar ritual down the platform.

"We have only a brief stop, here, but some mighty promising youngsters. Look them over."

"They know any trades?" asked a woman in a sunbonnet.

"Some, ma'am. It's intended that they learn trades . . . farming, smithing, carpentry. . . ."

Tom was impressed that here they stood, the adults talking about them as if they weren't even there, or as if they were livestock or circus animals. It was demeaning.

"Some can sing, recite, dance," the caretaker went on. "Some can read. . . . Tom, show them, would you?"

Embarrassed, Tom opened his Bible as he'd been instructed, and began the rendering of a passage from the Book of Matthew.

> The book of the generation of Jesus Christ, the son of David, the son of Abraham.
>
> Abraham begat Isaac, and Isaac begat Jacob. Jacob begat Judas and his brethren;
>
> And Judas begat Phares and Zara of Thamar; and Phares begat Esrom; and Esrom begat Aram;
>
> And Aram begat . . .

"Enough of this begatting!" interrupted a burly farmer. "I'm wantin' to take in a farmhand, not a goddamn preacher boy!"

Several of the other locals appeared embarrassed by the outburst, and drew away from the bully. He appeared to have been imbibing, though it was early in the day.

"Sir," said the caretaker indignantly, "we are not selling bonds of indenture. These are unfortunates who need food, shelter, guidance, and instruction in a trade. After your last remark, I would not consent to a placement with you. Go along, now!"

There was a murmur of approval from the other locals, and the bully shuffled away, muttering to himself.

"Now, to be quite serious, here," the caretaker continued. "Time is short. What sort of young men do you want to inquire of?"

"How about this one?" asked a motherly-looking farm wife timidly.

"She's lookin' at Davie, Nick," whispered Tom. "Are you gonna let her take him?"

"We don't have much say, Tom. I reckon we didn't see this comin', did we?"

Davie tried to hide behind Nick, but the woman coaxed him out with a gentle manner. She reminded Tom of his own mother, somehow, even with her sunbonnet and country clothes.

"Go on, Davie, talk to her," urged Nick. "She seems like a nice lady."

"Do I have to go with her?"

"Not unless you want to. Just talk to her."

"I want to stay with you, Nick. You or Tom."

"I don't know, Davie. That might not be possible."

"Wait a minute," said the husband of the woman who was trying to coax Davie out. He drew the caretaker aside.

"Sir, we lost two boys to typhoid last year. The missus has been grievin' ever since. This is the first time she's . . ."

He paused, eyes filling with tears.

"Maybe we could try both. I could use the help of the bigger boy, but I ain't just tryin' to get work out of him. Would we be expected to adopt them?"

"No, no! In fact, the society advises against it, for a year, at least. The children must be allowed to leave if they wish, or if things are not working well. Their situation will be reviewed in one year."

"Could we . . . I mean . . . would it be all right for us to take both boys?"

He gestured toward where his wife was still trying to coax Davie into the open. Her eyes were aglow, and she was smiling. Davie was responding with a timid grin.

"Haven't seen her like that for better'n a year," the farmer said, wiping his eyes with a blue bandanna. "What do we have to do?"

"There's a bit of paperwork. You report how things are going to your local committee. Your Dr. Talbot is the chairman, I believe."

"So I heard. But . . . Well, I can't read nor write, sir."

"No need. You make your mark before a witness."

"My wife reads a little," he offered.

"Good. That will help. Now, let me see if we can make another placement or two before we go. Tom, you'd better talk to me later. Maybe we can do better than 'begatting.' " He smiled.

The caretaker moved on to where a rough-looking man was running his hands over one of the boys. The scene was much like that at a horse trade, it seemed, with a prospective buyer checking for soundness.

"Sir, you are not buying a horse or a slave," he admonished.

"I don't want to take in no cripple, neither!" the man retorted. "Any more trains comin' through this spring?"

"I couldn't tell you," the caretaker said flatly, leaving the other to ponder the meaning of his answer. If he had the intelligence to do so, of course.

"Better be loadin' up," the conductor said. "They're about done takin' on fuel and water."

"All right! Back on board," called the caretaker. "You boys who are getting off here, stay with me. We have some papers."

Quickly, good-byes were said.

"Good luck, Tom. Me and Davie will be all right. We'll look after one another," assured Nick, clapping the younger boy on the shoulder. He stuck out his hand.

"And to you, both of you. You'll be fine, Davie."

"What about you, Tom?"

"Hey, they sell papers everywhere, don't they? Anyway, the man said we can go back next year if we want. But you'll be with Nick, here."

When the train chugged out of the station, there were three of the boys left behind: Davie, Nick, and a husky boy they didn't know, who had jumped at the chance to apprentice himself to the blacksmith.

Two of the girls had been taken by families in or near the small Missouri town. The caretaker explained to Tom that girls were somewhat easier to place, but that there were usually more boys, probably for the same reasons. Tom wasn't certain what he meant.

15

The train rolled on westward. There were a couple of stops in Missouri, and a few placements. Tom wasn't sure exactly when they crossed into Kansas, because it was night. The boys slept in the seats or on the floor of the car.

There were a few bustling towns, which all looked pretty much alike. At these older towns the train stopped for fuel and water, but there was no lineup. Leavenworth, Atchison, Lawrence, Topeka . . . The goal was to place children in the newer prairie towns. These, too, all looked alike. All were about the same age and at about the same stage of construction and growth.

There were fewer children in the lineup now when they straggled out of the cars and lined up for inspection. Sometimes it was held on the station platform, like their first lineup in Missouri. Sometimes, in a church near the station. Once or twice, in a new school building.

The caretaker had assisted Tom in the selection of a few more suitable verses of scripture to be read. It was quickly seen that some audiences were more reactive to certain passages. In a church setting, a different crowd from that on the station platform, Psalms worked well. He could always get a good reaction out of certain psalms.

> I will lift up mine eyes unto the hills, from whence cometh my help. My help cometh from the Lord, who made Heaven and Earth. . . .

Somehow there was comfort in that, and hope for the future, for him.

Meanwhile, the train chugged on across a landscape that was rolling and green. There were few trees, except along the streams. The towns were newer, usually still under construction. It was apparent that even the houses and stores that were finished were new. There was always the smell of fresh lumber and paint and tarred roofs.

Tom was becoming discouraged. He felt dirty and gritty from the long train trip, four days, now. The car smelled of unwashed bodies and spoiling food.

There were few children left in the car now. It had been painfully apparent that some were more desirable for placement. The most handsome and appealing had been placed quickly. A bright smile helped. Tom had tried to make himself presentable in every way he could, and he felt that he presented a good appearance. A couple of times he'd actually been selected for a more detailed interview, but then rejected.

He could see the reason in the eyes of prospective foster parents. When he stepped forward to talk to them, their faces always changed. It was never mentioned, of course. Always some other excuse, if they even bothered to voice one . . . *A bit younger boy, perhaps* . . . But he knew. He had seen the shocked looks on their faces. It was always when he stepped forward, swinging his game leg, nearly four inches shorter than the other, and crooked. It gave him a rolling, swaying gait that was almost simian, apelike, inhuman. It had been no disadvantage in the city. An advantage, even, sometimes. He'd not rejected pity, because it often resulted in bigger tips.

This was different. Even those who might have treated him well out of sympathetic understanding would only go so far. Ultimately, he was coming to a cruel realization: *Nobody wants to take in a cripple.*

There were few left in the car. One set of three brothers wanted desperately to stay together. Tom had heard their talk with the caretaker, who was counting on one of the towns ahead. Maybe two or three families near each other, he suggested. That would allow the brothers to remain in contact, attend school together. It seemed that it might work out.

Even John, the perpetual pessimist, had found a placement. It had been amusing to see an equally pessimistic complainer take a liking to him. The grumpy farmer seemed drawn to a boy with his own approach to life. The man's wife, almost his equal in complaint, did not hesitate to voice her own doubts.

"Prob'ly ain't goin' to last," she prophesied as the three of them climbed into the wagon for the trip home.

"You don't treat me right, I'll run off!" warned John.

"Be good riddance, I reckon," said the farmer as he clucked to the team and drove off.

Somehow, Tom felt certain that as unlikely as it seemed, that placement would work out. The caretaker had his doubts.

"I don't know about that one," he confided to Tom.

"He'll be all right," Tom assured. "I've known him a long time. He ain't happy unless he's complainin'."

"Well . . . Maybe. They can try it."

"I reckon they'll understand each other pretty good."

There did come a day when Tom was actually chosen. It was not really a pleasant solution to the seemingly endless train ride.

"Guess I'll take him, if he's all you got," said the dour-faced storekeeper. "Come on, boy."

"His name is Tom," the caretaker interjected. There was concern on his face.

"Whatever . . . He'll answer, I reckon, if he's to eat."

"Tom, best of luck to you," the caretaker said seriously. They had become well acquainted during the past four days. He drew the boy aside. "If you have any trouble, the banker is the head of the committee here. His name is Williams. See him if you need to."

"Come on, boy!" The man put his arm around his shoulder.

For reasons he could not explain, Tom was very uncomfortable with that.

The storekeeper's wife, equally dour-faced, was a forlorn-looking creature. They had no children of their own, but there was a boy in the house, a few years older than Tom.

"Go wash up, boys," said the woman tersely.

They did so at the washbasin on the porch outside the kitchen. Tom was grateful for the chance to splash water over his face and neck after the gritty days on the train. They dried on a dirty-looking gray towel, and reentered the kitchen.

Supper was frugal and not very appetizing, even as hungry as Tom was. Greasy salt pork lay in a puddle of watery drainage from a yellowish pile of a lumpy substance that was described as potato salad. He thought he'd tasted better around the fire back in the alley in New York. Hotel garbage was usually better fare than this.

He did gain some information though, during the meal. The boy, Caleb, was a nephew, who had been living with the Clarks for a year, helping in the store. He would soon be leaving to return to his parents in Iowa, and Tom was to take his place. Caleb said very little.

As darkness fell and they prepared to retire, Shem, the storekeeper, spoke to the newcomer.

"Boy, you'll sleep in the loft with Caleb till he moves on. That bed's big enough for two."

They climbed the ladder to the loft, and in the dim twilight Tom saw a mat of striped canvas ticking on the floor. It would be barely big enough for two.

"It's just cornhusks, not no feather bed," Caleb said. "It ain't bad, though."

Sometime later, as Tom lay trying to sleep, the other boy spoke again.

"Tom, I got to tell you a couple of things."

"Yes. Shem said you'd show me the job at the store."

"It ain't that. . . . Well, partly . . ."

"What do you mean?"

"Well . . . They'll talk big about takin' in an unfortunate boy to help him. That ain't exactly so. They're lookin' for a slave, I reckon."

"I don't understand. They've had a slave?"

"No, not a real slave, not a nigger. Never had one. I been their nigger, though, the past year."

It was quiet for a while. Tom didn't know what to say.

Finally Caleb spoke again. "Somethin' else, too, I reckon. You notice how ol' Shem likes to put his hands on you? Well, he ain't just bein' friendly. Don't be alone with him if you can help it."

"But . . . Your folks . . ."

"They don't know he's like this. Lord, I'm glad to be gettin' out of here." Caleb heaved a great sigh.

Tom was quiet for a little while, and Caleb spoke again.

"If'n I was you, I'd get outa here, fast as you can. Before day comes."

"Really?"

"Yep. Longer you're here, the harder to get out."

Tom crept down the ladder before daylight, carrying his cardboard suitcase with his other clothes and his Bible. He'd drop the suitcase if he had to. It would slow him up if he had to try to run. Now, he knew why he'd felt so uneasy about the storekeeper's touch. The man couldn't keep his hands off young boys. He pitied Caleb, related by blood. It must have been a dreadful year for him.

The sky was just beginning to pale in the east when he slipped into the alley behind the bank. Here, he half concealed himself behind a pile of boxes and trash and settled in to catch a few winks of sleep if he could.

When banker Williams arrived at the bank that morning, he noticed a boy sitting on the steps, holding a small brown suitcase hugged to his body. The boy was not blocking the entrance, just sitting there on one side. . . . *One of the orphans from the train?* Williams thought. . . . *Odd . . .*

The banker took out his keys and began to unlock the big door. As
he did so, the youth rose and approached him.

"Good morning, sir . . . May I speak with you?"

Now he recognized the boy. The one with a twisted leg and odd way
of walking. Too bad. But . . . hadn't he been placed? Yes, Williams was
certain of it.

"Come in," he offered. "What is it you want . . . ? But first, your
name?"

"Tom."

"Sit down, Tom." He motioned to a chair and removed his hat to
hang it on a rack behind his big desk.

"You are Mr. Williams?"

"That's right." The banker settled into his own chair and placed the
fingertips of both hands together, like a spider walking on a mirror. He
studied the boy. *Intelligent looking . . . Well mannered.* He waited.

"Sir, I'm off the train yesterday."

"So I assumed," the banker smiled.

"You're head of the committee?"

"Yes . . . You were placed here, right?"

"Yes, sir. But . . ."

"Just a moment." Williams rummaged in a folder on his desk. "Tom
. . . Tom Street, no?"

"I guess so. I didn't have a last name."

"And you come from the street, I suppose. But you were placed with
the Clarks. The storekeeper and his wife?"

"Yes, sir. I don't want to stay with them."

The banker studied him for a few moments, pushing his fingertips
together again and looking very thoughtful.

"Are you going to tell me why?"

"No, sir," Tom said quietly but politely.

The banker smiled. He liked the youngster's straightforward manner.
"Fair enough."

He had wondered about that placement anyway. There was something about the demeanor of that nephew who'd been staying with the
Clarks. The boy had always seemed sad and withdrawn. He'd understood
that Caleb would soon be returning to his own family in Iowa.

His own concern was not with another family's problems but with
the Children's Aid orphans.

"Well, let's see, Tom. The train's gone."

"I don't want to be any trouble, sir."

"Yes, yes. But you do have to be somewhere, no?"

A clerk had entered the bank and now Williams rose to take his hat
from the rack.

"Sam, I'm going on an errand. Back pretty soon," he called. Then, to the boy, "Come on, Tom."

They went along the boardwalk to an office a few doors down the street. The gilt lettering on the window proclaimed:

Dr. C.W. Lowry
Physician and Surgeon

"Doc," the banker called as they entered. "Can you give me an opinion, here?"

The doctor shuffled out of an inner office and glanced over the mismatched pair in the doorway.

"On which one?" he joked, straight-faced.

"This one." The banker pointed to Tom.

"Any special trouble, or do I have to guess?"

"Thought you might take a look at his leg, Doc."

"Hmm . . . Old injury?"

"I . . . I guess so," Tom mumbled. "Horse stepped on me, before I remember."

"I see. . . . Hmm . . . Fairly straight. Just short . . . Throws the pelvis off level."

"Can anything be done?" asked the banker.

"Well, no. Not surgically, that is. A built-up shoe would help a lot. He'd walk almost normal. Tell you what! Ask Ed down at the saddle shop. He fixes boots and shoes. Tell him three or four inches of build-up. He'll know. Here, wait a minute. . . . Lie down on the table, here, son."

Quickly, the doctor measured from point of hip to ankle bone on each leg.

"Yes . . . Three and a half inches. Tell him that."

The saddler's shop was a light airy place, with the powerful smells of new leather and neat's-foot oil.

"Sure," said the saddler. "I can fix that up in a hurry. He's leavin'?"

"No . . . Not sure yet, Ed. He's off the train."

"Figgered so. Well, you go on. He can stay here to get the shoe fitted."

The banker turned toward the door.

"I'll be back for you, Tom. We'll get some dinner, and see about what's next."

·   ·   ·

It was pleasant in the shop, watching the saddler cut a stack of matching billets of thick leather. He shaved and shaped, and finally began to nail the layers to Tom's shoe.

"There! Try that!" he said finally.

Tom laced and tied the shoe, and stood, more square with the world than he'd ever been. He felt taller. . . . He *was* taller! He drew himself up with pride and took a few steps. He didn't have to swing his hips in the lurching gait. It would take some practice, but . . .

"Ain't quite finished. Take it off. I got to rasp it down and polish it."

When the banker returned, the boy was sitting on the workbench, and the two were visiting comfortably. The saddler was demonstrating his tools as he worked, their use and care, and the boy was asking questions. Good, intelligent questions. How is the tooling done on the saddle? The sewing of harness? Boots . . .

The saddler took the banker aside.

"This is a smart boy, Will. You say he ain't placed?"

"Guess not. Why?"

"Well, I been thinkin'. He's showin' an interest. He's apt, maybe. With that game leg, some jobs he can't do. But I could teach him leather. Don't need good legs to do what I do."

"I don't know, Ed . . ."

"Mebbe we could sort of try it?"

"Maybe so. Tell you what. I'll talk to him about it and we'll come back. Much obliged for the work this morning. What do I owe you?"

" 'Bout a dollar, I reckon. But I'll forget it if this works out. I'd have to talk to the missus, of course."

"Of course. You do that, Ed."

He walked down the street toward the café, the boy at his side, walking fairly well on his "new leg."

"Work pretty well?" he asked.

"Yes, sir. Mr. Bowden was showin' me about the shop, the tools and all. Sure smells good in there. He let me take a few stitches on a saddle he was fixin'. . . ."

The boy rattled on, excited.

The banker smiled to himself. *Sometimes,* he thought, *things just seem to work out.*

16

Texas, 1867

"Ezekiel, where's your father?" called Naomi from the henhouse.

She carried a few eggs in her apron, held up like a bag with the folds in her left hand. The old black hen was acting broody again, fluffed up and threatening as she approached the nest. Well, maybe it was time to let her raise another brood. They were getting a few more eggs, with the greening of spring. The hens worked frantically at anything green just now. It was hard to keep them out of the garden yonder.

Zeke hadn't answered, and she stooped to look out through the doorway. He was standing there, looking a bit helpless, tired, and discouraged. About like she felt herself.

"I . . . I expect he rode into town, Mama."

She'd been pretty sure of that. She shouldn't have asked him. It was hurtful to talk about. It had been hard enough during the war, not knowing whether he'd come home at all, and with two young sons. Daniel, the youngest, had died that first winter James was gone. The husband of Rebecca Stone, on the next place, hadn't come home at all. He'd been killed in that last battle, clear down at a place called Palmito Hill, four hundred miles from home. It was there that James had lost his right arm. . . . And his spirit. It still made her angry to think that it was a completely useless battle. The war had been over for several days, but neither side had received the word yet, so far south of everything.

She'd been relieved that it was over, for a little while. Then it became clear that it was to be worse. Yankee troops occupied the once proud Texas Republic, stealing, bullying . . . The Radicals, who had sympathized with the North, were now in the catbird seat, gaining power and welcoming the damned Yankee carpetbaggers. In the scramble for political power, it sometimes looked like there was no leadership or organization. Just the oppression of military occupation by a foreign country. It was enough to make a body want to quit. James *had* quit, to all intents and purposes. He wasn't the same man she'd fallen in love with so long ago. Now he sulked, wouldn't talk, wouldn't touch her. . . . That hurt most of all.

Ezekiel, fifteen and big for his age, had been a godsend these last few years. Most of the work of the ranch had fallen on his young shoulders. Looking after the cattle, mostly. It hadn't been possible to keep up. They had steers three and four years old and never branded. Some hadn't even been cut. They weren't worth anything anyway. . . .

"Maybe you'd better go see about him, son," she called.

Both knew where he'd be. He'd be at the cantina in town, drinking and talking politics. Not politics, really. Just a bunch of white trash telling each other what they should have done to keep out the invading army of bluebellies. James had never been like that, or associated with them. He'd had pride and dignity, which was missing now, lost at Palmito Hill along with his arm. She hated to see him like this, drinking heavily and no longer caring.

Zeke ambled down to the corral and saddled his little mare, one of the few horses they had left. The Yankees from Fort Concho had stolen most of the better ones. Well, maybe it was Comanches. One was about as bad as the other, she figured. She maybe favored Comanches, even. At least they were honest about their horse stealing.

Her thoughts were interrupted by a call from Ezekiel.

"Here he comes, Mama!"

She stepped out the door of the henhouse, bumping her head on the lintel. She usually did when she tried to hurry. What was James doing back now? Usually, unless they went to fetch him, it would be after dark before he returned, dead drunk, with the horse bringing him home.

James waved to her. . . . (He hadn't done that for a while. . . . He *must* be drunk. . . .) He rode on toward the corral, swung down, and handed the reins to Zeke. He turned as Naomi approached, and actually smiled at her.

He'd been drinking some, but seemed fairly sober, she thought. There was a new light in his eyes, somehow. He looked more like his old self. . . . No, she mustn't get her hopes up, yet.

"Naomi," he said, "I'm thinkin' maybe there might be a way out of this!"

He reached to enfold her in his arms, for the first time since his return. At least, with this kind of fervor.

"James!" she squealed. "The eggs!"

•   •   •

A bit later, at the kitchen table, he explained in detail.

"I couldn't see no way out," he began. "Some of 'em are plantin' cotton, but that takes a lot of work, and . . . Well, you know." He lifted the stump of his right arm and let it fall. "Even the three of us couldn't handle enough cotton to make it. We don't have money to hire farmhands. What we got is cows, which nobody wants, 'cause everybody's got 'em, and they ain't worth nothin'. . . . Four or five dollars a head."

"I figure," Naomi interjected, "nobody sold any for a few years because the men were all off fightin' one another. The cows just multiplied."

"That's jest exactly it," agreed James. "Everybody's in the same fix. But I been talkin' to some folks."

To worthless white trash, Naomi thought. *What's this scheme goin' to be?* She waited.

"Well, I been talkin' to these fellers, like I said, and some of 'em over toward Waco have been drivin' cows to market. Yankees eat beef, too, you know."

"They *steal* it!" she snapped.

"Yes, yes, I know, honey. But farther north, they *buy* it."

It was the first time since his return that he'd used his pet name for her . . . *Honey.* Maybe it was a good sign. . . . But what did he have up his sleeve? She felt a twinge of guilt over having let such a thought flit through her head. *Empty sleeve* . . . But there had been a time when the two of them would have laughed over such an error. Laughed *together* . . .

"Zeke," James was saying, "how many head do you reckon we have?"

"Hard to say, Papa. There's a lot in the brush, there along the Concho."

James nodded. "But how many could we gather, with a few riders? Three hundred?"

"Sure, easy."

Naomi spoke, a bit of irritation in her voice. "But what's the point, James? There's no market here, and they're worth only a few dollars for hides and tallow."

"Exactly. But we can drive them to a better market."

"Where? St. Louis?" she asked sarcastically.

"It's been done!" he insisted. "Before the war. Not from here, but from a bit nearer. But there are closer markets. The railroads are comin' in. If you get a herd to a place where they can be *shipped* . . . Sedalia, Kansas City . . ."

"That's so far, James."

"Not really. Several herds have gone up the Old Shawnee Trail to

Kansas City. But the railroads are building west across Kansas since the war. The Union Pacific has a line that goes clean to a place called Salina, I hear tell. There's another. Atchison, Topeka and Santa Fe . . ."

"They can't go clear to Santa Fe!" she snorted.

"Not yet, but I'm thinkin' they will. Or somebody will."

"What does that have to do with us?"

"Well, with these railroad towns comin' in, it's a lot closer than the Missouri towns by way of the Old Shawnee Trail. A couple of drovers took herds last year, not northeast but straight north. There's an old trail that crosses the Indian Nations."

"Drive cattle through Indian country? James, that's crazy!"

"It's been done!" he insisted. "Most of those Indians ain't wild, Naomi. The Civilized Tribes . . . Well, the Cherokees even fought for the South in the war. They've got their own government, their own Light Horse Police."

"What's that to do with . . . ?"

"I'm comin' to that. They're chargin' ten cents a head for cattle cross-in' the Nations on the Shawnee Trail, we hear tell. But there's another old trail, leads to a trading post up in Kansas, on the Arkansas River. Almost straight north of here. Cuts a couple hunnerd miles off the trip. A half-blood trader, a Cherokee-Scotchman settled there, name of Jesse Chisholm. A lot of travel on this trail of Chisholm's now, through Fort Worth."

"Cattle? Is there a railroad?"

"Well, no . . . Not right there. A couple of herds have gone up Chisholm's trail, though. And that's the point, Naomi. Cattle are worth a lot more up there. Maybe forty dollars a head. Ten times what they are in Fort Worth."

"You're plumb crazy, James. You're not a drover."

Instantly, her heart sank as she said it. Here she was, putting him down, after the first sign of interest he'd shown in anything since the war.

"But, what's to lose?" she said quickly. "A few cattle, worth nothin' here. Who would you get to help?"

"Been workin' on that," he smiled. "If we get several of us, poolin' our herds, helpin' trail 'em . . . Me and Zeke here, the Simmonses over east, the Mangums up by the north fork . . . We can make up a herd, a few hunnerd from each ranch. We figure one rider for each two or three hundred cows. Extra horses . . . Drive a remuda along . . . Take a wagon to carry grub and bedrolls . . ."

"Papa, our cattle ain't even branded or sorted," Zeke protested. "I wasn't able to handle it."

"I know, son. You couldn't be expected to. I figger this, though. We get three or four ranches neighborin' here, help work each other's cows, do the brandin', and take the drive together. We could prob'ly get a herd of a thousand, easy. Not even sort 'em . . . Mother cows, calves . . . Leave the small ones, of course . . . Steers, bulls."

"Plenty of *them,* Papa. Been nobody to cut 'em."

"Yes . . . That's okay. Any that are too ringy, we leave behind, or shoot 'em to save trouble."

"You've done a lot of planning on this, James!" Naomi said. His excitement was contagious, now. She hoped it would last, and it began to look like it would. This was more like the man she married. . . .

"Zeke," James said, "come tomorrow, let's look over the horses, pick us three or four apiece. Then ride over to the Simmonses and talk to them about this. We can get some idea of a count on the way, maybe. Any critter big enough to travel . . . Them farmers and settlers comin' into Kansas will be wantin' to buy stock, I expect, to start their own spread."

Naomi rose and started to get dinner on the table. It was good to see her menfolk chattering excitedly about man things. About anything, actually. It had been a long time. . . .

She had reservations about the whole scheme. Even more about her boy's part in it. He was only a boy yet, in her eyes. But men had to grow up quickly in this time and place.

Basically, though, it was good. She'd seen the excitement in her husband's eyes, and there was a new thrill in the way he'd looked at her today, too. She'd feared that the loss of his arm had robbed him of his manhood. She'd even wondered if he'd had another physical wound that had damaged unseen parts of his body.

Today, she reckoned not. She'd seen an appreciative glance at her bodice and had contrived to show him a few inches of ankle as she sat at the table. Tonight, Naomi figured, might be the night she'd actually get her husband back from the war.

17

The Mangum boys were pretty good with a lariat. . . . *La reata.* They'd rope a calf, flank it down, and the men on the ground would have it castrated and branded in short order. Bigger animals would be caught by two ropers, head and heels, and stretched between the two horses while the work was done.

"Whose brand goes on this one?" yelled Zeke, trying to sort out the various irons at the fire and keep them all at proper heat.

"Dunno," Absolam Mangum called back. "His mammy ain't even branded. Gawd, they're mixed up in here! Look thar . . . Thar's a brand I ain't even *seen* before!"

"Looks Mexican," his brother Slim answered. "She's lost, I reckon."

"Vent her brand out and trail brand her," suggested James.

By agreement, unbranded animals whose ownership could not be established were branded in rotation with one of the four marks from the cooperating ranches. Completely foreign brands could be "vented," or canceled, by a slash burned across with a running iron. All animals destined for the drive would be identified by a trail brand, a circle about four inches in diameter stamped on the left ribs. This would prevent disputes over ownership as they traveled through country where other cattle might be encountered.

Zeke burned the bar-S of the Simmonses on the hip of the calf on the ground, and replaced the iron in the glowing coals. The Mangums' running M would be next, then their own upside down J Y joined after that.

"Better hold that one, boys," James called. "He's pretty small to travel."

The calf in question, along with his mother, was herded aside into open country. The growing herd of cattle that would make the drive was held loosely in a milling circle by other riders.

They had worked hard at this preparatory work for the past week. First at one ranch, then the next, four in all; the task was nearly done. The herds would be combined and headed north in another day or two.

"How many we goin' to start out with, York?" asked Old Man Simmons.

"Purt' near fifteen hunnerd, by my tally," James told him.

"We got enough riders?"

"Hope so. What you figure? One for every two or three hunnerd?"

"Sounds okay. That'd need mebbe seven or eight riders. Bingham's wagon'll do for the cook, he says. That Mexican hand of his can drive it and do the cookin'. You're goin', ain't you?"

"Reckon so. You?"

"Don't believe I'd better, James. I'm pretty gimpy on cool mornin's. I don't think these ole bones could take it. I'd slow you down. My boys can handle it."

"Let's see. That'd be two from each spread, countin' Bingham's Mex on the chuck wagon," mused James. "Mebbe we'd ought to have one more, jest to handle the remuda. There'd ought to be about thirty horses."

"That many?" asked Simmons, startled.

"I think so, Sim. If we don't let some graze as we travel, they'll start to lose weight. A horse has to eat about half the time to stay healthy. That was one of our problems in the war."

He hadn't talked much about the war to anybody since he'd been back. Maybe if they hadn't had to ride their horses to death, literally sometimes . . . Well, it was over now. . . . Hard to forget, though.

"I hear tell a cow will *gain* weight sometimes on a drive, Simmons. How you figger?" he asked.

The old man chuckled. "That's different, James. A cow gulps all he can hold as fast as he can, and then chews it later as he walks along or rests. Learned that, drivin' oxen. You watch. . . . An ox team's usually chewin' the cud as they move."

"Never noticed. I ain't been around oxen much."

"No matter. But where can we get horses? The Yankees . . ."

"Yep . . ." James sighed. "Well, Barnes at the livery in San Angelo has been bringin' in some Mexican mustangs, I hear. Got a half-breed nigger breakin' 'em. Mebbe I'll ride in tomorrow and see about it."

"Would he take a promise for payment?" Simmons asked.

"Don't know, but we'll see. Sim, I reckon we need to all set down together this evenin' to finish talkin' some of this out."

"That's the last one for this gather," called one of the riders as Slim Mangum shook off his loop and began to re-coil the *reata*. "Bingham's tomorrow?"

"Guess so. But let's meet there tonight to talk about it," James answered.

The moon, a day or so past full, was rising as they gathered at Bingham's just after dark that evening. Some details must be worked out, with the clear understanding of all parties. Old Man Simmons, as the eldest representative, presided.

"I expect," he began, "that we'd ought to have a trail boss, first thing. I'd vote for James York, here. We started with his idea."

"No, no, I . . . ," James began, but Simmons waved him down with a gesture.

"Sounds good to me," agreed Bingham in his gravelly guttural.

The others nodded, and it was done.

"Now he's goin' to San Angelo in the mornin' to try to pick up some horses," Simmons went on. "James figgers we'll need mebbe thirty head, and we count only half that many among us. That sound right?"

"Not right, mebbe, but true," growled Bingham. "Damn Yankees!"

"Yes, I know, Zeb, but we got to trade with them Yankees . . . sell 'em beef!" James interjected.

"I know, I know . . . I'll shut up, James. Sorry."

"No problem. I'm goin' to try to work out somethin' with Barnes, to pay when we get back. Zeb, is your wagon an' Mex cook ready to go? And where is he, anyhow? He'd ought to sit in on this."

"Gomez? Sure, I never thought of that!" He stepped to the door and yelled into the night. "Gomez! Come up here!"

He turned and shuffled back to his chair, settling his bulky frame again. Mrs. Bingham, a birdlike little woman who seemed completely mismatched with her giant of a husband, poured more coffee for everyone. They'd had three children, James knew, and all had died in infancy. Gloria Bingham's face showed some of her inner sadness, but her smile was ready and sweet.

A heavyset man with a swarthy face rolled through the doorway with a gait like that of a seaman. He could have been fifty or sixty, or even seventy. James, meeting the Mexican for the first time, now realized that the man was lame. This was why he would be a cook there, not a *vaquero*.

"*Buenos noches, señors.*"

Mrs. Bingham poured him coffee, and he lounged easily next to the doorway.

"There are the fellas I told you about," Bingham said with an all-inclusive wave of introduction. "You know some of 'em. Simmons, Mangum, York . . . York will be trail boss."

Their eyes met, and both nodded, an acknowledgment of introduction.

"We were talkin' about how many men, an' if we have enough, Gomez. The Mangums' two boys . . . Papa won't go . . . York and his boy Zeke . . . Two Simmonses . . . You and me . . ."

Gomez nodded.

"We're thinkin' maybe one more to handle the remuda," Bingham went on. "There'll be about thirty horses."

"That ees a good idea, boss. Where you gonna get him?"

"Don't know. You got any ideas?"

"No . . . *vaqueros* is scarce. Thass why so many cows, now."

"Well, we'll see. York's going to town tomorrow to see if we can pick up a few horses. He'll ask around."

"Thass good, boss."

There was an easy familiarity between these two men. James didn't know how long they might have been together, but they appeared to have a great deal of mutual understanding. The dominant tone of Bingham's dialogue with the Mexican and Gomez's constant use of the term "boss" were not what they seemed. There was mutual respect and understanding here. The implied relationship of servant and master was more like an inside joke between the two.

"How many cows?" asked Gomez.

"About fifteen hunnerd, we figure," James answered his query.

"Thass good."

At the livery the next day, James and Zeke sat on the cedar rail of Barnes's corral and watched the milling bunch of mustangs circle the arena. Between and among them moved a dark-skinned man, turning and showing them, sorting and displaying to best advantage.

"They're all broke?" asked James.

"Mostly. Some more'n others, I reckon. Coffee, there, can tell you. He's workin' 'em. He talks to 'em, seems like. And he'll tell you straight. Ef ever was an honest nigger, it's prob'ly Coffee."

"He looks fairly light skinned."

"Yep . . . That's why somebody named him 'Coffee,' seems like. Quite a bit o' cream in that cup." He chuckled at his own joke. "I expect he's got some Injun blood. Cherokee or Choctaw, mebbe. Don't think it'd be Comanche. He's more civilized."

"Was he a slave?"

"Dunno. But dammit, York, you ain't buyin' *him,* you're buyin' horses."

Both chuckled, and Zeke joined in.

"I know. I just wondered about how they were broke. He works for you?"

"For hisself, mostly. He caught these mustangs, I bought 'em from him, and he's breakin' 'em, so much a head. You can talk to him about 'em."

"I think I can see what I need to. How much a head?"

"Well, times is hard, James. You know that," the liveryman whined. "I gotta have twenty a head."

"They ain't worth that. Not *half* that. Ten?"

"You're jokin' I s'pose. Their hides alone are worth that. Tell you what, though . . . Take the whole bunch, save me from goin' broke on feed, you can have 'em for eighteen."

James snorted indignantly. This was all part of the game.

"For that pen of buzzard bait? Don't be silly, Frank. I only need about a dozen anyway. . . . I pick 'em, twelve dollars a head."

"James, you wouldn't want to be the cause of my kids goin' hungry, now, would you? I wouldn't starve your boy, here." He jerked a thumb at the embarrassed Zeke.

"Hadn't given the possibility of your starvation a lot of concern, Frank. Now, let's get serious, here. I get to pick 'em, twelve head, and for friendship's sake, I'll go thirteen dollars. Take 'em off your hands today."

After a bit more haggling, they settled at fifteen.

"One more thing," James added. "If I go that high, I want a favor. I pay when we get back from Kansas."

"That wasn't in the deal!"

"I know, Frank. But you know, times is hard. How about this . . . If we make it and sell somewhere up there, and make any money, I'll pay you sixteen. If we have to pay cash now . . . Well, I don't know if we can raise it among us. We might have to take fewer horses."

The liveryman thought only a moment. "Okay . . . We're all in the same fix. If you make it, it's gonna help us all work our way out of this. I'll do it. Sixteen, payable when you get back."

They shook on it, and the horses were sorted and penned separately by Coffee and Zeke.

"Where's your herd at now?" asked Barnes.

"Down on the Concho. Figger we'll start day after tomorrow."

The liveryman extended his hand again.

"Best of luck, James. And not just because I got money ridin' on it."

"I know, Frank. Thanks!"

•　　•　　•

They were about three miles out of town when a rider approached from that direction at an easy lope. It was Coffee. He reined in gently when he caught up and touched his hat brim in greeting.

"I heared you tell Mr. Barnes, suh, that you need a wrangler for yo' remuda."

"Well, yes . . . You know of somebody?"

"Yassuh. Me."

"You? Don't you work for Barnes?"

"No, suh. Not really. Them hosses is well enough broke."

"But . . . You don't know anything about us. Why would you want to go?"

"Know what I need to. And, I seen you pick horses."

James smiled and extended his hand. "All right, Coffee. You're our man. Is this goin' to rile Frank Barnes?"

"No, suh. He know about it. He say tell you I'm to look after his investment."

18

It took a few days to get the cattle accustomed to the trail. There were always a few steers or old cows that tried to turn back, slip away from the bunch, or hide in the brush to escape. Individual animals began to identify themselves by their habits. One old brindle steer could always be depended upon to "bush up" as the time for morning departure neared. It became routine to locate old Brindle each morning.

"He's more trouble than he's worth," growled Zeb Bingham. "Let's shoot the sombitch and save us time."

James chuckled. "Reckon we'll lose enough without doin' it on purpose, Zeb!"

There were others. . . . A mossy-horned old cow that snorted and threatened when approached. She'd never actually attacked anyone, but her attitude always suggested that it was imminent. "Better not trust ol' Snuffy there" became the byword.

Gradually, the troublemakers fell into the routine, or vice versa. In some cases it involved merely a brief glance to see that a particular animal was not departing from its usual behavior.

"They're gettin' us purty well trained, I reckon," observed Slim Mangum, hazing Brindle out of the brush one morning.

On the other hand, there were individual animals that provided a major advantage. After three days' travel, it was noted that one red roan steer always seemed to be in the lead as they traveled. In another few days it became routine for whoever was to ride point to locate that steer as they prepared to move out.

"Come on, Roanie! Let's get 'em movin'!" And, the roan steer would follow the point rider, as the others fell in behind.

The men became better acquainted quickly, and came to appreciate the strengths and weaknesses of the others. One evening, as they finished a meal, Ike Simmons belched heartily. "Damn, Gomez, that was fine!"

Gomez beamed. "My *señora,* she taught me all I know."

That appeared to be considerable. Gomez would collect plants along the way to flavor beans or stews. He had found wild onions, sage, and some other herbs to mix with his various concoctions. He could produce a surprising variety with the staples in the wagon, augmented by other items, and was constantly creative.

"There's a newborn calf out there," said Slim Mangum as he came in from night herding. "What do we do with it? It can't travel. Knock it in the head?"

"We could eat it," suggested his brother. "Right, Gomez?"

"Mebbeso. Lemme do some think about this. Catch it for me, an' I'll carry it in the wagon today."

He did, for three days, letting it nurse when they stopped for the night. Then he traded the calf to a local farmer for a supply of fresh vegetables and a bucket of eggs.

Thus began to develop a relationship, an esprit among the men.

"You have children, Gomez?" asked someone at the fire one evening.

"*Sí* . . . Four . . . Grown and married, back in Mexico. We go to see them maybe, some time, me an' Maria."

The cattle were quiet, a night rider circling the herd. It was a beautiful starry night. Coffee came in from the dark and squatted comfortably, pouring himself a tin cup of his namesake beverage.

"How 'bout you, Coffee? Any family?" asked Zeb Bingham.

There was silence for a moment. It had become custom in the postwar period not to question a man's past. There were too many with divided loyalties in a still uneasy country. Not long ago Texas had been a proud sovereign nation. . . . Now it was considered only a rebellious "province" by the federal forces of military occupation. It was safest not to ask of a man's past, which might reveal his political position. Sometimes it might reveal worse, after the lawlessness of the border war.

None of this likely pertained to a half-breed Negro horse wrangler, it was supposed. Still, they had begun to treat Coffee with the respect due a man skilled in his job. *He talks to 'em,* someone had once suggested, and this did seem to be true. A horse that had been worked with and gentled by Coffee showed habits and manners not found in many cow horses. It was as the liveryman in San Angelo had said, *he's good.* And any man who is good at his job develops respect among his co-workers.

In this case, however, an odd difference. One Negro, one Mex in the crew. It would not be amiss to ask such men about their past. To demand it, even. That would be different from asking a man who was "free, white, and twenty-one." . . . Such a freeman might have reservations about answering, and it would be his right to resent the inquiry. For the "lesser" man, an answer would be expected.

There was an uncomfortable silence, then. The trail crew had come to think of their fellow drovers as *men,* not as Union or Reb, colored or Mexican. *Men.* But no one was quite certain what was going on. Coffee finally broke the silence with a straightforward answer.

"No . . . No family that I know of. Never had time to set, much."

There was another awkward silence, and Bingham finally spoke, with his deep guttural chuckle.

"Ain't we one hell of a crew, though? Smaller'n most trail outfits, an' we got us a nigger hoss wrangler, a greaser cook, an' a one-armed trail boss!"

Insults are not necessarily insults among friends. A ripple of laughter erupted around the fire.

"Quiet!" growled Zeb. "You'll spook the damn cattle!"

They moved on, northeastward, passing east of Abilene and toward Fort Worth, gaining confidence as they gained experience. The routine became established in the minds of men, horses, and cattle. Some days, with good weather and level country, they covered nearly twenty miles. Most days were not that productive. A small stream, a strip of rough country, a threatened storm, any other distraction became a major delay. Some days they covered no ground at all, or even lost a little as stubborn steers tried to turn back. That was usually because of weather.

Past Fort Worth, they turned more directly north.

"Near as I can figger, we'll hit the Red River just north of Gainesville," James explained one evening. "That puts us into Injun Territory in a few days."

There was a serious silence.

"What they call the Nations?" someone asked.

"Don't reckon so . . . Not exactly, anyhow. Way I understand it, every tribe's got its own treaty with the Yankee government. The five Civilized Tribes is a little farther east than this. We might be on the lookout for Cheyenne or Kiowa or even Comanche."

Again, silence. Everyone was concerned but hesitated to be the first to say so.

"Well," said Zeb Bingham finally, "there's somebody ahead of us. We'll see how they make out."

They had seen the broad trampled path of a large herd, apparently on the same course. Judging from the age and condition of the cow chips along the way, the other herd was a few days ahead.

"Reckon that's about the size of it," James agreed. "From what I could learn, there's not much trouble on this trail to Chisholm's tradin' post. Farther east, the Cherokee have been chargin' a toll, I guess. We're more likely to run into the horse Injuns . . . buffalo hunters. They'd go at things a little different, I reckon."

As it happened, they were still a few days short of Gainesville when the point rider came loping back to talk to the trail boss. One of the flankers moved up to the point position, and they slowed the cattle while a brief consultation took place.

"Better come look, James," said Absolam Mangum. "A steer's carcass."

Attention had been called by a couple of buzzards circling overhead.

"What's the problem?" asked York. "The outfit ahead lost a steer? We've lost a few our own selves."

"Well, you take a look. This one's been butchered."

The thought flitted through James's mind that the outfit ahead had butchered a yearling to feed the drovers. Maybe to trade some meat to locals for vegetables or eggs or chickens. He touched a heel to his horse's flank and they rode forward.

A buzzard moved sluggishly away from a scatter of clean-picked bones a few hundred yards to the west of the beaten trail. Another circled overhead, and a pair of coyotes slipped away to watch from a distance.

"There," pointed Mangum.

James was startled. He had expected to see a carcass, fairly intact, stripped of the easiest and choicest cuts of meat. That would be the manner of trail-drive cooks or drovers. This carcass, however, had been stripped of every scrap of flesh, and the bones cut apart. Buzzards had found slim pickings.

"But . . . ," he finally realized, "what happened to the *hide*?"

"Yep," said Mangum solemnly. "What did? Must be, somebody took it."

Obviously, it had not been eaten by the scavengers of the prairie. It must have been removed by humans. But who would want a hide? It would be a nuisance to carry, and useless as it dried to flinty hardness in a day or two on the hot, dusty trail. There was only one logical answer.

"Injuns!" James muttered, half to himself.

"Reckon so."

There was a shout from Coffee, who was driving his remuda parallel to and a few hundred yards west of the herd. He beckoned, and the two drovers turned their horses in that direction.

"*Another* one?" James asked, more to himself than anyone.

This one, too, had been butchered cleanly and efficiently, and the hide was missing. Only the bones remained, with a few reddish scraps of meat clinging to the backbone.

"Injuns," said Coffee in a matter-of-fact way. "They took the hide and the sewing sinew from along the backbone there."

He was right, James reflected. Whites might take the hides in some circumstances, but not the sinew. That would be useful only to an Indian woman.

"Coffee, you seem to know about this. Tell me . . ."

"Not much, Mistah York. Been aroun', some. This ain't a chance kill. A huntin' party, mebbeso, with women along to do the butcherin'. They took mos' everything they could use. Even some of the innards, I reckon. Liver an' such. Coyotes an' buzzards don't get much here."

"How you figger it? This three or four days ago?"

The Negro nodded. "Sumpin' like dat. I figger mebbe the outfit ahead ran onto some Kiowas or Comanches, and struck a bargain of some sort. If there'd been a fight, we'd see more dead or crippled cattle."

"Makes sense, I reckon," James admitted. "Well, nothin' to do but keep movin'. Absolam, I'll take the point awhile. You go tell all the others what's up, but don't skeer 'em none. Jest let 'em know."

The young man nodded and reined away. James started to turn his horse, but then circled back.

"Coffee, you've had some experience with Injuns?" he asked.

"A little bit," the Negro said cautiously. "Why you ask me, suh?"

"Jest thinkin' about it. You know hand sign?"

"Some."

"Good. Might come in handy, don't you think?"

Coffee grinned, his broad ivory smile shining in the sunlight.

"Wouldn't be surprised, boss."

"All right, then. You tell me if there's anything you see that I'd oughta know about. Okay?"

"I sho' will, suh!"

There was, somehow, an unspoken agreement here. In this brief exchange there was a new understanding and respect.

James York was sure that in this man, he'd hired more than a horse wrangler.

19

"Don't nobody move, an' for God's sake don't nobody shoot!" the trail boss called. "Pass the word . . . Better circle the cattle, Slim!"

York was busily trying to move the outfit into some semblance of unity to handle whatever might come next. He wasn't ready for this, and hadn't seen it coming, though he realized now that he should have.

They were still a day or two short of Gainesville, as near as he could figure. Things were going well. They'd seen no more signs of trouble that might have afflicted the trail outfit ahead of them, whoever they might be. They'd discussed the Indian threat around the fire each night. It was acknowledged that, though they weren't really in Indian Territory until north of the Red River, there might be Indians anywhere on the southern plains. The army hadn't been very successful in keeping them corralled.

"An Injun ain't goin' to understand a line in the dirt, that he can't see anyway," Zeb Bingham said. "That's what the army's expectin' 'em to do. Don't mean much to a Comanche."

Zeb had been riding point this morning and motioned for the trail boss to join him as he topped a low rise. York spurred forward, motioning the lead flanker to slow the herd as he passed him.

"What you figger?" asked Zeb, pointing ahead as York drew alongside.

Three heavily armed and painted warriors sat quietly on horses barely a bowshot away. James glanced around the terrain and immediately realized a couple of things. First, that the wash of a wandering dry creek bed a few hundred yards ahead was occupied by at least forty more well-armed warriors. His other thought was that this was a very cleverly planned ambush. There was not another spot in sight where the Indian horsemen could have been kept hidden until the approach of the drive.

"Go get Coffee," James said to Zeb. "Tell him I need him right now."

"Looks like he's comin' already, James. I expect he can see what's happenin' from out where he is to the west, there."

A quick glance showed him that the Negro was loping toward them.

"Good . . . Zeb, you better go stay with the remuda. You know how Injuns like to steal horses."

Zeb reined away, and James looked to see how the outfit was positioned. Slim and Absolam were beginning to get the herd milling around in a more solid mass, but there were still cows strung out for half a mile behind. The Simmonses were pushing them along. With a father's concern, James tried to locate Zeke. Yes, there . . . The boy was riding near Gomez with the chuck wagon. Fortunately, it was early enough in the day that Gomez had not yet pulled ahead to look for a campsite for tonight.

James York assumed an air of dignity befitting a leader of the party and raised his right hand in the hand sign of greeting. Coffee had taught him a few simple signs as they traveled. He sat very still now, right palm forward to show that he held no weapon.

"That's good so far," said Coffee as he drew alongside. "Now, we walk the horses toward them, slow-like."

"Who are they?" asked James.

"I dunno. Kiowas, maybe."

The three warriors now walked their horses forward, and the two groups stopped, a few paces apart.

"We come in peace," Coffee repeated the hand sign already initiated by the trail boss.

The warrior in the center was a big man, dignified, almost haughty in bearing, and heavily built. He had a broad face and dark skin. . . . Darker, almost, than Coffee's. There was no question but that here was a leader of men. It was revealed in the proud tilt of his head and the determined angle of his jaw. He casually returned the sign as he studied the drovers before him.

Then, just as casually, he made the hand sign for question, and pointed to the milling hundreds of cattle behind the drovers. His meaning was plain:

"Where are you going with the cattle?"

"We are only passing through, my chief," Coffee signed. *"We mean no harm. How are you called?"*

"No need for sign talk," said the chief unexpectedly. "Let us use English."

York stifled a gasp. It had been a clever maneuver to catch the drovers off guard.

"I am Satanta, chief of the Kiowas," the big man went on. " 'White Bear,' in your tongue. Who are you?"

"I am called Coffee," the Negro answered. "Our chief, here, is called York."

Satanta nodded and spoke directly to the trail boss. "You wear only one arm. . . . You are a warrior?"

"I was . . . in the war."

"And you still lead. . . . Good. You are a warrior."

"I fight only when needed," said York carefully.

The Kiowa nodded again. "That, too, is good, One-Arm. A man should not kill only for the sake of killing, no?"

"That is true," James York agreed.

Satanta turned now to Coffee again. "You are their hand-talker?"

"Yes . . . I drive their horses, too, my chief."

"Our *boys* herd horses," Satanta noted, to no one in particular, but quite pointedly, as he turned back to York.

"You have many spotted buffalo," he noted conversationally.

"Yes, my chief," James agreed, taking a cue from Coffee's form of address. "We take them north to the other white man's country."

"The Long Knives?"

"No, not the army. Farmers."

The look of disdain on the face of Satanta told his opinion of those who grow crops instead of riding free with the wind to hunt.

"Anyone who wishes to buy or trade for them," York added lamely.

Satanta nodded again, pondering the situation. "I see. . . . It happens that *our* children are hungry. My wives are hungry. I have promised to bring them meat today, but we see no buffalo." He paused a moment to scan the distant horizon, and then looked back to York. "I see only spotted buffalo today. What shall I do?"

"My chief," Coffee broke in, "it would be our pleasure to trade, I am sure."

"Trade what?" Satanta feigned a puzzled look, and then his face lighted. "Ah! I know! A few spotted buffalo . . . My brother One-Arm has so many. . . . A few of them in trade for safe passage through the Kiowa Nation. You have a good thought there, horse herder. Maybe you throw in a few horses, too?"

The last remark was laced with just a touch of scorn. Horse herders were, among Kiowas, usually youngsters not quite ready for the hunt or for war.

"No horses," said York flatly. "We need them to herd the cattle."

"You know your needs, One-Arm. But these are good horses. Much better than we get from the army. Some of theirs are hardly worth stealing."

There was a veiled threat here, which James did not recognize. But Coffee did.

"At most times," said Coffee, "we would be proud to make a gift of horses to our brother, White Bear. But we need these, as our chief, One-Arm, has said. Maybe another spotted buffalo or two, in exchange for no horses now?"

"It is good," nodded Satanta. "Of course, I cannot promise that all my young men will know of this trade."

There was a suggestion of a twinkle in the eye of Satanta, and York realized that the Kiowa was enjoying this immensely. It was an inside joke, a part of the complicated trading game. He admired the strategy that the burly chief had devised.

"My chief," Coffee now said calmly, "we would wish you firm control over your young men."

Satanta was apparently caught completely off guard by this maneuver, but he maintained his stoic composure. Only a lift of his eyebrows betrayed his surprise.

Now, if any horses were stolen by Kiowas, it would reflect on Satanta's leadership.

"Let it be so," the chief grunted. "Now, how many cows? Six?"

"*Aiee,* we are poor drovers!" said Coffee quickly. "Maybe three?"

"Five," said Satanta firmly.

"Four?"

"No . . . Five, but you can pick them."

"It is good!" said Coffee.

He's done this before, thought York.

The same thought was reflected in the dusky face of Satanta, who knew and respected negotiating skills when he encountered them.

They got the herd moving again and cut out five steers from the drag. The Mangum boys drove them out away from the bunch and turned them over to young Kiowa riders.

White Bear nodded approval as he sat with Coffee and York, and there was actually a semblance of a smile as he waved and turned his horse away to join the rest of his party.

"There," observed Coffee, "is some kinda *man.*"

"You've met him before?" asked York.

"No . . . Heered of him, though. Reckon we'll hear more of him."

They turned to rejoin the drive as the herd straggled out again on the trail north.

·   ·   ·

Gainesville fell behind them and the Red River lay just ahead. James had been concerned about crossing with the herd, but now felt better. It was easy to see where others had crossed. Once more, he was grateful to the unknown drovers ahead of them whose trail was plain to follow.

"We'll cross before dark, and camp on the other side tonight," James decided.

That had worked out best. The cattle could drink their fill and bed down quietly while tired drovers caught their few hours of rest. Then men, horses, and cattle would be ready for a fresh start.

"That's Indian Territory?" asked Zeke at his father's elbow. "Looks pretty much like this side."

James chuckled. "What'd you expect? But Coffee says we might not even see many Injuns. We seen one o' their big guns already."

"How does Coffee know so much about Indians?"

"He's lived with 'em some, he says. Those tricks of his to gentle horses . . . Injun 'medicine' . . . Mebbe he *can* talk to horses, like some folks say. Well, let's cross!"

The crossing was made without incident. The chuck wagon had already crossed and Gomez had the cooking started when the roan lead steer plunged in, followed by the rest of the herd.

They were just settling down for the night as twilight fell, when Slim Mangum pointed to the north.

"Look! Somebody's comin'."

"Injuns?" asked his brother.

"Don't look like it."

Seldom had a figure looked more ridiculously out of place . . . A single rider, dressed in a dark business suit and a derby hat. Behind the cantle of his saddle was a loosely packed blanket roll. He appeared ill at ease on the horse, sitting like an inexperienced rider. From the derby on his head to the patent-leather shoes on his feet, he was a townsman, a man of civilization. What could he be doing here in the wilds of Indian Territory? The drovers stood speechless as the newcomer carefully circled around the herd and approached the fire.

"Good evening, gentlemen," he greeted. "May I speak to your leader? 'Trail boss,' I believe he is called."

"I'm the trail boss, I reckon," said James York. "Get down and set a spell. Supper's about ready."

"Thank you . . . May I camp with you tonight?"

"Shore," said James, smiling. "Sort of figgered you'd might want to."

The little man dismounted stiffly and clumsily, and began to unsaddle. He did appear to know a little more about that than they expected. He set the saddle and blanket roll aside and looked around questioningly.

"Jest turn your horse in with ours," James suggested. "Over there."

"I'll take him," offered Zeke.

"Thank you, son," said the little man. "Now, Mr. . . . ?" There was a question in his tone as he turned to the trail boss.

"York. James York."

"Ah! Yes. My name is Sugg . . . W. W. Sugg. Later, I would like to discuss some business with you."

James nodded, puzzled. He'd find out when the time was right, he guessed. But the man sure didn't fit his idea of a cattle buyer. What was he doing in Indian Territory?

"It's this way, Mr. York," Sugg began.

They had eaten and drunk coffee and the camp was quiet when the two sat down to talk. It was a beautiful moonlit night, a million stars overhead. The ripple of the river harmonized with the soft murmur of resting cattle.

"I work for a man named McCoy," he went on. "Joseph McCoy. I'd like to suggest that you deliver your cattle to his pens in Abilene."

Is the man crazy? James wondered.

"Uh . . . Mr. Sugg, we just came from down that way. Why would we—"

Sugg held up a hand in protest. "No, no! Not Abilene, Texas. I'm talking about Abilene, *Kansas.*"

"Hadn't heard of that one."

"Exactly! That's my purpose . . . to tell you of the advantages of delivery there."

"Your boss is a cattle buyer?"

"Yes . . . A shipper. Abilene is on the Union Pacific Railroad. Yes, there are other rail towns, but none with facilities like ours. Pens, loading ramps, cattle cars, feed available. Direct shipping to Kansas City, St. Louis, even Chicago. *And*"—he leaned forward confidentially—"it's *closer* than any shipping point on the other railroads."

"This McCoy work for the Union Pacific?"

"No, no. He just owns the loading facilities. Look . . ." He pointed to the sleepy cattle. "How would you get them into a car without chutes and ramps?"

"Well . . . Reckon I hadn't thought of that. . . ."

"Exactly. You'd hoped to sell them, though."

"Shore. Now, what if I wanted to use the pens and loading ramps, and ship them myself?"

"You could do that. We'd work it out. But then somebody'd have to go with the cattle. It's easier just to sell 'em in Abilene and forget it. We'll pay forty dollars a head, less a small fee for the pens."

Forty dollars? Ten times their worth back on the Concho?

"Well, I . . ."

"I don't want a decision now, Mr. York," Sugg protested. "Just letting you know."

"How do we find it?"

"Just head north. Straight on past Chisholm's store on the Arkansas River. Abilene's a few days beyond, on the Smoky Hill. Just ask as you travel."

"Thanks . . . We'll maybe give it a try!"

20

Sugg traveled with them for a day as they headed north across the Chickasaw Nation. Then he turned aside. He had heard, he said, of other herds, farther west, heading toward Kansas.

"I'll need to find them and tell them about our facilities at Abilene, too. Best of luck to you all!"

He rode away, cheerfully headed westward.

James watched him go, still somewhat amazed at how out of place the man seemed. Everything about him appeared ill fitted to the frontier and the rigors of a life in the saddle. Not many men would plunge alone into the unknown hazards of the Indian Nations just to sell an idea of someone else's.

Zeb Bingham, at the trail boss's elbow, summed it up. "You got to give him credit for spunk, York. Not many could do what he's doin'."

James nodded. It had been easy to size up the little man as a city dude, a tenderfoot who did not understand what he was getting into. Maybe, even, a little crazy. But there was more to the man, it seemed. A job to do, and he was doing it. James smiled as they watched the ridiculous figure in the derby hat, elbows sticking out, stirrups too short, stiff in the saddle. . . . But as Zeb said, he had spunk, and a job to do. They could only hope that the Cheyenne and Kiowas he might encounter would recognize and respect that.

·   ·   ·

They encountered a party of Chickasaws a few days later and negotiated a toll for crossing their national lands.

"Jesus!" exploded Slim Mangum. "Are we goin' to give the whole herd away afore we get to the railroad?"

"Reckon not," James told him. "If we did, it'd be better'n gettin' killed tryin' to keep 'em from stealin' 'em, though."

"You can give 'em *your* steers, then," snapped Slim.

"Hold on," Zeb interrupted. "None o' that! We all agreed. We're in it together. We elected James York our trail boss, an' he's the one with the say. I say we're gettin' off cheap, a few steers that weren't worth nothin' when we started."

Slim subsided with no further comment and turned away.

"We could hold another election," James suggested.

"Forget that kind o' talk," growled Zeb Bingham. "I'll handle Slim, if need be. We don't need no arguments."

They moved on, through an area where they weren't sure what to expect. The sketch map that James had made from hearsay back in Texas did not show who might occupy the region just south of the Kansas boundary and north of the Chickasaw Nation.

"One o' the other Civilized Tribes?" suggested Bingham.

"Don't know, Zeb. I just don't recall hearin' anybody say. Mostly, the ones I talked to knew the Old Shawnee Trail, and that runs quite a ways east of here. Creek and Cherokee country. Someplace, we'd ought to meet Osages, I guess."

"Well, so far, our trail's plain. The outfit ahead's markin' it with cow chips."

James smiled. "Yep. Shore hope they know where they're goin'! But I wasn't thinkin' so much of that. Just north gets us there. But I wondered how many more tribes or nations we'll meet up with."

"Reckon we'll see . . ."

They were in a country of wooded hills covered with scrub oaks, now. Between the ridges were wide areas of open grassland. Deer and elk were abundant, and Gomez managed to bag a couple of turkeys to vary their monotonous diet. Even with the above-average skills of the cook, a respite from salt pork, biscuits, and beans was welcome.

Ahead of them, the trail of the other herd still pointed straight north. They had enjoyed fine weather. Too good to be true, James feared. . . .

There came a day when dawn found a partly cloudy sky. The atmosphere was different, somehow. . . . Heavy, yet unsettled. The light breeze, usually at their backs, was variable, switching direction playfully, stirring tiny dust devils as it danced across the prairie. Scraps of cloud scudded across a watery gray sky above them.

"Thet's a weather breeder if I ever seen one," observed Zeb. "Mebbe we'd ought to camp early."

James agreed. He rode ahead to consult with Gomez, who nodded and pointed to a grassy valley near at hand.

"Ober there, maybe?" Gomez suggested.

"Looks good," agreed James. "We'll bed 'em down there."

By the time the herd was circling and beginning to settle, the air was still and quiet. There was a feeling of uneasiness over everything, including men, cattle, and horses. James noticed that the hairs on the back of his hand were standing upright, and his skin was tingling.

To the west, a low bank of dark clouds was building. It was an ugly gray-green color, laced with occasional flickers of orange. From time to time, a low mutter of thunder, a barely audible moan, sounded from the approaching front.

The cattle were restless, circling, lying down only to get up again.

"Hold 'em close, boys!" advised James, circling quietly to speak to each drover. "Don't know what's comin'!"

He glanced up at the approaching cloud bank, just as it was slashed by a brilliant streak of blue-white fire. He quickly began to count, to himself. . . . *Hunnerd an' one, hunnerd an' two, hunnerd an' three . . .* He reached *eleven* before the rumble of distant thunder punctuated his count. Eleven miles out . . .

Soon, another flash . . . *Hunnerd an' one . . .* this time, *ten miles* . . . Moving pretty fast . . . A thin mist of rain began to fall, partially obscuring his view of the looming cloud bank. He could no longer identify the individual flash of the lightning bolts.

There was a patter of larger raindrops now, and he began to sense that some of them were *bouncing.* Tiny balls of frozen ice, striking the ground, the grass, or leaves of nearby oaks with a louder, popping noise. At first, the hailstones were pea-sized, then larger, the size of marbles. With a sudden fury, rain pelted down, driven by gusts of wind and mixed with chunks of ice the size of hen eggs.

The cattle were lumbering to their feet in a panic, bawling in confusion. A few began to run, and the riders attempted to turn them back. That could be extremely dangerous.

"Let 'em go," yelled James, but his words were drowned in the fury of the storm.

He saw one rider rein aside, and the flood of the herd poured past him to charge the fringe of trees. The rest followed, spreading and scattering in panic as they went. He couldn't see the other rider through the curtain of water and ice.

"Here's another, over here!" Zeke called.

"Bring him in, son!" James shouted back.

The young man circled, waved, and yelled, and the bewildered steer broke out of the brush into the open. There he saw others of his kind, and galloped toward them.

The storm had passed, but the air was chilled, and the ground whitened in places with chunks of ice from the size of a pea to that of an apple. It would soon be dark, and the reddening western sky cast an eerie light across a landscape that had the appearance of a nightmare. Trees and bushes had been stripped of foliage by the hail. Broken branches hung precariously by shreds of bark. Here and there were bodies of rabbits and small birds struck down by the icy bullets of the storm. A small stream nearby had swollen and overflowed its banks, the rushing current crested by streaks and patches of white as the rising waters spread.

"Bring 'em out into this flat," James yelled. "As many as we can before dark!"

The cattle milled nervously, bawling as they circled.

"Here's ol' Roanie," called one of the Simmonses. "Thet ought to help some!"

The bawling became an advantage, as lost individuals followed the sound back toward the gather.

"I seen one bunch runnin' back south," Absolam Mangum shouted to James.

"How many?"

"Mebbe fifty . . ."

"Better go get 'em! Take a couple of other riders. . . . Here, Zeke, you go with Ab, there! Don't be out after dark ef you kin help it. . . . We got maybe an hour."

Gomez had managed to get a fire going near his battered chuck wagon. Its canvas top hung in shredded tatters from the bows. Men began to straggle toward the point of light in the gloom of the vast unknown prairie.

"Everybody accounted for?" asked Slim Mangum as he rode in.

"Dunno, Slim. Who's with the herd?"

"Zeb and Coffee. Guess we're all here. Anybody hurt?"

"Couple of sore shoulders," James answered. "Zeb's got a knot on his head."

"Hell, he had that before."

There were a few halfhearted attempts at a chuckle.

"How about the cattle?" Gomez asked.

"Hard to tell, I reckon," James admitted. "We'll know more when it gets light. Right now, I figger we can't account for more'n half of 'em."

"Prob'ly headin' back to Texas," said Absolam glumly.

"Might be . . . I figger we'll take a day . . . maybe two . . . round up all we can and move on. There's always a chance we can pick up some trail-branded strays on the way back home."

"Hardly worth drivin' 'em back, is it?" asked Slim.

"Depends . . . Let's see what we got left, an' then decide where we stand," the trail boss said.

Morning revealed a few stragglers heading in toward the main gather on their own. A quick count and an experienced estimate showed possibly nine hundred animals in all.

"Boss, there's cows strung out from here to the Red River, looks like," said Zeb, returning from a scout to the south. "They're movin' pretty slow now, though. I reckon two or three of us could backtrack for half a day, make a gather, and drive whatever we get back up here."

James nodded. "Prob'ly worth a day's travel. Let's do it. The rest of us will spread out and try to pick up some that's bushed up nearby. Who you want with you?"

"The Mangums, I reckon. Okay?"

"Okay, Zeb. If the cattle get restless, we'll drift 'em on north a ways. Good luck!"

"An' to you!"

The big man turned his horse and motioned to the Mangum brothers. The stream had fallen almost as rapidly as it had risen. The day was clear and the sky was clean-washed blue.

They found a few dead cattle, apparently felled by the larger hailstones. It was hard to tell, though. One old steer had almost certainly broken its neck in a fall into a small ravine. Another . . . Lightning? Maybe . . .

The gather near the camp netted nearly a hundred more cattle. Some of them limped, but could probably travel. Three horses, lost from the remuda in the storm, were also recovered. Coffee checked them over carefully.

"They's all right, boss!" he said with a grin.

Just before dark, Zeb and the Mangums returned with nearly three hundred cattle, driving easily.

"Reckon they jest spooked an' tried to go home," he reported. "Boss, there was more. Want us to try a gather in the mornin'?"

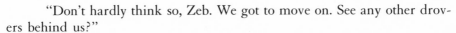

"Don't hardly think so, Zeb. We got to move on. See any other drovers behind us?"

"Not a sign, James. But we got to figger we ain't the onliest ones with this idea, huh?"

"Right! We know of at least one other outfit, the one ahead of us. Well, we'll see. We move on in the morning!"

21

"We must be pretty close to the Kansas border," observed James, studying the map that W. W. Sugg had given him. It was actually only a sketch diagram, a printed handbill with the proposed route to the McCoy cattle pens and loading chutes at Abilene.

"Don't see no markers," growled Zeb.

"Reckon there ain't any. Guess it don't matter much, though. Looks purty much the same on both sides."

"You s'pose we'll run into any of them bushwhackin' . . . what they call 'em? Jaybirds?"

"Jayhawkers . . . Sugg said there wasn't much jayhawkin' goin' on. Might be somebody might try to charge us a toll for passage."

"It ain't right!" snarled Zeb.

"Well, let's cross that bridge when we get there."

"There's a *bridge*?"

"No, no, Zeb. It's jest a sayin'. . . . Never mind."

Slim Mangum, who had been riding point, waved to his brother on the left flank to come forward. They conferred for a moment, and then Slim loped over to where James and Zeb rode.

"Riders ahead, boss. Looks like about ten of 'em."

"Indians?"

"No . . . White men. Don't seem in no hurry."

"Okay . . . Where's Gomez?"

"Up ahead. They're headin' for the wagon, I think."

"Is he campin' yet?"

"Don't think so. 'Bout time, though."

York nodded. "Zeb, let's go see what they're up to. Slim, jest keep the herd driftin'. Tell the others."

The drover turned his horse and loped away.

"Prob'ly be no trouble," the trail boss remarked, "but let's go see."

Gomez had stopped the wagon and was chatting comfortably with the riders.

"Hey, this my cozzin Ramon!" he beamed. "They took 'em cows to Abilene."

"Good!" said James. "Who's the trail boss?"

"Ober dere," Gomez pointed. "Name Johnson. They stay wid us tonight?"

"Sure! I want to ask them about the trail an' all."

A few hours later, with twilight deepening and the stars popping out one by one, the two trail bosses sat a little to one side, talking.

"You won't have no trouble," the newcomer predicted. "Trail's plain . . . Jest foller the tracks of thet outfit ahead."

"We been doin' that. 'Pears it's bigger'n ours, right?"

Johnson chuckled. "Right. 'Bout twice your size, I reckon."

"An' the pens and all . . . Purty good?"

"Top kind. They're good folk to deal with, looks like."

"I see a bandage or two on your crew. Trouble?" asked James.

Johnson grunted mirthlessly. "Not with the drive. Afterward, some o' the boys got sorta likkered up an' got to scufflin' some, with a couple o' the locals. The marshal busted a couple o' heads. No harm done."

York chuckled. "How far to Chisholm's?" he asked.

"Three, four days . . . Oh, yes, Chisholm's dead, though."

"Dead?"

"Yep. Food poisonin'. He et some stew that had set overnight in a brass kettle, I heered. Thet's bad. . . . Brass is poison, y'know."

"So I've heard. The tradin' post still there?"

"Yep, but empty. I guess his wife left. Pity . . . He was a good man. Some o' the boys say nobody ever left Jesse Chisholm's place hungry."

"I'd heard that. His wife's Indian?" York asked.

"I b'lieve so. Cheyenne, maybe. But he was Cherokee, hisself. Half-blood Scotchman."

"Well, no matter now, I reckon. How far beyond that is Abilene?"

"Don't remember, exackly. Mebbe a week, give or take . . . Given good weather, you'll do fine. Whose cattle you drivin'?"

"Our own. Bunch o' neighbors tryin' to make it by neighborin'."

Johnson nodded, and both were silent a little while, sipping coffee. Johnson's eyes strayed to James York's empty sleeve.

"The war?"

James nodded. "Palmito Hill . . . The war was over, and we didn't know it."

The other man shook his head. "An' it don't matter now, does it? But, all I want is the damn Yankee army out of Texas." He rose and stretched. "Guess we need another Sam Houston."

James was silent. Governor Houston had been virtually thrown out of office for not supporting the Confederate cause. Was this the same man who had defeated the Mexican army and founded the Republic of Texas? But he was dead now, Northern carpetbaggers were pouring in, and Texas appeared to be losing her identity as a sovereign republic. He didn't even want to think about it, or that once-proud Texas was under military occupation by a foreign army.

"Well," he said finally, "ef we can't lick 'em in battle, mebbe we can sell 'em beef."

"Yep. Hell of a note," said Johnson as he turned away.

They passed Chisholm's store near the junction of the Arkansas River with the Little Arkansas. Its inhabitants having departed, the place seemed without spirit itself. It was falling into disrepair. *Odd,* thought James, *how fast a house goes downhill when there's nobody livin' in it. Seems like it's got no reason to go on.* He had known that feeling himself, before he found this one, this attempt to drive cattle north. On northward, toward the rails at Abilene . . .

On the eighth day past the trader's, they saw the town ahead. The new cattle pens stretched alongside the tracks for a quarter mile, and more were being constructed. Lumber, practically nonexistent here, was being shipped in on the railroad on flatcars.

A rider loped out to meet them and asked for the trail boss.

"Reckon I'm him," James York offered. "Who be you?"

"Stuart . . . I work for Joe McCoy. I'll help you pen your herd. We need 'em in the holdin' pens on the end, there to the east." He pointed.

"Good enough!"

He turned and signaled to the flankers, who eased the herd in that direction.

.   .   .

They had never seen so many cows in one place. Pen after pen, all crammed full of cattle, even while men were pushing more through the alleyways and up the ramps into waiting cars. The animals were encouraged by the judicious use of long poles, used to punch stragglers along. It was apparent that the "cowpunchers" had developed a certain expertise for efficient loading of the cattle cars.

James York received payment for the cattle and held a conference in the shade of one of the new frame store buildings.

"How you want to do this? It's a lot of money. We got forty dollars a head, and our count was over thirteen hundred."

Zeb Bingham spoke up. "Reckon each family'd ought to take care of our own, hadn't we? I pay Gomez."

"Let's stay a day or two," suggested Absolam Mangum. "Take a bath, see some women. Buy clothes, maybe." He looked down at his own tattered jeans. "Mebbe even a drink or two?"

"Sure," James agreed. "We pay Coffee before we make the split, then each family's on its own until day after tomorrow. We meet here to start home, a bit after daylight?"

There were nods of agreement.

"You gonna stay at the hotel?" asked one of the Simmons boys.

"Don't reckon so," James said. "Don't look too savory. A bath, maybe, and then camp south of the tracks, there. Want to camp together?"

There were nods of agreement.

"How'd they pay you? In gold?" asked Zeb.

"No. Paper. Greenbacks."

"Well, seems like we'd ought to go make camp an' make our split there, instead of showin' it around town."

"Good idea. Let's move."

They gathered at the area where Coffee was holding the remuda.

"What about the horses?" Coffee asked. "You gonna sell 'em?"

"You kin sell thet damned ol' piebald I been ridin'," said Slim. "He's got the roughest gaits I ever seen."

Everyone laughed, but no one was really interested in selling off the remuda.

"Can you look after 'em some more, Coffee? We'll spell you if you want to go to town," the trail boss offered.

"Sure, boss. But I don't expeck to spend much time in town. Ain't certain I'd be real welcome."

There was an uncomfortable silence for a moment. No one was certain how a man of colour would be received here, and it might be better not to find out in a wrong way. Yankees were unpredictable where Negroes were concerned, talking big about equality and all, but not wanting them around.

• • •

The next day, walking the streets of Abilene with his father, Ezekiel York paused to read a handbill in the window of the land office.

"Look here, Papa. . . . The railroad's sellin' land, along the right-o'-way."

"Let's see, son . . . Homestead land?"

"No, it says here for *sale,* by the acre. How big is an acre?"

"Can I help you, gentlemen?" a voice spoke from the doorway.

"No," said James quickly. "We were just lookin'."

The man stepped outside, a well-dressed individual with a high stiff collar and embroidered vest over a starched white shirt. He glanced at the poster in the window and then to Zeke.

"I heard this young man ask," he said, "about an 'acre.' That's a square, a hundred and sixty square rods . . . six hundred forty of them to a square mile. The government has given land to the railroads to build on, and to sell for settlement. *People* are needed here. A dollar twenty-five an acre will set you up in farming."

"Don't b'lieve we'd be interested," James told him. "We're just visitin'."

"Of course . . . But look around! Come back if we can be of any help."

"Papa," said Zeke as they walked on, "couldn't we look at some of it? He said it's along the railroad, east of here."

James laughed, but there was time to kill while the younger men pursued their own interests. Why not? They saddled and rode eastward along the tracks for a few miles. It was early autumn, and the tall seed heads of the prairie grasses brushed against their knees as they rode. In places, the nodding plumes were taller than the horses' backs. It was a lush green country of rolling hills, with trees sparsely scattered along the watercourses. They paused at the top of a rise and studied the country. Each range of distant hills appeared a more bluish hue, until the farthest in sight, some thirty miles out, seemed to blend with the blue of distant sky.

Ezekiel was totally charmed by the sight. He had never seen such country. He felt, somehow, that he had come home.

"Papa," he said softly, "could we . . . ?"

"Son," said James firmly, "jest look at it! You buy it, you got nothin'! Spend all that money, you can't plow it, too many rocks. Look at how the limestone caprock comes right to the surface, there. Shore it's purty to look at, but not worth the price. Dollar twenty-five an acre! Nothin' but grass, and never be good for anything!"

He reined his horse around. "We better be gettin' back."

Zeke lingered another moment, watching the shadows of puffy white clouds creep across distant hills.

Mebbe, he whispered to himself, *but some day I'm comin' back for a better look.*

Then he too turned his horse and hurried to catch up with his father.

BOOK VI

THE CENTENNIAL
1876

FOREWORD

While the war had slowed settlement, it had also diverted the attention of the military from friction on the frontier between the Indians and whites. At the war's end, thoughts had again turned to the "Indian Problem." . . .

– The Territory of Arizona was paying a bounty of $250 for each Apache scalp.

– 1864: Colonel J. M. Chivington, with more than six hundred Colorado Volunteers, attacked Chief Black Kettle's band of Cheyennes, who were camped under federal protection near Fort Lyon and flying the American flag. His orders: "Kill and scalp all big and little; nits make lice."

Chivington's "boys" massacred some three hundred Cheyennes, mostly women and children. They displayed scalps, arms and legs of children, and other body parts on the stage of a theater in Denver.

– 1866: Captain William Fetterman: "Give me eighty men and I'll ride through the whole Sioux nation."

Shortly thereafter, Fetterman and exactly that number were killed by Sioux outside Fort Phil Kearny in Wyoming.

– 1867: General William Tecumseh Sherman of the "scorched earth" march through Georgia was now assigned to the plains. "The more [Indians] we kill this year," he stated emphatically, "the less will have to be killed in the next war."

– 1868: Survivors of Black Kettle's people, now camped on the Washita in Indian Territory, were attacked by Lieutenant Colonel George Armstrong Custer's elite Seventh Cavalry, virtually wiping out the Southern Cheyennes.

– 1869: General Phil Sheridan, meeting a chief with whom he proposed negotiating, was told that this was a "good Indian." "The only good Indians I ever met," Sheridan snapped, "were dead."

The warfare continued to accelerate. More settlers were killed and mutilated. Women and children were carried off.

"Yes, Mr. President . . . You sent for me?" asked the blue-coated general.

"Yes . . . Sit down, Mr. Sherman." The President turned and dismissed a young lieutenant who was acting as his secretary. "Close the door, please!" he called after the retreating figure.

"Yes, sir."

President Grant turned back toward his visitor and offered a cigar. "Smoke, Sherman?"

"I . . . Well, yes . . . Thank you, sir."

"You can drop the formality, Sherman. We're in this together, and this is a completely off-the-record meeting. I will be totally candid, and I expect the same. Understood?"

"Yes, sir."

"Good!" Grant paused to light his cigar and that of his visitor. He blew a fragrant bluish cloud into the air and settled back. "None of our conversation is to go beyond this room," he cautioned.

"I understand, sir. Have I . . . Is there something I don't know about, sir?"

"No, no, that's not it, General. I'm just looking for suggestions. The Indian problem . . . Each new killing brings more outrage on the part of the public. I'm looking for ideas, here. Tell me how the campaign is going."

"Yes . . . Well, it could be better, sir. It's like chasing smoke. . . . Reach out to grab it, it's gone. The Indians run, and come back another day."

"Cowards?"

"No, not at all, sir. Just clever. And brave! Some of my commanders call the plains Indians the finest cavalry they've ever seen. Quite unorthodox, though."

Grant nodded. "You had considerable success in cutting the Confederacy in two. Have you any ideas on this?"

"An entirely different situation, sir."

"I'm quite aware of that, General."

"Yes. But the reason our march through Georgia was successful was that it cut the enemy's supply lines, destroyed his support system."

Grant snorted. "These savages have no supply lines!"

"Ah, but they do, sir. Just not like ours. Tribes which depend on farming, you'll note, are already under subjugation. That *was* their supply line."

"But these wild tribes move around. They hunt."

"Exactly, sir . . . Hunt *what*? Mostly buffalo."

"Go on!"

"Well, Mr. President, the railroad has, in effect, cut the continent in two, hence cutting the herd in two. It was a great hazard during the building of the roadway, you recall, before the war. Stories of stampeding animals knocking trains off the tracks . . . But now, it's easy to put hunters near the herds, by rail."

"You're suggesting that we send hunters out?"

"Not send, exactly, though that's been suggested."

"Why not use the army? Ah, I see. They're needed for the fighting, of course."

"Yes, sir. It has helped considerably to have the Negro units in the field. Good fighters . . . 'Buffalo soldiers,' the savages call them."

"Why, for God's sake?" asked the President.

"It's a compliment; an honor. They look like a buffalo, to the Indians. Dark skin, woolly hair. And the buffalo is a sacred animal. But let me continue. There's quite a market in buffalo hides. Common ones bring three or four dollars. The rarer beaver-fur type, as much as seventy-five dollars apiece. That's about what the bicolored black-and-tans bring, too. There are some buckskin-colored animals, particularly in the northern herd, which bring up to two hundred dollars. They're not too attractive, to my thinking. A sort of dirty white . . . But *rare*."

"I don't see . . ."

"*Encourage* the hunting. Maybe even furnish ammunition . . . Unofficially, of course. The entire culture of the plains Indian depends on the buffalo. Take it away, he has nothing."

"Yes . . . How long do you think this would take?"

"I have no idea, sir. But I know there are far fewer buffalo on the plains than a few decades ago. We don't see them by the millions as the early explorers did. If we continue to push the 'hostiles,' as our scouts call them, while letting the civilian hunters reduce their . . . ah, 'provisions,' so to speak . . ."

"Yes . . . I see. You know there are voices in Congress protesting the 'wanton killing' of buffalo for hides, and the rotting of good meat. Some of the states are passing legislation."

"I know, sir. Idaho has such a law. Hard to enforce. A lot of sentiment *against* such legislation."

"Including yourself, eh?" smiled Grant. "Phil Sheridan agrees with you, of course. Well, perhaps we can stop some of the proposed legislation in committee."

– 1871: Wyoming passed legislation regulating buffalo-hide hunting.
– 1872: Montana and Colorado followed. The Kansas Legislature passed a bill prohibiting "wanton destruction of buffaloes," but it was killed by the governor's pocket veto.

These laws had little effect. The hunters, like their quarry, were far-flung and fast moving.
– 1874: Federal legislation to regulate the traffic in buffalo hides was allowed to die for lack of the President's signature. Other bills were tabled in committee.
– 1875: Nebraska passed protective legislation, and Texas was debating a similar bill.

General Phil Sheridan, commander of the military department of the Southwest, traveled to Austin to speak before the legislature.

"These [hunters]," he told them, "have done in the last two years . . . more to settle the vexed Indian question than the entire regular army has done in the last thirty years. They are destroying the Indians' commissary; . . . Send them powder and lead, if you will; but for the sake of lasting peace, let them kill, skin, and sell until the buffaloes are exterminated. . . ."

He further suggested, tongue in cheek, that a bronze medal be struck for the buffalo hunters, with a dead buffalo on one side and a discouraged Indian on the other.

1

Cawker City, Kansas, 1876

It was a bright day in early October, a warm, lazy Indian summer morning. It was the sort of day that one dreams of. Tall grasses on the prairie, changing to their respective fall colors. The sky was a clear clean azure blue with only a few puffy clouds scattered high above. Along the roadside, myriads of wildflowers of several types, all in the same shade of glowing gold, lent further brightness to the day. Other flowers, in all shapes and in various shades of lavender and purple, shone in contrast.

This beauty was lost on the young man who drove a team and a rickety farm wagon toward town that morning. His shoulders were slumped, largely from worry. He'd pick up a few supplies. Precious few, for money was short. He had a little wheat, and that was another worry. How long could he wait without risking too much loss from rodents? There was also his note at the bank, not due until January, but of great concern. He saw no way that he could pay it, unless he could shoot or trap enough furs to pick up a little money. And fur wasn't prime yet. He'd have to wait until colder weather thickened the pelts on the critters.

Maybe he'd run into a couple of the boys in town. Talking to young farmers with similar problems sometimes made him feel better.

"Hey, Wen! Wentin Wilson!" a voice called from the board sidewalk. "Where you goin'?"

"Store, I reckon," he answered, pulling in the team.

The other man stepped off the walk and crossed the dusty street with a purpose.

"Where you been? We thought mebbe the Injuns had got your hair."

"Nope. Not yet, anyhow."

Both knew that it was a joke, but there *had* been Indian attacks only a day or two farther west.

"Need to talk to you," said his friend. "Let's go huntin'!"

There was a crackle of excitement in his voice.

"Huntin' what?" asked Wilson. "Where?"

"Buffalo! Good market for skins. We'll head down toward Fort Dodge. The sutler there can ship 'em for us."

"But seriously, Rathbun. What *about* Indians?"

"We'll take a big party. I've got nearly a dozen, several wagons. Come on, go with us. You got nothin' goin' on at yer farm now."

That was certainly true.

"Come on . . . Park your wagon, and let's talk about it."

In an hour, Wilson was convinced. It might be just what he needed. At least, it would be exciting.

"I'll do it," he agreed. "When do we leave?"

"Mebbe two weeks. Got to get our outfits together," said Rathbun.

Almost a century later, a slim yellowed notebook written in pencil was found on the desk of William L. White at the Emporia, Kansas, *Gazette* after his death. There was no indication of who might have left it. It was a diary, telling of a buffalo hunt from Osborne County, Kansas, past Dodge City and into the Palo Duro region of Texas. It is signed "W. A. Wilson."

Thursday Oct. the 26 we left Osborn Co. bound for the buffalo country. Our out fit consist of 14 men, well armed 7 teames. We made 12 miles and camped. We pitched our tentes on Twin Creek and prepared Supper, laretted our horses, & retired. Friday = 27 = we wer on our way bi sun up and made 12 ½ miles & stoped for dinner on wolf Creek one horse in mi team bawked at every hill = we start again and pass through some beautiful country we made 15 miles this afternoon pitched our tents on a beautiful stream call paradise. The watter is extreamly salty, we haul fresh watter with us & our bread being exhausted baking & cooking. Saturday = 28 = we start at sun rise & make 8 miles a town on the K.T. railroad called Rusell where we finished bying our out fit and took dinner. Here I had the pleasure of

meeting mi old friend = wash Tennel – of Newwaverly,
Ind. Here we heard the Indians was 200 miles west of us &
one man & team turned back = George Haden bi name. 1 o
clock & we are on the move a gain. We made 15 miles and
camped at victora colony = owned bi rusians = we wer on
the move bi day light & made 12 miles & stoped at Hayes, a
military out post. Here uncle sam has quite a number of
soldiers = we stop on big creek for dinner. This is the last
town where we can get any thing to drink & the boys is
improving the opportunity by taking plenty of the obejoyful,
we went to the edge of town and took dinner. At two o
clock we started & drove to the smokey river, 12 miles from
Fort Hayes and camped. There is continualy a cloud of mist
or smoke arising from the rigver. Here is a fine spring & a
big spring for a ranch. We crossed the Fremont trail to day.
Monday oct. 30 – we wer up at four o clock & start at sun
up. We stoped on Big Timber for dinner after making 12
miles. We see two herds of antelope and a wolf = but did
not kill any. One of our party went back to town after his
coat & has not caught up yet. There is no watter in this
creek. We have a good suply that we fetched from the
smokey. = One o clock & we start a gain. we pass through a
dessolate dessert. The contry is all on fire. we traveled till 8
o clock & camped on Walnut Creek after traveling 20 miles
= hungry = sleepy & tired

Tuesday Oct 31 1876

We left camp at sun rise & drove 15 miles up Walnut Creek
and took dinner here. We struck a texas catle ranch &
traded for a pony. At two o clock we started up the creek &
drove 8 miles & camped. Here we found plenty of watter &
good feed for our horses.

Wednesday = November the 1 1876

It comenced raining at mid night. & continued raining &
snowing all day. At noon three hunters came to our camp
nearly froze. We gave them dinner & bought 26 Buffalo
hides & one quarter of a Buffalo bull. We wer well fixed
then. We stayed in camp all day

November the 2

The sun rose bright and clear this morning. This forenoon
we wer busy drying out bagag & bedding. Last night the
wolves wer so numerous & howled so, they caused our
horses to stampede. At 1 o clock we packed our baggage =
loaded = and started up Walnut Creek. We made 8 miles &

camped on the head watters of Walnut Creek. We fell in here with an other party of hunters.

Friday November the 3

We left camp at 8 o clock & made 12 miles & took dinner. Here we see our first bufflao. Miself & Mat Page. & Ed Rothbun sadled our poneyes & now for the chase while three others went up the cannon & shot three shots & the Buffalo came up on the divide & us three horse men after him. We run him a bout 4 miles & gave him up. We left camp at two o clock & made 5 miles on the head watters of Hackberry Creek & camped. We hauled our wood & watter with us. Here an other hunter joined us. It rained all night.

Saturday. Nov the 4 — we left camp at 8 o clock & made 10 miles & stoped on Pawnee River for dinner. There is no game in this country except Antelope. At two o clock we started a gain. The ground being very soft and heavy loaded we made 8 miles & camped on a small creek where we caught a coon & called it Coon Creek.

Sunday the 5 November 1876

We wer up in good time and cooked our coon & had corn cake & molasses & hooked up & started at 8 o clock & made 10 miles & stoped on Buckner Creek for dinner. Here we had a nice wolf cahse & a skunk chase. We captured the latter at one o clock. We started a gain & made 12 miles. Here we struck the Atchison Topeca & Santafee rail road & the great ArKansas river. Here we camped. We started at 8 o'clock up the river & struck Dodge City after driving 15 miles. Here we went in to camp & will remain till tomorrow. I am writing in the Eldorado Saloon. Here is all kind of gambling goin on = hundreds of dollars changing hands every hour. The women is on the streets drunk & smoking sigars. This is the Hardest place I ever saw in mi life.

Tuesday the 7 This is Election day & every thing is lively. We all voted — some one way some on other. We left town at 9 oclock & made 7 miles & took dinner. The boys is all on the rampage. A bout half is left in town & wait their return. = 1 oclock & we start on our way rejoyicing. Every body has a bottle & concily happy. We crossed Mulberry & a place called Kill Pecker. We made 12 miles & went in to camp (corn is 5 cts a pound hay is $40-a tun). Our wood is all exhausted & we burn Bull shit, or to use a finer phrase, buffalo chips. The boys is going to bed early. = They was out all night to the dance halls. Every thing is high 25 cts for a shave = 75 cts for cuting hair = whiskey 25 & 50 cts a drink.

Novem. Wednesday the 8 1876

we was on our way bi 8 oclock. Last night we put out poison & caught a silver grey fox & a grey wolf. These wolfs are very large. They mesure froom 5 to 9 ft in length & are very ferocious. We went 4 miles. There we struck Crooked Creek & took a fresh suply of watter & drover 7 miles and stoped for dinner. It would do your soul good to see the boys baking Bread with a fire made of Buffalo turds & it smells delicious. One oclock & we start a gain. There is plenty of antelope through here. They go in herds of 40 & 50. One of our party killed an antelope this afternoon. We made 10 miles & camped without any watter for our horses.

Thursday November the 9 76

This morning we wer on our way bi sun up. We got two silver grey foxes & one wolf last night. We made 12 miles & took dinner. At 1 oclock we start a gain. We went about 4 miles & struck a herd of Buffalo & killed 8 Buffalo. All lay on a half an acre – hair shit & blood all over. We skinned & took the best of the meat and went in to camp at dark.

Friday November the 10 1876

We was busy this morning in collecting the hides & baking up bread. We start a gain at 9 oclock. Our out fit had a few words & came near a fracas between H. Gibler & P.T. Rathbun. We made 8 miles & stoped on the Sand Hills = Mat Pages camp & Cimarron River for dinner. Two of our hunters went out this morning & have not came in yet while we eat dinner. I. & Ed. Rathbun came in having killed 5 buffalo. Mi self & 4 others went out & skined & brought in the meat. here we loaded a team & started it back to the Solomon Valey. we are in the Indian hunting ground & we keep a sharp look out.

Saturday Novber the 11 1876

We staked our hides & started at 8 oclock & made 7 miles & crossed the comarron river & went in to camp here. We will stay the rest of the day. Here is plenty of watter & good feed & plenty of Bull shit to burn. This afternoon was spent in reloading ammunition & washing. Two herds of buffalo came within ½ miles of camp, about 500 in each herd. There is 6 of us laying under the bank of the river just now. An other hunter on the south fired in to the herd & they stampeded, so we cussed the man & went to camp. One of our party is sick – P.H. Moore.

Sunday Novemb the 12

We concluded to stay here today & explore the country.
Miself & 3 others went up the Cimarron river about 20
miles. This river runs a southeast cours. We killed 19
Buffalo to day & returned to camp at 8 oclock. It
commenced raining and snowing & continued all night.
Today I killed mi first Buffalo. I shot two shots & it fell. I
went up with in fifty feet of it & it jumped up & came after
me & I run a bout three rods & put in a new shell & fired.
He bucked, Blew Blood & fell dead. I never was scared so
before.

Monday Nov the 13 1876

This is a cold snowy blustry morning. A hunter came to our
tent for something to eat. There is a great number of
hunters here – some has no tents nor any covering except
green hides these frose stiff. This is what the hunters calls
russling on the plains – a short life = but a mery one. A
portion of this day was spent in reloding shells & fixing up
amimition as we are with in 5 miles of the Indian Territory.
We keep our selves ready for fear of an attack. 3 miles from
us the Indians killed a hunter & where he is buried his
coffee pot stands all covered with his blood. His blanket &
camp kettle also stands there. He was killed 4 weeks a go.
There is abot 2000 Indians now out for a hunt. Mi self &
I.T. Rathbun killed a buffalo in the Territory. We tied our
ponies to the horns of the buffalo so as to be ready if the
Indians should come up on us. How ever we did not see
any. This has been a very disagreeable day – & the
appearance of a cold stormy night = which it was.

Tuesday Nov the 14 1876

This was a clear cold morning. Mi self & two others went
out in to the Territory. We did not see but two herds =
about 75 in a herd. We did not kill any. The buffalo has
gone south west on account of the wsevere north east storm.
We will not stay here long. We have no wood & bull shit is
very scarce. I have beene riding all day & am very tired.

Wednesday the 15 1876

We wer up early. The run rose clear yet it was cold all day.
5 of us went out & brought in the meat & hides which we
killed the 12 of Nove. We staked our hides & packed ou
kit & loaded our wagons, got our supper, lit our pipes
& sat down a round a Bull shit fire to shiver up solid
comfort.

Thursday the 16 1876

This was a clear cold morning. One of our hunters went out
& killed 10 Buffalo before breakfast. We staked our hides &
covered our meat, loaded our wagons, ate dinner & started a
south west cours through the Indian Territory. We made 10
miles & camped on the sand hills between the Cimarron &
Sharps Creek in the Indian Territory.

Friday the 17 1876

This was a nice clear morning we started at sun rise &
drove 15 miles to Sharps creek & rook dinner. The snow
has all disapeard. We stop here a couple of hours to let our
horses feed. We started at 2 oclock & had to drive through
the sand blow outs – the sand half way to the hub. We
drove till 9 oclock & made 15 miles & camped on Beaver
River in The Indian Territory.

Saturday the 18 1876

This was a nice clear morning. Here we found good feed &
waited to let them feed here. one of our hunters killed a
deer this morning. we left Beaver River at ten oclock &
made 8 miles & took dinner on the = Paladora – of the
Indian Territory. One oclock & we are on the move again
up The Palo Duro. We have seen very little game for 3 days
past except antelope. The Indians have run them so much
that they are very wild. We made 8 miles & camped. Here
We killed a wolf & one Buffalo.

Sunday Nov the 19. 76

The sun rose bright & clear. We are now nearing the suny
South & will be in Texas in two hours drive. We wer on
our way bi 8 oclock & we struck the pan dora Pass & made
8 miles & stoped for dinner. This pass is a nice little valley
with hills & mountains on each side. We passed the rifle pits
this fore noon-a place thrown up of earth for the protection
against the Indians. A long the tops of the hills is beautiful
cedars growin on each side of the pass which makes a very
picture spot. 2 o clock & we move a gain westward on the
dobia wall Trail. We made 12 miles & camped withe out
any water for our horses.

Monday Nov the 20 1876

This is dark cloudy morning. We wer on our way early this
morning on account of having no water for our selves or
horses. We expect to strike watter soon. we drove 3 miles &
found wood – watter in a bundance & a small place called
Hunter's Resort where they sell corn at 5 cts a lb tobaco, 2

collars a lb, powder and ammunition in proportion, flour 6 dollars a hundred. We went in to camp here. I saw buffalo hides piled up here as high as a house & hundreds stretched for drying. We are a bout 30 miles west of the indian territory in the state of Texas. This afternoon there is a good many hunters at these head quarters laying in supplies. This firm pays from 50 to 90 cents for buffalo hides & sell salt for $11 a barl. This afternoon we wer busy moldling bullets & fixing up our out fit ready for a hunt tomorrow.

Tuesday Nov the 21 1876

This was a cold cloudy day. We moved down in Locus Grove and went in to camp. I.T. Rathbun beieng sick we stayed here all day. I went up to the head watters of Palodoro to an Indian wigwam of the Black Foot & Shian tribe. They treated me very courtesly. They wer tanning buffalo hides. They invited us to dinner. They wer having a feast on roasted dog, but not being kindly disposed toward the canine breed I refused, not being hungry. Still it was three oclock & I had not eaten any thing since morning. I also visited a Mexican ranch stakaded securly a gainst an attack of Indians which are very numberous.

Wednesday Nov the 22 1876

It commenced raining last night and continued all night & rained all night & rains all day long. Out hunters that went out yesterday came in to day & had killed – 6 – buffalo. Our sick man is better to day. We have visiters to day, both Indian boys, Jim and Justice & Bad Jack from KiKomo. One has been here sic years on the frontier of Texas. He was in the fight between the Indians & hunters at Dobia walls. A bout 100 yards from our camp is the grave of Jack Jonson who was shot bi his partner a short time-a-ago. The wolves has torn his carcass out and cleaned the bones. His blankets wer raped around him before burying. He was buried bi the hunters. The boys is enjoying them selves playing cards while I write. We are now 130 miles from the line of New Mexico, 120 from Colorado, 69 miles west a little south of the Indian Territory & 800 miles from Kansas City. We expect to start south as soon as the weather settles. We have plenty of good feed for our horses. THe winter grass is green & nice. We have venison pot pie for dinner to day.

Thursday the 23 1876

This was a clear cold morning. We coralled our horses, hitched up, took on a suply of watter, and at 10 oclock started south. We made 12 miles & made a dry camp. 20 miles east of us there is 400 Indians & mexicans camped on wolf creek a hunting.

Friday Nov the 24 76

This was a clear cool morning. We wer on our way bi 8 oclock. We struck the Canadian River & went down it, made 12 miles & stoped for dinner. The rivers here in Texas, as well as in Kansas, run a south east course, concequently we call east down & west out. There is plenty of buffalo here but no good camp ground. One oclock & we wer on our way. We drove 6 miles & struck a herd of buffalo & killed 45 buffalo & drove 1 ½ & made a dry camp in a canyon. I say 10000 buffalo at one sight. Richard Bancroft was chased bi a cripled Bull this afternoon. We laughed & hollered at him. The nearer you come a getting killed on the buffalo range & then escape, the more fun it is for the hunters. It is real amusing to sit a round a Bull shit fire & hear the hunters tell of their many hair breadth escapes. I met a man yesterday who has not been in the setlements for 5 years. this same man killed a black bear near where we are camped to night. We have 37 buffalo to skin tomorrow morning.

Saturday the 25 1876

We wer out in good season this morning. We killed 32 buffalo this forenoon & took the hides & moved 2 miles & went in to a permanent camp on the Canadian river. There is plenty of turkeys & black tail deer & quailes. The country is very rough. Canjans extend 5 miles from the river. The banks in some places is 200 ft. perpendicular. Tired, Hungry, Sleepy & Blood from head to foot. There is some beautiful cedars growing along the sides of the canjons. A portion of the country looks as though it had been heaved up bi volcanic eruptions. In places the melted lava has run for ½ mile in different directions & many other noticeable curiosity which I have not space to anumerate.

Sunday the 26 1876

The sun rose bright & clear this morning. 4 of us started out on a prospect to Wolf Creek, a distance of 18 miles north east. We had not over 5 miles when we encountered a herd of buffalo & killed 22 and skined them & returned at sundown. Jack Sweethand & Howard Giblet killed 20. the plaines is covered with buffalo. These plaines is destitute of timber & watter. The buffalo range from 8 to 15 miles from the Canadian river on the flats. They come to watter a bout

every third day & then mostly in the night. When they leave
the river & start up the canyon it sounds like distant
thunder & can be heard for miles.

Monday Nov the 27 1876

This was a cloudy day. We wer out staking hides & cleaning
up the remaining dead Buffalo. Our hunters went out &
killed 17 Buffalo this fore noon. We skined & hauled a
portion of them in. We came in to camp at 8 oclock tired &
hungry.

Tuesday Nov the 28 1876

This was a stormy morning. the snow fell during the night
to the debth of one inch but it cleared off about 9 oclock.
The snow left and it was warn & pleasant. Our hunters
killed 32 buffalo to day. We skined them & came to camp at
dark.

Wednesday Nov the 29 76

This was a cold morning. Snow fell last night about an inch
deep and remained cold all day with a cold faw wind from
the north. We staked our hides & then remained in camp
the balance of the day.

Thursday Nov the 30 1876

The sun rose nice & clear this morning. However there was
a cold north west wind all day. We wer out today but killed
only 13 buffalo. The snow storm has taken them north. The
buffalo not like most animals go a gainst the storm

Friday December the 1 1876

This was a clear cold windy day. We skined the buffalo that
we killed yesterday & we killed 22 buffalo to day & skined
19 of them & came in at 8 oclock at night.

Saturday Dec. the 2, 1876

Made a mistake

Sunday the 3 December

This was a nice clear day. Mi self & Ed Rathbun went out
to hunt a steel which I lost. Being unsucksessful in finding it
we found aherd of buffalo & I killed 3 & Ed killed 5
making 8. We got lost & did not get in till 9 oclock tired &
hungry.

Monday the 4 1876

This was clear frosty morning. I & E.D. Rathbun went out
to bring in the hides which we killed yesterday. We took a
grey hound with us & while we wer out we caught a
buffalo calf a bout 4 months old & tied it & brought it in to
camp. He cut some lively pranks be fore we got him in. We

dryed out hides & loaded 100 buffalo hides & 1000 lbs of meat on a 4 horse wagon and tomorrow morning myself & John T. Rathbun starts for Dodge Citty. It will take about 20 days to make the trip. We are going after suplies.

Tuesday Dec 12

We struck Dodge to day. We have been 9 days on the road. A portion of the time was very disagreeable. John Moore was well when i left camp. we will start back tomorrow. We expect to start back to cawker city about the midle of January. The dance halls is in full blast tonight. When I come back to dodge city I will send Father 100 lbs of dried buffalo meet if the express charges is not two high. I am well & harty dirty-greasy & ragged. I am heavier now than I ever was. I weight 180 lbs. Tell Father that I will send him money enough to pay that note of mine that Pete Williams holds against me which is $110 due about the 1 of January. I dont want you to sell my wheat unless I write for money. The hole of our party has killed over 400 buffalo in 12 days skined & layed out the hides. Give mi regards to John Shreiffer. we are now camped on the salt fork on the Canadian River. When we go back we expect to move to Red River. This is a wild country and wild people in it. There is no law here except the gun & revolver or knife. There is any amount of Mexican Greasers and Sapnyards & Indians. With many wishes for the health & happiness of all of you permite me to subscribe miself yours affectionaly P.S. I want you to write as soon as you get this. Please dont delay & give me all the news. I will now close hoping to hear from you soon. Direct to

W.A. Wilson

Dodge City

Kansas

You will find the money that I expressed at C.T. Forgey & brother. It is expressed to John Wilson & express charges paid. Since I commenced writing I have seen the express master & he says that it will cost 8 dollar a hundred = to ship buffalo meat to Waverly so I guess that is two high, but if he wants some when you write tell me & I will send him a little = you will please lay this book away for refference should future occasion ever require it. I will not start back to camp until tomorrow morning because the man that came in with me is on a spree. We have bought 80

dollars worth of groseries & ammunition and feed. He
entrusted me to due all the business for him. There is a
good many hunters in now for suplies & they alla take a big
spree when they come in. Well I believe this is all so I will
close once more your truly W.A. Wilson

2

A personal letter from Dr. A. H. Mann, retired army surgeon of the Seventh Cavalry, written to a friend in later years:

Springfield, Ill.
Feb. 14, 1902

Dear Mrs. Wilson,

In your letter to Nellie you ask that I write you a history of my life with Gen. Custer. So many years have elapsed since then that incidents have escaped my memory. Had I have kept a more perfect diary of events, I might have written something that would have been interesting to you. I sat down to the task and by a few notes and by bringing my memory into play have succeeded in making rather a voluminous article. How interesting it will be to you I leave that for you to decide. Probably before you get through with it you will wish that you had never made that request of me.

My first experience with the 7th Cavalry was after being on duty with the 18th U.S. Inf. at Columbia, S. Car. the winter of 1871 and 1872. I was sent to Opelika, Ala. to the 7th Cav. One troop was stationed there commanded by Capt. Thos. B. Weir. I remained on duty there and Montgomery and Livingston, Ala. All that fall and in April 1873 I was ordered to Memphis, Tenn. to accompany Gen. Custer's command to Yankton, S.D. and then to return to Columbia. I went to Yankton and got fully into the

*middle of that famous blizzard that Mrs. Custer speaks of in "Boots
and Saddles", also when she mentioned your humble servant as
packing the precious stove pipe down to help them out in their
little cabin. Instead of returning to the Sunny South I got orders
from Dr. Head, Med. Director at St. Paul, to go with the expedition to Ft. Rice. I was detailed as Sr. surgeon to go up on the
steamer with the sick and supplies. Let me say here Mrs. Custer is
the bravest little woman in the army. She rode her horse day after
day with the General, and when any night she could have slept on
the steamer she preferred to share the tent with the General, rain,
sleet or sunshine. It was all the same to her. She is one of the
noble women of the 19th century. After I got to Ft. Rice, I un-
loaded my sick and supplies and found to my disappointment an
order from Gen. Terry to report to Gen. Custer for duty. I did so
and found myself instead of going back to the southland destined
for the Black Hills. Of course I was rather disappointed but as I
had been on the plains in earlier days in 1867 & 8, I thought what
others could endure I could. We went on our campaign. I will not
give you a full history in this private letter to you for I will send
you with this a diary of that trip as far as I kept it, and what I
can bring back to memory. It will give you one man's idea of the
campaign and if I censor the Gent a little it is no more than Capt.
French, McDougall, Weir, Hale and even Tom Custer. There was
none of us but what felt that there was no glory in a campaign of
that kind. Mrs. Custer if she would express her opinion would have
said the same thing. Where was the glory of battle when Lieut.
Crosby was shot down and scalped? Where was it when Capt.
Hamilton was killed by a squaw at the Battle of Washita? I have
got over the idea that there is glory in being scalped by the Indians.
When Gen. Warren fell at Bunker Hill, he exclaimed with his
dying breath that it is sweet to die for one's country. It is all right
in civil warfare, but to be slaughtered by the noble red man of the
forest is a different thing. As A. Ward or Josh Billings said, "Patriotism consists in being killed for your country and then having your
name spelled wrong in the papers." That is about the experience of
being killed in the Indian Wars. We started on our march to the
tune of Garryowen, the General's favorite tune, and bid good-bye
to those we left behind us. Fortunately I had no one to leave
behind me then, but I felt sorry for those who had. One sweet little
woman, the wife of an officer, took pity on the forlorn old bachelor
and kissed me good-bye. It was done in the presence of her husband
so I accepted it with heroic fortitude. We had got several days on
our march and had not seen an Indian. One day I was riding at
the head of the regiment with the General, when we approached a*

wooded stream. We were fired upon. The Gen. dismounted the command and we drove them out into the open country. We chased them several miles and whipped them in fine style. We lost 7 men killed and some wounded. I rode at the head of the regiment with the Gen. He ordered me to the rear twice, but I told him I did not know where the rear was. He had a horse shot under him but I escaped scot free. After the fight was over he put his hand on my shoulder and said, "Do you know what I ought to do to you?" I said, "No, Gen." He said, "I ought to place you in arrest for disobedience of orders." I told him, "All right. I have other assistants in the rear looking after the wounded and I was up there to look after him." His remark was that he had too much respect for bravery to put one in arrest, but if I had been killed my mother would have blamed him. My reply was, "General, my mother years ago gave me to the army and she would be very sorry to hear that I was a coward." We had no cowards in the 7th Cav. except I might say Major R. The rest that I enclose will give you an insight into my life when it meant something to be a soldier.

I wish that you and Mrs. Custer and I could meet once more. We could do some talking.

Wishing you success and good health and with love to yourself from Nellie and I

I remain

Your friend,
A. H. Mann

Harvey Mann removed his glasses and wiped his eyes. So many memories . . . He was glad that Nellie hadn't happened to step in to find him with his eyes filled with tears brought on by the memories.

He took a deep breath and replaced his glasses. Where had the years gone? He was past sixty now, and wasn't sure *when* he'd grown old. From one day to the next, seemed like . . . His thoughts drifted back to a day in the spring of 1872. He'd spent the winter in South Carolina with the 18th Infantry. . . . A nice place to winter, after having spent time on the frontier in Colorado, Kansas, and Nebraska, in the Department of the Platte.

The years and the posts where he'd served had a tendency to blur together in his memory, now. After the Platte, there had been duty in Mississippi and Arkansas, and his enlistment had run out in 1869, when he was still only twenty-seven.

He'd been in the army since he was nineteen . . . a third of his life. . . . First as a private in the 26th Illinois Volunteer Infantry. He'd caught the eye of the regimental surgeon, who recruited him for a hospital steward and helped him to "read medicine" as an apprentice. By 1864, he was assigned to an assistant surgeon's rank with status as an officer. He was promoted to surgeon the following year.

After the war the military went through a period of reorganization. Even reenlistments were slow to be approved because of the backlog of paperwork in Washington. While waiting, he'd opened a medical practice in Toronto, Kansas, where he had relatives. He'd barely settled there, however, when his reinstatement was approved and he was assigned to the 7th Cavalry at Fort Stephenson, Dakota Territory. That's where he'd met Captain Fred Benteen, an older man who was a respected professional soldier. They had remained friends.

A short while there, and then back to the sunny South . . . Collinsville, South Carolina, where the 7th was engaged in enforcing Reconstruction under martial law. That had been good duty. . . . The weather was comfortable in winter and not intolerable in summer, compared to the extremes of the Dakotas. He had hoped that this assignment would last a long time.

But on the plains the war with the Sioux had been growing hotter. Red Cloud, having outmaneuvered and defeated the army at every contact, had struck a separate peace treaty, which he never broke. New names had appeared in the newspapers, new leaders among the Sioux. Harvey had remembered some of them from his previous tour of duty at Fort Stephenson . . . Crazy Horse, Rain-in-the-Face, Spotted Tail, and the spiritual leader, Sitting Bull. . . .

He pushed the letter aside and picked up the diary he had mentioned in the letter to Mrs. Wilson. Idly, he leafed through it, the thoughts of a young man. . . . Some of them sounded foolish now. Others wise beyond years . . .

3

The Black Hills Expedition from July 2 to the Ft. Rice Dakota Sept. 10th, 1874 from the diary of A. H. Mann

Since the return of the Yellowstone expedition on the 21st of Sept. 1873, Gen. Geo. A. Custer's rather restless spirit had been at work to devise a plausible excuse to enable him to visit the Black Hills with another and similar expedition of the years previous. The unknown laurels and so to enable him to gather these laurels (no matter at what cost of labor, trouble or life) it became his study by day and night. The honor of his country weighed lightly in the scale against the glorious name of Custer. The hardship and danger to his men as well as the probable loss of life were worthy of but little consideration when dim visions of an eagle or a star floated before the mind of our Lieut. Col. The great ease with which the Indian kept out prying pale faces. The mystery which surrounded the Black Hills range. The few who had been and seen gave this section of Dakota such an interest that our long haired chief had determined to organize an expedition and if possible fathom the unexplored secret, the mystified mystery and as a matter not to be overlooked again. Encircle the name of Geo. A. Custer in fresh leaves of laurel. His first application for permission to carry out his plans was refused most emphatically by the War Dept. It seems that the Sec. of War thought of our country's honor, and had this at heart more than the intensive gain to be derived and refused to have anything to do in the matter. Having learned that he could not influence the powers that be at Washington he repaired to Chicago and interviewed Gen. Sheridan. Little Phil gave him his sympathy at that time but nothing more as the appropriation would not cover the expense of an expedition, but here is where the sagacity of Gen. Custer came into play. He showed by figures that his proposed expedition run on his plan would not only be no expense to the Government but an actual savings investment provided however he was placed in command. The arrangement proved irresistible. The U.S. forgot its honor, forgot its sacred treaty then in force between the Dakota Sioux and itself, forgot its integrity and ordered an expedition for the invasion of the Black Hills. The object the Gen. stated to the different agencies along the Missouri River would be one of peace. For this purpose ten troops of Cavalry, two companies of infantry, three Gatlin guns, and one 10 lb. Rodman gun and 75 Indian scouts with 126 mule wagons were massed at Ft. Lincoln, S.D. The latest pattern of improved carbines were issued, 200 rounds of ammunition per man, and all to assure the Indian that we want peace and nothing but peace. It is true that Indians had previously broken their contract with the Government time and again and could have been treated as enemies long since, but on the other hand considering their lack of intelligence and as wards of the Government it appears strange to me why a Government as powerful as ours should be the first aggressor or in other words why we as a rich Government should not have bought up the Black Hills and by so doing saved the lives of hundreds of soldiers and Indians, and by so doing make an honorable peace with the red man. I have no love for an Indian but the white man of former days has made him what he is today. We all know the treachery of Indians for the past 20 years, but former history does not class him as so debased since the Canadian French and renegade Americans got amongst them. I saw one fair sample of the noble red man in 1867, that was Spotted Tail, a chief, also Red Cloud but unfortunately for our men, Red Cloud defeated us at the Ft. Phil Kearney massacre in 1867.

* * *

His thoughts drifted back again to the thrill of the old days on the prairie, the guidons fluttering, the band playing the lilting strains of "Garry-owen". . . . He turned a page or two and began to read again.

We left Fort Rice, Dakota with 10 troops of the 7th U.S. Cavalry (Custer's regiment) one company of 17th infantry, U.S. Co. and 20th U.S. Inf., 3 Gatlin guns and 75 Indian scouts, Gen. Custer in command. Gen. Forsythe and Col. Fred Grant were attached to the staff. They were members of Gen. Sheridan's staff and came from Chicago to go with us. We also had Capt. Ludlow, chief engineer, of Gen. Terry's staff and Professor Davidson (Botanical Prof.) Ellingsworth (Photographer) and Prof. Winchell (Geologist) all noted men in their professions and several others accompanied us as members of the scientific corps. The march as explained in orders was to be conducted as follows: The wagon trains to move four abreast if the ground admitted. One troop of cavalry to move in advance of the column, four troops of cavalry to march on either side or flank of the troop and about 300 infantry. The two companies of infantry to cover the rear of the train. While the last company of cavalry, acting as rear guard, would follow the column one half mile. This method of moving a large command is the safest known. The first case of the commanding officer is the safety and comfort of his command, for without sufficient supplies and ammunition the command is useless. Gen. Forsythe was placed in command of the right wing and Lt. Col. Tilford of the left and Capt. Sanger 17th Inf. of all of the infantry. The medical department consisted of doctors Mann, Williams and Kimball. We carried supplies for two months and ammunition for 30 engagements. On July 1, Gen. Custer, who up to that time had remained in Ft. Lincoln, came out to the camp and assumed command and issued the order to move at 8:00 A.M. The soldiers who had been here over ten days and compelled to take their horses two and one half miles to water morning and evening and were nearly eaten alive by mosquitoes that assembled nightly over our camp. They were rejoiced at the prospect of moving though we believed that death awaited probably many of us in the front. At 9 o'clock A.M. July 2, the companies wheeled by fours into line of march, guidons flying in the breeze, the band playing our battle quick step Garryowen, the officers dashing up and down with an air of importance, the men full of chatter and cheerful, and as we cast our eyes for the last time on Ft. Lincoln, up the valley we saw the ladies of our command, the wives of officers and soldiers waving their handkerchiefs in sad farewell. And just as we left the last ridge that overlooked the valley, the men gave three hearty cheers whose echoes must have been heard by the anxious women watching us from the fort. A soldier and his wife are liable to be parted at any minute and for any length of time in the morning, at the noon day meal or at the dead hour of night. Whenever duty calls he must obey and go. The poor wife, sick or well, or dying, she bids him farewell with how heavy a heart God and himself only know. She cries as tho her heart would break for he goes on the trail of a marauding tribe of Indians, and she feels sure that he will have to fight ere he returns. And now as he is hastily preparing, she fears that she is looking upon him for the last time upon this earth. In her love for him she imagines all sorts of mishaps such as being prisoner among the red man and being tortured and burned at the stake, the child now clasped to her breast, now clasped to the husband's heart may be an orphan perhaps twenty hours hence. Such is a soldier's farewell parting on the frontier.

The first day's march took us over well known ground where we had hunted antelope time and again until we knew every swell of the ground as well as the red man did. Mules in the different camps were strangers to such heavy work as they were called upon to perform, for the wagons were loaded heavy and we saw some very amusing scenes at bucking that displayed to perfection this long-eared animal's tenacious stubbornness. The odometers scored fifteen miles as our first day's march and that was considered by the infantry as a fair day's work. A time for Reville was now 2 A.M. An officer in command of an exposition must post his sentinels and use all due diligence in the enemies' country. He must establish his calls with a vow to the safety of his men and horses and his personal comfort is not to be considered. The allowance of rest and sleep will be regulated by time and circumstances. Frequently, when a day's march has been protracted until an uncomfortable late hour at night by bad roads, we would arrive in camp hours after dark. And by the time they attended to their horses and got their own suppers, it would frequently be midnight when two hours sleep would have to reward them for 22 of hard labor. Exposed to sun and heat, thermometer at 110 degrees (at that time Montana is cold in winter and red hot in summer) as Mrs. Custer remarked nine months winter and three months late spring, but spring humps at once to summer with the intense heat. It is one of the finest countries to emigrate from that I ever soldiered in. Perhaps the day will come that we will be proud of Montana but not now. Some other day, knowing that these hardships were unavoidable, the men endured them with a stoicism that a citizen in the States would have thought impossible. No man knows what he can endure until he is tested. We had sickness with other things to contend with. The constant strain on the nervous force and mental and physical was likely to break down the constitution of soldiers not too robust, but compared with life in the barracks, it was far healthier on the march than so much innocuous disquietude in garrison, for in garrison men eat, sleep and do not take sufficient exercise, hence, more sickness.

Our general course of travel from Ft. Lincoln was to southwest. Occasionally we had to divide on account of roads and gullies.

The second evening found us encamped on a tributary of the Little Heart. There was no wood, so the men had to go two miles and carry a sufficient supply on their horses to last until morning.

July 4th we crossed the old trail made the year before and gave the boys a topic for discussion. Would we see a finer country than last year? Would we meet as many Indians as we did before? God help us!

We did to our sorrow meet a party of Sioux Indians. They were eager in their protestations claimed to be out hunting. This we discredited, but as orders have been issued for us to act simply on defensive, we did not disturb them. They were evidently posted here as a corps of observation of the movements of our expedition. That this party was not on a hunt alone was evident as none of their squaws were with them. And without the fair sex, it is well known that no Indian chases the antelope over the plains. He would as soon forget his pony, gun or tomahawk as to think of killing game and not have his squaw there to carry it home for him.

"Right". Oh, thou noble red man, when you reach your Happy Hunting Ground, may your squaw also reach a haven of rest is the sincere wish of "Yours Truly".

My diary of the campaign ends here. Suffice it to say that after a campaign lasting until August 30th with a few fights with the enemy and a few on our side killed and wounded, we returned tired, dusty and glad to once more look upon our homes at Ft. Lincoln.

I will not weary your patience with some more reminiscence. After my return from Cuba at the close of the Spanish Am. War, I got hold of a book, a school boy history, of life on the plains including the account of the duel between Yellow Bear, an Indian sub-chief, and Buffalo Bill. A great imagination that some cheap novelist has is quite amusing to parties who were eye-witness to these scenes. This duel took place some 3000 miles from where the author of it was raised and likely years before he was born. For his information or that of others who may be interested, I will state that I was an eye-witness of the encounter. It took place in June, 1874, on a branch of Little Big Horn of Rosebud River. I was at that time in charge of the medical department as senior surgeon of Gen. Custer's staff. We met the Indians in Yellowstone Valley and while Generals Custer, Crittenden, Stanley, and Col. (now Gen.) Otis were in consultation with the most prominent chiefs Big Sitting Bull, Gall, Grass, Rain-in-the-Face, and Long Soldier, both sides were quiet but with the same quiet that a cat watches a bird for we had no faith in the honesty of the Indians. We never could trust to their honor in those days and I fail to do so now. It was while the pipe of peace was being smoked in Gen. Custer's tent that Yellow Bear, thinking to make himself a great brave, advanced towards our lines and in his braggadocio manner said that he was a great chief and that he would take the white man's way of adjusting any difficulties. He would meet any white brave half way and fight him like the white men do, and if he was killed, his party would leave the country open for the Blue coats to explore the Black Hills. But if he was the victor then we must go back to Ft. Rice.

A person that was not acquainted with the bombastic ways of the Indian would think that we had no show to advance into the Yellowstone country, but Yellow Bear found a foe worthy of his steel. To the credit of the soldiers I will state that a sergeant of an infantry regiment stepped out of the ranks and offered to accept the challenge, but Buffalo Bill, the bravest of the brave, took his gun in his hand and walked to the front. He told the Sgt. that he had an old quarrel to settle with Yellow Bear and that he considered it his fight. There was but one shot exchanged. Cody, as he always did, made a sure shot. Yellow Bear's bullet passed so close to Cody's head that the concussion knocked him down, but being only momentarily stunned, he shortly rose to his feet and with gigantic strides he reached the body of his adversary, and to serve the Indian with his own medicine he took the scalp of Yellow Bear and waved it before the enemy. It is seldom thought, even thirty years ago, that a white man would scalp an Indian much less later, but when people understand that the old tradition was with an Indian a life for a life and that to save the scalp of a dead Indian was his sure guarantee to the Happy Hunting Ground, you'll see how they value the scalp. They value it as a Protestant does the prayers over a dying friend, or the Catholic the holy water and the unction. So it is not strange that they will risk their lives in battle to save the scalp of their dead comrades. Yellow Bear's greatest trophy would have been Buffalo Bill's scalp and it would have immortalized him had he been successful. Therefore, I cannot denounce Cody as some people probably do.

We will refer to Custer's battle as this dime novel speaks of it. I have read the history of that battle as written by several different authors. They were not there nor within 2000 miles of the Rosebud at this time. What information they got they pumped out of some renegade Sioux at the price of some tobacco or a square meal. And of all the liars walking the face of the earth commend me to the Redman. Annanias was suddenly cut off for only one lie and if the same punishment was meted out to the Indian they would be beautifully less in numbers today. If a person at this late day is particularly interested in that last battle they can find its true history in a book written by Capt. Godfrey of the 7th U.S. Cavalry. I do not much like to refer to that massacre on the Little Big Horn June 25th, 1876. God knows that some of the bravest men in the army shed their heart's blood on that battle field. It is past and gone, the requiem has been sung over their lonely graves, the bugle has sounded taps, or lights out and the surviving comrades have bidden farewell forever as they silently marched away. Gen. Custer there made the mistake of his life, but when we remember his glorious achievement in the Shenandoah Valley, let the mantle of charity gently cover his mortal remains at West Point. For his mistake on the Rosebud he, soldier-like, paid the penalty. He could have at one time saved his own life but like a true soldier and patriot, he preferred to die with his men. Had he been victorious no greater hero would have been presented to modern history than the gallant Lt. Col. of the 7th Cavalry. Had the great Napoleon beaten the combined powers and the elements at Waterloo, Lord Wellington would have sunk into oblivion and the eagles of France would have flapped their wings over the lion of England. I dare not wish to say anything against Mother England, she has always been a proud and powerful nation, but the guns of Santiago and Eleana made her respect us and duly opened their eyes to naval enterprise in the Orient. Sometimes it takes American gunpowder to let foreign nations know who and what we are.

Referring again to Buffalo Bill I must write of him as a gentleman, a brave man, and one who is fully respected by the Government.

There was another brave scout, but he sacrificed his life in our first battle in the Black Hills. That was the unknown Charlie Reynolds. He received an Indian bullet in the brain. Nobody knew his history, but no one at the age of 32 years did more for his country than he did. He sank to his eternal rest, mourned by all the command and loved by all. As I said, we knew nothing of his history, but we knew him as a true comrade and a brave man. And as the bugle sounded the last farewell over his grave, there was many an honest tear that fell for Charlie.

In closing this history I will say this no matter what critics say of Gen. Custer as being reckless, but as one of his staff officers for nearly three years no word of disrespect or censor will ever be uttered by me. I speak of him as a true friend and a brave officer, one who through all his years of army life was ever ready to risk his life with his men. He did not say, "Go in, men!" but "Follow me." Wherever the most danger was, there was Gen. Custer. Let those who criticize him put themselves in his place and see how much better they would have done. In the years to come history will do full justice to his heroic deeds and his name will be enrolled among the list of our greatest generals. The son of austerity rose in splendor over the crags and valleys along the Little Big Horn that June morning, but went down in bud more than Napoleon's Waterloo. It is surprising to me with what indifference a present generation reads the history of that fatal day a quarter of a century ago, but it remains to the survivors of that fight to ever keep green the message of their departed comrades. As we drop a tear over their lonely graves let us hope with the poet:

That their bodies are dust
Their good swords rust
Their souls are with their God
We trust.

4

He closed the book, tossed it on the desk, and sat for a few moments staring out the window. He rose and walked restlessly around the room, limping only slightly from his old wound. It had been a long time since he'd stirred his memory that deeply. The bullet below his knee was a reminder, of course, but that was only a daily nuisance, and a weather indicator in times of storm. It didn't fester nearly as badly now as it used to. It had helped when, a few years ago, he'd managed to fish out of the draining wound a scrap of blue woolen uniform, driven clear to the shattered bone by the bullet. . . . The lucky shot, as it turned out . . .

It had been in the spring of 1876, when he was stationed at the Grand River Agency in Dakota. Everyone was bored by the inactivity, though it was assumed that there would be a campaign of some sort later in the year. Although strictly speaking it was against regulations to leave the post, several of the officers had from time to time engaged in impromptu hunting trips for antelope in the surrounding prairie. It had been partly due to the attitude of the Custers.

That was one of the troubling memories, the friction among the officers of the 7th. Two factions . . . that of the old-line officers like his friend Fred Benteen; the other, the exuberant Custer and his brother Tom. Some had tried, in later years, to make that a factor in the ultimate outcome of the campaign, but Harvey Mann had never thought so. True, some of the men still grumbled about the fracas on the Washita in '68. . . . Custer had pulled out, leaving nineteen men still engaged. Those left behind had met with an unenviable fate, which was resented by the anti-Custer faction.

But mostly, it had been a matter of personality conflicts. That, along with the inescapable resentment over loss of rank at the end of the War Between the States. George Custer had been demoted from brevet brigadier general down to captain. Now, back up to lieutenant colonel. He still preferred to be called "General" by his officers. Tom Custer, once a brevet lieutenant colonel, was now a captain. But Mann himself had accepted the decrease in rank from surgeon to assistant surgeon at his reenlistment with no qualms. It was the way of things.

Now, it was the way of things to be bored at the inactivity. It was rumored that the next campaign would begin in June, but to while away the time the officers, especially the Custer faction, would organize a small hunting party from time to time. Sometimes it would be only one or two officers, with perhaps one of the Indian scouts as a companion. That was what Harvey Mann had decided to do as a result of the frustrating boredom. An afternoon away from the agency, with one scout as his companion . . .

It was not considered necessary to inform anyone. There were no orders *against* such activity. A couple of miles outside the agency, Mann and his companion were startled when a couple of armed warriors suddenly rose out of a grassy ravine. This should have been no cause for concern, since the purpose of the Grand River Agency was to administer Indian affairs. The scout raised a hand in the salute of greeting.

Just then, Dr. Mann recognized one of the men. None other than Rain-in-the-Face, wanted under a federal warrant for his predatory activities. At almost the same instant, the Lakota chieftain realized that his identity was known. He raised his rifle. . . .

"Don't shoot, Rain-in-the-Face!" yelled Dr. Mann.

Even as he did so, he threw himself to the side of his horse and jerked the animal around. The scout was already fleeing. Rain-in-the-Face snapped off a quick shot as Mann put spurs to the horse and sprinted for the post. He felt something strike his leg, but the pain did not come until a few moments later.

Arriving at the agency, he went to his dispensary and examined his leg. A clean round hole in the blue trouser leg, and one in his own skin to match it . . . Perhaps a hand's span below the knee on the lateral side. He cleaned and probed the wound, discovering that the Sioux's bullet had struck the bone of the upper fibula, shattering it.

The enormity of the event sank home as he realized that he had amputated limbs for similar gunshot wounds. Standard procedure was amputation for penetrating wounds involving destruction of bone.

However, he reasoned, he could still walk. The fibula at this level is not a weight-bearing structure. Maybe he'd be lucky and survive the inevitable infection. He decided not to report the incident to regimental headquarters at Fort Lincoln. Maybe he'd be healed by the time the campaign started. Besides, he thought, there were undoubtedly regulations that dealt with private hunting expeditions. An unfavorable report such as this would be hard to justify. He cleaned, cauterized, and dressed his own wound, and said nothing about the incident in his reports.

Healing was slow and painful. He limped about the agency in the course of his duties, changing dressings as necessary. The leg festered and drained, improved only to flare up again.

By early summer, when orders came to depart for Montana, his leg was still not well enough to withstand long days in the saddle. He was forced to admit his indiscretion, telegraphing headquarters to do so. Immediately the department wired back a demand for more details about his injury.

Harvey realized that by not reporting the incident at the time, he could probably be subject to court-martial. He telegraphed back his resignation, which was accepted without further official inquiry.

Saddened and regretful, he headed back toward civilization, while the 7th Cavalry marched into history, pennants fluttering and the band smartly playing the strains of Custer's trademark marching song.

A few short weeks later, Dr. Mann was engaged in opening a private medical practice in Chicago when he heard a newsboy hawking the headlines of the day. . . .

**Custer's 7th Cavalry Massacred by Indians in Montana.
Two Hundred Dead**

Numbly, he hurried outside to buy a paper in the street and read the shocking news of the fate of friends and acquaintances.

As he read the skimpy details of the massacre, the strains of "Garryowen" whispered through his memory. George Custer had taken the drinking song of the old Irish town and made it his own. How well he remembered the words . . . The lavish dinner parties back at Fort Lincoln, hosted by the Custers, had sometimes become drinking bouts. Tom Custer would lead, and the other officers would join in the singing . . .

Let Bacchus' sons be not dismayed,
But join with me each jovial blade,
Come booze and sing and lend your aid,
To help me with the chorus.

Instead of Spa we'll drink down ale,
And pay the reck'ning on the nail,

No man for debt shall go to jail
From Garryowen in glory.

It was a little later that he realized how his own life had been spared. Oddly, in an attempt to *take* it. His life had been saved by an old enemy . . . *Rain-in-the-Face.*

5

Ezekiel York stood on the street corner in Kansas City and watched the Negro minstrels perform. There were three of them: one older man who played a harmonica and two youngsters. One of these danced, while the other sang and provided a castanetlike rhythm with a polished pair of bones held loosely between his fingers.

> I went down South with mah
>   hat caved in,
> Singin' Polly-wolly Doodle all the day.
> Comin' back home with a pocket
>   full o' tin,
> Singin' Polly-wolly Doodle all the day.
> Fare thee well . . .
> Fare thee well . . .
> Fare thee well, my Fairy Faye
> For I'm gwine to Louisiana
> For to see my Suzianna
> Singin' Polly-wolly Doodle all the day

The dancer was expert at his vocation. Zeke watched in wonder as the boy shuffled and turned, performed jumps and whirls and leaps that seemed impossible for human flesh and bone. *He doesn't even seem to have bones in his legs,* Zeke thought to himself. *Just rubber, bending any way he wants!*

> Grasshopper settin' on a railroad
> > track,
> Singin' Polly-wolly Doodle all the day,
> A-pickin' his teeth with a carpet
> > tack,
> Singin' Polly-wolly Doodle all the day.
> Fare thee well . . .
> Fare thee well . . .

The grinning vocalist was equally skillful, and the crowd was laughing at his antics and his facial expressions as he created appropriate verses. It *had* been a bad grasshopper year, at least in some areas. It had hit the farmers much harder than it had the cattlemen. But everyone agreed that it was probably an unusual season.

> Goober-nut settin' on a railroad
> > track,
> His heart was all aflutter,
> Aroun' the bend come Number Ten,
> Toot, Toot! Peanut butter!
> Fare thee well . . .
> Fare thee well . . .

The crowd roared with laughter at the improvised lyrics. Goober nuts, or peanuts, had been brought from the South by returning soldiers and were a source of great amusement to the public. A *nut* that grows in the ground? It had not yet been determined just where they could be grown. Warm climate, sandy soil . . . Not in most of Kansas, it seemed. The sandy parts might be too dry, or too far north.

The minstrels paused for a rest, and the crowd began to disperse, many dropping coins into the hat between the old man's feet.

"Thankee, ma'am . . . suh . . . ," he nodded to each contributor.

Someone brushed against Zeke, and his reflexes jerked into action. The pickpocket pulled back, but his wrist was held fast in the iron grip of the tall drover.

"I . . . I din't do nothin'!" the thief yelled. "Leggo o' me!"

He was a scrawny, pimply-faced white teenager. York wondered whether he had been in league with the minstrels or merely an opportunist. Probably the latter, he decided.

As if to confirm his conclusion, the older Negro spoke. "Ah'm sorry, suh! He ain't with us." He turned to the culprit. "Go on, now," he scolded. "You nothin' but white trash!"

The thought crossed Zeke's mind that this, too, could be part of the act, but still, he thought not. There were genuine looks of resentment on the brown faces of the younger minstrels.

"An' you ain't nothin' but a damn nigger!" hissed the pickpocket.

"Quit it!" demanded Zeke, releasing the wrist. He fished a coin from his pocket and handed it to the youth. "Now, go get somethin' to eat. You bother these folks again, I'm comin' after you."

A policeman elbowed through the knot of people.

"What's the trouble here?" he demanded.

"No trouble," Zeke told him. "Sort of a misunderstandin' here, is all." He dropped some more coins into the old man's hat and turned away toward the stockyards. He understood the people there better than he did city folks.

He wasn't sure just what he was doing here. Maybe he just had to see a little of the world. They'd usually just sold their cattle at the railhead at the end of the drive. It had been a profitable business. Sometimes two herds a year, after the route became more familiar. They'd used different shipping points, too. The Santa Fe had built tracks to Newton and Wichita and Dodge, and that had cut a hundred miles or more off the distance they used to drive to Abilene on the Union Pacific. Zeke couldn't number the thousands of cattle they'd pushed up the trail since that first desperate drive in 1867, which had saved the Yorks' ranch and those of neighbors. A lot of those cattle had worn the Yorks' Bar-Y brand.

They'd bought out the Simmonses' spread, imported some new bulls to breed up the wild longhorn stock, and expanded the Bar-Y. By some standards, they still weren't a big outfit. Not like the two-hundred-mile spread of Don Luis Terrazas across the Rio in Mexico. Don Luis, one story related, had once been asked if he could supply as many as four thousand three-year-old heifers.

"Certainly," replied the old Don. "What color do you prefer?"

Or the old Santa Gertrudis ranch, now called the King. Zeke had seen a lot of cattle wearing their Running W brand, which the Mexican *vaqueros* called the "Little Snake."

He'd seen a lot of country, too. It had been his job to scout out the best possibilities for shipping, as new railroads, pens, and loading facilities evolved. Some drovers were considering driving as far as Wyoming, it was said, but the Bar-Y hadn't considered that. There was still too much Indian trouble. That Custer thing, only this summer . . .

Zeke could foresee that the day of the big cattle drives was all but over. Railroads were thrusting clear into Texas now, and they could ship from there. Probably be a few long drives into Wyoming and Montana before the tracks reached there. A lot would depend on the Indians, he reckoned.

He wasn't sure what he wanted. His father, James, who had really built the Bar-Y, had died two years ago. It seemed like James had never quite recovered his health after his war wounds. He'd led the first three trail drives north, but everyone could see that he'd been pushing himself. Zeke and his mother had been glad when James admitted it and stayed behind.

Now, he was gone. The widow York was still attractive, and there was no shortage of potential suitors. Naomi had been cautious, but last spring had married Hiram Goodman, an old friend from before the war. He'd become a widower a few years ago. Zeke thought it was a good arrangement, but it left him in an awkward situation. He was twenty-five now, but he'd never married. Never found the time for much courting, it seemed. There were very few available women, and even fewer that would interest him.

The newlyweds would live in Hiram's big house, and there seemed to be no point in Zeke's living alone on the Bar-Y. But he had to think it out . . . travel a little. . . .

He bought a paper from a newsboy on the corner and glanced at it briefly in the shade of a tall brick building before heading back to the stockyards. He was intrigued by an article about the Centennial Exposition in Philadelphia. The centennial of the birth of the nation! There were etchings of artists' sketches of the buildings and the exhibits. Wondrous new machines . . . A reaper that could also *bind* the sheaves . . . A printing press that operated with a continuous roll of paper rather than loose sheets . . . Thomas Edison's newest miracle, a telegraph that could send two messages at the same time *on the same wire* . . . There was even a device said to transmit *voices* over a wire, called a tele-phone. . . . An engineer named Corliss had designed the largest steam engine in the world, with a self-operating governor to prevent a "runaway" accident. . . . A new company called Westinghouse was demonstrating an "air brake" for vehicles including trains, which could provide much more stopping power than conventional mechanical leverage.

There were also pages of description of exhibits from many states and foreign countries. Those from the West were primarily agricultural. He paused at the etching of a Kansas display. . . . Corn, wheat, mammoth vegetables and fruit, and a special display of fine-quality broom corn. Interesting, he thought. Maybe he'd go on to Philadelphia to see all this for himself.

But for now, he'd think about some supper. There was a good steak house down by the yards. There usually was in most towns, he'd noted. One thing cattlemen did understand and relish was eating. From drovers just off the trail to the cattle barons who were establishing their kingdoms, they knew good beef and how to enjoy it. And, in a town with a shipping point, there was access to the finest. The larger the town, the more dignified and high-class the establishment. Near the really big yards there might be several such establishments. Some were little more than saloons catering to drovers. "Cowboys," some called them now. Other places offered the finest in decor, service, and cuisine, like the gentlemen's clubs of more civilized regions. The term sometimes used for these more dignified establishments was "cattlemen's club."

Zeke didn't care much, but he had found one he liked here. The food was good and they understood the drover. He'd been in Kansas City only a day. He'd taken a hotel room near the yards, which offered a bath and a convenient barber, and divested himself of accumulated grime from the trail and the train. He'd purchased some fresh clothes and turned his soiled ones over to a Chinese laundryman near the hotel.

Now, after his stroll downtown, he arrived at the restaurant, hungry from his walk and the encounter with the pickpocket.

"Yes . . . Mr. York, isn't it?" asked the well-dressed waiter who met him at the door. "Table for one?"

"Right both times," Zeke smiled. It was still a new experience to be treated with such respect, and he hadn't decided whether to enjoy it or to be embarrassed.

It was early, and there were only a few people in the dining room. He glanced around as he was seated at a small table against the wall. The location offered a good view of the rest of the room. At a far table, three cattlemen were attacking large steaks with enthusiasm, even as they carried on a lively conversation. At another sat two men, one a well-dressed gentleman, the other a leathery drover. They were enjoying a leisurely meal, talking calmly. . . . Probably a ranch owner and his trail boss, Zeke figured.

Near the table where he had just been seated, an oddly assorted trio sat. There was food on the table, but no one was paying much attention. Two women and an older man . . . One of the women, Zeke noticed, was young and quite attractive. Quite possibly the best-looking woman he'd ever seen, in fact. She was doing most of the talking, and seemed to be troubled about something. The other, a striking, dark-haired woman of middle age, said nothing but seemed to be listening sympathetically. The man, although somewhat older, appeared tanned and healthy, a man of action. He could be anywhere from fifty to seventy, Zeke thought. He, too, listened intently, nodding from time to time. He was well dressed, like the raven-haired beauty beside him. The younger woman's garments tended toward the plain and utilitarian. . . . Maybe traveling clothes, Zeke decided. Idly, he wondered about the nature of her problem, and hoped that she was finding the help she needed.

The waiter arrived with the first course of his meal, and he could not resist his curiosity.

"Who is the gentleman at the other table?" he inquired casually.

The waiter glanced over and lowered his voice as he spoke.

"That's Mr. Sterling, sir. J. D. Sterling. Early settler."

"What's he do?"

"His business? Lots of things, I'm told. Railroads . . . Started in freightin', I guess. Scout on the Santa Fe Trail before that. He's the 'Sterling' in Sterling, Van Landingham and Company. Big in river steamers before the war. Shipping cattle, now."

"I see. . . . And the ladies?"

"Oh . . . The dark one's his wife. They come in once in a while."

"The other?" Zeke tried to sound casual, though his interest burned.

"Don't know. She's new. From out of town."

"A relative?"

"I don't know, sir. I can try to find out. . . ."

"No, no, never mind. I was just curious."

"Yes, she's quite attractive, sir." There was only the slightest hint of sarcasm in the waiter's tone.

The trio departed just as the waiter brought his steak, and Zeke settled down to serious eating. He was just finishing his coffee when the waiter approached with a conspiratorial air.

"The lady's name is Evans, sir. She's looking for a missing relative, and had hoped that Mr. Sterling, with all his connections, could help her."

"Oh. I see." Zeke was somewhat embarrassed. "Thank you."

He started to ask if the lady's quest had been successful, but . . . Well, he'd have seen a little joy of some kind in those blue eyes, would he not? He had to assume that her efforts had been unrewarded, and he felt sorrow for that. In an unaccountable way, he wanted this Miss Evans to possess happiness that matched her beauty. Or was it *Mrs.* Evans? He hadn't noticed whether she wore a ring. . . .

No matter, he'd never see her again. He left the waiter an extra tip for his unsolicited effort and stepped out into the dusky twilight. He'd start home tomorrow, he figured. Or, maybe not.

6

The woman he had seen in the restaurant continued to pop into his thoughts unexpectedly. He remembered the way she moved, her mannerisms, her sad smile, and his heart ached for her, in a completely inappropriate way. He had wanted to *help* her in whatever search she had found herself. . . . A ridiculous, boyish thought. Well, at least he hoped that she'd found some help in Mr. Sterling and his wife.

This preoccupation with a woman he had seen only once and would never see again began to bother him. He tried to shove it aside, but it kept creeping back. On the street he saw a woman at a distance and hoped that it would be the woman from the restaurant. Then he was disappointed when it was not, and angry with himself that it mattered.

Evans . . . That was the name the waiter had told him. She appeared to be about his own age, but was she married or not? He didn't even know. He wondered what her first name might be, and none seemed to fit. . . . Maggie? Jean? Elizabeth? He was embarrassed at the game he found himself playing. He felt like a schoolboy, writing the name of the pretty girl in the front row on his slate.

He dreamed of her that night. Not an erotic dream . . . just an encounter in which she smiled at him with a sadness that spoke of frustration and helplessness. His heart went out to her. He wanted to help her, protect her, shelter her from harm and make the sadness disappear from that lovely face. He enfolded her in his arms and rocked her gently, crooning to her as to a troubled child. She lifted her face, looking directly at him with deep blue eyes that held not only gratitude but love and . . .

He awoke, startled, shaking with nervous emotion. *Am I losing my mind?* he wondered. This was completely illogical. This woman in his dreams must be simply that . . . a dream. There was no way that he could know anything about the real person that was embodied in the Evans woman. The dream woman was simply created in his mind and *looked* like the woman in the restaurant. He muttered a mild profanity, aimed not at the woman, but at himself, for allowing such irrational thinking to influence even his dreams.

Zeke sat on the edge of the bed for a little while, then tried to go back to sleep, and finally got up. By a shaft of moonlight at the window he looked at the pocket watch that had been his father's. . . . A couple more hours till dawn . . . Restless, he lay back on the creaky bed to consider his next move.

He quickly decided against one of the things he'd thought of earlier, the Centennial Exposition in Philadelphia. It had seemed like a good idea, but he was already having trouble with strange thoughts and dreams. Maybe it was the big-city surroundings. If so, Philadelphia would probably be worse. *Yes,* he thought, *that's probably it.* . . . If he could just get back to his own sort of country, he'd feel better. Maybe even get the disturbing thoughts of the woman he'd seen only once out of his head. Well, he *had* seen her twice, he told himself, once in the dream. . . . *But you can't count that, stupid!* his other side protested. Maybe he *was* going mad. . . .

He lay there until dawn, staring at the square of moonlight that marked the window of his room. When the sky began to turn a yellowish gray he rose, washed his face and hands at the bowl on the dresser, and dressed. It was growing light now, and as he stepped out on the street a rooster crowed, somewhere beyond the yards. It was a welcome sound, a reassurance that his world still existed. He'd check the train schedule when the agent opened the ticket office. Meanwhile . . . Well, might as well have some breakfast . . .

The cattlemen's dining room was open, and he found that he was hungrier than he had imagined. Steak, eggs, and biscuits with thick white gravy seemed to hit the spot, washed down with strong black coffee. Not as good as Gomez brewed, maybe. But he'd always savored Gomez's coffee under an open sky after a tough day in the open. . . . Or, *before* a tough day, or both. He smiled to himself. This must actually be pretty good coffee, to remind him of the Mexican cook. He sipped another cup, paid his tab, and sauntered down to the railway depot to check the schedule.

He didn't have any urgency about his travel, with no one to go home to. Maybe he'd just ride the tallgrass country for a few days and look it over. He still felt an attraction for the area, as he had on that first cattle drive when he was just a kid. Yes, that's what he'd do . . . pick up his horse at Wichita. . . . He'd left his guns and bedroll outfit there at the livery, too, and just carried a valise with a clean shirt, soap, towel and a razor, and his papers for the herd. And now, with his family ties in Texas in a new situation, maybe now was the time to look at some of the Kansas rangeland. He was sure it wouldn't be as good a buy as when he'd looked at it with his father, but maybe . . . Well, it was worth a look. He could afford to invest, when he found just what he wanted. His mother was settled, and he could sell the place in Texas. Maybe to his stepfather, if Hiram wanted it. Somebody would. But he needed to find just the place up here. He knew what it would look like . . . good water, grass, a place to put the house, with a good spring for household use. . . .

The agent handed him a timetable, which he managed to figure out after a little study. It appeared that the train he wanted would be at about 9:30. He verified this and bought his ticket, and went back to the hotel to check out and pick up his luggage.

The railroad car was new, one of the improved models that the Atchison, Topeka and Santa Fe boasted. There was an air of gentility about it, with upholstered seats and bright new paint on the woodwork. Overhead was a professionally lettered sign:

**Please refrain from shooting
buffalo from the windows while
the car is in motion.**

Zeke smiled, a little sadly. That day was gone, for practical purposes. Maybe the sign was only to impress the easterners who seemed to be pouring in.

He tossed his valise into the overhead rack and sat down. People were boarding from both ends of the car, filling the seats quickly. . . . A salesman with a sample case . . . A young couple with a baby . . . A weather-beaten farmer and his equally weatherbeaten wife . . . Two young women whose clothing and painted faces advertised their trade . . .

A young Negro poked his head inquiringly into the car, and the conductor reacted quickly.

"Wrong car, boy! The one at the back there is for colored!"

The Negro immediately ducked his head in the subservient manner that was familiar to Zeke. He'd seen Coffee do it, to get himself out of a threatening situation when they were driving cattle and encountered hostility. The Negro drover would assume the personality of a Southern darkie to avoid confrontation. Zeke had asked him about it once, and Coffee had merely shrugged.

"Saves arguin', Zeke, and a heap safer. I know what I am, an' you know, but a fella like that don't care to know. It's jest a way to git by."

Now, he saw this young man put on the same act.

"Yassuh, yassuh," he mumbled. "Thankee, suh."

The Negro withdrew, and the nearby passengers chuckled at such ignorance.

Zeke wondered what had ever happened to Coffee. If he did find just the rangeland he wanted, he'd need some help, and he couldn't think of a better man. Maybe he could locate him when he went back to Texas. It would be worth a try.

His thoughts were distracted by the entry of a woman carrying a carpet-sided valise. At first he thought his eyes were deceiving him, but no . . . It *was* the woman. She had occupied his dreams and most of his waking thoughts since the episode in the restaurant. Just now, the expression on the beautiful face had changed from that he had seen before. Now it was one of irritation and impatience. It took only a moment to realize the cause. Behind her followed a big, loutish man, crowding her along. He was well dressed but unwashed, and a three-day growth of stubble on his flabby jowls contributed to his disreputable appearance. A fat cigar jutted from between his stained teeth.

Is this the man she was looking for? Zeke wondered in amazement. If so, *why?*

Then he realized . . . They were not together. The lout had spotted a woman traveling alone and was attempting to become a companion. Zeke's temper began to flare. If he had it figured right, this lady needed a hand, and it had nothing to do with her original quest. Her whole attitude said that she could probably handle this situation, but she shouldn't have to. He rose and stepped into the aisle, directly in front of her. He tipped his hat and made a slight bow, using his best manners.

"Miz Evans!" he exclaimed. "How nice to see you again! May I offer you a seat?"

There was a short pause while she sized him up. If he'd guessed wrong about the man bothering her, it was over, and he'd lost his own seat to boot. The face of the lout flushed with anger under the whiskers and grime, and he appeared about to speak.

Just then, the woman smiled and spoke, taking her cue flawlessly.

"What a pleasant surprise," she cooed. "Thank you, Tex."

His heartbeat quickened. He'd called it right! She slipped gracefully into the seat.

"Now wait a minute!" the lout mumbled around his cigar. "I . . ."

Zeke drew himself up to full height and took half a step forward, jutting his chin toward the man.

"Yes?"

The other's stare faltered and broke. He seemed to lose interest in challenging a well-built drover.

"Nuthin'," he mumbled as he shuffled off, looking for a seat.

Zeke slid into the seat beside the lady, embarrassed and not knowing what to say. Now he *really* felt like the schoolboy. . . . He was rewarded with a friendly smile.

"Thank you again," she said. "Now, who *are* you, and how do you know me?"

"Ezekiel York, ma'am. You called me '*Tex*'?"

She smiled. "It seemed I should call you something." She glanced at his hat and boots. "You're a drover . . . from Texas, I supposed."

"You're right, of course. And I saw you with the Sterlings in the restaurant."

"Oh, yes, I remember now. You know the Sterlings?"

"No, not really . . ."

He couldn't tell her that he'd been so bold as to ask who she was.

"Oh," she said, a little bit disappointed. "I thought maybe . . . But they were very kind."

The look of sadness and concern crept over her features again.

"I . . . I don't want to burden you with my problems . . . but, I'm trying to find my husband."

The thought crossed his mind that any man who would leave this woman must be crazy. There must be more to the story, and he waited. And he now knew . . . *Mrs*. Evans. He'd used the Southern-drawled "Miz" advisedly, due to the situation. It could have sufficed either way. Yet there was a certain disappointment. . . .

"David went to Kansas City in March to buy cattle," she went on. "Brood stock. He's interested in crossing the British breeds with the long-horns. But he didn't return when he expected. I wrote the hotel where he stays sometimes, but he hadn't been there. I came looking for him."

There was a trace of a tear in her eye, but the tilt of her chin was still defiant.

"I guess he never reached Kansas City."

7

This was not a pretty picture. The thought that maybe this David Evans had abandoned his wife had crossed Ezekiel's mind earlier, but not now. A stable, settled cattleman with a plan for his ranch would not leave all that and a lovely wife, surely.

"He was carrying money?"

The moment he asked, he regretted it. He had no business asking such a question.

"I'm sorry, Mrs. Evans. . . . I had no right. . . ."

"It's an honest question," she admitted. "Yes, he was. He didn't trust banks, entirely." She sighed. "Of course you're thinking that it was a foolish thing."

"Well . . . I can understand it."

What he couldn't understand was how the man could pull himself away from such a woman. But men do, for a variety of reasons, and he must not fault the missing husband. An Indian friend had once told him that one should not judge another "unless you've walked a mile in his moccasins." He thought, however, that the moccasins of David Evans must have felt pretty comfortable. Still, one never knows. . . .

"Do you have children?" he asked. That should be a safe question.

"No, not yet."

That told him that she had not given up. She still considered her husband alive.

"Mr. Sterling suggested that I hire a detective," she went on. "He gave me a name. . . . One of the Pinkertons' people. But . . . well, it's costly. Frankly, I don't think I can afford it. So, I guess I'll search a little for myself."

His heart went out to her. He wanted to help her, but *how?* He couldn't offer her money, of course. Or offer to go with her.

"How will you do this?" he asked.

She shrugged, a tired little gesture. "Well," she said finally, "it seems he never got to Kansas City. So I guess I'll backtrack. . . . Stop at each town he'd have passed. I'm going to stop at Lawrence now. Then Topeka, Emporia, Strong City, Florence, all the towns between. Did he get this far?"

She showed him a map with the route of the A.T.&S.F. railroad cutting across the prairie toward Wichita. It was a logical approach, but a tremendous task.

"How was he traveling? By train?" Zeke asked.

"Yes. He intended to, anyway."

"That should help some."

"I hope so. I have this picture. . . ."

She opened her purse and took out a tintype photograph of a nice-looking man in a Union uniform. He wore a full mustache and a stern look. Everyone had a stern look in a photograph, he'd noticed. It seemed to him that somebody's picture ought to look like they were having a good time.

The most notable thing when she opened the purse, however, was a glimpse of a little pocket pistol. It was a double-barreled Remington derringer, 41 caliber, nickel plated with ivory grips. A ladies' gun . . . He had no doubt that the lady knew how to use it. He felt a little better about her safety as she traveled. But not much . . .

The conductor came through the car, punching tickets, and Mrs. Evans showed him the tintype. He studied it a moment.

"Don't think so, ma'am. Hard to tell, from one of these. Soldiers all look pretty much alike in uniform."

"But he's not a soldier now," she protested.

"Yes, ma'am, I understand that. Did he still have the mustache?"

"Yes, he does."

Again, Zeke noted that stubborn refusal to admit that her husband might be dead. She was pushing it a little too hard. He *does,* she had said. How was she to know he hadn't decided to shave it off? Still, he envied a man whose woman was so fiercely loyal and trusting. He envied the man in the tintype for more than one reason.

In his own heart, he knew that there was very little chance that David Evans was alive. On the train, in the night, someone could have clubbed or stabbed him as he dozed, taken his money belt, and shoved the body off on a remote stretch of track. In a rough or brushy area or on a trestle crossing a stream, it might not be discovered for months. Maybe never.

What would Mrs. Evans do? More important, who would help her, look after her? She appeared pretty self-sufficient, but a woman alone was at a distinct disadvantage. If there was no word of a missing spouse and he was presumed dead, and it was acceptable for her to remarry, she probably would, and he felt a strange jealousy rising against whatever man she'd choose. Another thought came. . . . Maybe she'd go back to wherever she started.

"Where do you come from?" he asked.

"Indiana."

She hesitated, and he was afraid that she saw his logic in asking.

"But . . . ," she went on, "I love the prairie. Some folks don't, I know. But there's something about it. Maybe some people are meant to be in a place, and know and understand it. How it *feels*. And others . . . Well, some will never know."

There was a dreamy look in her eyes for a moment. He wanted to say that he, too, had felt the call of the tallgrass region, and felt its spirit. He was afraid he'd sound stupid.

"Yes . . . ," he said softly, and was rewarded with a hint of a smile.

"You're stopping at Lawrence?" he asked, returning to a more conventional topic.

"Yes. I'll try each town. Each stop narrows the area of David's disappearance. Eventually, I can narrow it down. . . ."

Both fell silent, and for a little while there was only the doubled *click-click . . . click-click* of steel wheels on steel rails. Ezekiel knew that they must be nearing Lawrence. It was only an hour or so out of Kansas City by rail. By horse, a couple of days. He did not want to see her leave the train, yet had no excuse to avoid the parting. His ticket was to Wichita, hers to Lawrence. He considered for a moment getting off the train anyway, but what explanation could he give? She knew that his destination was farther on.

"Mr. York . . ."

"I . . ."

Both spoke at once after a long silence, and they both laughed nervously.

"You first," he insisted.

"I . . . I just wanted to thank you for your kindness, Mr. York. It was quite chivalrous for you to have challenged that bully. I could have handled him, though."

"I'm sure of that, ma'am," he smiled, "and my name's Ezekiel. Zeke, to my friends."

She smiled. "Thank you . . . Zeke. And I'm Catherine."

There was an uncomfortable silence again, broken by the call of the conductor for the stop at Lawrence.

"Ma'am . . . Mrs. Evans . . . Catherine . . . I wish you all the best in your search."

Privately, he was not sure what he wished. Mostly, for this magnificent woman's future happiness. Of one thing, he was certain. He could have no part in it. If she actually found her husband, he did not even want to know about it. If she did not, it would still be months before she could be certain. Years, maybe. He had no idea where he'd be by then.

They were slowing into the station.

"Through passengers have twenty minutes," the conductor called. "We'll take on water here."

The train ground to a stop, brakes squealing, and people began to move. Zeke rose and walked with Catherine Evans, helping her down the steps to the brick platform. They turned awkwardly to face each other, out of the mainstream of traffic to and from the depot. Zeke felt a tingle of excitement, mixed with sadness that he'd never see her again. How could he feel such a closeness to someone he'd just met? It was as if he'd known her always. The oddest part was that he felt strongly that *she* felt it, too. They looked into each other's eyes . . . there was so much left unsaid. . . .

"Can I . . . ? Is there anything I can do for you?" he asked.

"No . . ." Her voice was husky and there was a trace of a tear in her eye. "I . . . I'm fine! Where will you go now?"

"Don't know. Back to Texas, I reckon. My mother's there. See some country on the way. Got some affairs to settle."

Actually, he was more at loose ends than before. He wasn't sure who he was or what he wanted.

" 'Board!" called the conductor, and people started climbing back into the train cars.

"Guess this is good-bye," he said. "I'd better go. Again, good luck."

"And to you, Ezekiel York! Thank you."

She stuck out her hand, not as a woman might, limply and helplessly, but as a man might do. . . . A handshake on introduction or at the completion of a business transaction.

He took her hand. It was a firm, even handshake, as he would have expected, and just at the last, a little extra squeeze as she looked directly into his eyes. There was so much in that tiny bit of extra pressure . . . an acknowledgment of the depth of a relationship that could never be and in fact had never been.

He leaped back on the steps of the car and turned to wave at the slim figure standing on the platform. A hand was raised in farewell, and it was all he could do to keep from jumping from the train again.

Instead, he turned back into the car with a ridiculous feeling of bereavement. How *could* he feel this way about a woman he'd known for only an hour, and whom he would never see again?

8

The first couple of hours on the train had been exciting, thrilling, at times little short of wonderful. After the departure of Catherine Evans, there seemed to be little significance in anything.

It was only a few minutes before Zeke began to berate himself. He had neglected to learn an address, even a general area where he might locate her. It had seemed too forward at the time. She was a genteel, married woman, while he was merely a drover. His use of social graces, taught by his mother, had been adequate for the occasion, but he had been off balance, uncomfortable with the situation. *Damn!* He hadn't given her the slightest clue about how *he* might be reached, either. There had been opportunities to do that. He thought of each part of their conversation and reviewed it in his mind. *Yes, there I should have said . . .*

But he hadn't. The more he thought, the more he was certain that he must have come across to her as a country bumpkin. Yet, there *was* that last look as they parted, the gentle squeeze of the hand. . . .

He thought of leaving the train at the next stop, but realized that it would be impractical. He would then have to find a way back to Lawrence. That would be a day's travel by horse, and she would probably be gone by then. Maybe he could find a train going back, but that, too, would take most of a day. He fumed at his stupidity. He might have lost the best opportunity of his life.

Finally he came to the conclusion that this potential romance was simply not meant to be. It was too precarious a circumstance, merely two people whose trails had crossed by chance. They had traveled the same road for a short while, and now both would go on, living their respective lives. It had been a pleasant interlude, marred by Catherine Evans's personal tragedy. He would always wonder, and always hope for the best for her.

Lonely and discouraged, he found the train trip boring and uncomfortable. He stared out the window at the magnificent tallgrass prairie without seeing it. It was late July, and the big grasses were pushing tall seed stalks upward. Already, some clumps of the bluish stems were three to four feet in height, and would double that in a few weeks. The yellow-plumed Indian grass would not be far behind. He had been enthralled with this phenomenon in other years, but now, lost in his self-pity, did not even notice.

At Topeka, the conductor, in answer to another passenger's question, said that they had been following roughly the route of the old Santa Fe Trail. Now, however, the train's route would bend to the south, away from the Trail and across the Flint Hills. There were frequent stops for fuel and water.

There was a decent meal at the Harvey House dining room in Topeka, another at Florence, where Fred Harvey had opened a training school for his Harvey Girl waitresses. There was even a hotel there for those who elected to stay over.

Ezekiel was in no mood to appreciate such niceties. He wanted to get away, to forget what might have been. He arrived in Wichita, retrieved his horse and saddle roll, and headed for Texas, his heart still heavy.

By the time he crossed the Red River from the Indian Nations into Texas, Zeke was feeling better. He still thought of Catherine Evans often, but not with the disturbing intensity that he had known before. Now, it was a sad, nostalgic tug at his heartstrings, a regret for what he should have said or done. Only occasionally did she enter his dreams. She had probably gone back to Indiana and would marry some easterner, he tried to tell himself, with only partial success. But under any circumstances, she was lost to him.

His interest in a cattle operation of his own was revived as he neared familiar territory. In San Angelo, he inquired around for Coffee, the Negro wrangler, and found him breaking Mexican horses for sale to the army. Coffee reacted favorably to his questions about a job in the tallgrass country.

"It's a long way from a done deal," Zeke assured him. "But if you'd be interested, let me know where I can find you when the time comes."

The horseman nodded. "I sho' will, Zeke. Ef I ain't here, I'll leave word here at the livery, as to where I be."

.   .   .

On to the Concho . . . He found his mother and Hiram well settled and apparently happy. It came to mind that probably there had been no time in Naomi's troubled life when she was quite so secure. She had fitted well into the role as the wife of a prominent rancher. Hiram seemed to worship the ground on which she walked, but was not overbearing about it. Zeke was glad to see them as a good team who enjoyed each other and a future as secure as one could be.

After a supper cooked by Lupe, an ample-bosomed and ample-hipped Mexican señora of indeterminate age, the men returned to the patio. Hiram offered him a cigar and a light from a sulfur match.

"Your mother will join us," his stepfather assured him. "She's never gotten over the idea that *she* has to clean up after a meal."

The two chuckled comfortably. Zeke was wondering how to approach the subject of the Bar-Y when Hiram spoke again.

"Zeke, have you thought what you'd like to do with your Bar-Y spread?"

"Well . . . No. Not exactly," stammered Zeke, caught off guard. "Is there a problem with it?"

"No, no. It's not that. We used it to pasture two-year-olds this past year. Heifers, mostly."

"Yes, I know. Anybody living on it?"

"I've got a foreman there, and a few hands. It's better to have a place lived in. Looks like the drives are goin' to be over pretty soon, though. I wondered if you'll be wantin' to live there and settle down."

Zeke was interested that Hiram's thinking was much along the lines of his own.

"I'd been thinkin' about that, Hiram. You're right. . . . We can ship from Fort Worth pretty soon now, by rail. Some are talkin' drives to Montana, but I ain't that eager to draw it out. Let the Kings and some o' them do that part."

"So you figger to settle here?"

"I ain't sure, Hiram."

How could he approach what was on his mind?

"Well, I was wonderin' "—Hiram spoke cautiously—"if there's any way you'd consider selling it. To me . . . It holds some sentiment for your mother, I'm sure. Or do you want to sell it at all?"

"How does she feel about it? And Hiram, I'm not even sure how the title reads."

"I've checked that. It's a bit vague, but you're an heir, or issue, or somethin'. At least half of it's yours, I reckon. We can get the legalities set straight. She'd like to do that, I think."

Just then Naomi appeared at the door, wiping hands on her apron.

"Talking business, boys?"

"Well, in a way," answered Hiram.

She pulled a chair closer on the patio and sat, settling herself comfortably.

"What do you think, Ezekiel?"

"About what, Mother?"

"About selling us your interest in the Bar-Y. Or do you want to take over any interests in it?"

Zeke was caught off guard. He had intended to bring this up, but they were ahead of him.

"I'd like to have you near," she went on, "but Ezekiel, I know you've always liked that tallgrass grazing country. Is it really true that the grass grows taller than a horse?"

Zeke laughed. "Yes, Mother, it is true. I've seen it."

"I had the idea you'd probably settle there after the drives are over."

"How did you know?" he asked.

"Your father knew. He saw it on your first drive. He was thinking of that Kansas land for crops. You saw it as graze, to *fatten* cattle."

"I . . . I guess so. Or to raise 'em. He knew all about this?"

"He knew a great many things, Ezekiel. I think he even picked out Hiram for me."

Zeke gasped. "What?"

Hiram and Naomi giggled like children, and he took her hand.

"Yes," she went on. "James used to mention what a fine man owned the Circle H, and what a pity he had no wife."

"Mother, I never realized . . ."

"Of course not. You weren't supposed to."

"Did you know this, Hiram?" asked Zeke.

"No, we'd never really met," Hiram chuckled. "I saw her in town, and asked after her."

"About the same with me," Naomi added. "But look, son. . . . Let's talk about the ranch. Do you want to partner with Hiram and me?"

He'd thought that he had known what he wanted, but this was moving pretty fast.

"Let's sleep on it," he suggested, "and talk tomorrow. Guess I wasn't quite ready for this."

By morning, his head was cleared somewhat, and they talked. It was an amiable negotiation, with everyone feeling uncommonly generous toward the others.

Title to the Bar-Y would transfer totally to the Goodmans, for an agreed-upon sum. Livestock would be divided proportionately. Naomi would work with the lawyers to file the necessary paperwork.

The men would sort the cattle, Zeke choosing a hundred of the best three-year-old heifers for breeding stock. Together, they'd choose a few young bulls, to be turned in with the females in December.

Meanwhile, Zeke would return to Kansas to try to locate available land. He now could be more specific, knowing exactly how much he could afford to invest. He really hoped for about ten thousand acres, but he'd have to see. . . . Maybe more, maybe less.

9

zekiel left immediately for Kansas. He decided to winter there, to
see what sort of seasons he'd be dealing with in a ranch operation.
He'd never seen it except in late spring and summer.

By horse, train, and overland stage, he crisscrossed the entire central
part of the state. He studied maps, talked to farmers and ranchers, and
became familiar with land values. By early October he had a fair idea of
what he wanted.

The state, he now realized, was much dryer in the western shortgrass plains. The eastern part, especially southeast, was heavily forested and
hilly, much like southern Missouri and Arkansas, or Arkansaw, as some
called it.

But the tallgrass country, the rolling Flint Hills that had first called to
him, occupied the middle portion of the state. Most of it had never felt the
plow, and never would. The limestone caprock, laced with the veins of blue-
gray flint that lent the name, would prevent it. Tall grasses . . . Clear
white gravel streams fed by springs . . . Along the streams, cottonwood
trees, and in the canyons and gullies, mighty oaks, walnut, locust, and sycamores grew.

October was beautiful . . . warm, still days, cool nights, and a myriad of
colors. Zeke was astonished that the grasses as they ripened assumed a variety of colors. Big bluestem, or turkey-foot, took on a reddish hue, in contrast
to the golden yellow of the Indian grass. Little bluestem, a soft pink . . .

There were numerous shrubs on the rocky hillsides with startling colors, too. The staghorn sumac became a brilliant scarlet; fragrant sumac, less conspicuous. A plant called *wahoo* by the natives shone forth in yellow and pink splendor. Prairie dogwood growing alongside was a darker, duller gray-purple by comparison.

Winter could be severe, he was told, but manageable if a person planned ahead. The nutritional qualities of the prairie hay were considered superior for winter feed. He was also informed about the burning of the grass in the spring.

"You've got to burn the grass," one rancher told him. "Keeps it clean and pure. Comes back better, thick and lush. Cattle do better on it. About April's right. Injuns always done it, to bring back the buffalo, I reckon."

"Every year?" Zeke asked.

"Well, no. Jest when it needs it."

"How do you tell?"

"Just gets so you know. When there's a lot of trashy dry stuff in it, I guess."

As he acquired a better feel for the area, he began to check on the availability and price of land. It was, as he suspected, a bit higher than when he and his father had looked at it nearly a decade ago. Two to three dollars an acre, now. But cattle, too, were worth more. He had the resources to invest, and the cattle to stock the range. He began to contact land offices as he traveled, describing his needs.

"I've got somethin' might interest you," one told him. "Twelve or fifteen sections, as I recall. Maybe nine thousand acres. Some good improvements on it. House and barn; corrals."

"How does it happen to be for sale?" asked Zeke.

"Absentee owner. Don't recall exactly. Went broke from mismanagement, maybe. You can't manage a ranch here like you would an English country estate."

Both chuckled. There had been some who had tried exactly that, complete with riding to the hounds on foxhunts. They had discovered that this was hardly the country for a gentleman farmer.

"Want to have a look?" the agent asked.

"Sure. Why not?"

"Good! It'll take all day, though. It's about ten miles out. Tomorrow be all right for you?"

"Guess so."

"All right! I'll have a buggy."

"Fine. I'll take my horse, though. I might want to explore a little."

"Of course. I'll meet you here at the office, say an hour after daylight?"

•   •   •

It was one of those days that linger in the memory as one of the finest in a person's life. The sky was clean, pure, and still, with just a touch of the coolness that announces autumn. Indian summer . . . The smell of ripeness in the air seemed in perfect harmony with the dim blue haze over distant hills. It was as nearly perfect a day as he had ever seen.

It seemed perfectly appropriate, then, when the dim wagon tracks they were following topped a hill to reveal the scene below. A farmstead, or more properly, the headquarters for a ranch. This was definitely not the plaything of an English gentleman farmer, but the result of the honest toil of loving hands. He could see the dream. Behind the barn there rose a sheer cliff of limestone, some fifty feet high, which formed the back wall of the barn. Stone from the cliff had been used for the lower story of the barn itself, and for corrals. The hayloft was framed of wood and shingled by a careful workman.

The house might leave something to be desired, but he quickly realized that it had been erected as a temporary shelter while the critical ranch buildings were being constructed. It was a rough frame-and-board structure with a canvas roof. The canvas was tattered now, deteriorating from loneliness as any home does when no longer inhabited. There were weeds in the yard, attempting to choke out a bed of iris and daylilies, and a few struggling hollyhocks. He could visualize the site where a more permanent home would stand.

The entire farmstead faced south and would be sheltered from winter storms by the cliff and a heavily wooded gully. There was even a spring flowing out of the limestone hillside. He tasted the water and found it sweet and good.

"Belongs to an old widow woman, it seems," the agent said. "I don't know much about it, but the family wants to sell. There may be some wild cattle on it, and they go with the place."

"How long has it been abandoned?" asked Zeke.

"Not sure. Couple of years, maybe."

It was time to do some horse trading.

"Well, the house isn't much," Zeke said tentatively.

"That's true," said the agent quickly, "but it has great possibilities!"

"A lot of work . . ."

The other man laughed nervously.

"You don't look to be afraid of work," he ventured.

"I'm not, but I'm looking for value received, too. This is a big investment for somebody like me."

"You're looking for a loan?" asked the agent, a hint of alarm in his voice.

"That's not what I said. If the price is right, I'll pay up front, with a bank draft from Texas."

"I see. . . . Well, I'm sure we can work something out. Meanwhile,

I've an idea. It will take some time to negotiate the terms with the owner, and all. You'll need to go to Texas, possibly, but not until we've finalized the contract. Would you be interested in living on the place while the arrangements are under way?"

The next few weeks were filled with glorious excitement. Ezekiel rode over the hills, estimating the numbers of cattle, finding hidden springs and canyons. There were deer, turkeys, and quail in abundance, and fish in the clear streams.

One of his favorite spots was the top of the hill that formed the cliff behind the barn. He would climb there sometimes to watch the autumn sunset over the ranch that would, he hoped, be his. He had never seen such sunsets. He discovered a dim foot trail around the shoulder of the hill, and had the strong impression that someone had previously climbed this hill many times from the house below to watch such sunsets.

Unable to avoid the obvious needs of the place, he began to do minor maintenance on the corral, and to patch the worst of the damaged canvas on the dwelling. The weather was growing colder, and he cut some firewood, stacking it conveniently by the east-facing door of the structure.

When he rode into town for supplies in mid-November, he learned that the owner had agreed to terms.

"The widow wants to come here to complete the transfer," the agent told him. "We can have the paperwork all ready, do the signing here at the office. Is there any way that the bank here can be of help to you in this?"

"Possibly . . . But I'll want to go to Texas, visit my folks, take care of that end. . . . I'll spend Christmas there, and then come back. You'll want some earnest money, I suppose?"

"It's customary, Mr. York."

"Of course."

"Now, winter travel may be a matter of difficulty. Would it be satisfactory to you to postpone the actual meeting to complete the signing until spring?"

"I was thinking of that, myself," Zeke agreed. "Say, April or May?"

"Good. We can agree on a date later, depending on when the widow wants to attempt the trip. She may be feeble, I don't know."

It was April before the proposed meeting was arranged. Once the documents were signed, he would return to the Concho to drive his brood herd northward to the Flint Hills with Coffee and another cowboy or two.

He was mildly curious about the elderly owner who would be selling. Was the ranch lost because of mismanagement on the part of a son, or perhaps a son-in-law? Everything he had seen about the place led him to believe that its operator had been a good, hardworking man. There must be more to the story. And why did this widow insist on traveling to Kansas to complete the transfer? Well, the elderly often have strange twists in their minds. . . .

It was a gloomy morning, with a light drizzling rain falling, as he rode to the livery and unsaddled his horse. Good for the grass, but unpleasant for travel, he was thinking as he checked his pocket watch and walked toward the agent's office. He'd be just about on time for the ten o'clock meeting. He stepped through the door, removing his hat and slicker to hang them on the hall tree.

The agent came out of an inner room, hurried, nervous, and with a strange look on his face.

"She's here already," he announced in a half-whisper. "Not what we expected at all . . . I had no idea . . ."

He led the way into the inner office, where a woman sat primly, hands folded in her lap.

"Mrs. Evans, this is Mr. York, our buyer. . . ."

Neither of them really heard him.

"Catherine?" Zeke blurted in disbelief.

"You?" she gasped at the same instant. "*You* are the buyer?"

Both burst into delighted laughter, while the puzzled agent stood in open-mouthed amazement.

Then Ezekiel sobered. Under the circumstances, he had no right to feel so elated. "I'm sorry, Mrs. Evans . . . ," he mumbled uncomfortably. "This must mean that your search has been fruitless."

Now she, too, became serious. "Yes. I guess I knew it already, but I . . . Well, I spent a lot of money in the search. I had to sell. My . . . my husband has been declared dead. He loved our ranch so. . . . I'm glad that you're the one . . ." She faltered. "I'm pleased that you've taken a liking to it," she finished more formally.

There was so much that he wanted to say, so many things that he wished to tell her. He now knew whose feet had made the path up the hill to the summit where the sunsets were the most magnificent. Embarrassed, he glanced to the window.

"Looks like the sun's comin' out," he pointed. "Guess the storm's over."

"Yes," she said, her voice low and soft. "It looks like it."

AUTHOR'S COMMENTS

This book and its preceding volume, *Tallgrass,* have been a great adventure. I've been asked how long it took for the research, to which I can only admit "all my life," and more. It's a collective experience embracing several generations and many families.

People sometimes ask where a writer gets ideas. (No writer really knows.) In this case, the opposite was the problem. There was far too *much* material. The book had been under contract as a single book of 200,000 words, about the size of this volume. A historical novel; the working title, *Kenzas.* But a major problem arose. There was so much early history that the manuscript was nearly to contract length before I realized that the story was not yet even approaching the Civil War period. It was elected to divide it in two, calling the early years *Tallgrass,* and to create a sequel, this present volume, which has had the working title "Tallgrass II."

I still liked the *Kenzas* title, but it didn't fit as companion to *Tallgrass.* Such whimsical suggestions as *Taller Grass, Shortgrass,* and *Burnt Grass* were rejected out of hand. My editor and longtime friend, Pat LoBrutto, called attention to the two major features of our country that had impressed him: tallgrass prairie and our prevailing south wind, which gives the area the name *Kansas,* sometimes translated "south wind place." Consequently the title of this volume, *South Wind.*

All of the stories in these volumes have some basis in fact. I talked to the granddaughter of "Karl Spitzburg," the Swiss seminary student who rebelled and ran away, and to the descendants of the freed plantation slaves who traveled west. One family still proudly displays the big iron kettle in which they cooked on the trail. I met people who had come west on the "Orphan Trains." Consider the scene in which "Ezekiel York" and his Civil War–veteran father argue the possibilities of the tallgrass Flint Hills for ranching. It was told to me by an old cowboy, over a campfire in those same hills. It was *his* family story, and the stream on which we were camped bears his family name.

The account of the sinking of the steamer *Arabia* is taken from newspaper accounts and from visits to the *Arabia* Museum in Kansas City. There, salvaged artifacts are displayed, including the saddled remains of the doomed mule.

Ezra Willett, hiding in the haystack from Quantrill's raiders, was my grandfather. The flag sewn by Nancy (Landis) Willett in the story is still in my family. By an odd quirk of fate, a great-uncle of my wife's rode *with* Quantrill.

One of our daughters married a grandnephew of Dr. Harvey Mann of the Seventh Cavalry, and I had access to his letters and his story. A few years ago, an account was published describing Mann's encounter with Rain-in-the-Face, and an "encysted arrowhead" in the *hip* as his souvenir. I think it more likely that the Sioux chieftain carried a rifle, as most warriors did by this time. The Mann family tradition describes a bullet wound in the lower leg, and I have written my account that way. Dr. Mann did return to Woodson County, Kansas, after his brief practice in Chicago. He died in a hotel room in Kansas City in 1915, en route to visit an old army colleague at Fort Leavenworth.

There is a Cherokee saying that "the world is filled with stories, which from time to time permit themselves to be told." It is my privilege to be permitted to take part, in a small way, in that telling.

Don Coldsmith
"Kenzas," 1997

SOURCES

American Encyclopaedia, 1883

American Heritage *Book of Indians,* 1961

Andreas, A.T. *History of Kansas*, 1883

Arnold & Hale *Hot Irons,* McMillen, 1943

Connelly, *History of Kansas,* American Historical Society, 1928

Emporia *Gazette* (microfilm files), 1977

Family oral histories . . . McNaughten, Landis, Howell, Coldsmith, Willett, Mann . . . others

Gard, Wayne *The Great Buffalo Hunt,* Alfred A. Knopf, 1959

Mann, A.H., personal letters, 1902

Mann, A.H., unpublished diary, 1870s

McPherson, James M. *What They Fought For,* Anchor-Doubleday, 1995

Smithsonian Institution, Bureau of American Ethnology, *Handbook of American Indians,* 4th Edition Government Printing Office, 1912

World Book Encyclopedia, 1965